PRAISE FOR AWARD-WINNING AUTHOR
SUSAN CRANDALL

WHISTLING PAST THE GRAVEYARD
A National Bestseller

"A coming-of-age story as well as a luminous portrait of courage and the bonds of friendship. . . . Susan Crandall tells young Starla's story with pitch-perfect tone, evoking 1963 Mississippi and its struggles with a deft hand. Like Harper Lee's *To Kill a Mockingbird* and Kathryn Stockett's *The Help*, *Whistling Past the Graveyard* is destined to become a classic."

—*New York Times* bestselling author Karen White

"Crandall delivers big with a coming-of-age story set in Mississippi in 1963 and narrated by a precocious nine-year-old. Young Starla is an endearing character whose spirited observations propel this nicely crafted story."

—*Kirkus Reviews*

"A delightfully complex story about defying the odds to find the gifts we have tucked inside us."

—*Shelf Awareness*

"Crandall threads historical detail throughout the book as the struggles of the civil rights movement are vividly portrayed. . . . Crandall's young narrator captures the reader's heart."

—*Library Journal*

"*Whistling Past the Graveyard* is a multilayered saga that can be enjoyed by teens and adults alike. It has a cinematic quality that will make readers wish for a screen version. And you can't say better than that."

—BookReporter.com

"This is a work of imagination in the mind of a nine-year-old child that might remind you of Harper Lee's *To Kill a Mockingbird* or Kathryn Stockett's *The Help*. . . . It's a real winner!"

—Liz Smith, *The Chicago Tribune*

"A luminous portrait of courage and the bonds of friendship, this coming-of-age story is as endearing and spirited as they come."

—*Shape*

"I would recommend this book to those who enjoyed *The Secret Life of Bees*, *The Help*, and *Saving CeeCee Honeycutt*."

—Teacher's Choice

THE FLYING CIRCUS

"Crandall's *The Flying Circus* is a fascinating story of love and loss set against the colorful background of barnstorming 1920s America. Every detail sings, and every character will touch your heart in this rip-roaring tale of three daredevils on the run, each with something to hide, drawn together by a desire to conquer the skies as well as their own demons."

—Melanie Benjamin, *New York Times* bestselling author of *The Aviator's Wife*

"Exciting adventures abound when three unlikely misfits take to the skies. Friendships are challenged, lives are risked, and dark secrets threaten to tear the trio apart as they barnstorm across America's heartland. A spirited, bighearted tale."

—Beth Hoffman, *New York Times* bestselling author of *Looking for Me*

"An engaging road saga."

"An exhilarating, memorable flight into the world of barnstorming in the 1920s, with all the twists and turns of an aerial acrobat. Compelling characters and a fascinating setting make this journey a sheer joyride. Satisfying and delightful!"

"*The Flying Circus* is Susan Crandall at her best—a colorful, rich, and historical tale of the early years of flight. Heroes and villains and an achingly sweet romance will pull at the reader's heart long after the last page is turned. I loved this book!"

"Crandall has crafted a wonderfully charming, memorable and thought-provoking read."

"Deeply moving. A richly drawn story of love, loss, and redemption with characters as finely tuned as the planes they fly."

"Historical fiction with appeal to both romance and adventure fans."

BOOKS BY SUSAN CRANDALL

the *Myth* of PERPETUAL SUMMER

SUSAN CRANDALL

G

GALLERY BOOKS

New York   London   Toronto   Sydney   New Delhi

G

Gallery Books
An Imprint of Simon & Schuster, Inc.
1230 Avenue of the Americas
New York, NY 10020

First Gallery Books trade paperback edition June 2018

GALLERY BOOKS and colophon are registered trademarks of Simon & Schuster, Inc.

For information about special discounts for bulk purchases, please contact Simon & Schuster Special Sales at 1-866-506-1949 or business@simonandschuster.com.

The Simon & Schuster Speakers Bureau can bring authors to your live event. For more information or to book an event, contact the Simon & Schuster Speakers Bureau at 1-866-248-3049 or visit our website at www.simonspeakers.com.

Interior design by Jaime Putorti

Manufactured in the United States of America

10 9 8 7 6 5 4 3 2 1

Library of Congress Cataloging-in-Publication Data is available.

ISBN 978-1-5011-7201-4
ISBN 978-1-5011-7202-1 (ebook)

In memory of my mother, Margie Beaver Zinn
Finishing a book isn't the same without you

the *Myth* of
**PERPETUAL
SUMMER**

PROLOGUE

August 1972
San Francisco, California

I kneel in front of the small black-and-white television, my face close to the screen, breathless at the newscaster's words. A mug shot appears. Blood rushes hot, and my head goes fuzzy. Now grown and far too thin, that face still holds a distinct echo of the boy I so loved. My brother Walden . . . lost to me for years, now labeled a killer.

Memories as thick as the air and mud and secrets of our Mississippi childhood sit heavy on my skin. Even though my three siblings are scattered, miles away and years out of mind, they dwell in a place as deep inside me as my own heart. Perhaps our extraordinary bond comes from the strain of madness that runs in our blood, the love and hate tangling until they're braided into an unbreakable rope, a lifeline and a noose.

As far as I have run, as many times as I have reinvented myself, my childhood has snaked through time and wrapped around my throat.

Have I been a fool to hope that at least one of us survived unscathed?

It's time to admit that, perhaps, the blood that knotted love and hate may have, in the end, made murderers of us all.

1

August 1972
New Orleans, Louisiana

I delude myself into thinking I am where I am today because of clear choices and controlled decisions. In the chaos of my childhood, that's all I dreamed about, power over my own life. But in the dark of night, when I lie alone in my apartment in Pacific Heights, shrouded by mist and distant foghorns, I'm forced to admit I am only a seed. At first blown to Los Angeles on the wind of someone else's dream, and then rooting in San Francisco, where I was dropped by a different someone. But I *have* rooted well. That, at least, is my doing.

Yesterday, after the newscast that named my brother a murderer, I called my boss at the Buckman Foundation. I'm in charge of public relations; a position gained by tenacity, dedication, and, admittedly, the fact that Mr. Capstone likes me. That job is my whole life—and I'm not using it as a turn of phrase.

The Buckmans are old money. Even in the progressive atmosphere of California, old money is just as prideful and unbending as it was in the South. Fortunately, James is a common last name, so Mr. Capstone, who never misses a morning or evening news broadcast, didn't make the connection when I requested time off for a family emergency. His tone was concern laced with what sounded like surprise that I even *have* a family. He assured me Keith and Stan are happy to step up while I'm gone. Which is *not* a comfort. They both believe a woman has as much business being an executive, junior or otherwise, as a monkey. They're continually looking for ways to kick the ladder out from under me and leave me hanging by my fingernails.

My life, perfect and organized just yesterday morning, is now a tangle of worry and uncertainty. On the flight, I made a list in my current sketchbook of the scarce, yet disturbing, details I've discovered about Walden's situation. As I walk through the New Orleans airport, a group of three shaved-head, white-robed Hare Krishna step in front of me, flowers and pamphlets extended in their pale, bony hands. Even though my home city is full of such groups, I've never paused to really study those selling street-corner prophecies. Now that Walden's name has been linked with the Scholars of Humanity—a group with a leader being investigated by a now-murdered journalist and a compound deep in the Louisiana swamps—I pause to look into their eyes, searching for what ignites their doubtless devotion. But all I see are lost children who consider themselves enlightened, saved and saving others.

I empathize, I do. After all, I was a lost child, too.

Then I think about Sharon Tate. Although I met her only once, the news of Manson's butchers shook me to the core. The girls who did the killing, delusional and brainwashed, devoted to a madman, singing like children and dressing like schoolgirls throughout their trial.

And now my own brother is accused of a crime nearly as monstrous.

I don't know how he could be capable of such a thing.

But you do know, don't you? Just like they say back home, blood always tells.

Even under the canopy of ancient trees, the heat is oppressive in the historic Garden District of New Orleans. The stately old houses with their deep porches and floor-to-ceiling double-hung windows are closed up, no doubt cool and serene on the inside. I hear the soft burble of a splashing fountain in one of the gardens concealed behind an aged brick wall and wrought iron gate, creating an illusion of relief from the heat. In defiance of appearing weak and ordinary, even the wisteria refuses to wilt.

The irony isn't lost on me as I stand in front of the ironwork double-gate in front of Ross Saenger's home seeking his family's wealth and power to save my brother. The wealth and power I resented—as I'd resented Ross himself—so deeply and for so long. My sketchbook listing the meager facts is tucked in my tote, and a much longer list of appeals and entreaties piles up in my head. I am ready to beg. On my knees if necessary.

I do not look forward to this reunion. But this is about what Walden needs, not my wounds and grudges. Truth be, I cannot blame Mrs. Saenger for what happened in '63. It was her kindness that saved our family—right before it tore us apart.

I feel a little faint and wish I'd pulled my hair into a long ponytail at the nape of my neck. I'd forgotten how Southern air coats the skin and weighs the lungs, how the stillness carries its own mass. I regret my polyester double-knit vested pantsuit and long for the yellow cotton sundress of my youth. Nausea grips my empty stomach and I want to turn away. But this is Walden's best hope.

The grandeur of this house stands out, even in this neighborhood, two-and-a-half stories of brick solidity and symmetry tucked behind an iron fence and a tall, carefully sculpted hedge. Porches span the front of the house on both floors, trimmed in turned posts and filigreed ironwork. Marshaling myself, I open the gate, cross the walk, and climb the marble steps. I stare at the black door and study the beautiful leaded glass transom over it. I set down my suitcase beside a shiny black ceramic pot filled with red geraniums and ring the bell, desperate to get out of the heat. It hits me, stupidly and belatedly, that Mrs. Saenger might not be home. The street is quiet, the only sound the ever-present whirr of cicadas in the ancient trees. I regret my haste in letting the cab go.

As I wait, the drumbeat of my desperate heart scatters my carefully laid-out words like starlings from a wire. I must slow down my thoughts or else babble like a madwoman when Mrs. Saenger appears.

But when the door swings open, it isn't Mrs. Saenger. It's Ross. And thought ceases altogether.

"Good—" His arresting blue eyes are pleasantly expectant, as if he's anticipating a neighbor or a friend. He's even taller and broader-shouldered than when I last saw him in '63, his light brown hair longer.

My mouth opens, but nothing comes out. I'm fourteen and tongue-tied. I'm sixteen and broken.

His expression slowly morphs into surprise. "Tallulah James? Oh my God, is that you?"

"Hello, Ross." My vision is getting gray around the edges.

"You're alive!"

He thought I was dead?

"I . . . there's been . . ." I feel myself listing to one side, the grayness pushing deeper into my vision. I'd prepared myself to face Mrs. Saenger. Not him.

My knees wobble.

He reaches out and takes my elbow. "Come in out of the heat." He plucks my gold suitcase off the porch and guides me inside. "You look like you could use something cold to drink. Have a seat in the living room and I'll bring something. Coke? Tea?" He lets go of my elbow in careful stages, as if he's afraid I'll collapse.

"Just water, please." I barely feel my feet as I move into a room that screams old money: crystal chandelier, matching chintz sofas (tastefully worn and inviting), oil portraits of ancestors, carved marble fireplace, gleaming silver on the bar cart, and fine, thick area rugs underfoot. This place is just as I'd imagined it when I was hating my older brother, Griff, for abandoning me to live here. A perfect life. A movie set. Not with me where he'd promised to be.

When Ross returns with the glasses of water, I practically down mine in one gulp.

He sits on the sofa opposite me and settles his elbows on his knees, linking his hands between them. I have trouble looking directly at him. He's a man now, but I can still see the boy I pined over. And I feel that old burn of resentment.

He says, "For the past nine years, I've imagined the worst. It's quite a relief to see you alive and well." The note of judgment in his tone raises my hackles.

I take a slow breath. "I am quite well, thank you. I've made a good life for myself." *Alone. On my own. No thanks to you or Griff or my grandmother.*

"You could have called to let us know you were okay. Griff was out of his mind with worry," Ross says.

Griff made his choice. Just as Granny James made hers. Only Margo's abandonment wasn't a surprise; she just lived up to expectations. "I left a note so no one would think I'd been abducted by aliens or alligator poachers." The look on his face tells me my attempt at lightening the mood fell flat. "Honestly, I'm surprised Griff even knew I was gone. Besides, he's hardly in a position to complain about someone disappearing." I'm a little shocked at my own counterproductive childishness.

"*He* didn't disappear," Ross says. "He was right here. And you knew it."

"So, where is he now?" I imagine him all Ivy League–educated on the Saengers' charity, living well, with a wife and adoring children. He can probably help Walden better than I.

Ross holds my gaze. "I have no idea where he is."

I blink. "What?"

He leans forward, his shoulders holding the set of bad news. "He was never the same after everything that happened in Lamoyne— your dad, the accusations. After his high school graduation in '65 he packed his things and left in the middle of the night. Broke my mom's heart."

Cold fear creeps up my spine. All this time, I imagined him in the loving arms and stability of the Saengers, part of a happy family. "You have no idea where he went? He never contacted you?"

"No. Must be a James family trait." There is bitterness in his voice.

"Hey! I might owe Walden and Dharma, but I'm not going to apologize to *you* for the choices I made!"

He raises his palms to me. "Fair enough."

I remind myself I'm here as a beggar. "I actually came to see your mother. Is she here?"

"No."

I wait, but he doesn't elaborate. "Will she be home soon?"

"No. She and Dad died three years ago. Car accident."

"Oh, Ross. I'm so sorry. I had no idea." I've kept everything about home frozen in time. And, I realize, I've been deliberately *not* thinking of the possibility that some people may be gone. What about Gran? My beloved Maisie?

"Of course you didn't. Because you didn't let anyone know where you were."

"I came to ask her—now you, I suppose—for help." He stiffens slightly, so I'm quick to add, "Not for me. For Walden. He's in serious trouble. I didn't know where else to turn—"

"I saw the news."

"Do you think your mother's cousin Sam will be willing to help? He did so much for Griff. Or maybe he can recommend another lawyer? I don't want Walden left in the hands of . . . of a—" Suddenly, I smell my little brother's baby shampoo, feel his hand in mine, recall the trusting way he looked at me. "A c-court-appointed lawyer."

I feel clammy. I reach for the glass of water, only to discover it's empty.

Ross stands and hands me his. "Here. I haven't touched it."

As I take a grateful drink, the obvious occurs to me. "I suppose *you* can recommend someone, being a lawyer yourself." *Please don't let him offer to take the case. Who knows what the fallout would be?*

He gives me a smile that tickles a memory of the way he used to make me feel. "I'm not a lawyer."

"I thought it was a *foregone conclusion*." The phrase springs from the past.

His eyes soften. "Good memory. As it turns out, I bucked the family expectations and became a psychiatrist."

"Didn't know you were even interested in psychiatry."

"Circumstances spurred it."

"Oh." I shift uncomfortably, suddenly feeling as if I'm under a microscope. "Sam, then? Do you think he'll help?"

"I already called him. His calendar is full, and Walden's case will be time-consuming. But his daughter Amelia is willing." He must see the concern on my face because he adds, "Unlike me, she's always *wanted* to be a lawyer. She's a barracuda."

I have reservations. And I'm ashamed to admit one of them is that she's a woman. I know firsthand how preconceived notions create an uphill battle. And this is the South, where women are still supposed to be wearing pearls and aprons and going to the beauty shop twice a week. What if we get a male chauvinist pig for a judge?

"I don't want to sound ungrateful," I say. "But maybe I should look for someone with more experience. I'm not asking for a handout. I intend to pay."

"You could easily get someone with more experience. This is a high-profile case with national attention. Lawyers will come after this case like a shark after blood in the water," Ross says. "But Amelia is really good. And she cares about the outcome, not the media exposure she'll get. She can devote the time. *And* she's not asking for a huge retainer. She's already contacted the Orleans Parish jail to get in to see him."

I don't admit it, but that retainer would be a problem. I have a little savings, but I'd have to borrow the rest. And going through that kind of credit scrutiny will be blood for the sharks in my own particular waters—Keith and Stan are already circling at the foundation.

"Have you called your grandmother?" he asks, his voice more neutral than his eyes.

"No." I almost can't ask the question, but the wrongness of my assumption about Mrs. Saenger blindsided me. "Do you know if she's still at Hawthorn House?"

"As of last Christmas she was. She sent Griff birthday and Christmas cards here, even after I wrote to tell her he was gone."

The relief that rushes through my veins tells me I love her far more than I resent her. Still, just the thought of that emotional conversation makes me sway.

"But when I called yesterday," he says, "there was no answer. Do you want to try now?"

I should say yes, of course. But I don't have the strength.

"You don't want to talk to her." Ross has not lost his ability to see inside me. He'd been that way since the moment he saved my life.

"I'd rather not. Not right now."

The look that crosses his face makes me feel like a wayward child—and I suppose in a way I am. But at the moment, I can barely form thoughts into words.

Ross nods. "I'll try again. You look ready to drop. Have you eaten or slept?"

"I can't eat. The mere thought of food . . ." I shudder.

"Let's get you upstairs. You can take a hot bath and get a nap."

"I'll call a cab, get a hotel. Then I should go see Walden. He needs to know he's not alone."

But he is alone, because you left him.

"Don't be ridiculous. You'll stay here. And there's no way you'll get in to see him today. Amelia hasn't even gotten in yet." He's already in the front hall, picking up my suitcase.

The thought of going back out into that sweltering heat makes me dizzy. I'm not sure I can even drag myself up the long, curved mahogany staircase.

I follow him to a bedroom with ice-blue draperies, bedspread, and filigree on the wallpaper. Just looking at it makes me feel cool and calm.

"There's a private bath through that door. Get some rest, you're going to need it."

As he's backing out of the room, I say, "Don't let me sleep long. I want to go see him as soon as—as—" I put my hand over my eyes.

The first tears I've allowed since this all began start to fall. I turn away and wave Ross from the room.

I hope he doesn't try to comfort me. I'm too worn to ward it off and too weak to not crumble.

After a couple of seconds, his soft footsteps move away and I hear the door quietly close.

I reach into my purse and pull Griff's lucky arrowhead out of the zipper pocket. Then I curl on my side on the cool bed, clutching it to my chest, and allow myself a regret-filled cry.

I dream of a storm-filled sky, lightning bolts and tree-stripping winds. A dark swirling twister barrels down on me as I chase Walden, his blond hair bobbing ahead of me, a bright spot in the dimness. We're surrounded by endless acres with no shelter. The roar is right at my back, the wind ripping at my clothes, snapping my hair in my face. Then the noise rises over my head, the funnel skipping over me. Then descending, plucking Walden from the earth, his small feet still running as he hangs in the debris-filled air.

I wake yelling his name.

Feet thud up the stairs and down the hallway, stopping abruptly at the bedroom door. I hear Ross's hand on the knob before he pauses, then knocks. "Are you all right?"

"Yes." A drop of red falls onto the wide bell of my pants, standing out against the argyle design. I open my hand to see I've squeezed the arrowhead so hard I'm bleeding. "Oh shit!"

The door bursts open, and Ross is by the bed before I can blink. "What happened?" He heads into the bathroom, returning with a thick blue towel. When he tries to wrap my hand, I pull it toward my chest, careful so the blood doesn't drip onto the bedspread. "It'll ruin it."

Confidently, yet gently, he takes my hand and flips the towel around it. "It's a towel, for God's sake, not an heirloom." Then he looks in my eyes. "Lulie, did you . . . ?"

The sound of the nickname I haven't heard in years sends a clammy shiver across my skin. "Did I what?"

"Try to hurt yourself."

"Of course not!" The idea of him trying to dig around inside my head irritates me. "If I was going to kill myself, I'd have done it in San Francisco where nobody would find me until I was good and dead."

He surprises me by laughing. "Only you, Lulie." After a pause, he says, "At least you answered one of my many questions."

"And that is?" I pull my hand and the towel from his grasp.

"Where you're living." He raises a brow. "Alone?"

"Very. By choice, if that's your next question. And I'm not isolated in a filthy apartment filled with a hundred cats. I'm quite normal."

There's something in the way he looks at me that makes me uncomfortable. I shift and get off the far side of the bed.

"Normal is what I always wanted for you. Of course, *normal* is a relative term. And quite separate from *happy* or *content*."

I head to the bathroom to run some cold water over my hand and rinse off the arrowhead. "Quite content," I say over the sound of the running water. I adore my job, my apartment. I have acquaintances, not the emotional entanglements of deep friendships.

I look in the mirror and see him leaning against the doorjamb to the bathroom. "So how *did* you cut your hand?"

I finish rinsing the arrowhead and hold it up for him to see, but I keep my eyes on his reflection, not the real man.

"Unusual good luck charm," he says.

"Talisman," I correct. "I don't believe in luck."

He steps closer behind me. "Do you still have a place to cast your anger and your fears?"

I am so startled that I turn to face him.

"You're not the only one who remembers." His gaze holds mine for a second, then he turns. "I'll get some bandages for your hand."

As I listen to Ross walk down the stairs, I wonder—if I'd continued to toss my fears into a river, would things have turned out differently for all of us?

* * *

I've changed to the coolest clothing I brought, a flowered halter dress that felt totally acceptable in California but seems overexposed as I walk into the kitchen of this old Southern mansion. If Ross is shocked, he hides it well. He sets a grilled pimento cheese sandwich on the kitchen table and nods for me to sit.

Funny, I'd forgotten all about pimento cheese. Just like I'd forgotten about the weight of the air.

"It's too hot for this," he says. "But Mom always made it when things got rough."

"Thanks." I know if I take a bite, it will grow in my mouth until I choke on it. I pick up half and try to at least look like I'm going to eat it. As Ross is getting glasses of sweet tea, I wonder which of the four chairs around the table was Griff's when he lived here.

Has he seen the news? Is he on his way back home?

Even if he has, Walden is mine. Mine to protect. Mine to save. He and Dharma were always mine to care for.

I pick a few pinches off the sandwich and drop them on the plate in an effort to make it look like some of it is disappearing. "Did you know my uncle sent Walden back to Lamoyne?"

I relay yesterday's conversation with Uncle Roger.

"Walden was unhappy." Uncle Roger *sounded every bit as distant and snobbish as my mother always described—before she amended her assessment when she needed to dump her kids on him, a man none of us had ever met.* "We sent him back to his grandmother after two weeks."

"You separated the twins?"

"It was for the best. We adopted Dharma—she's made our lives a delight. She's in New York, on Broadway." His voice lifted with pride.

"And her twin is headed to prison because you gave up on him after two weeks! He was a traumatized nine-year-old! How could you be so heartless? You need to get him a lawyer—"

"Whoa, whoa, whoa there, little lady. First of all, you do not tell me what to do. Second, Walden is not my concern."

"Do it for Dharma," I say. Your delight. *"This will break her heart."*

"I doubt that. She hasn't seen him for nine years."

My hand tightens around the receiver. "Can I have her number? I need to call her."

"No, you cannot. Dharma needed a clean break from all that madness down there. That's why I've thrown away every card and letter you've sent."

"You did what?" *I wrote those letters so they would know I still loved them. I never expected a response, because I never included a return address.*

"Her time before she came to us is irrelevant. Do not, I repeat, do not drag her into this in any way. Her life has nothing to do with her brother's, or yours—or my feckless sister's for that matter."

"No. I didn't know that," Ross says. "Griff never wanted to go back to Lamoyne. He couldn't stand you not being there."

"This all could have been avoided if Gran had let me stay." The bitterness of her betrayal is just as choking as it was then.

"Listen, Lulie, there was no good solution back in '63. Not for any of you." By the way he pauses, I know I'm not going to like what is coming. "As soon as you're done picking at that sandwich, we need to leave for Lamoyne. I finally tracked down your grandmother. She's in the hospital."

Despite Ross's assurances that Gran's situation is not life-threatening, my pulse pounds in my temples and my hands fidget as I ride in the passenger seat of his Mercedes toward Lamoyne. I try to calm myself as I listen to Don McLean sing "American Pie," glad for the noise of the radio.

"I'm not sure I would have thought to call Mr. Stokes." The admission is slow in coming, mostly because calling him is the most obvious thing to do and it didn't cross my mind.

"When I didn't get her at home after several tries, I decided I'd better do something. I mean, a lot could have happened since Christmas. And this business with Walden—"

"Are you sure it's just high blood pressure?"

"That's what Mr. Stokes said. When I spoke to her on the phone, she called it 'a little episode.' We'll know for certain soon."

My stomach drops to my ankles. After all this time, I'm going to face her—and all my assumptions are likely to be blown out of the water.

"I hope her blood pressure doesn't skyrocket at the sight of me."

"She loves you, Tallulah."

A long time ago, I believed that without question.

At the sign announcing seven miles to go, my mouth goes dry. I realize I'm as nervous about seeing my hometown again as I am about seeing Gran.

And I don't relish doing either under Ross's observant eye.

We've made the turn off before I realize he's taking us past Pearl River Plantation, a route he could have easily avoided by staying on the highway.

Long strands of Spanish moss reach low over our heads, a veil shrouding the secrets I left behind. Foliage crowds the narrow road, its density so pressing I feel as if we're going to be crushed. Living in the city, I'd forgotten how closed in a person can feel while still being outdoors. I open the window, only to be met with air so thick it feels solid and the sour smell of vegetation rotting in the humidity. Dark brown water fills the narrow drainage ditch running parallel to us. I see something slither into it.

I thought I'd faced returning to the South when I arrived on Ross's front steps. But the shock of seeing this place robs my body of breath and chills my skin. Before we left New Orleans, I put on the matching short, puffed-sleeved jacket so I won't give Gran a coronary with my halter dress. I pull it closed over my chest. *This* is my homecoming, here in this quiet isolation, amid the leafy green vines that shape trees into monsters, on this dusty road I walked for over half my life.

My time in California ceases to exist. My professional success evaporates. I am a powerless child.

As we near the lane to my old home, I swear Ross is purposefully slowing down. At least he doesn't point it out like a tour guide of my past.

I can't help but look. The painted sign is warped and peeling, the lettering no more than a washed-out memory of the vibrant

green it used to be: PEARL RIVER PLANTATION—PECANS AND
BLACKBERRIES—OWNERS: DRAYTON AND MARGO JAMES. I close
my eyes and I see ten-year-old Griff standing in the heat with his
ruler, swatting mosquitoes until he had the lettering perfect.

The mailbox is missing, the graying post leaning away from the
road. The lane is so overgrown I can barely see where it used to be.

All these years, I assumed Gran was still running the orchard,
even if the house was vacant and overtaken by mice. But the farm is
a ruin. By now the blackberry canes are impenetrable and wild, and
foraging animals are well-fed on the pecans. Our generation killed
the James family legacy once and for all.

It seems I created fanciful lives for all those I left behind, lives
that had no basis in reality.

Myths.

2

January 1958
Lamoyne, Mississippi

The Mississippi sky is angry; all swirling gray and spitting. Tiny white ice balls hiss against the stage set up in front of LaFollet Hall at Wickham College—well, in just a few minutes it won't be LaFollet Hall anymore. It will be James Hall, a lasting tribute to our family. And the James family, at least our little branch of it, can use all the respectability it can get its hands on. This has only recently come to my attention—last spring, after my tenth birthday, to be exact. Daddy demands specifics when presenting oral arguments. I never used to notice the sideways looks and the whispers around town, or how people abruptly stop talking when they think I'm in earshot. But lately things have changed. Or I've changed. I'm not sure which.

Daddy is a history professor here, just like Granddad James and Great-Granddad James before him. Anybody can donate money, Daddy says, but the James family has committed their lives to this "bastion of higher education." Which, when I really think about it, makes me wonder why there hasn't been a James Hall before now.

Griff (who's just a year older than me, but a whole lot more cynical, according to Daddy) was the first to point out that a lot of

things about this honor don't add up. First, he said, Christmas break
is a mighty strange time for a building dedication, when everything
is deserted and dark. Dedications come in the spring, when nature
decorates the campus with giant ivory magnolia blooms and bright
azaleas. And then there's the *reason* for the name change; something mysterious dressed in whispers and snippy answers. For this
being such an honor, it sure has a big cloud of stink around it.

I asked roundabout questions, but all I got was a whole lot of
cold shoulder. Two days ago, Granny James took me by the arm and
leaned in close, the way she does when she's either dead serious or
sharing a secret. My hope for a secret was squashed when she used
all three of my names. "Tallulah Mae James, it is unbecoming to
question one's good fortune. We'll hear no more about it."

Well, I knew sooner or later adults always blab about what Gran
calls *things that must never be mentioned*. You'd think they'd be better at keeping things to themselves, with their rules and maturity
and all. Sure enough, last night I overheard Daddy talking on the
phone. Turns out Jacob LaFollet was a *Communist*, so the name had
to change "posthaste" (which is the same as PDQ, but Dad likes
old-fashioned words).

I reckon the posthastedness is why I'm out here in a sleet storm,
shivering in anklets and black patent leather shoes.

As I watch from the stage, the Spanish moss is getting stiff, frozen drips from the twisted arms of the old trees. My hands inside
my white rabbit muff are the only warm things on me.

This muff is the best thing I got for Christmas. Naturally, it
was from Granny. When I opened it, Margo—she hasn't let us call
her Momma since the twins were born—had a hissy fit, saying nobody needed to wear a poor rabbit's fur and that both Granny and I
should be ashamed. Granny told her to get down off her high horse
before she got a nosebleed. In a polite voice, of course. Granny is
always polite, even if the meaning of her words cuts deep. Margo
gave Granny the stink-eye and lit a cigarette, which Granny hates
because proper Southern ladies *do not* smoke. That's the way it is
between them.

I keep the muff hidden in the way back of my closet, just in case Margo gets it in her head to get rid of it. She's like that. Daddy says she's a woman of *conviction* and *principles*. Maybe so, but I think sometimes she just wants her own way.

I peek at the newspaper photographer in the first row. He's not looking at Daddy, the star of the show. He's looking at Margo. Everybody *always* looks at Margo. Instead of wearing a nice dress, coat, gloves, and a church hat like the other ladies, she has on tight, tight black pants and a fluffy mohair "ski sweater." (I guess it's okay to steal the hair off a goat but not a rabbit.) Why does she always have to stick out like a kangaroo at a tea party?

She's from up north, although I've overheard some people say they think she came from another planet. She is special. Extraordinary. Daddy reminds us all the time. Lately, though, I've been wishing raising blackberries and pecans at Pearl River Plantation—or even the fact that Dharma and Walden are twins—was enough special for her.

Even this morning, on the James family's special day, she had Daddy stop the car when we got to campus. "Let me off at the curb. I need to see someone about the rally for Africa before this absurd waste of money."

"Today?" Daddy's voice was sharp, and I braced myself for a fight. *Please, please not today.*

"This is *important*, Drayton."

Daddy's ears turned red, but he let her off at the curb. And I finally let out the breath I was holding.

When we pulled into his faculty parking spot, Granny James was already standing there, dressed in her funerals-and-weddings clothes, waiting under her big black umbrella.

She waved a gloved hand at the weather. "So much for the great myth of perpetual summer."

According to Granny, Northerners have a lot of misunderstandings about the South. Like how folks shivering up there in Vermont and Minnesota think we're picnicking in warmth and sunshine all winter long—perpetual summer. She takes a great deal of pleasure in setting Northerners straight whenever she gets the opportunity, which mostly presents itself with Margo.

"You all look quite elegant. If only your grandfather were here to see this day." Even though Granddad died in a hunting accident when Daddy was ten, Gran keeps him alive with her stories. "James Hall," she said it like it held some kind of magic. "A family tradition. And you'll be next." She patted Griff on the shoulder.

"I'm going to be a newspaper man," Griff said. "Like Clark Kent. In New York or Chicago. I'll write about things that are happening now, not stuff from a hundred years ago."

"Up north? Gracious, Griffin!" After shaking her head, she said, "When your father was your age he wanted to fly airplanes, the next week it was to sail around the world, then it was to become an African safari guide . . ." She waved her hand to indicate the list went on and on. "But you'll see, just as he did, tradition, that's what's important to a family."

"If I was a boy, I'd teach history at Wickham." I was sorry I said it even before I took another breath. I don't even like history.

"Oh, Tallulah, you'll support the James family tradition in other ways, ones more suitable to a young lady." Then, as if unsuitability brought her to mind, she asked, "And where *is* Margo?"

Daddy took Granny by the elbow, and we all started walking. "She'll be right along."

"Drayton! Can't she just—"

"It's fine, Momma. She'll be here." He didn't sound very convincing.

Griff and I hung back. I said, "I'm so mad at Margo for ruining Daddy's big day with a meeting."

Griff kept our umbrella pointed into the wind as he shrugged. "What did you expect?"

I guess he's given up. But I haven't. Someday the French will get out of Algeria and Margo can stop protesting and just be our momma again.

As we waited to be called up to the stage, Griff said, "I wonder when Dad decided he wanted to be a history professor and work the orchard?"

I shrugged. "Does it matter?"

"What if it happens to me? I want to live in a city. Do something exciting!"

"Yeah." I laughed and nudged his arm. "Be Superman."

"Clark Kent! Superman's not a real person. I'm not stupid."

Clark Kent isn't real, either, but I suppose there are people who do his job, so I stayed quiet.

A few seconds later he said, "I just don't want to be like Dad."

"Why not?" Daddy is as close to perfect as a person can get.

"I think he wishes he was somewhere else."

"Maybe when he was a kid. Not now."

"Oh yeah? Just the other day when he and Margo were fighting, he said that her life wasn't the only one that got ruined. He gave up what he wanted, too."

Truth be, Daddy and Margo can have some real window rattlers. "That's silly. He has all the James family traditions. He has us. Maybe gave up a motorcycle or something." There never seems to be enough money, so that made sense.

"Now *you're* being stupid."

"Griffin!" Granny hissed in a rough whisper and pointed toward the stage steps. "Go fetch Dharma."

Griff shoved the umbrella into my hand and went to pull Dharma off the platform steps before she reached the top.

She kicked and squirmed as he brought her back, knocking loose the bows and braids I spent a half hour on this morning. "I want to tap dance!"

She's been taking lessons—Granny's idea, to "give her fondness for drama a place to vent." Now Dharma is crazy for it, clattering around all day long on the hardwood, demanding we watch her "shows," driving us all out of our minds.

Griff and Gran got busy shutting down Dharma's hissy fit. Granny said, "Tallulah, there's a comb in my pocketbook." She held out an arm, and I took it off her elbow.

The pocketbook is one she saves for the best occasions. It's not heavy like her everyday purse, because she only puts the bare necessities in it just before she leaves the house. The wind tugged at the umbrella, so I set the pocketbook on the step so I could flip the clasp one-handed.

There was a folded hanky on top. As I lifted it, something fell out and clattered against the wooden riser. A gold necklace with a large locket. I know all of Gran's jewelry, she likes to tell me the stories that go with each piece—and this one looks old and full of stories. But I've never seen it.

"Tallulah!" She let go of Dharma, and snatched the locket off the step. "I said I wanted a comb!"

"Where did that come from?" I asked.

"Just do as I say and hand me that comb." She slid the necklace into her coat pocket.

I know how to read the atmosphere, as Daddy says. It's an important skill when you live in a town where everybody thinks your mother is from another planet. So I see right quick Granny's not going to be telling me stories about that necklace.

Margo finally shows up as the dean finishes his speech, the eyes of everyone listening to the dean shift to her, and I am so embarrassed I want to sink into the stage. But Daddy looks so happy when she takes his hand that I find some forgiveness.

Just before we're all frozen to death, Daddy goes to the podium. He hands his umbrella to Margo, then takes off his hat before he speaks. Sleet gathers like salt in the sharp part of his dark Brylcreemed hair. Even with the dressing, I see his cowlick is trying to poke up.

As I look beyond the small crowd, I see Mr. Stokes and Maisie off at the edge of the quad, holding hands and dressed in their Sunday best. It's a little bit of a shock to see their dark faces on campus, but Mr. Stokes and Granny James go way back to when they were both children at Hawthorn House. And me and Maisie are best friends, even though we don't see each other much except in the summer. I take my hand out of my muff and give her a secret wave down at my side. Maisie smiles, so I know she sees it.

Dad only says about three sentences, then the dean shakes his hand. And that's that. LaFollet Hall is now James Hall. A big banner is pulled to cover the limestone engraving over the front doors.

The newspaperman calls, "Dr. James, can we get a shot of the family?"

Dharma jumps right up there; she loves having her picture taken. I nudge Walden to get him to move forward and stand beside her. Griff and I stand right behind the twins, and Granny takes her place between us and Daddy.

The newspaperman looks up from his viewfinder. "Where's young Mrs. James?"

I feel Granny stiffen. She hates it when people call Margo "young Mrs. James."

When I turn, Margo's nowhere to be seen. "She had to get out of the weather," I say quickly. "She's taking a cold." Some folks don't understand the importance of getting France out of Algeria.

Dad puts his hand on the shoulder of my wool coat and squeezes a little. I'm not sure if it's a warning that I'm in trouble for fibbing, or a thank-you for making a good excuse.

We all smile big, fake picture-taking smiles for the newspaper. I pull my hand out into the cold and take Granny's. Even through her gloves I can feel her warmth, or maybe I'm just imagining it because I always feel warm when she touches me.

She gives my hand a squeeze, and I'm almost glad Margo and her beatnik clothes aren't here.

When we get home—without Margo—Daddy stands on the blue-and-white-checkerboard asbestos tile in the kitchen with his coat on, like he can't figure out what to do. He's deflated and low, the happy leaked out of him when Margo disappeared.

"I'm so proud of you, Daddy," I say. "You gave a fine speech."

He doesn't look at me when he says, "Thanks, kiddo."

I look at Griff, raising my eyebrows and giving him a head jerk to join in, but he just shrugs and goes to his room. Griff always backs me up, even when he thinks I'm wrong . . . unless it has anything to do with Margo.

Well, *somebody* needs to make Daddy feel better. "Gran's right. Margo was disrespectful. She should be ashamed!"

Daddy's gaze flashes my way and his shoulders snap straight. "You *will not* speak of your mother that way. You get to your room and think about all the good, important things she does."

His hateful tone stuns me. I stand there, unable to move.

"You heard me. Go!"

Dharma comes into the room, all sweetness and sunshine. She has some sort of radar that lets her know two things: if one of us other kids is in trouble, and if one of us is getting too much attention. She slips right up against Daddy and wraps an arm around his leg. His hand comes to rest on the top of her head.

I try to explain. "But, Daddy—"

"*You* should be ashamed! I want a list by tomorrow morning of the things your mother does to make *your* world a better place."

I heard him and Margo fighting the other night, and *he* said she was neglecting the family and needed to stay home more. Now he's acting like she's perfect and *I'm* bad.

Dharma looks up at him. "*I* love Margo."

My heart slams against my ribs. I run to my room, tears stinging my eyes. I know better. Talking about Margo always makes Daddy forget all his own rules about logical debates and presentation of facts. He loves her more than *anybody*, even us kids.

I throw myself on my bed and bury my face in my pillow. The *fact* is, Margo was selfish, no matter what Daddy says.

I lie there with my notebook and pencil, listening to the weather beat against the house, my heart filled with disappointment. This was supposed to be a good day. A day that was going to change our family back to the way it used to be. Before Margo decided it was more important to look after Africa than it was to look after us.

Instead of the list I'm supposed to write, my pencil begins to sketch on its own, as it often does. The lines and arcs, swirls and shading begin to take shape. Soon I see it's a carousel. From my favorite day *ever*.

I was only five, but when I close my eyes, I can still smell the hot sugar from the cotton candy wagon, hear the breathy toot of the calliope in the center of the leaping horses. The beachside amusement park was filled with colorful lights and sugary treats—and happiness.

Momma, this was before the twins, before she was Margo, held me by the waist on a horse that leaped so high I got dizzy. Griff galloped beside me all on his own. Momma's bright laughter cut through all other noise as she watched Daddy stand on the horse in front of us with his arms outstretched to keep balance as it rose and fell and whirled. We were a team then, us Jameses, so we all ignored the grouchy old operator when he shouted for Daddy to sit down. Finally, the man pulled the lever, the music notes dragged slow, and the circling came to a coasting stop. He made us get off, but Daddy didn't get mad. He just laughed and took us to the next ride, then the next and the next, until the park closed and Daddy carried me on his shoulders, exhausted and sticky, to the car.

Griff comes into my room and looks at my notebook. Then he smiles. "That was a good day."

As he says it, I realize just how long it's been since our family has had a good day.

"But there wasn't a storm." Griff points to the page.

In the background, I've drawn dark swirling clouds and angry crashing waves. Jagged lightning streaks in the distance.

"No, there wasn't," I say. "That came after."

As far back as I can recollect, there were no storms in our house on Pearl River Plantation until after that trip to the amusement park. But that first one was a horrible, raging thing that rattled the windows and shook the walls.

Griff had been acting like his shadow was creeping up on him all week, jumpy as a cat in the dog pound. He was like that: seeming to know trouble was coming before it walked through the door.

Daddy tucked me into bed as usual, but it felt strange, because Momma wasn't just in the other room. She was nowhere—well, she was somewhere, but not here.

Griff and I had spent the whole sweltering day lazing in the shade and hanging our heads inside the blackberry refrigerators. It was too hot to eat lunch, so we hadn't bothered coming up to the house. When we finally came in, hungry as bears, the sun was sinking low. The house was empty except for the dirty dishes piled in the sink and Momma's radio playing on the kitchen counter.

For the first time in days, Griff was still and quiet. "She's probably gone to the store," he said.

"But Daddy has the car."

"Maybe Mrs. Buell picked her up. She's always offering to take her."

"Momma said she'd rather starve than take a ride from Mrs. Buell. Momma says she's a hippopotamus."

"A hypocrite, not a hippopotamus, you goof." He ruffled my hair, like he did when he was teasing me, but his eyes weren't laughing.

He got busy scraping the last of the peanut butter from the jar, making us sandwiches. Then we watched *Kukla, Fran and Ollie*, my favorite show. By the time Daddy got home, I'd kind of forgotten Momma wasn't there and went to bed just like always.

A loud noise startled me awake. I sat up in bed, looking around. My room was bright from the moon.

Something thumped in the house, and my heart beat fast and scared.

Then Momma yelled—I didn't understand what, but it was an awful noise. I jumped out of bed, threw open my door, and ran toward her voice.

When I got to the living room, a book almost hit me in the head.

Daddy had blood running down his forehead.

Momma was yelling, shrill, angry words.

And then Griff was there, pulling me from the room.

Daddy yelled. Words so full of anger I couldn't understand them.

"Come on, Lulie!" Griff held my arm so tight it hurt, tugging me out the kitchen door and across the damp grass.

He didn't let go as we ran out to the orchard barn.

"What's happening?" My words were smothered in his pajamas as he grabbed me in a bear hug.

"It'll be okay."

I pushed him away. "Daddy was bleeding!"

"He's fine. Forget about it."

"I can't! I can't forget! They . . . they . . ." I started crying too hard to talk.

He turned on the hose and held it for me to take a drink. I finally caught my breath.

"Come on," he said. "I want to show you something." He took my hand, gently this time, and we left the barn and headed toward the pecan orchard. Everything looked silver in the moonlight. Silvery and cold, even though it was still daytime hot. He talked the whole way, about nice things, things we'd do before school started and I went to kindergarten—find me an arrowhead down by the river (Griff found his last fall), tie a rope onto a tree so we could swing ourselves into the swimming hole, go on a Labor Day picnic with Tommy Murray's family (he and Griff are best friends like Maisie and me, but Tommy's white, so they get to spend more time together). He got me thinking on so much, I was barely crying anymore.

"Here it is," he said as he stopped.

We were at the corner of the orchard, the trees in lines like soldiers at our backs. He took me right to the edge, where the ground fell to the river below. I felt the cooler air, smelled the mud, heard the easy movement of the water.

"Are you still scared?" he asked.

I want to tell him I'm not, but I never lie to Griff.

"It's okay," he said.

I opened my mouth and a little hiccup came out, the leftovers from crying. "Not as scared as I was."

"Close your eyes and wrap it up in a tight ball."

"Wrap what up?"

"The scaredness." The silver of the moonlight shone in his eyes. "Go on now. Close your eyes."

"Don't let go of my hand," I said, afraid I'd lose my balance and tumble into the river.

"I won't. Swear on my arrowhead."

That's his most serious promise, so I close my eyes.

"Now wrap it up in a tight ball."

"Okay."

"Now open your eyes and throw that ball into the river."

I look at him.

"Do it. It's gonna sink under the water and get carried all the way out to the gulf. It'll be gone forever."

"How do you know it'll work?"

"The river has magic. Indian magic. It gave me my arrowhead, didn't it?"

I nod.

"Okay, then. Throw it."

I pulled my hand from his and hurled that ball as hard as I could.

"Good!" He laughed a little. "Next time you can just use your mind to throw it. You don't have to use your hands." He ruffled my hair. "Feel anything different?"

My heart wasn't thudding. The knot was gone from my throat. "I . . . I do feel a little better."

"It'll get better the farther the ball goes downriver." He took my hand again. "We'll stay in the barn tonight." We start back through the orchard.

As we lay side by side in the barn, just before I fell asleep, he whispered, "Just remember, when I'm not around, the river will always make everything okay."

3

I'm not much for thinking on the Jameses who came before us; I'm usually too busy trying to deal with us Jameses who are here now. But in the two weeks since the building rededication, the whole *James family legacy* is stuck in my head. No matter what I'm doing, it buzzes around in there, landing on my arithmetic problems and interrupting my concentration when I'm studying for the spelling bee (winning is going to be my "suitable" contribution to the family legacy).

I keep thinking of each of our lives as a long rope with different knots in it. There were a lot of knots in Daddy's rope before any of us kids were born, so I can't say for sure that he *doesn't* think his life got ruined like Griff said. Ruined! Such a horrible word. And Daddy says words are the weapons of great men, so he always chooses them carefully, even when he and Margo are fighting.

Gran says I stole my curiosity from one of the barn cats. But I just want people to be honest, like she says I must be. She's usually happy to answer my questions, probably so I don't go asking anybody else about *things that must never be mentioned*. So I decide to go to her house after school to find out more about Daddy's life getting ruined. Because, if it's true, maybe Griff *needs* to be worried about getting stuck on the farm and being a professor. After all, he's eleven already.

After the dismissal bell, Griff and Tommy are waiting for me at the stairs that lead down to the front doors. Lamoyne Elementary looks like it belongs in a horror movie with bats flying around the bell tower. The other side of town, where the lawyers and doctors live, just got a fancy new school, long and low and modern. Gran says we should be glad we don't go to the new William Faulkner Elementary because our school is rich with history and tradition. It's also got grooves worn in the wooden steps, soot from the coal furnace, and mice bothering the cloakroom, but I reckon that's all part of the tradition.

"C'mon, Lulie! Tommy got a new puppy," Griff says. "His name's Buster."

Most times Tommy and Griff let me tag along on whatever they're doing—unless it's shooting BB guns or digging through the city dump for stuff they can use to build go-carts and inventions and the like.

"I'm gonna go check on Gran," I say. "I'll meet the puppy to-morrow."

Griff eyes me for a minute, looking to see if I'm hiding something from him, even though he knows neither of us keeps secrets from the other. Then he shrugs. He and Tommy take off at a run as soon as we're out the door.

It's warmed up real nice for February. I'm checking the bare trees for the first spring buds as I walk around the corner of the school building. As I clear the corner, I'm just about knocked off my feet. My lunch box and my booklet of spelling bee words fall to the grass-bare ground.

"Watch where you're going!" Grayson Collie says, and gives me an extra shove.

I take two steps backward to keep from falling.

I want to say something sassy, something that'll make him feel as bad as he tries to make other people feel; maybe something about the way his second teeth overlap his crooked front ones, or the way he picks his nose all the time.

I don't, though, just like I don't dare bend over to pick up my stuff. I learned the hard way not to turn my back on Grayson. He's big for a sixth grader because he was held back in fourth grade (supposedly because he missed so much school on account of having pneumonia, but everyone knows if brains were leather, Grayson wouldn't have enough to saddle a june bug).

"Where's your retard brother?" he says, looking around. Grayson mostly picks on coloreds but makes an exception for me and Griff. He's easier on me when Griff's around. Griff fights back.

No one can see us where we stand. My heart hammers while I make up my mind if I should run. Can I make it to the street before he catches me?

He takes a step closer.

I squeeze my eyes closed. I hear crumpling metal, then his laughter and his cloddy feet running off.

I open my eyes. My lunch box has a foot-shaped dent in the top.

I collected Coke bottles along the sides of the roads for a whole summer to get that *Sky King* lunch box. I'm mad enough to run after him. Luckily, my brain kicks in before I do. All I'd end up with is something else broken.

Last summer Maisie told me a colored boy's arm ended up in a cast just because he didn't get off the sidewalk fast enough when Grayson and his toadies came along. But even if that kid had been white, Grayson still wouldn't have gotten in trouble. Blame never sticks to him, on account of his daddy being the police chief.

Once I'm sure he's not coming back, I pick up my spelling bee booklet and brush off the dirt. I leave the lunch box right where it is and head toward Eudora Avenue. If I take it home, I'll have to explain how it got ruined. If I do that, Griff will look for a way to get back at Grayson. And Chief Collie has a particular dislike for Griff for some reason. I'd rather carry a brown paper bag for the rest of my life than have Griff do something that will get him in trouble with the chief.

Eudora Avenue is the prettiest street in the whole of Lamoyne. It's lined with giant arching trees and has big grassy islands with flowering bushes and fancy lampposts. It's even pretty when everything is winter-bare. All of the best stores are on it, including our

one hotel, Mr. Hayes's drugstore, Potter's Hardware, and the Southern Belle Dress Shop. As I pass Bertram's Candy it smells like warm
butter and sugar (Gran says Bertram Beecher uses a fan to lure in
customers). If I had a dime, I'd go in and buy a piece of fudge, but I
tell myself the smell is almost as good as tasting it.

Down past Bertram's is the fancy building that used to be First
Planters Bank. We don't pass this building without hearing one of
Gran's stories. Granny's Great-Granddaddy Neely gave it life years
before the War between the States, her granddaddy used it to save
our town during Reconstruction, and her daddy rode it to its death
in the Depression. My favorite story is about the time her granddaddy took down a robber with a pistol all by himself, saving his
depositors from losing their fortunes.

Now there aren't any more Neelys, not since Granny became a
James.

In the next block is the big Western Auto where my bicycle
lives. I step into the shade of the deep V-shaped alcove that leads
to the front doors and there, in the display window between the
car tires and rifle racks, sits Sadie (I've already named her), the
most beautiful red bicycle I've ever seen. I'm bumping my knees on
the handlebars on the one I'm riding now, a hand-me-down from
Tommy Murray's older sister. I know a new sixty-dollar bicycle isn't
likely in my future, but a girl can dream.

As I'm standing there, admiring the two-tone seat, the shiny
wire basket over the headlight, and the rack over the rear fender,
there's a ruckus on the street behind me. A car horn honking over
and over, short and long blasts. Underneath that, voices are singing
loud.

I step back onto the sidewalk—along with a lot of other people
stopped in their tracks and drawn out of stores. On the other side
of Eudora Avenue, a car is weaving too close to the parked cars on
one side, then to the island on the other.

It's *our* car! Daddy's driving. And singing! I'm so happy to
see him smile, my heart floats a little lighter. There are at least
eight people in the car with him, students by the look of them,

packed so tight that body parts are sticking out the rolled-down windows.

I hear a man behind me. "I knew it. I just knew it. That damn Drayton is just like his uncle George—a James through and through."

A little shiver runs down my back. I hold still, hoping they don't notice me.

"Bad blood, I say," an older voice says. "Only a matter of time. Wonder what ever become of that crazy George?"

"Ain't no great mystery far as I'm concerned. Looks like Drayton got hisself the short end of the James family stick—"

I spin around. They're in the door of the Western Auto. "At least my daddy is an educated man and uses proper English!"

Both men look as surprised as if I'd sprung up out of the sidewalk like a fast-growing weed.

The older one pokes his gnarly cane in my direction. "You watch it when talkin' to your elders, young 'un." He looks old enough to have fought in the War between the States, like a shrunk-up apple with white scraggly hair sprouting all around his head and out his ears. Too bad the Yankees didn't get him.

"C'mon, Vesper. Leave the child be." It's another voice. I look past the hateful old men and see Mr. Hayes standing in the door with a shiny galvanized bucket in his hands. His brown eyes are kind as ever. "She's got enough troubles, and I need to pay for this and get back to work."

I hold my tongue because I don't want to sass in front of Mr. Hayes. He's always nice to us and sometimes gives me and Griff free penny candy.

All three of them go back into the store. And by the time I turn to the street, the horn is blocks away. I duck my head against the stares of people in the street and hurry on, buzzing mad, and not just at the old cooter. Margo gives people enough to talk about in this town. Even if he was having fun, Daddy was driving reckless. And Granny wouldn't like it. She says a man in Daddy's position should behave dignified and scholarly.

As I chug along, fuming like a locomotive, those men's words rattle around in my head. Why'd they call Uncle George crazy? And what were they talking about, *bad blood?*

Now I have more questions for Gran.

Granny lives on the opposite side of town from us. I walk the dirt lane that runs through the tunnel of tree branches and ends at her saggy front steps. Hawthorn House backs up to the river and is big and old and kind of rickety, but Granny tells how it used to be when she was a child, polished and grand. Now, the wind whistles through the gaps around the front door that has cracked and peeled and been repainted so many times it looks like gator hide. Daddy is always offering to replace it, but Granny won't hear of it. She says the worn-out-ness of it reminds her of "family come before." Everything about this house honors the Neely family. I think she loves this house even more than the house on Pearl River Plantation, where she went to live with Granddad as "a young James bride." We live in that one-story clapboard house now; the pecan orchard and professoring at Wickham are Daddy's birthright.

Even though she lives here, Granny still organizes the orchard work, because Margo isn't much for what Daddy calls "agrarian pursuits." Each of us kids has a job—even the four-year-old twins, not that they're good at them. Gran says it doesn't matter, that it's the principle of learning responsibility. Walden takes his work seriously, like he does everything. Last fall, when he was supposed to be picking up stray pecans that missed the collection wagon, we found him up on the roof of one of the orchard sheds because he saw some up there. He's like that: he'll do anything to make the people around him happy. Dharma, on the other hand, pretty much ignores her chores no matter how fun we try to make them look. Gran says Dharma will come around. But I think Dharma is like Margo: not very interested in pecans.

As I come through the front door, I hear the ticktock of the grandfather clock standing under the stairs in the hallway. Gran's newspapers are on the little table next to the front door, the daily crosswords pulled out into a special pile but unmarked. I've never seen the crosswords back up for more than a day. A nervous flutter goes through my stomach.

I check the kitchen. The sink is filled with evidence of sick food—dirty china teacups and saucers with toast crumbs.

"Gran?" I head up the stairs. I hear her radio playing softly in her bedroom. "Granny, it's me."

"In here, sugar." Her voice is croaky.

Her room smells of Vicks VapoRub. She's pushing herself up in bed, her flannel nightgown buttoned to her neck. President Eisenhower is talking on the radio about the new Cuban government and that dirty communist, *Fi-del* Castro.

She glances out the window. "What time is it? Drayton hasn't come already, has he?"

"No, ma'am," I say. "I walked here on my own after school."

"It's too cold to be traipsing all the way out here."

"It's warm today."

"Well, you can just stay here until your father stops on his way home. I won't have you walking around alone after it starts to get dark, young lady."

I stop myself before I say that Daddy and Margo don't mind if we're out after dark as long as we use our noggins. Griff told me to stop being so honest with Gran about everything, it just makes her worry and usually sets off a fight between her and Margo.

"That's what I planned," I say, but I think Daddy might not show up today. I wonder if Margo made him so sad that maybe he'd had a nip. He keeps a bottle of bourbon in his desk drawer for a "little pick-me-up" when he's feeling particularly tired and low. If he did, I think maybe he had too much.

"Could you please turn off the radio?" Gran asks. "So much worry in the world. And bring me some aspirin, will you?"

I take care of President Eisenhower and Mr. Castro, then go to the bathroom and get fresh water and two aspirin. After she takes them, I fluff her pillows so she can sit up and visit more easily.

"Do you want to play cards?" I ask. Granny is a stickler for manners. I can't just hop into my questions.

"You're so thoughtful, Tallulah, but I don't feel up to cards today."

My stomach flutters again. Stacked-up crosswords. No cards. She must be sicker than I thought. I sit in the upholstered chair, thinking about those men at the Western Auto and eyeing the bottom shelf of her night table where the old black photo albums sit.

It just now comes funny to me that Gran is always talking about family and traditions but never Uncle George. Only that he left Lamoyne a long time ago.

"Uncle George was firstborn, right?"

She sits up a little straighter and gets a cloudy look on her face. "Why on earth are you bringing up George?"

I tell her how the men at the Western Auto said something about bad blood and Uncle George. I don't tell her *why* they were talking about the Jameses in the first place.

Gran's lips press together, like she does when she's perturbed. "You shouldn't be hanging around Western Auto, but yes, George was older than your Granddad." But she doesn't start off on a long story about the funny things George did as a boy, his accomplishments, and how he fits in our family like she does about everyone else.

"Is he dead?" I ask.

"Why would you ask that?" Her voice cracks from her cold.

"Well, you said, he *was* older. Like he's dead."

"Oh, I suppose I said that because he's been gone for so long."

"So? Did he and Granddad have bad blood like those men said? Is that why he left?"

She looks like she's parsing her words, finally she says, "There's another meaning—" She stops. "You need to stop listening to gossip. It's rude and unladylike."

"But why—"

"Hush now," she interrupts. "No good ever comes of listening to rumors." She lowers her chin and gives me that look, the one that both shames me and makes me feel like I'm special.

I want to ask how I'm supposed to tell if something's a rumor if I don't know what really happened, but not after that look. Instead, I reach down and pick up the photo album with *James* written on the cover in spidery white script. "Can we look at pictures of Granddad and the old Jameses?" Maybe I'll see a picture of Uncle George and see if he looks like a crazy loudmouth.

"Of course. Hop up here." As she makes room for me to sit beside her, she starts coughing. I pat her on the back until it passes, then hand her a tissue to blot the tears the coughs squeezed from her eyes.

I open the album to the first page. There's a thick, yellowed picture of about twenty people standing in front of the wide steps up to the porch of our house at Pearl River Plantation. It's less warped and worn than it is today, but still not what most Yankees think of when you say plantation house. No Tara for sure. Sitting on a half-raised basement that used to be the kitchen, it doesn't even have a second story, let alone a "grand staircase." Nowadays people would just call it a farmhouse and avoid the confusion. But there's the James family tradition, so it stays a plantation.

"That's the extended James family. This is your Great-Granddad James." She places a red fingernail on a whiskered man standing behind a woman in a chair. "Your Granddad is on his momma's knee."

"Why is he wearing a dress?"

"That's the way they dressed babies back then. More comfortable and easier to change diapers."

I look at her, trying to figure out if she's just making that up so I won't think Granddad was a sissy.

"So, which one is Uncle George?"

"There, up on the porch with his arm wrapped around the post."

He looks to be around the twins' age. I wonder why he wasn't with the rest of the kids down front. It's hard to see his face with him so small and shaded by the porch.

"So if George is older, why didn't he get the orchard and become a professor instead of Granddad?" Even I know it's the firstborn son who's supposed to get all the stuff—even when you're not living in a castle.

For a minute, Gran just sits there. Then she finally says, "Let's just say George wasn't well suited to either one."

"What does that mean?" *Crazy George.*

"He wasn't"—she paused—"an intellectual like your grandfather. And as for Pearl River Plantation, well, he was just too . . . scattered. And he didn't have a good wife like me to do the organizing." She winked.

"So where'd he go and what *did* he do?"

Her eyes cloud, and she looks like she's taking a walk in the past. Finally, she says, "One day, he left without so much as a goodbye. Like I said, he was . . . undependable."

"He left, so Granddad *had* to be the professor? And you both had to take over Pearl River Plantation?"

"Your grandfather didn't *have* to. He *wanted* to."

"But the legacy. *Somebody* had to be the professor. And then Granddad James died and Daddy had to be a professor instead of climbing mountains or guiding African safaris."

"It wasn't like that. There were other things—" Suddenly she stops talking, tilts her head, and pats my hand. "As we become adults, our views change. It's not that we give up our dreams—reality sometimes changes them for us. You'll see."

None of this sounds good for Griff. And it certainly doesn't explain why Daddy said his life was ruined. But Gran has that look in her eye, so I leave the subject there for now.

"I want to see another picture of Uncle George. One that shows his face better."

"There aren't any more."

"Why?"

She pauses, like she does when she's making up her mind if I'm old enough to hear something. "Your great-grandmother took his pictures out of the albums after he left. Destroyed them."

"If Griff ever decides to move away, we're not getting rid of all his pictures!" I decide right then and there that if anybody tries to, I'll snatch them up and hide them.

"No, no, of course not. Your great-grandmother was a very rigid woman. Not very tolerant of . . . imperfections. If things turned out to be a disappointment, she just pretended they didn't exist."

"Uncle George was a disappointment?" Because he was a loud-mouth? Or because he was undependable? I start to turn the pages of the album and, sure enough, there are tiny white corner holders without pictures on several of the black paper pages. And some of the other pictures aren't regular size, like they had part of them cut off.

"Poor George." Her words are a breathy sigh. "He was so lively. But no one understood him."

"What does that mean?" I ask.

Gran blinks and shakes her head a little. "It just means he didn't fit in and decided he'd be happier if he moved away." She closes the album. "You know, I'm feeling a little hungry. Would you mind making me some cinnamon toast and tea? Then we can play some cards."

I'm so happy that she's feeling better I put the photo album on the foot of the bed and hop up. "Sure!"

I'm in the kitchen with my hand in the breadbox before I suspect she just wanted to stop talking about Uncle George.

The streetlights are on and the stores closed as I pass through town. The cube clock on the corner of the bank says it's ten after six. As I pass, I look into Hayes Drugs to see if Mr. Hayes is still in there, sweeping up and restocking shelves, so I can wave to him. But it's dark, except for the dim light behind the lunch counter. I *can* see my favorite thing in the store, the giant yellow ceramic lemon that dispenses lemonade.

On down the block, the traveling yellow lights that surround the marquee at the Roxy Theater make my shadow do a wavery little dance on the sidewalk. *Vertigo* is playing again. I want to see it, but not enough to take twenty-five cents that can go toward saving for one of those new Hula-Hoops at the five-and-dime.

I'm crossing an alley, practicing wiggling my hips for when I get a Hula-Hoop, when I hear a bang. Turning, I see Griff flying out the back door of Billiards and Beer, a pool hall I know no kid is supposed to be in. Even standing this far from the back door, it smells like an old deep fryer and warm beer. Gran calls it a human cesspool (not one of the vocabulary words Daddy gives us each week, so I had to look that one up on my own) and says it should be burned to the ground.

Griff sprints in the other direction, his jacket whipping in his hand. I've just opened my mouth to call to him when the door slams open again, so hard it smacks the brick wall. Two men come out with pool sticks in their hands. They skid to a stop at the other end of the alley.

They can't catch my brother. Not only is he fast, he's wily. He knows more hiding places around this town than a stray cat.

One of the men yells, "We'll find you, you little son of a bitch!"

Language like that out on the street where ladies and little kids can hear proves Granny is right about this place. I bet they spit on the sidewalks, too.

When I get home, there's no sound of Walden clomping around in his Bat Masterson outfit, Dharma's tap shoes, or the smell of Margo's lit cigarette. Griff is sitting watching *Lassie*, like he's been there for an hour.

"Why were you at Billiards and Beer?" I ask.

"I wasn't."

"I saw you!"

"Whoever you saw, it wasn't me," he snaps, and crosses his arms over his chest.

"It was so you!"

"Was not. And stay out of alleys when it's dark."

"Gotcha!" I point a finger at his nose. "How do you know it was in the alley and dark if it wasn't you?"

He's always mad when I outsmart him. For a minute, he sits there grinding his teeth. Then he says, "I was working."

"You can't work at a bar! You're a kid!"

"Oh yeah?" He reaches in his pocket and pulls out a handful of crumpled bills.

"Jiminy Cricket! How much?"

He stuffs the money back in his pocket. "Not enough."

"For what?"

"Emergencies . . . and baseball cleats. Last year's are too small."

Griff is really good at sports. But Margo says it's more important to use our money to free Algeria. I say what good does it do to
live in America if you can't play baseball?

"What kind of emergencies?" I ask.

He gets up, goes to open the refrigerator, and points inside.
"Like this. We need to eat."

I peer inside. There's a milk bottle empty but for a clotty ring
in the bottom and a shriveled apple with a bite out of it (Dharma,
no doubt). Just looking at all that emptiness makes me hungry in a
place so deep it doesn't feel like my stomach at all.

I want to point out that the wad of money in his pocket isn't doing us any good because the stores are all closed. But it's kinda nice
to have somebody worry about me, so I stay quiet.

He goes and gets the box of Sugar Jets off the top of the refrigerator and shakes it. It sounds almost empty. Then we sit side by
side on the davenport, eating dry cereal out of the box and watching
TV until Daddy comes home with a sleeping twin on each shoulder. He looks like all the smiles and songs and horn-honking have
been wrung out of him. The twins must have had dinner at the
sitter's. My stomach is still grumbly, so I'm a little jealous—even
though Mrs. Collins smells like mothballs.

While I help Daddy tuck them into bed, I tell him my worry
about Granny not being well for orchard season.

He shrugs. "She will be."

"What if she isn't better when the blackberries need picked?"
Granny's the only one who knows where to order supplies and what
workers to hire for the harvest and which ones are nothing but
trouble.

"The birds can have the damn blackberries this year!" His tone
is so cross that I run to my room.

After I'm in bed, I can't stop thinking about the orchard. Gran's
been trying to teach me about pruning the blackberry canes, but some-

times I still can't tell a primocane from a floricane. If I cut down the wrong ones, we won't have any fruit. And the pecans. The trees only produce a big crop every other year, and this year most of the trees will have a big one. How will we get all the work done? The farm is in our safekeeping for future Jameses. We can't be the ones who ruin it.

Granny always says I worry three steps ahead of where I need to. She says keeping your eyes fixed on the mountain you might have to climb is a good way to fall into a pit right in front of your feet. But the harder I try to stop worrying, the worse it gets.

Suddenly I feel so lonely for Griff that I wrap myself up in my quilt and head to his room.

Daddy started to add the ductwork for central heat back when I was five and hasn't got around to finishing it. Granny says Daddy has "sporadic enthusiasm" for projects. Like two years ago, when he started to invent a new kind of pecan sheller. He barely slept for working on it. But his enthusiasm left town and the half-finished machine is growing rust behind the orchard shed—next to the un-used bricks he's been collecting from knocked-down buildings for years to pave our driveway.

When I open the door, Griff's on his belly with his arms thrown wide, sound asleep.

I curl up in a ball at the foot of his bed, in the space between his feet and the wall. Even with the quilt, I'm cold.

Maybe my shivering wakes him up, because in a bit he says, sleepily, "Lulie? What's wrong?"

I usually only come in when Daddy and Margo are having a row. And then I'm busy with calming Walden. I've never figured out how Dharma sleeps through them.

"What if Granny isn't better when it's time for pruning and fertilizing?" I ask.

"I swear you're the only person who can worry about a tornado on a sunny winter day. Dad will figure it out if Gran can't."

"Daddy said the birds can have the blackberries this year!" I surprise myself by how loud I am and quickly cover my mouth with the quilt.

"He didn't mean it."

"What if he did?"

"Dang, Lulie! The parents say stuff they don't mean all the time. Stop worrying. Dad won't let the farm get ruined."

"But we need to—"

He surprises me by leaning forward and giving me a hug. Griff isn't a hugger like Walden. "We can't do anything about the black-berries or pecans tonight." The hug ends with a little shove. "Go back to bed."

"I feel better when I'm with you. I'll be quiet. I promise."

"You're crowding my feet." He reaches under his pillow. "Here." He presses something into my hand.

When I feel the coldness and the jagged edge I know exactly what it is. His arrowhead. He treats it like a diamond and never lets anyone touch it, not even Tommy.

"It has big Indian magic," he says seriously. "You can keep it until Granny's better."

"Truth?" I stare at the chiseled stone in my hand.

"Truth."

I wrap both of my hands around it and hop off the bed before he changes his mind.

"Thanks, Griff," I whisper as I hurry back to my room.

A couple of weeks later, Daddy is teaching a late class and Margo is off at one of her meetings, so Griff and I put Walden and Dharma to bed. It takes both of us to wrestle Dharma and run a toothbrush over her teeth. Once the twins have settled down, Griff and I elbow each other for room at the bathroom sink.

"I heard Mrs. White and Mrs. Adler talking today. I was in the cloakroom and they didn't know I was there. They said you'd better start getting to school on time or they're calling the truant officer," I say.

"I'm not truant. I show up."

"Late!" Griff doesn't understand how much better off we are if we stay invisible. "They said we're not *properly supervised* and our clothes are dirty." Granny James would have a stroke if she heard that—besides, our clothes aren't all *that* dirty. "They're talking about calling a social worker."

"That's stupid. They're just old biddy gossips. Besides, school's a waste of time," he says. "It's making us a bunch of robots."

Lately Griff's taken to repeating Margo—at least about the stuff he wants to be true. He's not so keen on her *Christmas is nothing more than a way to get people to spend their money on useless junk and distract them from the real problems in this world.* Or *Television is arsenic to a child's mind.*

"Dad says formal education is important," I say around my toothbrush.

"That's because he'd be out of a job otherwise." He takes the cup from the holder and rinses. Then he hands it to me and dries his mouth on a towel he picks up off the floor. "And they don't talk about us because I'm late for school. They do it because we live in a run-down house and Margo is . . ." He stops. "If we were rich, nobody would talk about us."

Apparently, Griff isn't into Margo's *Capitalism is a ravenous monster devouring our souls*, either.

I spit and rinse. I'm putting the cap back on the Gleem when Griff leaves the bathroom and shuts the light off on me. He loves doing that, leaving me standing in the dark with a dripping toothbrush. I leave the bathroom and walk into the cold hall, toward my bedroom. Our house feels empty, even with me and Griff and the twins in it.

I feel a little ashamed for wishing Margo tucked us in bed at night and packed our lunches in the morning. But some days I guess I'm just a selfish girl.

A while later, I hear a car in the driveway and headlights arc across my wall. I go into the living room and wait. Daddy comes in and stands in the middle of the room with his hat in his hand. "Margo not home?"

"No," I say. "She said her meeting will be late so she'll stay with a friend."

The words seem to hit Daddy's shoulders like stones. His eyes close. He stands there kind of swaying for so long, I think maybe he's fallen asleep. Then he rubs his eyes with his thumb and forefinger. "'Yet the soul maintains its deathly sleep and the heart bleeds from a thousand wounds.'"

"What?"

"Hugo Wolf." He shakes his head and hauls his heavy legs off to his bedroom, closing the door behind him.

I dread what's coming. Daddy's moods usually settle in for a while once they arrive. And *shadow time* is the worst mood of them all.

After that night, Daddy pretty much disappears into his whiskers and his dark, closed-up bedroom.

And Margo just plain disappears.

4

May 1958

Griff says you can get used to a sharp stick in the eye if it's there long enough. But I can't get used to Margo not being around at all. I know it's stupid to miss her, because she wasn't home much and didn't hardly do anything for us anyway. Still, it doesn't feel right in our house without the smell of her cigarette smoke or the sound of her and daddy talking late at night.

Not long after Margo took to the wind, Gran had a little sit-down with Griff and me. She made it clear Margo's whereabouts are no one else's concern and we're to keep family business to ourselves. She also told us we have nothing to be ashamed of. *Ashamed*. That means Margo is up to something sinful. But at least it means she's not kidnapped or dead.

Of course, everybody in Lamoyne who wouldn't say two words to my face about Margo before she disappeared wants to ask after her now that she's not around. So I came up with a good, shameless reason for her being gone. She went back up to Michigan to care for a sick aunt.

After a while, people started asking too many questions, so I decided my excuse needed some legs. Now I say that Margo volunteered for the Red Cross and had to leave for Africa straight *from*

Michigan. That's how volunteering works. You go when they need you.

People generally look surprised, and not always convinced. But at least the questions stop. Which makes walking around town a whole lot less like dancing on a hot skillet.

I'm headed to the Farm and Feed to pick up the order of pectin for the upcoming jam making. Passing an alley in the neighborhood near the school, I hear a cat yowl in pain. I follow the sound. It's coming from a garage with its door open to the alley.

Just inside, Grayson Collie is sitting on the concrete floor, taking a lighter flame to the whiskers of a cat he's tied to a toolbox.

"Hey! Stop that!" The words are out before I think.

Grayson looks up. "Fuck off, or I'll come out there and set you on fire." He holds the lighter closer and closer to the cat's paws, staring at me as he does.

My body goes as hot as if it *is* on fire. I snatch up a rock and send it sailing right into the middle of his forehead.

He drops the lighter and grabs his head. I see blood through his fingers.

I run in, yank the twine off the cat's neck, scoop it up, and run like the devil.

Grayson is shouting horrible things. I hear his feet pounding the ground.

The cat is squirming and yowling. I keep running, arms tight around it.

Car tires screech.

I turn. Everything goes slow. I'm frozen, watching the shiny bumper come closer, closer.

It stops just short of me.

The cat wriggles free and takes off. I can't move.

"Are you all right?" A man's voice.

I look up from the bumper.

Mr. Hayes is out of his car, hurrying to me. "Tallulah! You can't just run into the street like that." His hands are on my shoulders, then he takes my wrists and holds out my arms. "Was that your cat?"

My knees are jelly. I look at the blood welling up along the cat scratches. "No. I saved it." I look back into the alley. It's empty.

"From what?" Mr. Hayes is taking a handkerchief and dabbing at the blood.

I almost tell, then I remember that after I reported Grayson to the principal for shoving me off the monkey bars we got a rock through the front window of our house. "Some kid was hurting it."

Mr. Hayes looks down the alley with a frown. "Who? Where was he?"

"I'm sorry I ran in front of your car. I'll be more careful." I pull my arms from him and hurry off on rubbery legs.

I hope Grayson's too worried about somebody finding out he was torturing a cat to come after me. I'll have to watch my back for a while, though, just in case.

That night, I'm lying in bed with my arms and legs spread wide so none of my parts are touching because it's so hot, studying the shifting lace of moonlight through the trees. For the whole day, my insides have been buzzing like one of Mr. Stokes's hives, thinking of what *might have* happened to both me and that cat.

Finally, I hear Griff walk to his room and close the door. He stays up late reading hot rod magazines. He and Tommy have been collecting parts from the junkyard and storing them in the old smokehouse out back. By the time they're old enough to drive, they plan to have a dragster ready to "ride the curbs."

I peel my sweaty self from my sheets and go to his room. He doesn't look up when I open his door.

"I know you're awake," I whisper.

He tucks an arm behind his head. "What's the matter?"

"I don't know." I can't tell him the real reason for my buzzing, he'll get mad—and get even. Since I've been working in the blackberry cane at least I don't have to explain the scratches on my arms.

I sit on the foot of his bed. I just need to be near him for a bit, that'll calm the bees in my chest.

He doesn't say anything, just waits like he always does for me to spill my guts.

"Do you still want to go to a big city and be Clark Kent?" I ask. The question aggravates those bees like a bear paw after a honeycomb. If Griff leaves, I'll be all alone on nights like this.

"Maybe. I want a place where I'm who I am because of me, not because of Margo, or Dad, or Great-Granddad Neely, or anybody else. Been thinking on California. Everything is new, not chained to the past. And it's the hot rod capital."

"The whole state? I thought a capital had to be a city."

"The only part that counts is LA."

"Because of Hollywood?"

"Because of everything about it. You can be anything there. Anything at all. And it's sunny and dry." He pats the bed. "No damp sheets."

"Well, like Gran says, it's too early to be making those kinds of decisions."

"I reckon." He sighs and puts his other hand behind his head. "So what's really keeping you awake?"

"That was it." It wasn't when I came in, but it certainly is now. "I don't want to wake up one day and you'll have disappeared, too."

"Oh, Lulie, she doesn't deserve you missing her. It's nothing but fights and embarrassment when she's here."

I think he just wants to remember the bad so he doesn't miss her himself.

He goes on, "Dad will get over shadow time. The talk will die down. Things will be better than ever. You'll see."

"Good. If it's better than ever, you won't need to leave." I head back to my own bed before he can say any more.

We're two weeks into summer vacation, and I'm up with the birds. Not because I want to be. It's harvest time. Blackberries might not look dainty, but they are as delicate as snowflakes. Got to get them off the cane and into the refrigerators before the heat of the day.

Pick them a day too early, they're sour. A day too late, they're mush.

The early rising is only tolerable because Maisie and I pick side by side, then spend the whole rest of the day together—that is, unless her momma has work for her at Judge Delmore's house. Maisie's momma works there as a cook. Sometimes Beulah, the housemaid, has extra outdoor sweeping or woodwork washing for Maisie. I don't like the way Mrs. Judge Delmore talks to Maisie and her momma. She's one of those ladies whose nose is stuck so high in the air it's a miracle she doesn't trip over everything. As Gran says, there's never an excuse for unkindness.

Most girls have a best friend of their own color, but Maisie and I are salt-and-pepper best friends. She's almost always got a good amount of humor in her, unless her daddy's in a mood. That's one thing that makes us such good friends, the way we both have to check the wind around our houses before we know how the day's going to go. I guess you could say we understand each other, which is important in friendship. Gran says things will change in time for Maisie and me. Ridiculous. That's like saying things will change between Griff and me.

Before I go out to the orchard barn, I stick my head in the boys' room. I don't want to wake Walden, so I tiptoe in and shake Griff by the shoulder. He takes a blind swat and catches me in the nose.

"Hey!" I loud-whisper. "I'm just trying to keep you out of the doghouse. Better be in the barn by the time Gran gets here." If there's one thing I hate, it's Griff being in trouble—it almost feels worse than when I'm in trouble myself.

I give him one more poke from arm's length and hurry toward the door. He buries his face in his pillow and mumbles, "Coming."

I can't dally around prodding him. If I'm late Gran makes me and Maisie pick in different spots to remind me to be responsible.

Next, I open Daddy's door. His room is dark because he closed the shutters on the outside and keeps the drapes tight. It smells like phys ed and Billiards and Beer all rolled into one. I don't remember the last time I saw him anywhere but in this bed. He's on his back with an arm thrown over his eyes. Gran says he'll come around when he's ready, and to leave him be unless he isn't breathing. I walk over and put my finger under his nose. He is.

As I eat my bowl of cereal, I'm feeling pretty low. I can't wait to see Maisie. No matter how bad I'm feeling, she can always get me to laugh.

Dew sparkles in the rising sun as I come out the back door. I feel better already, just being out of our house. Sometimes it feels so heavy I'm surprised it doesn't collapse on us while we're sleeping.

I walk toward the barn, which sits off from the house, between the pecan orchard and the blackberry fields. Every step away from our house lightens my mood. I feel even better when I set eyes on Mr. Stokes—and then a little worse when I don't see Maisie at his side. In addition to being Maisie's Granddad, Mr. Stokes is Gran's right-hand man in the orchard. He's our bee man, too. He brings his hives every spring to make blackberries for us (pecans are wind pollinated, and he says the bees respect that) and honey and beeswax for him.

"Mornin', Mr. Stokes."

"Mornin', Miss Tallulah."

"Fine day," I say. It's always best to mind manners before asking a nosy question.

"Indeed."

"Is Maisie coming today?"

"She be along."

I'm relieved and a little worried. Her daddy gets rough with her when she sasses. I won't know if that's the case until I see her, though, because Mr. Stokes is almost as bad as Gran when it comes to *things that must never be mentioned*.

Since I've been thinking this morning on different colored friends, I've taken count. All of Griff's friends are white. And Daddy's friends are all white. I never see Margo's friends. They could be purple for all I know. But I can't quite figure Gran and Mr. Stokes.

"You and Gran have known each other a long time, right?" I know Gran likes Mr. Stokes and respects him, because us kids are supposed to use the same manners on him as we would any white person. But being friends is something entirely different.

"Since we were children bedeviling my mama and your Mamo."

"Did your mother work for Mamo all her life?" I ask, hoping Mamo didn't treat old Mrs. Stokes the way Mrs. Judge Delmore treats Maisie and her momma.

"Pretty much. They run a tight ship, those two. Was back when Hawthorn House was still somethin'." A pleased smile curves his mouth. Gran likes to tell how ladies fought one another for an invitation to tea or to be included on the Christmas party guest list. But that was before the Great Depression ate up all of Great-Grandfather's money and finished with his pride for dessert.

"Were they friends, Mamo and your momma?"

He's quiet for so long I almost ask again, but when I glance up at his face and see the quizzical look on it, I know he heard and is just parsing it out, as he does.

He finally says, "I'd say they had a strong respect for each other, those two ladies. But friends . . ." He shakes his head. "Not in those days."

"Things were different?" I can't believe it. Margo says nothing's changed in Mississippi since the first slave was dragged here in shackles.

"In some ways," he says slowly. "Some the same."

"You and Gran seem like friends."

He stops dead. "We do?" Then he tilts his head. "Don't let folks hear you say that."

"You're not friends, then?"

"I reckon that depends on what you mean by friend."

"Well, Tommy and Griff"—my yardstick for all friendships—"spend lots of time together and keep each other's secrets and will get in a fight to defend each other, so I guess that's what I mean."

He's quiet again, looking off in the distance. Finally, he says, "If that's so, then I reckon you can call me and your granny friends. Just don't go doin' it out in public."

I wonder what part of my definition provoked the distant look and what made him finally decide his answer was yes.

Today's a lucky day—for me, not so much for the orchard—because the picking is light. Gran always says we're one bad harvest ahead of the taxman. Maisie and I have our berry pails cleaned and stacked long before lunchtime. Her momma usually packs a lunch for her and me and Mr. Stokes. Well, she packs enough for Griff, too, but he's always in a hurry to meet up with Tommy. I'm pretty sure Tommy's mom keeps a lunch ready for whenever Griff shows up—she's one of those mothers who's always trying to feed you. Not like Margo.

Griff takes off on his bicycle, and Maisie and I get permission to take our lunches down by the river for a picnic. Well, Maisie gets permission from her Pappy Stokes, I'm what Daddy calls a free-range kid, better to learn how to be responsible for myself.

As we walk slow and easy through the shade of the pecan orchard, Maisie's singing. Which is another thing I love about her, if she wasn't my best friend, I might even be jealous of her voice. Griff says I can't carry a tune in a bucket. He always tells me true about things like that.

After her song is finished, she asks, "Still no Margo at your house?"

"Nope." I like the way the *p* pops but can't use it around Gran or Daddy, because *nope* isn't an actual word.

We walk on, quiet with each other, scaring off a rabbit or a squirrel every now and again. Gran keeps the orchard floor neat by hard work, not by letting livestock graze like some do. Which means we can look at the sky as we walk and don't have to keep an eye out for manure.

Finally, Maisie asks, "Think she'll ever come back?"

I know Maisie's heart; she's not just nibby-nosing like the rest of Lamoyne. Still, I can't bring myself to speak what I'm afraid is true, so I shrug. Which is also a forbidden answer around Gran and Daddy.

"Does it go away, the missin', the longer she's gone?"

"No." I'll only admit this to Maisie. I make Daddy and Gran think I'm not sad over it. Daddy is sad enough already. And Gran's always trying to fill us up; I don't want her to think she's not enough.

But she isn't. And I don't understand why.

I say, "It's crazy, but I feel Margo *not* being here way more than I ever felt her *being* here."

"Maybe not so crazy. Momma says people never miss a thing till it's gone from them."

Maisie's momma is like Daddy in that way, always saying thought-provoking things. Sometimes Daddy's answers to my questions are so longwinded that I forget what the question was by the time he's done trying to make me figure it out on my own.

After a moment, Maisie asks, "Why're we goin' this way?"

Since we're settled into being best friends for life, I've decided to show her my secret place by the river. Griff is the only other person in the world who knows about it.

I stop and look at her, holding up a pinkie finger. "There's a magic place. You can't tell anyone."

Her eyes are wide and serious as she links her pinkie with mine. "I swear."

I nod and we march on. Thinking on secrets and friends makes my curious nature think of Gran's slippery ways when it came to Uncle George. "Did your Pappy Stokes ever talk about Daddy's uncle George?"

"Who?"

"Guess that answers my question."

We reach the place where the pecan trees are the oldest, and the rail fence meets from south and west, and the land drops away toward the river.

"Here we are." I stand and look around, *reverently*, as Daddy would say. Sometimes I'm thankful rather than vexed over Daddy's weekly vocabulary words. Like right now, when no other word but *reverent* could describe how I feel.

Maisie looks around, bewildered. She hasn't understood the magic yet.

"Here." I climb on the rail fence, then reach up and pull myself onto a thick branch of the most perfect pecan tree that ever sprouted. This is *truly* my secret place, off the ground and farther away from the world.

Maisie follows me and we sit quiet, side by side, looking at the river.

"Now I see," she finally says, hushed and respectful. Then she knocks her shoulder into mine. "Thank you for bringin' me."

"That's not all." I reach into my pocket for the safety pin I tucked in there when I got dressed this morning. "This is the place we're going to be blood brothers—or sisters, I reckon."

"What do you mean?"

"Last month, Tommy and Griff did the ceremony to become blood brothers. That means you might not be born from the same people, but you're linked just the same. It's a forever promise."

Maisie nods solemnly. "If you think it'll work, then I'm ready. What do we do?"

"I prick each of our thumbs with this pin and we squeeze out a drop of blood. Griff said the proper way is to slash across your palm, then shake, but then you have to explain why you have a cut, and blood brothers are secret and sacred."

"I'd rather have a thumb prick anyhow, if you're sure it'll work the same."

"Griff says the important part is the promise and the mixing of blood."

Maisie keeps her eyes on mine as she holds up a thumb.

"Ready?"

She nods.

I stick my thumb first, then hers. I'm happy to see that our blood is exactly the same color. It makes me think this will work for sure, even though our skin is different.

We press the blood spots on our thumbs together. "Blood sisters," I say.

"Blood sisters." Maisie's face is serious enough that I know she's putting her heart in it, which Griff says is important.

Once it's done, we sit for a while watching the river and I can tell something inside me has changed. I think something inside Maisie has, too. We *are* sisters.

The Saturday before the Fourth of July, Gran and us kids come home from the grocery store. The twins make straight for the tractor-tire sandbox. I lead Gran and Griff into the house, each of us carrying two big paper bags. Gran's talking about this week's case on *Perry Mason* as we walk through the back door. And there sits Margo, big as you please, at the kitchen table smoking a cigarette and reading a book.

I stop dead and blink, just to make sure she's not a mirage. When I open my eyes, she's still there, dressed head to toe in black. Her eyelids are black, too—makeup, but not the kind any mother around here wears.

She's here! Really here.

Before the three of us find the voices she startled out of us, she says, "What's wrong with Dray? He won't get out of bed." She sounds like she just saw us an hour ago, and not four long months.

My mouth goes cottony, and my heart beats hard and fast. I want to drop my bags on the floor and throw my arms around her. But I hear Griff breathing behind me, deep and shaky, and I'm afraid to move.

Gran's voice is low and cold when she says, "Drayton has been ill." I swear if I turn I'll see puffs of frost coming from her mouth.

Margo's head snaps up. "Ill? What do you mean, ill?" There's a look on her face I've never seen. She looks . . . scared. "Has he seen a doctor?"

"There's no medicine for what ails him." Granny steps beside me and thumps her bags on the table. "You just take off, leaving him with four children . . . it's *too much* . . . too much heartbreak."

Griff drops his bags on the kitchen counter. Then he turns around and walks back out the kitchen door slamming it behind him.

The sharp sound makes me jump, but Gran stays as still as a tree stump.

Margo's back straightens. "He knew I *had* to go to San Francisco! I was going to die here! Those people saved me." Her hand caresses her book like it's a baby.

"Really, Margo, you cannot tell me that you were crusading for a *cause* in San Francisco these past months. That was pure selfish folly."

"If you're trying to blame *me* for Dray crawling into bed and not coming out, then you'd better rethink it. You know how he gets in a mood. And my being here doesn't change it one bit. What's it been, a couple of days?"

"Nearly four months. He's had to take sick time from the college. If he's not better by fall classes . . ."

Margo's eyes get so wide you can barely see the black around them. She shoots out of her chair and runs to Daddy's room.

Gran puts an arm around me and pulls me close. "Your children are just fine," she calls after Margo.

Her words pour over me like icy water. I realize Margo hasn't even *looked* at me.

My knees are shaky, and a darkness pools in my heart. All this time . . . and she doesn't even *see* me. I'm afraid I might throw up, but I swallow hard instead, not wanting to move from Gran's tight hold. My fingers slide into my pocket to wrap around Griff's arrowhead.

With one hand, Gran flips closed the book Margo abandoned on the table. Then she groans.

On the Road by Jack Kerouac.

"Is that a bad book?" I whisper.

"There aren't any bad books, Tallulah." She hugs me tighter. "But there are books that give a woman like your mother damaging ideas."

From Gran's comment and the title, I figure it's a book that encourages people to leave home.

Gran and I don't talk while we put away the groceries, me shaking like a willow in a windstorm and Gran thumping cans onto the shelves and closing the cabinet doors harder than usual.

I keep looking at the doorway, hoping Margo will come back, give me a big hug, tell me how much she missed me and promise never to leave for so long again.

But the doorway stays empty.

5

In all of my years away, I believed this moment would never come. I wrapped myself inside the steady rhythm of my life in San Francisco, leaving Lamoyne and all that happened here safely outside my chrysalis. And so, I find myself shockingly unprepared for the emotional onslaught of seeing the ruination of my old home.

My equilibrium doesn't return after Ross and I pass Pearl River Plantation. He's quieter than he's been on the entire trip from New Orleans. Out of respect? Because he's swallowed up in the memories of the autumn that changed us all? Or is he simply tired of a one-sided conversation? As much as I've tried to converse with some polite regularity, my words grew sparser as the miles closed between me and my old life.

As we get nearer town proper, I take my pencil from my purse and shift my gaze to the pad on my lap, coward that I am. I need to save my reserves for seeing Gran.

I place the lead tip on each of the details I've learned about the Scholars of Humanity as I read through them: (1) The cult lives in a compound tucked deep in a Louisiana swamp. (2) They identify themselves as "a beneficent society dedicated to height-

ened spiritual awareness and psychological enlightenment."
(3) The name of their leader is Westley Smythe. (Sounds like a
bookworm, an introvert, a small man who folds in on himself.
Not a *charismatic*—the word choice of the latest news report—
leader so convincing that his disciples will murder to protect him.)
(4) Walden is one of three followers arrested for setting fire to
Jonathan Moore's residence, with Mr. Moore inside. Presumably
because Mr. Moore, a nationally recognized journalist, was investigating Westley Smythe.

My pencil begins to stray. I sketch the new face of my brother.
A hard, worn face, framed by wild-looking long hair, aged beyond
his nineteen years. But I draw his eyes as I remember them, kind
and caring, open and trusting, not the empty soulless ones of the
mug shot.

"Remember"—Ross's voice startles me from my thoughts—
"he's a man, not the little boy you remember. He can stand on his
own."

I move my hand to cover the drawing.

"You're even better than you were as a kid," he says.

"Better?"

"Drawing. Griff always thought you'd become an artist." He
pauses, as if he's waiting for me to say something. Then he adds,
"Did you?"

I shake my head, too choked up by the memory of Griff spending his hard-earned money on art supplies for me. "I just doodle
around."

"So, what *do* you do?"

"I work for a charitable foundation that supports the arts and
education." I leave it unnamed, safer that way.

"What do you do for them?"

"PR mostly."

"Well, you got an early education in that field." He says it kindly,
and yet I flinch.

"I'm ashamed of it now," I say. "I was no better than Gran, concerned about what other people thought."

"Look at me," he says.

I slowly drag my gaze to him. *His eyes are the same.* And I know his heart is the same, too. Life has twisted and reshaped me, but Ross is the same as he was back in '63. His kindness and willingness to help a friend put me in this car today. It's also what sent me on the road when I was sixteen. I know it's wrong to blame him. And yet, if he hadn't come into our lives, things might have played out differently.

"You were a little kid. And don't *ever* be ashamed of the things you did to protect yourself and your family."

I manage a smile and nod. And yet those old wounds begin to bleed.

Riverside Hospital sits on the edge of town, the curved drive still shaded by stately magnolias. It has a new wing. A modernistic thing of sharp angles and glass that ignores the existence of the utilitarian-fifties brick building to which it's attached, as well as the thirties-era limestone building with art deco curves attached to that—a Frankenstein of architecture.

Ross pulls up to the new metal-and-glass front doors. "You go in. I'll park the car and give you some time with your grandmother before I come up. Room 317A."

My throat is too tight to talk as I get out of the car. The dissonance of the building, the assault of the heat, and the stifling blanket of humidity team up with my nerves, and my stomach pitches. I almost retreat back into the cool, protective solidity of Ross's Mercedes. But I press on.

The hospital smells of ether, alcohol, and floral bouquets, not helping my stomach one bit. I pause outside the door to 317. Only bed A is occupied, so this woman I do not recognize must be Gran. She is asleep, her thin white hair flattened and mussed. Her liver-spotted hand rests on the near-concavity of her stomach. Gran was always so careful to wear gloves because a lady's hands always tell her age. I step closer. The familiar wedding ring, loose on her finger, erases the denial my mind is grasping for.

My gaze shifts back to her face, searching for something of my hardy, well-groomed grandmother.

Her papery lids flutter open. She blinks and stares at me for a second, then she smiles and I recognize her completely. "Tallulah, oh my dear child." Her voice is thinner, reedier than before. "I've been so worried."

A worry she could have so easily prevented, but I don't say that, mostly because I can't speak at all.

A middle-aged nurse comes in and picks up the chart from the foot of the bed and looks at it before stepping between us and wrapping Gran's arm in a blood pressure cuff. As she pumps it up, she eyes first me, then Gran, and says, "So how is the family reunion coming?"

Without waiting for an answer, she sticks the stethoscope in her ears, but her eyes keep sliding from her watch to me and back again. After she makes her notes on the chart, she straightens the bedsheets. She then fusses with the flowers, the entire time casting surreptitious glances at Gran and then me. The action brings back a flood of unwelcome memories of Lamoyne's whispers in my youth.

Both Gran and I hold our silence until she gives up and walks out of the room.

"What a busybody. Just like her mother," Gran whispers to herself. Then to me she says, "Everyone in Lamoyne will know you've returned within the hour. You shouldn't have come."

Gran may look changed, but her foremost concern is still what people think.

"Ross insisted," I say, unable to admit my real, panicked concern for her health. "He's afraid I'll have regrets."

Gran's lips work for a moment. "Regrets are the monsters under the bed."

"You say that like you have experience." *Please tell me you're sorry and you wish you hadn't turned me away.*

She straightens slightly, and I see her reach for the dignity that has guided her entire life. "Oh, I have regrets aplenty. But none when it comes to you."

I feel as blindsided now as I did then. "None?"

"Not one." Her eyes hold mine, a hard, unyielding edge in them. Her face changes. I recognize it as the one she used in public when she was cultivating an image that was no longer a reality. She looks me up and down. "You have hippie hair."

My hand goes self-consciously to my near-waist length strands, and I'm angry with myself for doing it.

Then she adds, "And clothes."

"Well, in California it's just hair and clothes, Gran."

She offers a terse nod of concession. "So tell me about your life. Ross said on the phone you're living in San Francisco."

Pleasantries. I want to scream. "I am." I withhold details like a starving mouse guards a seed. I think of the ruined orchard. To- gether she and I could have preserved it. We could have kept it going—for Walden, for the Jameses who should have come after. "You told Ross on the phone you had a little episode. Looks to me like you've been laid flat."

She shrugs and points to her overnight case sitting on the bu- reau. "Can you hand me my lipstick? I don't want to look a fright when he comes up."

I move toward the case.

"The compact mirror, too, please, dear."

I hand them to her. "So? Is it just blood pressure, or is there more you're keeping secret?" I put enough emphasis on the word *secret* that her hands freeze as they twist the lipstick tube.

"It's just blood pressure. The doctor says I can go home tomor- row. Would you and Ross wait so I can ride down—" Her voice drops to a whisper. "To see Walden?" She swipes on her lipstick. Her voice returns to normal volume. "I can take the bus back home."

"Walden is all over the news, Gran. The cat's out of the bag. No need to whisper."

"Well, we don't need to draw more attention to it."

"How did he end up in a cult?" I ask, more bluntly than I'd planned.

"Oh, I don't believe any of that for a minute. I met Mr. Smythe. He's a good role model for Walden. His organization gave Walden purpose, a place to serve, a place to gain self-confidence."

"You don't seriously believe that?"

"You don't have any idea what's gone on here. Would a call have hurt you?"

I think of all the times I had the phone in my hand. But once I finally found the forgiveness, I couldn't find the courage.

"And would it have hurt you to let me stay?" I ask.

"I made my choices based upon what was best for you, not for me."

The color is rising in her cheeks. I don't want to be the one to send her blood pressure skyrocketing, so I drop it.

Gran seems glad to let it lie, too. "Walden has been so much better since he found the Scholars."

"Better than what?"

"You know Walden. Always such a good boy, doing his best and not causing trouble. He never felt like he did anything good enough to overcome—the tragedies." The last two words are hushed.

Is that truly how Gran remembers that domino-fall of horrors? A tidy little bundle. The tragedies.

"How long has it been since you've seen him?" I ask.

"He's been so busy with his work, it's probably been six months or so."

"Have you spoken to him on the phone?"

"Well, no. But Mr. Smythe makes sure he writes once a month. It's usually quite short, you know boys aren't much for letter writing."

I hear shoes squeak in the hall. Nurse Busybody is just outside the door, fiddling with a small cart filled with tiny white paper cups. She looks down the hall and smiles. I hear Ross say hello.

I say, "You do know that journalist was investigating *wonderful* Mr. Smythe for fraud, or money laundering, or tax evasion, or kidnapping, or wrongful confinement, or all of the above."

"Hush, now. We'll talk about this later. In private." She smiles and reaches out to Ross as he comes in. "Haven't you turned into a handsome man. It's good to see you. We have so much to catch up on."

I want to scream. "Gran! We're here because Walden needs help. This isn't a reunion."

She looks hurt, and I feel small and hateful.

She quickly regains her composure and looks at Ross. "I'm sure Tallulah is tired from all her travel. I was just asking her if you two could stay in Lamoyne tonight. Tallulah can stay at my house. And there's that nice little motel out on the highway for you. I know it's an imposition, but I'd like to ride to New Orleans with you tomorrow. I'm afraid I don't drive anymore." She offers a self-deprecating smile. "My eyes aren't what they used to be."

My heart hurts, seeing her deterioration. It was so easy to just believe she was the same person as when I left.

"Tomorrow's Sunday, so I don't see why not," Ross says. Then he turns to me. "I called Amelia from the lobby pay phone before I came up. She's scheduled to see Walden tomorrow. His arraignment is set for Monday morning. We won't be able to see him until after that. She did speak to him on the phone and instructed him to refuse questioning without her present."

"How was he?" I'm a little taken aback by the desperation in my voice.

"She said he sounded extraordinarily calm for a person in his circumstances."

Gran says, "He's calm because his conscience is clear. This misunderstanding will get worked out."

"Oh, Gran—"

"Let's not tire Mrs. James out," Ross says. He takes her hand and squeezes it. "Get some rest. We'll be back in the morning."

"Bless you for bringing Tallulah." She looks past him, to me. "The house is unlocked, just like always. I'll need clothes for tomorrow and my bag packed for the trip. Make sure you bring my navy suit and my white pumps. It'll look nice for the courtroom."

Before I can express my frustration at her concern over something as trivial as how she *looks* in the courtroom, Ross takes my arm and guides me toward the door.

"Oh, Tallulah," she calls.

I turn.

"Call Dharma. And find Griffin. He needs to come home. Let's show that we're all behind Walden."

"It's a big world. Hard to find a needle in a haystack."

"I know that all too well, Tallulah. I looked for you for years."

I march from the room, staying ahead of Ross so he can't see my tears.

As I'm in the hospital lobby restroom splashing cold water on my face, I look in the mirror, trying to see myself through Gran's eyes. My hair is much lighter, longer, and straighter. My face makeup-free but for a swipe of mascara. But the rest of me is still there; Ross certainly had no difficulty in recognizing me. But then, Ross isn't concerned that I'll further tarnish the James family name with my West Coast ways.

It doesn't matter. I'll be gone from this town tomorrow.

Ross has brought the car up to the front doors. His brown head is bent over a notebook perched on his rust-colored pant leg—no paisley shirts or plaid pants for this guy.

"Mind if I ask what you're madly scribbling there?" I ask as I get in, a diversion from discussing Gran. As a rule, I don't pry, lest I be pried upon.

"Just something for one of my cases. My best thoughts come when I'm not staring the problem directly in the eye." He closes the notebook and tucks it under his seat, then puts the car in gear. "I don't remember where the motel is."

"There's no reason for you to stay in a motel. Just drive to Gran's."

"Nope."

"Seriously, Ross. We're both adults—and we stayed alone at your house, what's the difference?"

"This is your hometown. People talk."

I can't stifle the bark of laughter. "I do believe I'm long past ruination around here."

He looks uncomfortable and sounds reluctant when he says, "I'm more concerned about your grandmother." He's quick to add, "No offense to you."

I think of Gran lying in that bed, a ghost of her former self. A natural part of nine years of aging? Or did this town and all that's gone on strip her down one layer at a time? I remind myself that she has to live here. I don't. Not anymore. "Pull out of the parking lot and take a left."

The motel has aged even more poorly than Gran. We roll to a stop, bouncing and rocking in the potholed once-graveled parking lot. The single-story concrete block building holds only a few scabs of turquoise paint. The faded plastic marquee letters clearly haven't been changed for years: SHORT-STAY RATES DAILY/HOURLY. The *D* hangs drunkenly askew.

For a moment, we both just stare at the warped orange doors and stained curtains in the windows.

"I don't think this is a good idea," I say.

"It's just one night. It'll be fine." He sounds like he's trying to convince both of us. "I'll check in and then we can make a run to the drugstore so I can pick up some essentials. You can take the car out to your grandmother's and pick me up in the morning." He puts his hand on the door latch.

I grab his arm as a rat as big as a raccoon waddles up to one of the orange doors, noses it a bit, then moves to the next. "Hell no. You're not staying here."

He sits tight, resolve on his face as he watches the rat try a couple more doors.

"Start the car and let's get out of here."

At last, he capitulates. But only if I drive from town to Hawthorn House with him lying in the back seat in case someone sees us pulling into Gran's lane. Southern chivalry knows no bounds.

Now that I'm driving, I can't divert my gaze from things I'd rather not see. I feel squirmy as we drive past the high school, which also has an incongruous addition tacked onto it. The baseball diamond looks the same as when Griff pitched from the mound, the Lamoyne Lion mascot on the half-walled sheds that serve as dugouts look freshly repainted. The football field, I see, has been renamed for the man who was superintendent of schools when I was a kid. I hated him, not because he was mean but because he always looked at me with so much pity in his eyes.

The town looks as tired as I feel. The islands along Eudora Avenue, once meticulously maintained, need to be mowed and the bushes trimmed. Amberson's Appliance and Callahan Shoes both have their windows soaped over. JCPenney and Sears, Roebuck have tried to spruce up their storefronts with shake-shingled awnings and new metal-and-glass doors. I can suddenly feel the cold of the worn, ornate brass door handle of the Sears store under my palm as I made my seasonal visit to pick up the Christmas catalog. I did it every year, and us four kids would spend hours poring over the pages, making wish lists that were never fulfilled.

I take in and let out a deep breath.

I can hear Ross shift in the back seat, as if he'd been looking at me. I'm more careful to keep my breathing normal.

On a Saturday there didn't used to be an open parking place for blocks. Now plenty sit empty in this prime block, yawning holes in a line of crooked teeth. Western Auto looks just the same as it was when I used to visit Sadie in the front window.

My fingers start to cramp as I near the old First Planters Bank building and Hayes Drugs, and I realize I have a death grip on the steering wheel.

The bank building, now housing an antique store, is just as I remembered, a monument to a vanished family name. The reminder of all of Gran's losses chokes me a little.

I'm flooded with relief when I see Hayes Drugs is still Hayes Drugs, unchanged and as sharp and vibrant as ever. As we pass, Mr. Hayes steps out onto the sidewalk in his white short-sleeved pharmacist's coat and lights a cigarette. A tall man, his back is now curved. I wonder if the stoop in his shoulders is from all the years of bending over handing free penny candy to forlorn children.

I feel a tear trickle down my cheek and lift a shoulder to wipe it away before Ross notices.

* * *

Just like our house on Pearl River Plantation, you can't see Hawthorn House from the narrow road that passes it. I'm surprised how my anxiety recedes the second I turn through the crumbling stone pillars and onto Gran's lane. No racing heart. No dry mouth. No clenched hands. The worst is behind me. I feel more like myself than I have since I saw the news in San Francisco.

As I drive the Mercedes through the overarching trees, I say, "You can sit up now, Sir Lancelot."

Ross sits up, but I can see in the rearview he's still intent on his notebook, so I leave him be.

When the house comes into view, it's just as it was when I left, no better, no worse. And it warms my heart to see it.

I'm first through the door. Ross hangs back, as if he knows I need a moment alone. I stop in the foyer, my feet frozen as I feel as if I stepped back into my fourteen-year-old self.

The house smells the same: a distinctive blend of cinnamon, lemon oil, and a hint of Chanel No5.

The grandfather clock is quiet, unwound or broken.

My gaze moves to the door of the small closet. Slowly, I reach for the brass knob, my heart hammering as if I'm in a horror film. The hinges oblige my imagining and creak as I open it. There, tucked in the front corner on the floor, are three canning jars, their red-checked ribbons gray and fuzzy with dust, the jelly darkened with time.

I pick one up and sit hard on the floor. Hard enough to draw Ross from the porch.

"Are you okay—Wow, is that . . . ?"

"She left them here," I whisper. Gran cleaned closets like clockwork every spring. "All these years and she left them there."

He sits behind me, his bent knees on either side. His hands settle on my shoulders. I resist at first, but finally allow him to pull me against his chest, taking meager comfort in sharing a memory with the only other person who knows the lengths I was willing to go to in order to hold my family together. I'm thankful he doesn't now, as he didn't then, point out the futility of such a naive gesture.

As his arms come around me I'm suddenly struck by how much I've missed the warmth of human contact.

His hands wrap around mine holding the jar with Gran's name on it in my girlish printing. I realize those mayhaws I picked when I was fourteen *did* change everything. Just not in the way I'd planned.

6

May 1961
Lamoyne, Mississippi

Spring is my favorite time of year. Summer vacation is fun and all, with no school—which allows for a break from walking on eggshells—the magic of the orchard and Maisie and spending long days on the farm. In the spring, you're standing on the edge of a thousand possibilities that *can* come true. For the whole month of May, I'm so filled with anticipation that I have trouble falling asleep. Well, anticipation for summer mixed with a dose of nerves about the upcoming seventh-grade spelling bee. I still haven't landed a blue ribbon, and this is my next-to-last year. I want to contribute to the James family legacy and make Dad proud. He says words are the most powerful weapons in the world and we need to learn to wield them wisely. And a blue ribbon might get Margo to notice me for longer than the time it takes to tell me to watch after the twins.

Even though last night's sleep was rough and short, I wake early. Golden light from the rising sun is shining through the window, setting the swirling dust motes on fire. I blow a breath in that direction. It seems to take it a long time to reach them and redirect their movement. I wonder if life is like that, changes come from disturbances from so far back you've forgotten they happened. Dad says history is like that, too, dominoes set in motion in one era toppling those in the next.

The dust slows and settles back into its lazy pattern.

Rolling over, there's a lump under my back. I reach around and pull out one of Dharma's rubber-toed Keds—a hand-me-down from one of the other kids who gets babysat at Mrs. Collins's house. My Keds never have enough life to make it through the summer, let alone get passed on. Gran says it's because I'm a tomboy, which lately is followed with a warning that now I've turned fourteen, it's time to stop running with Griff and Tommy; time to develop more ladylike pursuits. Why do girls have to change and boys don't?

I hear Dad singing in the kitchen—lately he's been in what Griff and I call his *shiny time*; he's fun and sparkly and we look forward to him coming home. As long as I can remember, his spirits have been like a roller coaster, high and low and speedy turns. Shiny time is the best of all his moods.

I toss the shoe onto the floor. It's ended up in my bed every night this week because I've been studying so much that I wake up Dharma by spelling in my sleep. I can't figure out how she sleeps through the hurricane of our parents' fights but a little whispered recitation of letters wakes her like an angry dragon.

When I sit down at the kitchen table, Dad sets a plate in front of me with a wave of his hand. "Voilà, mademoiselle."

"*Merci*, Papa."

I've only eaten two bites when he sits down across from me and says, "I have something I want to talk to you about."

Before long, we're in an argument. Although Dad would call it a debate.

"'It's not fair' is *not* a rationale, beanpole," he says. "I have no idea what that means." His voice is smooth as buttermilk, which sets off white-hot sparklers inside me.

"Why are you being so obtuse?"

"Obtuse!" He slaps his knee. "That's my girl! Now"—he nods—"your argument."

An expectant look comes to his face as he laces his fingers over his stomach. He's teaching us to be good debaters, to argue with solid facts, not wishes and supposings. I hate it. And I don't want to present an argument. I just want to go camping with Griff and Tommy on Memorial Day weekend.

"This is all Gran's doing, isn't it?" Who else would care if I go? Nobody, that's who. Nobody but Gran with her "you've come of an age for a young lady" lectures and constant cautions about "people's perceptions."

"Again, not a rationale. And pointless."

I take a deep breath and close my eyes, trying to capture a thought from the thousands tumbling in my head. Something reasonable. Something unquestionable. When I open my eyes, I keep them steady on Dad's. "First of all, if I wanted to misbehave in an unlady-like way with Tommy"—I shudder a little at the idea; Tommy's like a brother—"I wouldn't have to go on an overnight campout to do it."

Dad shakes his head. "Not relevant to your position—which is, why you *should* be allowed to go. You've just given me a reason to forbid you going *anywhere* with the boys."

I grit my teeth. "You never forbid me to do anything."

"Correction: I never have up until now. You're growing into a young woman. That changes everything."

"Why should it? You've always trusted me. Just because I'm fourteen doesn't mean I've lost my good judgment." Dad can't argue with that, not after spending my whole life making sure I *developed* good judgment—quite often the hard way.

"Now *you're* being obtuse," he says. "It's not just *your* judgment that is at issue here. I don't want you to get into a situation that's out of your control—"

"Griff will be with me! How out of control can things get? And it's *Tommy* for goodness' sake."

"Do I hear *emotion* driving your voice?"

Nothing ruins a debate with Dad more quickly than being emotional. My next argument has to be logical and calm, or he'll send me off to "think on it."

I clear my throat, stalling while my thoughts come into line. "I'm the one Gran puts in charge when she can't be around. And I'm the one who has never been brought home by Chief Collie. I'm responsible and always to school on time. I keep good grades. I think I've proven myself with my behavior and have earned the right to go camping with my brother. In fact, you should *want* me to go so I can supervise *him*."

I hold my breath while I wait for a reaction.

Finally, he smiles. "Well done, beanpole."

My heart lifts. "I can go?"

"No. But you put up a good argument. That's what counts." He gets up and ladles more pancake batter into the skillet.

"A good argument should ensure the desired outcome." It's always good to use Dad's own lingo on him.

"Not true. Plenty of flawless arguments still result in an undesired outcome. Just look at the Supreme Court."

"I don't give a fig about the Supreme Court! I just want to go camping!"

"It is totally inappropriate for you to go camping with boys, brother or not. You've come to the point when appearances count, whether we agree with the concept or not."

A red-hot fury takes my breath away. "*I'm* not the one everybody in town talks about!"

"No camping with the boys." He smiles and winks, like we both just thoroughly enjoyed ourselves.

I let my fork clatter to my plate and slam out the door. What good does it do to present a strong and logical argument if it's going to be completely ignored? And what good does it do to follow the rules, use good judgment, if you still aren't going to be trusted and get to do the things you want?

I almost wish Dad was in his shadow time—then he wouldn't know, or care, where I am.

Mother's Day is Sunday. Usually, I have the twins draw Margo and Gran each a nice card, while Griff and I sneak around town snipping flowers from various gardens—never too many at one place so they're not missed. But I have a much better idea for Gran and Margo this year.

About the only thing I've ever heard the two of them agree on is their love of mayhaw jelly. The fact that mayhaws are Southern makes Margo's fondness for their jelly surprising. I don't bring it up, though, because there aren't many things Margo and Gran can talk about with any kind of accord.

The tiny apple-like fruit isn't even as big as our blackberries, so it takes a lot to make a good batch. Last year we had the biggest haul ever. Gran and I went out in her little boat, up the river a piece, to a place where it spreads wide and gets swampy. That's where the best mayhaw trees grow. It's also where we got so chewed up by mosquitoes that we were both scratching ourselves raw by nightfall. Gran's right eye swelled shut. Margo said it was worth it because that was the best batch of mayhaw jelly Gran ever made. Gran said nothing was worth getting encephalitis. Of course, she was just being contrary because it was Margo. We've been chewed-up plenty of times and none of us have ever gotten encephalitis.

Cooking in Gran's clean, organized, well-equipped kitchen is better than cooking in ours, where dirty Tupperware cereal bowls and food-crusted plates are always piled everywhere. (Margo's not much for cooking. If it were up to her, our stove would never get lit.) I can hardly use Gran's kitchen, though, without ruining the Mother's Day surprise. So yesterday, while Dad was upstairs helping Gran unclog the bathtub drain, I sneaked her recipe, some of her canning jars, and a big pot out of her kitchen and into our trunk. I barely had it closed when Dad and Gran came out the front door.

I could tell by the sour look on Gran's face they were in a disagreement.

"Drayton, really, must she be so *blatant* about it? It's like she *wants* to stir up trouble."

"That's the whole point," Dad said in his calm, logical (and misleading) professor voice. "Things don't change if they aren't shaken up."

"This entire issue is too volatile to take much shaking without an explosion, and that won't help *anyone*."

I made myself small and still. Unlike Dad and Margo, Gran never argues about "adult matters" in front of us kids. And I wanted to know what they were talking about.

Dad put his hands on Gran's shoulders. "Momma, things have to change down here."

"Well, it doesn't have to change overnight. People need time to adjust. Our generation—"

"Has changed *nothing*. The generation before changed *nothing*. Most of the laws passed in Mississippi since the Civil War have had one purpose, to keep the Negroes in their place. Poll taxes. Literacy tests."

I should have known this is what they were talking about. Margo has been spoiling for a fight with everybody in town since she started working for civil rights. She's just nutty over President Kennedy, which is likely the reason for her new interest in Negro matters.

"Now you're talking like *her*," Gran said. "In absolutes. I respect the rights of Negroes. They should be allowed to vote unmolested and unintimidated. But all this other . . . the forcing of everyone to share the same space." She shook her head slowly. "It's too soon."

"It's the law, Momma. *Federal* law. What's going on here is *wrong*."

Gran sounds flustered when she says, "Certainly at times things are unjust, but—"

"That *but* is the problem!"

I didn't like the *but*, either, but I didn't dare open my mouth and draw attention to myself. Even though I want things better for Maisie and Mr. Stokes, everything about Margo's new work for civil rights frightens me.

Just over a month ago, she went up to Jackson to a protest for some Negroes who were arrested for using the white-only library. The "Tougaloo Nine," she called them. Police used clubs and attack dogs on the crowd outside the courthouse—which was mostly

Negroes, so nobody said much about it. Margo came home unhurt, but more determined than ever. Still, she promised she'll be here for Mother's Day. But I swear she looks like a wild-eyed horse ready to bolt. Just like she did when I was ten.

"Those men shouting damnation to race mixers and pointing fingers at imaginary communist plots are paranoid crazies," Dad said.

"They're afraid, Drayton!"

"Of what? They hold all the power."

Gran took Dad's hands off her shoulders and held them tight in her own. "Yes, they do. Think, Drayton!" She gave his hands a little shake. "Think! You could lose your job if you get mixed up in all of this. Wickham is *private*—separate from the dictates issued to public universities. Your daddy and granddaddy put their lives into that school. It's too much to risk. Let other people fight this fight."

"We need to help, not sit here and watch the rest of the country burn."

Burn? My stomach flipped. How could Dad even want Margo anywhere near something so dangerous? I wished she was back fighting for Algeria again, a place so far away that the violence can't touch her.

Maybe the bus riders won't come to Mississippi. Maybe the Negroes here are happy with their own supermarket, seats on the bus, and segregated schools. My history teacher says they are, that it's all the work of agitators from up north trying to tell us what to do; that the Negroes don't want to come to our schools. *Kind should live with kind*, he says. *It's that way in all of nature.*

I sure don't want it that way. If Maisie went to my school, I'd have one friend I could trust.

But even though I want Maisie at my school, I don't want Margo arrested and sent to Parchman Farm, or attacked by dogs. If change is coming anyway, maybe Gran's right. We should just wait. Stay safe.

When I give Margo the jelly for Mother's Day, I'll try to convince her to stay away from sit-ins and the fights and the buses.

Maybe she can be like she was for Algeria, someone who writes papers and goes to meetings and visits Washington, DC, to talk to the government. Maybe when she sees how much we love her, she'll stay home.

As I leave for school the next morning, I meet Mr. Stokes coming to check on his hives.

"Mornin', Mr. Stokes."

As he passes, his dark hand tips his white bee hat with its netting all gathered up on the brim. "Good day, Miss Tallulah." His bee gloves are tucked under one arm.

Mr. Stokes knows everything about nature and how one thing depends on another and how God's creatures instinctively know the special part they play.

I stop and turn around. "Can I ask you something?"

He half turns to me, his head tilted to the side. "Of course, Miss Tallulah. You know I always answer your questions."

"It's about nature."

He nods. "I know some about that."

"You said all bees are born knowing their place . . . I mean their jobs, what flowers make the best honey and when they bloom, and what hive they belong in."

"True."

"And they don't ever go doing another kind of bee's job, right?" He taught me all about what drones, workers, and queens do. The drones seem pretty much like freeloaders to me. But I guess them dying right after their single job is done and being left out to starve in the fall might be nature's way of evening out the scales.

"No, miss, unless the hive goes queenless or gets ready to swarm—when some of the workers start turnin' into queens and take on the egg-layin' work."

"And you said they don't go dallying around with wasps and yellow jackets, even though they're similar creatures."

His eyes get narrow and curious. "You sure you wantin' answers 'bout bees? Or somethin' else on your mind?"

This happens all the time: Mr. Stokes sees through to the secret questions that I'm afraid to ask. Maisie says it happens to her, too. I try to think how I can ask my question without sounding like I'm either being disrespectful or an agitator.

Finally, I shrug. "Never mind." I start walking before he can ask me again. "Have a nice day . . . and tell the bees I said hello." This is a joke we have, that he's teaching me bee language—even though sometimes it seems like Mr. Stokes actually *does* know how to talk to bees.

"I will," he says. I take a couple more steps before he calls, "Anytime you want to continue this conversation, just let me know."

I wish I was brave enough to ask Mr. Stokes outright what he thought about mixing the races, but he and Maisie are my friends, and I don't want him to think that them being colored makes any difference.

After last period, I'm standing at my locker trying to pull out my science book without dumping the whole stack on the floor at my feet, when I hear Grayson Collie's deep, troublemaking voice.

If the start of my day was any indication of what's about to come, this isn't going to be good. A kid spit at me in the lunchroom, calling our family horrible things. I put on my best imitation of Gran—who believes well-bred Southern ladies must rise above and swallow our ugly words—and said, "Jesus says we must love all mankind." That boy's family is churchgoing, so how could he argue with that?

He didn't. But he did spit at me a second time as he walked away, this time actually hitting my loafer. I waited until I was in the bathroom stall to wipe it off.

People at school are nastier to me than they are to Griff. He has a way of shucking off the shame and insults like dirty clothes. And now that he's the star of Lamoyne Junior High's football and baseball teams, everyone acts like they were never mean to him at all. Except for Grayson Collie. He's so jealous of Griff's elevated status, he goes double after him now—triple after me.

I lean a little deeper into my locker and hold my breath until Grayson passes—it's something I've always done, holding my breath until the bad moves on.

The next thing I know, my locker door slams against the side of my head, shoving me sideways and clattering my brain between the door and the other side of the locker. Electrified spots glitter before my eyes.

Before I can even turn around, I hear running feet and an angry growl.

There is such a flurry of shouting and noise and movement behind me, I cringe deeper into my locker, my hands protecting either side of my head.

When I don't feel any blows, I slowly twist to look.

The backs of Grayson's toadies are disappearing down the hall and sliding around the corner.

Griff and Grayson are on the floor, a tornado of grunts and fists and feet.

I don't know what to do. Griff isn't quite as big as Grayson, but he's all muscle and no fat. Still, I've never seen Griff hit anyone before, or even get in a yelling fight—he outtalks, outmaneuvers, and outsmarts instead. Grayson is a born fighter; his knuckles regularly sport the proud splits and bruises to prove it.

I take a half step toward them, reaching out in a useless effort to break them up. Grayson's foot catches me in the ankle and sends me falling against the lockers. Before I can get myself steadied to make another attempt to help Griff, he gets the upper hand and is wailing on Grayson so hard that I hear something that sounds like a bone crack. Whose, I don't know.

I look up and down the hallway, worried Griff's going to get in trouble. Then I remember there's a teachers' meeting and everyone is on the other side of the building. For a shameful few seconds, I just stand there, liking the idea of Grayson Collie getting what's coming to him.

That's when I realize Grayson's pretty much stopped fighting back.

"Griff! Griff, stop!"

He keeps punching.

Grabbing a handful of his shirt, I tug, but it's like trying to move a tree.

Finally, I get a hold of his ear and give a sharp tug. "Stop!"

When he looks up at me, he doesn't look like Griff at all. His eyes are so wild they scare me. Blood is running from his eyebrow into his left eye. His bottom lip is split.

My hand settles on his shoulder, gentling as I would a wounded animal. "Let's go before someone comes."

That seems to clear his head. He stands, chest heaving. He looks down at Grayson, who has rolled over on his side, clutching his ribs and spitting blood onto the polished floor. "Leave my sister the hell alone."

I'm tugging on Griff's arm as I kick my locker closed behind me—my science book long forgotten. "Come on!"

As we hurry out of the school, I ask, "What if he tells?"

"He won't."

"He might."

"Then he'll have to tell why we got in a fight in the first place." Griff wipes the blood from his eye and swipes his hand on his dungarees.

I don't say anything, but I'm not so sure.

We're about four blocks from school, and I'm just getting the jitters out of my stomach.

"I need your help," I say.

"I just helped you." His left eye is turning purple. Most of the blood from his face is now smeared on the tail of his plaid shirt.

"No, you didn't! You think Grayson's going to leave me alone now? You're crazy. He's going to be worse."

Griff steps close to me and looks down. "If he bothers you again . . ." He doesn't finish, but his bruised hands ball into fists.

"Dad says we need to use our brains, not stoop to meet an ignoramus on his level."

"Easy for him to say. He doesn't have to put up with all the bullshit we do."

I think of the disapproving way people sometimes look at Dad lately. "You don't know that."

Griff grits his teeth. "I can't wait to get out of this stinkin' town."

My heart gives a scared jerk, and my hands and feet shoot with tingles. "You won't leave me, will you?"

Griff sighs. "What do you want, Lulie? I've got someplace to be."

It's Friday, so there's no baseball practice.

"You hustling again?"

Last month Chief Collie brought him home for hustling pool at the roadhouse outside of town. "You know Daddy said he'd tan your hide if you ever did anything like that again." Which was almost as startling as Griff being brought home by the police chief; Daddy has never spanked any of us. He makes us explain ourselves and our "logic," then he talks and talks and talks and *talks* until you want to scream just to get him to stop.

"How about you mind your own business?" he says.

"If I'm your business, then you're mine."

"*What* do you want?"

I explain my Mother's Day plan—but I leave out the part about convincing Margo not to carry on the fight for the Negroes. Griff gave up on trying to change Margo's mind about anything a long time ago. Lately, he's taken to treating her like she's invisible, even when she is home.

"I need you to take me out in Gran's boat to get the mayhaws for the jelly," I say.

I get excited all over again. I'll give the whole batch, half to Margo, half to Gran, at our Mother's Day crawfish boil. Then I'll get Margo to promise to stay home. I keep telling myself it's just to keep her safe. But sometimes in the dark of night I get a hollow in a place that Gran, no matter how she tries, can't fill. If I can show Margo how much I need her, maybe she'll not only stay home but she'll also actually start *seeing* me.

Griff says, "Getting Gran more work to do doesn't sound like much of a present."

"*I'm* making the jelly. I already have the stuff at home. I just need you to help me with the boat."

"Can't." He turns the corner and walks off.

I'm worried. First the fight. And now just leaving me standing here with no way to get my mayhaws and no explanation why. He used to try to bamboozle me, make up innocent-sounding stories, trick me with niceness.

I stare after him, mad as a poked gator.

I'm only supposed to take the boat out with Griff (Gran's strict rule), and I don't have much time. She went up to Pelahatchie to visit a cousin, and I have to get the boat back before she gets home on the seven o'clock bus.

Well, I've watched Griff enough to know how to start the boat and drive it. That little motor barely moves as fast as a turtle. How dangerous can it be?

7

It's near four o'clock when I walk up to Gran's weather-beaten house. The branches of ancient live oaks in the front yard are thick, some twisted so low their elbows rest on the ground. Their shade makes for a sparse and patchy lawn. I notice that one of the upstairs window shutters is sagging out of square and the balcony over the front porch is drooping at one end. For a moment, I can see what people who don't love her see, a place ruined by time and bad luck.

I shake off such disrespectful thoughts and go around the house, through a lopsided arch heavy with peach-colored roses, past the covered-up well, to the shed near the river. The shed's as old as the house and in even worse shape. The whitewash has long turned a ghostly shade of gray. The hasp and hinges on the door are furred with rust. It's filled with cobwebs—probably home to a couple of snakes and river rats, too. I'm pretty brave when it comes to creepy things, but spiders make me cry silent, horrified tears.

The hasp is stuck, so I hit it with a rock a couple of times to loosen it. A little breeze kicks up, the heavy kind that tells you it's coming up a storm. I hurry, yanking the door from its swollen jamb. The hinges let out a noise like a screech owl. As soon as I get the door open, a dark shape swoops out straight at my head. I duck fast, a squeal squeezing past my lips.

A bat. I feel silly. And yet I still run a hand through my hair just to make sure it didn't land to set up housekeeping.

Once my heart settles, I wait a moment, in case any of its bat friends want to make for freedom. Peering in, the only break in the dark are a few lines of weak light sneaking through some cracks between the shrunken planks; no way to see webs or their makers. I take a second and find a stick in the yard. As my feet edge into the shed, feeling their way along the hard-packed dirt floor, I wave the stick around in front of me, a magic wand to clear out spiders and their traps.

Three steps in, I pause to let my eyes adjust. Unlike the tidy house, the shed is disorganized, the floor covered with piles and strays so you have to step carefully. A heavy-handed wind slams the door closed behind me. I can't see to move. I swear I can feel spiders crawling all over me. I squirm, bat wildly around my head and swipe my hands across my arms and shoulders. I hear a high-pitched whine, and it takes me a second to realize it's coming from deep in my own throat.

"Stop it," I whisper. "Just. Stop."

I stretch my arm out behind me. My palm touches the door and I push. Outside, I grab a big rock and jam it under the door. I tell myself the ruckus I just made sent all the spiders into hiding and walk boldly back inside. It takes me a minute to find the tadpole net we use to scoop the mayhaws off the water. Then I gather the galvanized buckets and pick up the gas can. *Light.* I shake it. Not even a slosh. I hope there's gas in the motor's tank.

Just as I'm walking back out, I spy Granddad's rubber chest-waders hanging on a hook. Leaning over a broken Adirondack chair, I reach for them. The waders are so heavy I almost fall onto the chair when I pull them from the nail.

Finally, I get out on the dock with my equipment. The bottom of the boat is full of water.

First Griff's fight. Then him abandoning me to do this alone. The stuck door. That bat. The weather. No gas in the can. Now the boat full of water. Gran always says when obstacles keep landing in your way, it's God telling you you're on the wrong road.

I stand there for a minute, deciding. Then I drop the net, bucket, and waders down into the boat. I run my purse, shoes, and socks back up to the house and leave them just inside the kitchen door, pulling Griff's arrowhead from my purse. Slipping it into the pocket of my wraparound skirt, I run my fingers over its reassuring dips and points.

The first couple of times Griff asked for his arrowhead back, I came up with excuses to keep it; an upcoming test, the spelling bee, warding off a hurricane, anything in which luck might play a role. Finally, he stopped asking. I figure he's either grown out of needing a lucky charm or just reckons I need it more. And I do—to start this cranky boat motor.

Using an old rusty coffee can we keep in the boat, I bail out as much water as I can. Then I unscrew the gas cap on the faded green Evinrude motor and look into the hole (a really smart girl would have looked before she bothered to bail). I rock the boat a little to tell where the gas level is. Not full, but I figure it's plenty.

I'm sweaty from the bailing. The breeze feels good and will help keep the mosquitoes from swarming, which will make it worth getting wet from a little rain.

Now the last hurdle, that motor. I go through the steps I've seen Griff do hundreds of times.

Turn on the choke. *Check.*

Pump the blub to prime the motor. *Check.* I give an extra squeeze just to be sure.

I grab the rubber T handle and give a yank. The T jerks free from my hands, stinging my fingers. I lose my balance and fall backward. I brace for the shock of water, but my shoulder hits the dock, launching me back into the boat. I bounce off the plank seat and onto the wet bottom, landing on my backside with a little *sploosh*. I shake off the sting in my hands and wait for the boat to stop rocking.

It always looks so easy when Griff does it.

I get back to my feet, placing them wide on the bottom of the boat. I grab the cord handle with a better grip. Concentrating on keeping my balance, I pull again.

The motor just gasps a couple of times before it dies.

I feel the time ticking away.

Two pulls and the motor catches. Blue smoke comes out. Then it sounds like it's going to die again.

The choke!

I flip the little metal lever. Once the choke is off, the motor runs nice and smooth. I take a moment to be proud of myself.

Unhooking the rope from the cleat on the dock, I push off and head upriver toward the mayhaw grove.

Who needs a brother anyhow?

Just thinking about Griff gets me worked up. We've always been like biscuits and honey, one of us never really right without the other. Even when he and Tommy occasionally exclude me, I don't feel left out. But lately he doesn't even tell Tommy what he's up to. I think about talking to Daddy about it, but that feels perfidious (Daddy's vocabulary words are getting more and more obscure).

As I watch the water ripple past, I think about Sunday and my stomach gets fluttery. This will be the best Mother's Day ever. Much better than last year, when Daddy was deep in his shadow time and Margo stayed home from the crawfish boil just to spite Gran because they were arguing over what to *do* about Daddy's shadow time. Margo was sick of it and said he needed doctoring. Gran said he needed a wife who supported him and, given time, he'd come around like he always did. Gran was right about that last part, at least.

This year, even with the Negro argument wedged tight between them, Gran and Margo are able to be in the same room without sighs and huffing and nasty looks (apparently Gran's rule that ladies never show unpleasantness applies only to words). I'm beginning to think all that word stifling might make things fester. Margo is never bothered by festering words. I wonder if that might be the one thing about her that I should try to take after. Heaven knows there isn't anything else in her I want inside me.

The second I have that thought, I'm breathless and heated by shame. There are plenty of things in Margo that are admirable. Her sense of justice for the underdog. Her commitment to making the world better. Big, significant things.

Even as I try to convince myself those things are more important than making dinner and tucking kids into bed, I'm shocked by how *resentful* I feel.

Griff treating Margo the way he does, like she's no more than a stranger in the room, begins to make sense. What if next year *I* stop noticing Margo?

Mother's Day might be my last chance to tie our family back together before it flies apart completely. If I can make Margo see how her being gone leaves a hole nobody else can fill, if this weekend will help keep Daddy in his shiny time, if I can convince Griff to give Margo another chance, then maybe, *maybe* it's not too late.

Moving against the current of the spring-swollen river, it's taking longer than I remember to reach the mayhaw grove. Off in the west, the clouds are getting darker. The air has turned still and heavy, which tells me the storm a'coming is going to be bad. Even if I turn around now, I could still get caught out. And if I don't get the mayhaws today, the clouds might dump enough rain that most of them could be swept away.

It's hard to tell exactly where I am; the river isn't familiar to me like the roads. Not much changes in the thick green woods from mile to mile. I heard a bobcat a while back, its creepy cry reminding me how alone I am and how far from people. It also reminds me how many sizable wild critters live out here, every one of them used to making themselves invisible as they're on the hunt. I take comfort in being in the middle of the river away from bobcats (not that they do anything to people but give them goose bumps), and bears and boars (both of which are considerably dangerous to a fourteen-year-old girl without a brother or a shotgun). Of course, being in midriver doesn't help with gators and snakes. I keep a keen eye for floating logs—the kind with two protruding eyes.

Over on the left bank, I finally see something that tells me I'm almost there. A hunting cottage perched on thick piles. It's not like the splintery little shacks folks around here use to hunt and fish. Gran said this one must belong to someone from up north with more money than sense; nobody needs a fine place like this, painted white with a deep wraparound screened porch to use for a few days once or twice a year. It even has a little cleaning and gutting shed near the water. Gran bets they're the kind of city people who just shoot and catch, then pay someone to deal with the messy work. A small, yet expensive boat is tied up to a fine dock and covered with a fitted canvas tarp. It's even named *Crescent City Queen*. How fancy.

I set my sights on the right bank, looking for the place where the ground gets so low that the river oozes into the woods. A big push of wind sweeps from the west, rippling the water and shaking the leaves overhead. I catch myself leaning forward, as if that will make the boat move faster. I will the storm to take its time as the grumbling sky argues for a faster arrival.

Finally, the right-side riverbank swings away. I guide the boat over to the wide shallows. The water near the edge is dotted with yellow and red floating mayhaws. I cut the motor and pick up the net as I coast into the tiny bobbing fruit. A gritty scraping tells me the boat has grounded. I realize I'm on a sandbar dumped by the sluggish creek that winds from the soggy woods.

First, I do the easy-peasy job of scooping what I can reach. One bucket is about half full by the time I've gotten all I can from the nice safe boat. The thunder creeps closer. Occasionally the air brightens with a flash. I'm running out of time.

The bayou is clotted red with mayhaws, fast harvesting for sure. Good thing I brought Granddad's waders. Snakes mostly run off rather than chase, but I'm happy all the same to have a layer of rubber between them and my skin.

I untie my skirt, glancing around like a fool to make sure nobody is seeing me in my slip, then laugh at myself, because the only eyes around belong to birds and raccoons. The boat being grounded makes it steady as I step into the chest-waders. Once I get the suspenders adjusted to their shortest length, they fit nice and snug on my shoulders.

As I step over the gunwale, I get a little shiver—and not just from the coolness of the water passing through the waders. I keep an eye out for scaly eyes floating in the lazy water of the bayou.

Grabbing my net and the empty bucket, I start slogging toward the thickest area of floating fruit.

Suddenly I see a ripple off to my right. A sharp yelp bursts from my throat. The snake—a cottonmouth by the way its entire body is on the top of the water—glides away from me. I take a deep breath and I move forward, splashing more than necessary and singing "Itsy Bitsy Teeny Weeny Yellow Polka Dot Bikini" at the top of my lungs. Gran would not approve.

While I scoop and dump I think about overhearing Dad and Margo talking in the middle of the night one day last week. Their voices were soft and floating through the darkness that stretched between their bedroom and mine. Dad asked if she would consider spending the whole summer at home. He's worried Griff's running too wild. *Changing.* That word made me shiver a little under my sheet.

She laughed. "Isn't that what we want? For them to learn from experience? He'll figure out the boundaries. We taught him to *think.*"

"I know. But what if . . ."

"What?" she asked.

"What if he doesn't? What if he's inherited . . . bad genes from my side?"

"Don't be ridiculous, Dray. There's no such thing as bad genes. And if you really believe there are, you should have let me get an abortion when I wanted to."

"How can you say that?" Dad sounded as shocked as I was.

Did she want to get rid of all of us?

She was quiet for a minute. "It's not fair that a woman has to be trapped by her own body. Men can enjoy themselves without a thought of the consequences."

"Those *consequences* are our *children!*"

I held my breath while I waited for Margo to apologize. But she said, "All I can say is thank God for the pill. Women are finally as free as men." In a moment she added, "Don't be mad, Dray. I shouldn't have said that. I wouldn't . . ."

I kept waiting for her to confirm with words that she would not have aborted any of us. But the silence hung heavy—just like my heart.

Dad was quiet for so long, I thought he'd either fallen asleep or was too mad to talk to her anymore. Then he sighed. "What if he needs limitations right now?"

"Then you're welcome to set and enforce them." Now she sounded snippy, not soft and happy.

"You know I have summer classes, a double load because Michaels is on sabbatical. And thesis advising. Maybe if you were just around keeping an eye on things. Only until school starts again in the fall."

She said, "I'll think about it."

Think about it. All she needed was a little nudge. I decided, too, those words confirmed she didn't wish she'd ended us before we came into this world. All the more reason to show her how much she means to us.

Excitement squirms around my insides afresh and I gather the fruit faster. My bucket is heavy and full when the wind gives a good kick and the first fat drops of rain hit the water.

It's impossible to hurry when you're knee-deep in water and the muddy bottom sucks at every step. I take my time as the rain blows in sheets and plasters my hair to my head. I keep bowed, my eyes on the water right in front of me. The surface looks like it's boiling. When I lift my face and shield my eyes to see how far I am from the boat, my heart drops to the bottom of the waders.

The wind and rain have moved it off the sandbar and it's edging into the river current.

"No!" I scream and throw my shoulders into my forward movement. All I accomplish is nearly falling face-first into the water.

I hear Dad's voice, feel him tapping my temple. *"Use your noggin!"*

Let go of the bucket; drop the net.

But I can't. Letting go is letting go of Margo. Everything depends on this batch of jelly.

"Help!" I yell against the wind. "Help!"

Stupid waste of energy. Think. Move. Get that boat!

I make it over the sandbar. The boat is edging toward the middle and starting downriver.

The water is at my chest now and getting deeper. I hold the bucket high and let go of the net, using my left hand in a swimmer's stroke to pull me forward. The rain slaps my face, blurring my vision.

My toe snags something, and I pitch forward. The cold rushes against my belly, my bare legs. The bucket tips on the water, the red mayhaws spread and scatter on the current.

I flounder, grabbing to save handfuls of fruit, trying to get my feet under me. Water takes my breath, fills my mouth. I can't find the bottom. My fists slap against the water.

I can't get to the surface.

The waders are pulling me down.

My eyes are wide under the murky water.

I kick again. Reach for the surface. My lungs burn.

Take off the waders!

I try to push the suspenders off my shoulders. They're even tighter than before.

My eyeballs are going to explode.

If only I had the arrowhead. Its magic would save me. Magic . . . Griff's magic . . .

My arms fall still.

I feel light, buoyant—even as the water tugs me down.

Calm. I pull it close, welcome the serenity, the peace.

Why was I fighting? I wrap myself in the wonder of sweet clarity.

Softly drifting. Drifting . . .

8

Suddenly the serenity is ripped away; a blink, a lightning flash. I reach for the retreating comfort with greedy need, turning from the clenched fist of pain in my chest.

Rough hands pound my back.

A boom vibrates the air, the ground under me, rolls through my body.

I'm forced onto my side as I cough and retch.

"There! That's it!" The unfamiliar voice is calm. Assured. The hands move with confidence. Another thud on my back. "Get it all out."

A spurt of foul-tasting water comes out of my mouth. I wheeze in a squeak of a breath.

"That's it. Relax. Breathe." The man's voice is raised, not in panic but to be heard over the wild wind and slashing rain.

I try, but my lungs feel like twisted sponges. Breath is pain.

I manage a small gasp. Then I cough up my innards: lungs, liver, intestines, maybe even my toenails.

"Give it a minute," he says. "It'll get better. Slow and easy." A soothing hand settles on my left shoulder. There's a pain in my right; a rock pressing from the ground. I shift and lean against the knees behind me, taking the pressure off my shoulder, but the hands keep me on my side.

I try to mentally unfurl my lungs and allow the slow flow of breath.

"There. Better." A hand cups my forehead, pulling my wet hair from my face.

I can finally open my eyes. Rain splashes in the mud before my face . . . and there's something big. And pink. I blink. It's a refrigerator on its side, buried to the Frigidaire logo, discarded here or floated on high water. A beached pig.

That strikes me as insanely funny. When I laugh, it sets off more coughing.

When I finally stop, the man asks, "Can you sit up?"

I raise myself on one elbow and nod weakly, the dip of my chin sending a muddy runnel of water into my right eye.

He holds my shoulders and braces me from behind as I sit. "As soon as you feel like you can make it, we should get in the boat." As if to reinforce his words, lightning explodes a nearby tree.

With a scream, I curl in on myself. My ears ring and I'm momentarily blinded. The sharp smell of scorched wood and something metallic stings my nose.

Finally, I look over my shoulder at him. Not a man. Sixteen? Seventeen? His hair is plastered with rain. There is mud on his face. And his eyes are the bluest blue I've ever seen.

"Wait right here!" He gets up and runs into the river, diving flat and swimming to a boat rocking on the stormy water. The *Crescent City Queen*.

I take a wild look around. Raw chunks and splinters from the tree are all around me. Gran's boat is gone.

"Oh no!" I croak the words. The mayhaws. Griff's arrowhead.

The boy is a fast swimmer and is already pulling himself up into his boat. He hoists the anchor. It comes up dripping mud from the river bottom. The motor rumbles. It moves toward the bank. He cuts the power. He drops the anchor on shore and is back at my side.

"My boat!" I shout.

"We'll search after the storm. Can you get up?" he asks, his voice buffeted by the wind and words slurred by the rain.

A wall of wind bends the trees. I hear a sharp snap, followed by a low, woody groan.

"Let's go!" He pulls me to my feet.

Clutching my fists to my chest, I start to take a step, registering for the first time my naked legs and soaked white blouse. My knees buckle.

Keeping a strong arm around my shoulders, he catches the backs of my knees and carries me to the boat, lifting me high enough to sit on the gunwale. I wait, as if I can't figure out how to move on my own as he pushes off and jumps in. After he helps me to a soaked cherry-red-and-white upholstered seat, he starts the powerful motor and we head downriver, me hunched and huddled into myself, the storm and the woods fighting like titans all around us.

Every boom of thunder and slash of wind takes me back. Back to another storm.

I was nine. Angry slaps of rain and rough shoves of wind battered our house on Pearl River Plantation. Inside, in the living room, there was a hurricane; raised voices and breaking glass. Three-year-old Walden clung to me as we crouched in my pitch-dark closet. He smelled of sweat and baby shampoo. His cries slowed to sobs as I pressed one ear against my chest and covered his other with my hand.

I wished Griff was home.

I'd learned to sense the mood between my parents. They were extreme, fully one way or the other, no regular days, no middle ground. Obsessive, Gran called it, the way they saw only each other, sometimes with eyes of love, sometimes loathing, but always full to the brim.

I'd been barely breathing for hours, hoping the buzzing tension between them would burn itself out (on the lucky days, it did) before it turned into an explosion of angry words and broken dishes. This was an unlucky day, the worst of the unlucky days yet.

Daddy hadn't slept for days; I'd heard him up knocking around all hours of the night. But he was full of energy. It seemed bothersome for him to be packed inside his own skin. He talked constantly, wild and scattery, going too fast to put in all the words. That was how this fight started, with too much talk, too many ideas.

Margo finally yelled, "Enough! You sound like a lunatic!"

He got mad. Fireworks mad. The anger quickly spread to Margo, a forest fire hopping from tree to tree. From the things they were shouting at each other, I wasn't sure if *they* even knew what they're fighting about. Which meant there was no way for it to come to an end.

I edged the closet door open with my shoulder and peeked through the crack. Dharma sat on the floor of our bedroom, humming to herself and calmly playing with her baby doll.

An ashtray went whizzing past our open door, shattering somewhere down the hall.

"Dharma, come in here," I said softly.

Dharma kept humming, her hands calm as they patted her doll's back, her body rocking gently, her eyes closed. Dharma never hid when our parents fought, she made her own closet inside her head.

Margo and Daddy flashed past our doorway, Margo's face red with rage as she spit out hateful words, her fists slamming into Daddy's chest as he tried to grab her wrists.

At that moment, thunder crashed, and I wished the storm would turn into a tornado and blow our house away.

Shivering in the boat, I keep my head down, protection against the pelting rain, but not against memories of storms past.

The boy angles the boat toward the white-painted house. He cuts the motor and drifts, jumping onto the dock, whipping the rope around the cleat, then knotting it with the speed and surety of experience.

I'm barely on my feet before he's holding out a hand and shouting, "Come on!"

Placing one bare foot on the driver's seat I keep my arms folded against my chest as I try to step onto the dock. I teeter, nearly falling backward before he grabs my elbow and tugs me to safety. He doesn't let go as he hurries me toward the long flight of steps that lead up to the screened-in porch.

I don't like him walking behind me, not with my wet see-through slip and outline of white panties in his face, but have no choice because the stairs are narrow. When I reach the screened door, I stop dead, Gran's voice in my head cautioning me never to go into a house with a boy alone.

"Open it and go in!" He gives my back a nudge. "Hurry up."

I turn. "Well, it's not like we're going to get wetter!"

He shakes his head, water dripping off his chin and reaches past me, turning the latch and pushing it open and gently shoving me through. The porch is as fancy as the boat, filled with white wicker furniture with aqua-colored cushions.

"Coming?" He's walked around me and opened a French door leading to a brightly lit kitchen.

Grasping my hands together under my chin, trying not to look like I'm covering up the fact that my bra shows through my wet slip and blouse, I follow. He disappears down the hall, leaving a trail of wet tennis-shoe prints on the polished pine floor and me dripping on a braided rug by the door.

"Here." He comes back into the kitchen and hands me a plaid flannel shirt and a pair of men's pajama bottoms. "It's the best I can do. There's a drawstring in the pants. The bathroom is down the hall. I put a towel out in case you want to shower."

Something about his eyes paralyzes me. Or maybe I'm just stunned not to be dead.

He holds the clothes closer to me and gives them an encouraging shake, as if I'm a frightened dog needing to be wooed to a treat.

I swallow hard. My chest burns.

"It'll be easier to take them if you let go of those." He nods toward the fists tight under my chin.

I look down and slowly open my hands. This whole time, I've had the mayhaws I grabbed from the water in my fists, clutched as tight as if they could save me.

Staring at them, I gasp. Then a sob jerks from my throat. This handful is all I have, nowhere near enough to save my family.

With hiccups and gasps, I try to explain how important they are.

I see he doesn't understand, but he pulls me to him, hugging me awkwardly, my arms and the handfuls of mayhaws caught between us.

I realize I sound like Dad during his hurricane time, when he can't seem to go fast enough to keep up with his brain, when he buys things we don't need and can't afford, setting off fights. For a second, I'm afraid that a hurricane time has taken me. But as the boy pats my back and tells me everything is all right, I begin to slow down, both breath and thought.

Finally, he lets me go. "Maybe you should just sit down for a little bit first." He directs me to a turquoise vinyl kitchen chair with chrome legs.

"I'm too wet."

"It won't hurt anything." His smile encourages me to sit down. "I'm Ross Saenger."

It's weird introducing myself in a wet blouse and underwear. My cheeks get hot. "Tallulah."

"Tallulah . . . ?" He raises a light brown eyebrow as he draws out my name.

He's even more handsome than I thought. I feel even more exposed.

"James. Tallulah James."

He smiles again. He has nice teeth. I wonder if they're naturally that way or from braces. I bet Dharma will need braces. She wants to be onstage. Famous. Like Shirley Temple. I watched one of her movies on *The Late Show* the other night. Is Ross old enough to be out here all alone?

My mind is bouncing again. Maybe being without air messed me up. I try adding some simple numbers in my head. That part seems to be working.

"Nice to meet you," he says.

He must not see the crazy in my eyes.

"But sorry about the circumstances," he adds.

"How did you . . . ?" I look toward the river, rough under the storm.

"I saw you go past in that dinky boat right before the storm hit. I was getting the *Queen* uncovered to go check on you when I heard you scream."

I screamed?

Then I remember. "It was a *squeal*," I correct. "I was just startled by a cottonmouth."

"Well, it's a good thing you were *startled*, otherwise I might not have been there when you went into the river after your boat."

"I didn't see you."

"I was still pretty far away when you bobbed under the first time. Sorry about the waders, I had to cut the straps to pull you up." He patted a wicked-looking hunting knife stuck in his belt. "I was cleaning up in the fish house."

The waders. Gran treats everything that belonged to Granddad with the same reverence she does the family Bible. *When we honor and respect his things, we honor and respect him.* She's downright zealous about it. Now the waders are gone. Granddad's boat is gone.

Maybe it would have been better if I had drowned.

I turn on the shower in the cottage's black-and-white-tiled bathroom, wanting to rinse the river taste from my mouth as much as the mud from my skin and hair. When I step into the tub and under the hot stream, I lift my face to the spray. The flush of water takes my breath. I jerk back, pressing myself against the cold tile and forcing my panicked gasps to slow. I stand for a moment, pushing away the pressure in my chest and the feel of the dark water sucking me down.

When I finally step back into the stream, I'm careful to keep my face out of the water, wash quickly and get out. The storm outside has started to settle. The rain still rattles the tin roof, but with less fury. I stand for a moment wondering if I'll panic like that every time I wash my face. Gran says you never forget the traumatic things, but they grow softer with time. I always thought the most awful thing time would have to wear down for me was Dad and Margo's fights. But the river proved that oh-so-wrong.

The towel I drape around me is so thick and soft. Luxurious. I never had any idea the true meaning of that word until this towel. I hold it a little more tightly, breathing in its lovely, fresh smell.

Leaning over the pedestal sink, I wipe the steam off the mirror and peer closely. I'm surprised. I look like my regular self. Shouldn't the fact that I just about drowned less than half an hour ago show?

I think of Ross, the burning concern in his eyes, the way he made me feel safe even when I was coughing up half the river. I look more closely at my reflection, turning my face from side to side, wondering if I might pass for sixteen. Not that it matters. It's not like I'll ever see him again.

A knock on the door startles me.

"Are you all right? The water's been off a while."

"Fine!" I look to make sure I locked the door. "I'll be out in a minute."

I hear Ross's footsteps move away and realize I didn't hear him walk up. Maybe he's a perv and was looking through the keyhole. Maybe he broke in to this house. Maybe he's a murderer on the run. He was already getting the boat uncovered when he heard me squeal. Why would he care if I was caught out in a storm? And why would he have put that wicked-looking knife in his belt? Maybe he saved me just so he can torture me and kill me slowly. Some people are sick like that.

I almost slap the hysteria out of myself. Ross is too handsome, his blue eyes too sincere, to be a killer.

Once I'm dressed in the flannel shirt and pajama bottoms, I roll up the sleeves and the legs—just in case I have to run for my life. Then I unlock the door and peek carefully around the doorframe. It doesn't hurt to be cautious.

Ross is in the kitchen, standing at the counter. He's changed to dry clothes, Levi's and a white T-shirt, looking like a high school quarterback, not a murderer.

"Mom always makes hot tea after a traumatic event," he says, as he pours water from a teakettle into a cup. "Can't say it ever helped me after a bicycle crash. But still . . ." Glancing down to the tea bag dangling from his fingers, his expression says he just realized something. "I guess it gave her something to do other than relive the blood, stitches, and broken bones."

"Jeepers, how many bicycle crashes did you have?"

I set my blouse and folded slip on the back of one of the turquoise chairs and run my hand through my wet, tangled hair. I wish I'd nosed around in the bathroom for a comb.

He shrugs. "Dozens."

"Are you a daredevil? Or do you just have really bad balance?"

He laughs. "Depends on who you ask."

"So, this is your cottage?"

His brow crinkles. "Yeah. My parents' anyway. Why else would I be here?"

"You don't sound like you're from up north."

"I'm not. Why would you think I am?"

I shrug, too embarrassed to tell him Gran figured no right-minded Southerner would have a fine place like this just for hunting and fishing. And there isn't anything else to do out here in the boonies.

"I'm from New Orleans." His pronunciation confirms he's not lying—*N'awlins*. "My grandfather built this place back in the day. Dad says it's a waste to keep it for a couple of hunting trips a year, but Mom doesn't want him to sell it—family history and all. She had to promise to use it on a regular basis to get him to keep it. We were supposed to be here for Mother's Day, but Dad got called to New York on business. Mom went with him. I'm here to let the plumber in tomorrow morning. Leak under the kitchen sink."

"Don't you have school?" I don't want him to be so old that he's out of high school.

"You a truant officer or something?"

"No! I just—"

"I was joking. I cut classes today. Private school. Dad is a big donor, so I get a lot of slack."

"Oh."

He bobs the tea bag in the mug, then lifts it to me. "Want it?"

"Thanks, but I need to find my boat." *Please don't let it have sunk from the downpour.*

"Yeah. Okay." He looks out the window. "Let's give it a few more minutes. Looks to be clearing in the west."

"The longer we wait, the farther away it's going to be. We should have gone right away, while we were both still wet."

"You did hear the *Queen*'s motor, didn't you? Even if your boat doesn't get hung up on anything, we'll have it chased down in no time. No need to get drenched again for a five-minute difference."

At least the current should have moved it in the direction of Gran's—

A fresh bolt of panic shoots through my heart. What if it floats past Gran's house after she gets home from Pelahatchie? What if she finds my stuff in the kitchen and thinks something horrible happened?

It did.

I shove that truth away, suddenly embarrassed I needed to be saved. I'm a good swimmer. Daddy taught me to figure my way out of situations. And still, there I was, too shortsighted to throw out the anchor when I got out on that sandbar and too stupid to take off the waders before I went into deep water. If the boat's sunk, I'll have lost both it *and* Granddad's waders. And all of it is going to be for nothing if the mayhaws are gone.

"Let's go. Right now!" He looks startled, so I add, "Please."

He sets the tea on the counter. "Okay, then."

As we walk down the steps to the dock, the sprinkles end, making me wish I had waited thirty more seconds and not yelled at him.

The sun breaks through the clouds, starting the river to steaming; rolling ghostly wisps that make me think of pirate ships. Ross backs the boat into the river and heads downstream, the bow plowing through the rising silver mist. I stand holding onto the windshield, hating my helplessness, scanning the river with a mix of dread and hope.

"Hey." He looks over at me. "We'll find it. I promise."

Minutes pass as the *Crescent City Queen* speeds down the river, churning a brownish froth behind us. I have no idea how far we've gone. The only landmark I can recall between here and Gran's is the railroad bridge just upriver of her place. I grow nauseated with fear that we'll see the bridge's ironwork before we find the boat.

"There!" I point through the mist to where the little boat's nose is shoved into the green-leafed branches of a newly fallen tupelo tree. "Oh my God, there it is!"

Ross sidles the *Queen* close and cuts the engine.

"Let me just change," I say, my heart so full of relief that my voice squeezes high.

He makes a show of looking down at my skirt laying in three inches of water in the bottom of Gran's boat. "No need to put that wet stuff back on. I can come and pick up my clothes tomorrow. I'm staying through the weekend anyway."

The last thing I want is for him to show up tomorrow and spill a single secret from the ever-growing pile today is accumulating.

"No, really, I've been enough trouble." I grab my wet clothes and scamper over the side, happy to see the bucket half-full of mayhaws is also safe. My frantic fingers locate the arrowhead in the pocket before I wring the water out of my skirt. "Turn around." I spin a finger.

"Just wear the stuff home."

"Turn. Around."

I'm pretty sure he rolls his eyes as he obeys. I wrap the skirt around me before I take off the pajama bottoms, holding onto one of the tree branches to steady myself. Then I turn my back. I give Ross's flannel shirt one last pet before I take it off and replace it with my wet blouse.

"Okay."

I hand his clothes to him. As soon as he takes them, I shove his boat away. "Thanks!" I try to sound flip and upbeat. "For saving my life and all. I'll return the favor someday."

He laughs. "I sure hope not!"

As I'm bailing out some of the water, he calls to me, "I'll follow you home, make sure you get there all right."

"No!" I calm my voice. "That's not necessary. I'm almost there anyway."

Unfortunately, there's no need to convince him, because when I pull the cord to start the motor, I can't get it running. I open the gas cap and see there's only a thin rainbow shimmer left in the tank.

"I guess I need a tow." As the words leave my mouth, I'm calculating the skinny odds of beating Gran home.

The sun is down when we pass beneath the rail bridge, its rusty skeleton black in the long twilight shadows of the trees. Bats are starting to dart after mosquitoes. I send a skittish look toward Ross. Now that I know he's a Southerner, asking him to set me loose so I can paddle the rest of the way would be wasted breath. "*A gentleman never leaves a lady unescorted when darkness approaches.*" Gran drummed it into Griff over and over, always reminding him that *I* am to be counted as a lady. I wish Ross would go faster, even though he's already explained that he can't while towing my boat and with dusk settling.

All hope of keeping my secrets evaporates when I see two forms standing on Gran's dock, each with a lit flashlight. Gran and Griff.

Ross cuts the engine and glides in, tossing a rope to Griff.

"Tallulah! Thank goodness!" Gran calls with her hand patting her chest. "We were just about to call the police."

I want to melt into the river. If she called the police, the whole town would know about my stupidity. Grayson Collie is always blabbering stories his dad brings home from work. Oh yeah, he would love to spread this one around, especially after Griff beat the crap out of him today.

The whole idea of Grayson gets my blood up. Which is a good thing, because being mad at him pushes away the lump rising in my throat from seeing the anxiety on Gran's face. She has enough to worry over with the orchard and Dad's hurricanes and shadows.

My Mother's Day surprise is ruined. Suddenly the whole idea seems silly.

Griff's strangely quiet, not admonishing me and spilling the beans about my plan.

I might be able to save face if I can get my story out before Ross ruins everything with the truth.

Gran hugs me, then holds me at arm's length. "What were you thinking, taking the boat out on your own? And why? What were you doing?"

I send Griff a searching glance and he shrugs. Did he keep quiet for me, or to protect himself?

"I was fine, Gran. It just came up a storm." I pluck at my wet clothes, glancing at Ross untying Gran's boat and pulling it to Griff. "Then I ran out of gas. Lucky for me, Ross was out and gave me a tow home. His family owns that *nice* hunting cottage upriver."

Ross slides a look my way. I ignore it and pray he plays along. When he jumps onto the dock and comes to stand before Gran, my heart is about to thunder out of my body.

"Ross Saenger, ma'am."

Out of the corner of my eye, I see Griff taking the bucket of fruit from the little boat and hiding it behind a bush. I feel guilty for doubting him.

"Well, young man," Gran says, "we're indebted to you. Tallulah isn't supposed—"

"I thanked him, Granny James. Properly. I'm sure he needs to get going. It's getting dark."

"Well, then, we shouldn't keep you." She smiles. "We do appreciate your gallantry."

I shudder at the old-fashioned word, but it's so like Gran that it makes me feel warm inside, too.

"Yes, thank you, again." I mentally urge him to get going.

He starts toward his boat, but Griff stops him with an outstretched hand. "Thank you for saving my baby sister."

I want to punch him for calling me *baby* in front of Ross.

Ross shakes his hand. "Glad I was there." Then he jumps into his boat.

I'm so relieved I want to kiss him. Most boys would want to tell the whole story, soak up being a hero. I wait for the motor to rumble, only then will it be impossible for more questions to come from Gran's mouth.

My heart sinks when she calls, "Oh, Mr. Saenger!"

He looks up. "Yes, ma'am."

"We're having a crawfish boil on Sunday. I know it's Mother's Day, and you'll likely be wanting to be with your own mother, but we'd be most pleased if you could join us, even for a short while. Just a small way of repaying your kindness."

I cringe. That will mean more questions about the stranded boat.

And I don't want this boy around reminding me of my stupidity, bothering me with his handsomeness. At the same time, I hope he says yes.

I'm turned upside down when he nods and gives me a smile.

9

Saturday Margo and Dad take the twins to see *One Hundred and One Dalmatians*, giving me fresh hope that maybe our family is turning a corner and the mayhaw jelly can make a difference. Besides, I went to a whole lot of trouble getting that fruit. I don't want to have almost drowned for nothing.

Losing that full bucket cost me. There's only enough to make three jars. As I'm readying the glue-on labels (I want to write something special so every time Gran and Margo look at the jars they think of how much I love them), I pause and chew on the end of my Bic—*writes first time, every time*—pen. Gran is "disappointed" in me, which is much worse than her being angry. And she doesn't even *know* about the waders. The gift of *two* jars to her while Margo gets only one might be best; I'm more likely to get back in Gran's good graces than I am to keep Margo planted on Pearl River Plantation for the entire summer.

While I'm thinking, Griff comes in the kitchen. He almost seems like his old self when he plops in the chair beside me.

"Thanks for not spoiling the surprise," I say, even though I know if he told Gran where I'd gone, he also would have had to admit he knew about it and let me go alone.

He shrugs. "I should have taken you."

I sit up a little straighter in my chair. "I was fine! I don't need to be treated like a baby." I surprise myself with how loud I am, as if yelling it will make it more true—which is exactly what a big baby like Dharma would do.

It makes me mad that I obviously *did* need Griff to keep me safe.

I turn the tables on him before he asks me anything more about it, or Ross Saenger. When Griff shook Ross's hand as if they were friends, I had a strange feeling, a kind of pride tangled with a little bit of jealousy. It makes no sense. I'm half dreading Ross coming to the crawfish boil tomorrow. The other half of me can't wait to see him again—which is absurd because the chances of him not telling the story of me drowning are too small to calculate.

"If you had gone, I'd have put your name on the label, too." Even as I say it, I realize what a paltry offering (Dad's phrase) this is, not at all the grand gesture (again, Dad) I had in mind, a full year's worth of jelly for each of them. "Where did you have to be that was so important, anyhow?" Then I add, "Not that I needed you."

He looks like he's making up his mind whether to lie to me. I don't like it one bit, this new, untruthful Griff. Finally, he says, "I have a job."

"A job? You promised Daddy no more—"

"Relax! I'm not hustling pool. It's a real job, at the Sinclair station by campus."

"Then why are you keeping it a secret?"

"Because I'm saving the money to leave, and if Margo finds out she'll probably need to 'borrow some' for the bills. Remember how she sent the grocery money to Tibet and then robbed our piggy banks?"

"And made us promise not to tell Gran," I add. That was the worst. And here I am with another secret I'm keeping from her. Is this how you turn into a bad person? One tiny secret at a time?

"Leave—like go to college?" I ask. "But you can go to Wickham for practically free." I know Griff wants to go to college away from home, but I can't bear the thought of it. I sometimes wish he wasn't such a good athlete, so a scholarship wouldn't offer a chance to go away to school—pretty selfish of me.

"I quit baseball."

"And you didn't tell me! When?"

"Two weeks ago."

"Tommy knows?"

"I made him promise not to tell you. I don't want a big deal over it. I just want to be left alone." After a few seconds he stands. "And I'm *not* going to college. I just want to get the hell away from here . . . away from all of the crazy shit in this family!"

I'm so shocked that I can't say anything. I sit there and blink as I watch him slam out the screen door, his black high-top sneakers thudding down the back steps.

Margo's been as skittish as a cat in a room full of rockers since someone called this morning to tell her the Freedom Riders are heading to Birmingham. After she hung up the phone, she was all wild-eyed, pacing and smoking. I tried to distract her with talk about the crawfish boil and the surprise I have for her. I'm not sure my words actually sank in, but she's here at Gran's—at least for now. I get the feeling she'll be gone as soon as the last crawfish is picked out of its shell.

I'm supposed to find Griff so he and I can shuck the corn. I've already set Walden and Dharma to scrubbing the redskin potatoes. The second my back was turned, though, Dharma ran off. I hear her practicing her tap in the dining room for the show she wants to give this afternoon.

I push open the creaky screen door and go down the warped and splintered back steps in search of Griff. Margo and Gran are each standing next to a purge tub, stirring the crawfish gently with their paddles. Their words are anything but gentle. They're arguing over me.

"Really, Lavada, what do you have against self-sufficient women? Griff was taking the boat out when he was *two years* younger than Tallulah. Shame on you for denying her the experience just because she's a girl."

As much as I don't want them fighting, today of all days, I admit I feel some satisfaction over Margo's argument. I continue slowly across the yard, pretending I'm not listening.

"Don't try to make me feel narrow-minded! It wasn't an 'experience,'" Gran says. "It was dangerous. And foolish. And against the rules."

"Rules." Margo gives a little chuckle, flicking ash off her cigarette in an exaggerated way that draws attention to the fact that she's smoking. "Children constrained by rules never discover their own capabilities."

"But they do find their *limits*—once they've passed them! It's our job to safeguard them, to make decisions until they're old enough to make them on their own. She could have been struck by lightning. That boat could have been overcome and sunk in that downpour—"

"Admit it, the only thing you care about is how things appear: *What will people think?*" She's taken on an exaggerated Southern accent. "A young girl out on the river alone. Scandalous! Pos-i-tively *scan*dalous!" Margo flutters her hand in front of her heart.

Her making fun of Gran makes me want to go slap her. But I just clench my fists and dig my fingernails into my palms.

Gran's cheeks are getting red, but she doesn't say anything, mostly because Margo just keeps going. "Besides, the only thing your *rule* would have changed is that Griff could have been struck by lightning, too. And nothing *happened*. Besides, if it scared her, it does more good than all the forbidding in the world can. Now she'll think twice before heading out with a storm coming."

"You are missing the point!"

Griff sneaks up behind me and startles me by whispering in my ear. "I saw your face when you showed up Friday night. Something *did* happen. Something that scared you."

I whip my head around, ready to deny it, but when I look in his eyes, I can't.

"What was it, Lulie?" I see a trace of fear in his eyes. "Truth. What did that guy save you from?"

I open my mouth to tell him enough of the truth to not be a lie. Only a choked sob comes out.

Slapping my hand over my mouth, I make a dash for the dock, the place I sit and ponder at Gran's when things are weighing on me. But the sight of the river only makes the muddy taste of its water come rushing back into my mouth.

I stop short of the dock, gasping, choking, a hand fisted against the pain in my chest.

Then Griff is there, wrapping me in a hug so fierce it brings a pain of its own.

Me crying is something Griff isn't used to. I can tell he's not sure what to say, so he just shushes me like a baby.

That makes me mad enough to stop. I push him away and wipe my eyes. "I'm fine." I sniff. "Fine."

"Did Ross do something—"

"No!" My cheeks flush with heat. I know what Griff is getting at; Gran would use the delicate term *get fresh*. "No. He saved me."

I tell Griff the whole story, not liking the little noises coming from the back of his throat when I get to the point where I gave up and let the water take me. I've just finished telling him what happened at the Saengers' cottage—leaving out my brief, silly suspicion that Ross was a murderer—when I hear the deep sound of Ross's boat approaching.

I turn my back to the river and wipe my eyes with the heels of my hands. "Don't you dare tell him I was crying."

Griff just looks at me.

"Swear on your arrowhead!"

He shakes his head and rolls his eyes. "I swear."

I face the river again.

As I look at Ross, the anticipation that kept me awake last night comes rushing back. I spent my sleepless hours trying to draw his face, but I couldn't get the blue of his eyes right, even with the pastels Griff bought me.

My heart beats faster and my skin tingles all over as the boat nears. I can't wait to hear Ross's voice again, to look into those amazing eyes. At the same time, I want to bolt and run for the house.

Ross smiles and waves, and I raise a self-conscious hand before I shift my gaze to Griff. I'm nervous about what he'll say to Ross, now that he knows what happened.

But all I see is a new look of admiration in Griff's eyes. "I'm glad you made it," he says.

Ross cuts a concerned look to me, confirming my face is red and blotchy from crying. Then he smiles and says, "Who could turn down a crawfish boil?"

I should be relieved. But my heart is still galloping around in my chest, my ears are buzzing, and parts of my body feel so electrified that I wonder if I'm about to faint. I'm torn between aggravation and appreciation when Griff leads him toward Gran's house. I follow along, not sure where I fit in. I'm grateful when we reach the house and Walden runs up and takes my hand.

"How are those potatoes coming, buddy?"

As I sit on the back steps, watching Ross and Griff pitch a baseball back and forth (turns out Ross is a sophomore and on the varsity baseball team), I get a little ticked off. Ross is *my* guest, and Griff has totally taken over, leaving me to shuck the corn by myself. I'm tempted to go tell Gran that Griff quit baseball so she'll drag him off to interrogate him in private.

Just when I've worked up the nerve enough to do it, Tommy comes into the yard, his beagle, Buster, trotting at his side. Buster sees the ball in flight and shoots into the air, snatching it before it hits Griff's glove. Then he runs off, tail wagging, stopping a few yards away waiting for someone to chase him.

While Griff tries to get the ball, I hurry over to Tommy. I'm glad he's shorter than Griff or Ross, so I can talk into his ear without being too obvious. "Why didn't you tell me Griff quit baseball?"

Tommy squints toward Ross. "Who's that?"

"You first."

"Because he didn't want me to. Now who is that guy?" There's an edge to the question.

"Ross Saenger. He's *my* guest." Just saying it gives me a little shiver. Mine. "He gave me a tow when Gran's boat ran out of gas on Friday afternoon."

Tommy's gaze snaps back to me. "You took the boat out alone?"

I straighten my shoulders. "Yes, I did."

Griff has the ball back from Buster and is wiping the dog slobber on his Levi's as he comes closer. He dips his chin. "Tommy."

By the tense way Tommy is standing, I can tell something is off between them.

Griff says, "Didn't think you'd come."

"Why wouldn't I? I come every year." There's a challenge in his tone.

Griff shrugs, then calls Ross away from playing with Buster to introduce him to Tommy. I'm just about to ask Ross to come into the house and help me bring out the stacks of newspaper to dump the cooked crawfish on when Dad comes around the corner with a bag of ice over his shoulder.

Then I see Dad arrived with more than the ice. He hefts the bag off his shoulder and plops it on the ground near the cedar bucket holding the crank cylinder for the ice cream. "Look who I found at the bait shop!" he says, like he's just discovered Santa Claus visiting from the North Pole.

Two girls, probably from the college, are right behind him. They have teased hair, polished fingernails, and are wearing pedal pushers with blouses tied just above their navels, showing a pink ribbon of skin all the way around. Their laughing stops when they see the yard full of people.

"Yowza," Griff says under his breath, and nudges Ross with an elbow.

My ponytailed, gangly fourteen-ness is suddenly too much to bear, and I want to melt into the grass.

One of the girls seems to recover before the other. "We were about to get stuck fishing with the boys, but Professor James was nice enough to invite us to the crawfish boil." I'm pretty sure I see the girl bat her eyelashes at Dad. "He even paid for our friend's bait. Such a nice man."

Margo comes and stands right in front of Dad with her hands on her hips. "Nice man, huh?" Then she turns to the coeds. "I'm *Mrs.* Professor James." Then she waves her hand toward us kids. "Mother of his *four children*." She turns toward Gran. "And this is his mother." She lowers her voice, as if sharing a secret with the girls. "She's quite old-fashioned." There's something in the set of Margo's shoulders and the tone of her voice that is unfamiliar to me. And she called herself Mrs.! She usually corrects people when they do that, reminding them she has a name of her own.

I wait for Gran to interrupt, offer her usual open-armed hospitality. But she stays quiet.

"Don't be inhospitable, Margo," Dad says. "It's such a grand day! Have you ever seen such a cerulean sky? We have a bounty of food . . . and these young maids have never had the pleasure of dining on crawfish! Can you imagine? I admit, neither are Southern-grown, but seriously . . . a travesty." He shakes his head.

The muscles in Margo's cheeks tense as she steps nose to nose with him. "Just remember, Dray, *I* was one of your coeds once." Then she kisses him. Not a sweet peck like parents are supposed to have, but a long, embarrassing kiss.

Dad picks up Margo, swinging her in a circle. "Carpe diem, my love. Carpe diem!"

"Drayton!" Gran's voice is harsh and angry. She's never angry with Daddy. Then she turns to the girls. "I do so apologize, but I'm afraid the food won't be ready for quite some time." I can't believe Gran can lie so smoothly, without a single twitch. "Perhaps you young ladies would like Margo to deliver you back to your friends after all?"

"Come on, come on now!" Dad rubs his hands together. Then his eyes widen, like he's just gotten a wonderful idea. "Let's all go swimming!" He's already unbuttoning his shirt with one hand and grabs the hand of one of the coeds with the other as he pulls her

down the slope to the dock. "Yes! Swimming." Then he starts singing, "'Shall we gather at the river, the beautiful, beautiful river . . .'"
His belt flies through the air and lands in the grass. Then he lets
go of the girl's hand and spins around, throwing his hands over his
head. "I can walk on water!"

I stand horrified as he reaches over and tries to untie the coed's
blouse. "Let's get you baptized."

She bats his hands away and runs back toward the house, her
eyes filled with surprise and—I can barely believe it—fear.

The other coed is calling, "Come on, Babs! Let's get out of here!"

"Come to me!" Dad yells. "Can you not feel it? The power of the
water?"

I lose track of the girls because I can't take my eyes off my father.
He's down to his boxers and one sock.

Gran is shouting, "Drayton Neely James! Griffin, go stop your
father!"

Without his shirt, I see how skinny he's gotten, each rib and
knob of his spine standing out under the pale skin.

Dad reaches the dock and kicks his boxers off. I cover my eyes,
my whole body screaming with shame.

"Life is a river!"

I hear a big splash. He's either belly-flopped or laid out and
fallen in backward. I turn and run into the house, my skin flaming
with embarrassment.

Fifteen minutes later, Ross comes to find me curled up in the
front porch swing. "Um, I just wanted to see if you're okay."

I'm too mortified to even look his way. "I don't know . . . this
isn't . . . he's never—" I cut the words off, remembering him driving down Eudora Avenue with a car full of people a couple of
years ago.

When I get the nerve to look at Ross, I see his clothes are wet.
"What happened?"

"Griff and I had to go in after him. He fought us." He points to
a blossoming bruise on his cheek.

"Oh my God." If only I could disappear in a puff of smoke.

"Your grandmother said he must have had too much *celebration*." He laughs a little. "It's not a big deal. Once my dad put on my mom's fur coat and hat and red lipstick and sang Bessie Smith songs at a New Year's Eve party at our house. It happens."

"It's not drink." Dad's soared past his shiny time. The hurricane is here.

Ross tilts his head and gives me a look that says he thinks I'm a foolish child. "It doesn't matter, Tallulah." He sits next to me on the swing.

"Where are Griff and Tommy?"

"Trying to talk your dad out of taking the dock apart because there are some rotted boards. He said he wants to rebuild it with an upper deck and he thinks he's figured out a way to build a boat lift out of old tires and a block and tackle in the shed. He seems quite determined."

"*Ugh.*" I cover my face.

"I should probably go."

Without thinking I grab his hand. "Don't!" I have to fight the urge to put my head on his shoulder and cry. "Please. Stay." I pull my hand back. "Gran would be so disappointed if you missed the boil."

He chuckles. "She does seem to be intent on keeping to the original plan. She just put the vegetables in the pots."

"If you leave, she'll think you've been offended and that would bother her even more than Dad's behavior."

"Well." He takes my hand in his and smiles at me. "Can't have that." Looking in his eyes, I can see that Ross Saenger is going to be a knot in my rope. There will always be a dividing line in my life; before he pulled me out of the river and all that comes after.

Gran manages to serve dinner just like always, despite the fact that Dad's down at the dock with a claw hammer and a crowbar prying off boards. We all eat, but it's a strange time. Griff and Tommy are oddly quiet—and not just because they're stuffing their gullets. Not so strangely, Gran and Margo are acting like two like-charged magnets. But I close it all out as I listen to Ross. He's been

so many places, done so many things. It's obvious his family has *a
lot* of money, but he doesn't act like it. Even when he's talking about
ski trips and flying to Europe, there's a humility to it, an air of
gratitude to his parents. He talks about his mother—a real mother,
who remembers birthdays with homemade devil's food cake, makes
hot tea after bicycle accidents, and is there to talk when life gets
complicated—and I'm so jealous I almost cry. For the *third* time
today. A new record.

Some time later, their tension seemingly dissolved, Griff leaves
to spend the night at Tommy's house. I'm pretty sure Griff was
driven by Dad's hurricane, which is bound to get worse. I can still
hear him knocking around in the shed.

I walk Ross to his boat, almost forgetting how horrible parts
of today have been. But my easiness with him evaporates. I'm self-
conscious about everything, my childish hair, my clothes, the way
I'm walking, the sound of my voice.

Ross stops and turns to me before we reach the gap-toothed
dock, and suddenly I can't breathe.

"Thanks for today," he says, those blue eyes locked on mine.

"Sure." *Clever.* My cheeks heat up again.

Then he stuns me by kissing me on my temple.

I stand there like an idiot, not sure if it was a thank-you kiss, a
brotherly kiss, or a real kiss. So I hurry to untie his boat and cast
him off.

Right before he starts the motor, he smiles and says, "I'm glad I
met you, Tallulah James."

I stand there dry-mouthed, with my heart thundering, watching
his boat until I can't see it any longer. Finally, I calm myself down
enough to walk back to the house and help clean up.

By the time we have things in order, Dad has set up three camping lanterns and is insisting on working on the dock through the
night. Gran looks at him with worried eyes, but the persuasion,
the logical argument I expect to come, doesn't. Margo loads up the
twins and suddenly I don't want to go home and face Dharma's
nightly bedtime tantrum—which Margo ignores, so it goes on and

on and on in the darkness of our bedroom. Thankfully Gran invites me to sleep over, a rare treat of it being just Gran and me . . . if you don't count Dad out there tearing the dock apart in the night.

Gran goes to bed first. She seems more tired than normal. Considering the day, that's not surprising. When I finally head upstairs, I pass the front hall closet and remember.

With a heaviness in my chest, I open the door and look at the three jars of mayhaw jelly, red-checked ribbons around their necks, sitting where I'd tucked them when we arrived, waiting for the right time to present them as gifts.

10

Jelly or no jelly, I was a fool to believe there was a ghost of a chance Margo would be home with us this summer. It's only June, and her attention is already split—not between us and civil rights, but between civil rights and banning nuclear weapons.

An hour ago, she got wind that a new bunch of Freedom Riders are coming to Jackson. Ever since that horrible bus burning over in Alabama on Mother's Day, she hasn't stopped complaining that she wasn't there. What does she think one woman can do against dozens of angry men swinging clubs and throwing firebombs, anyway? Why isn't registering Negroes to vote in Lamoyne enough for her? It's certainly enough to make people around here angry. It took Griff half a day to scrape off the nasty words someone painted on our car windshield.

When I asked Margo that question, she said that kind of I've-done-my-share attitude is why there's still a problem. If every person stood up for what was right, people like her wouldn't have to do it all. I couldn't argue with that. Still, I'm scared sick as she takes her suitcase and rushes the twins out the door to drop at Mrs. Collins's so she can head to Jackson with her group of demonstrators.

Just last week Margo was mad as a wet hen when Dad came up the driveway honking the horn of this shiny new Chevy convertible we can't afford. Now she's plenty happy to throw her suitcase in it and just leave.

"I want to go!" The desperate words bubble up before I'm aware they're coming.

"Tallulah, you're too old for a babysitter." She opens the back door and Walden climbs right in. His eyes are sad as he looks at me, but he's not complaining. Dharma stands pouting with her arms crossed across her chest, until Margo reminds her that Mrs. Collins is waiting to see her new dance routine.

"Not to Mrs. Collins's!" I shout. "I want to go to Jackson with you." When she puts on her angry lips I add, "I want to stand up for what's right, just like you say we should." I *do* care about the Negroes being treated fairly; I really do. I care about Margo's safety even more. And, to tell the truth, I'm tired of trying to be the same as everybody else. If I'm going to be different let *me* earn it, let *me* do something that counts. Besides, if I get involved with Margo's work, we can spend more time together.

"Don't be ridiculous," she says. "You know the blackberries are coming on. Granny James and Mr. Stokes need you for the harvest. I'm certainly not going to have time to watch you."

Watch me? I can't remember the last time Margo *watched* me. She barely looks at me.

I suppose I should just be glad she's not leaving me to take care of the twins, too. I'm already having to pick double because Griff's new job takes him away every day.

Margo is at the driver's door. "Tell Dray to pick up the twins when he gets home." I don't know why, but her never calling him Dad or Daddy to us like everybody else's mother does to their kids is starting to make me itch on the inside, a place too deep to scratch. "Mrs. Collins will be expecting them at least for the rest of the week." She starts the car and shoves it into reverse, letting the clutch out so fast it hops, leaving me to stand there with a belly full of dread, certain something bad is going to happen.

Late in the night, when I've only just gotten Margo-worry out of my head enough to fall asleep, Dad comes in and shakes me awake. Face rough with stubble, he's still wearing his clothes from yesterday, shirt untucked and wrinkled, there's a dark stain on the front. He puts his fingers to his lips and motions for me to come with him. He's jittery, the energy popping and sizzling from his skin. I think for sure something's happened to Margo.

With my heart racing, I get up and follow him into the kitchen. He paces, shifts, and shrugs, his body in constant motion. There is a feverish look in his eyes, glowing in the low light cast by the small bulb on the back of the stove. A scattering of papers is on the table; wildly sketched charts, diagrams with so many crisscrossing lines they look like spiderwebs. When I step closer to get a better look, he startles me by throwing himself across them, arms spread wide, chest against the tabletop.

"No! It's too dangerous." His voice is a coarse, panicky whisper.

"What's too dangerous?"

"You can't know too much, but *someone* has to be aware." His eyes cut to the dark window, then back to me. He lowers his voice further. "In case something happens to me."

"What are you talking about?" That dread that has been boiling in my belly gets fresh fire.

"I can't believe it's taken me this long . . . recorded history meaningless . . . so obvious . . . saints and kings and religion . . . manipulation most sinister." He's forgotten the dangerous papers on the table and is now pacing circles, running his hands through his hair and talking so fast he's not getting all the words out. Hurricane.

I lean a little closer to the table. One of the papers is covered with dates, some with red circles around them, some with blue, a few with green X's.

He steps between me and the table. "Don't."

"Why did you wake me, if you don't want me to see any of this?"

"Someone has to know." He glances at the window again, as if expecting someone there. "About the manuscript."

"What manuscript?"

"*My* manuscript. You can't tell anyone. Too explosive." Then he suddenly stops, leans to my ear, and whispers, "It's controlled by *the consortium*."

"What's controlled by the consortium?"

"History. What we're allowed to discover. They hide the lessons. Ensure war. Polarize."

"How can history be controlled?" Is he not making sense, or am I just too rattled from being jerked from sleep?

"It's in the manuscript. Locked in a file cabinet in my office closet." He walks to the window and looks out, then whispers, "What we know is not *history*."

"What did you mean 'in case something happens' to you?"

"They'll stop at nothing."

"Who?"

"Haven't you been listening? The consortium!" He takes me by the shoulders and holds my eyes with his agitated gaze. "Tell no one." He waits until I nod, then says, "Go back to bed." I leave the kitchen. Hurricane time can be confusing, but I've never been scared like this before. I should talk to Griff about it in the morning.

Except Dad trusted me, not Griff, with his secret. And he said I can't tell *anyone*.

Before the sun burns off the silver mist of night, I have the twins fed and dressed and ready for Dad to take to Mrs. Collins's. Easy enough since I never went back to sleep because now I'm worried about *both* parents. If Dad is right about history being manipulated, I hope his book is easier to understand than he was last night.

When he comes out of his room (still in the same coffee-stained shirt) the fear I saw in his eyes last night is replaced with a burning excitement as he talks a mile a minute about how he's figured out perpetual motion. Maybe it's like Griff says, sometimes Dad's just full of bullshit. Or maybe Margo has finally made him lose his mind. I wish I knew, because I hate wasting my energy worrying about something that's all in his head—there's too much real stuff to worry about.

I think I've figured out what to do about Margo, though. So the wakeful night wasn't a total waste.

Right after Dad leaves, I turn on the radio (Dad says today's

music is an offense to the senses and the intellect). I'm dancing to Del Shannon singing "Runaway" and rinsing cereal bowls
when Griff comes shuffling into the kitchen with his hair sticking up every which way. It hurts my heart how much I miss him
being around like he used to be. Ever since school got out, he's
either working at the Sinclair or with Ross, painting the Saenger
cottage.

Griff says Mrs. Saenger is just like Harriet from *Ozzie and Harriet*. So I can't blame him for wanting to be there and not here with
hurricanes and Dharma fits and berry picking. Still, I don't like the
gut-punched feeling it's giving me, like he's living in a world different from mine.

"It seems like you could stay home at least one day and help
with the picking," I say, a little startled by the hatefulness in my
voice. But it's just wrong that Griff can go off to his job and get
paid when I have to work the orchard for free. Most days, I don't
even have the joy of working with Maisie because she's at Judge
Delmore's more and more.

With that thought, I catch my breath. I love the orchard. I
should be happy to work in it. And jealous of my own brother?
What's wrong with me?

Suddenly I'm spinning. Wobbling. A gyroscope. A boat without
a rudder. A kite without a tail.

A girl alone.

My bare toes curl against the sticky tiles and I bite my tongue,
determined not to let him know what a sorry person I've become.

Griff looks at me with concern. "What's wrong?" Then he pulls
me into a hug and pats my back—like I'm a baby.

I shove him and take a step back. "What do you care? Just go to
your job. Spend all your time with Ross. It doesn't matter to me."

He looks as shocked as if I'd smacked him with a baseball bat.
"What the hell? I was trying to be nice."

"You think a hug is going to make a difference? You're leaving! You don't care about the orchard, or Gran, or the James family
legacy." *Or me.*

"What are you talking about? I'm right here."

"For now. But you said you're leaving as soon as you get enough money. And then what? I'll be stuck here taking care of Walden and Dharma, picking blackberries, hulling pecans, listening to Dad and Margo fight, and dealing with all the bullshit around town. It's hard enough with you here. But you're leaving me to do it alone." I stop, honestly stunned by all that came out of my mouth.

He stands there for a minute looking like he's never seen me before. "I . . . Lulie, I didn't know—"

"I'm sure you didn't. You haven't been here enough to notice if the barn burned down."

He puts his hands on my shoulders. "I won't leave. Not until you can go with me. I promise. I'll stick around and work. I can take a couple of classes at Wickham after graduation if Dad pushes it. Then, after you graduate, we'll go to California. It's full of young people and great music and beaches. Everyone does what they want, not what *generations* dictate they should. We can get a little apartment in Huntington Beach. I'll work on movie people's expensive cars. You can get a job at Disneyland. We'll have a life where nobody knows Margo, or Dad, and the police chief isn't up my ass."

Me, leave? Suddenly it's as if someone opened the drawbridge of the castle where I'm prisoner. I can't walk through it yet, but now it's open and I can breathe. Griff will take me away from here. I'll be free.

I look out the window.

"What will happen to the orchard if we go?" I've never really thought of another kind of future.

He shrugs. "The same thing that happened before we were born. Someone will take care of it. Walden loves it. It should be his anyway. In five years he'll be old enough to take on some of the responsibility."

I start to say I love the orchard, too. Then it strikes me. I feel something else, something much, much stronger. The ugliness of the way this town looks at us outweighs that love. Or maybe I only love the orchard because of Gran and Mr. Stokes and Maisie. But there will be a time when they're no longer here. The orchard will be so different. And the town will be the same.

"You swear you won't leave me?" Five years. If things are going to get better around here they will have—for both of us. If not, we have a plan.

"I swear," Griff says, staring me in the eye. "I won't leave you."

I throw my arms around his neck. Griff has *never* broken a promise to me. I'm so light I'd float away if he wasn't holding on to me.

We step apart. He opens the refrigerator for the orange juice and milk. And, just like that, we're back to our usual selves. But deep inside I'm different, I look at Griff differently—well, not differently, but like I always used to. Like we're a team. Now and forever.

I say, as if nothing had changed, "Margo went up to Jackson."

"So, what's new?" He pours Wheaties into his bowl and shovels on the sugar.

"I'm afraid she's going to get hurt. You saw what those men did to the Riders last month."

"Margo's too selfish to get herself hurt on account of others. She'll be fine."

"She's dedicated."

The milk bottle is in his hand and he pauses to look at me before he pours it. "Yeah. Okay. Fine. Believe what you want. But don't waste your energy worrying about her. She's not worth it. She'll always look out for herself first." He takes his cereal bowl and heads back to his room.

I put the milk bottle back in the refrigerator and decide Griff's not going to be any help in my new plan for Margo.

As I walk to the orchard barn, dew wets the toes of my Keds, turning spots of the navy-blue fabric to near black. The sun is starting to bake off the fog from the tops of the trees, but the mist is still strung low over the ground, pooling thick in the low places. The catbirds are singing. A quiet calm seeps into my chest, replacing the buzzing panic I've been feeling since Margo pulled out of the drive yesterday. There isn't anything more beautiful than the orchard this early in the morning.

The barn smells of old wood and dry pecan husks. The refrigerators hum in the background as I get the picking pails ready. Mr. Stokes arrives, bringing the bad news that Maisie is working at the judge's house today.

He says, "She's looking to get on full with the judge soon as she's sixteen. Their maid is close to seventy, opportunity opening up."

"And not work here *at all*?" Panic rockets through my veins. Sixteen is only a year away for Maisie.

"You don't think a woman can live off working harvest, do you? She got to look to her future."

The way he says it makes me feel selfish. But the orchard forever without Maisie is unimaginable.

As he and I leave the barn with the pails clinking against one another (I can only carry four by the handle, but Mr. Stokes somehow manages eight), I think of Margo up in Jackson, fighting for civil rights. I can't imagine Gran ever treating Mr. Stokes with the disrespect Margo says all colored people suffer in the South. I wonder if Mr. Stokes is secretly hating us white people, too scared to do anything else. I'd hate it if he felt that way.

I'm sure Gran would consider the whole topic to be one of the *things that must never be mentioned.* So I'd better get at it before she gets here.

"Mr. Stokes?"

His gaze slides over to me without him turning his head. I've noticed he does this when he's suspicious of what's going to come next. "Yes, Miss Tallulah?"

"Margo says your people . . . colored people . . . hate Mississippi."

"Mississippi my home, just like it's yours."

I can tell by the look on his face he's deliberately misunderstanding the meat of my question.

"What about having things separate?" I ask. "Would you rather it be that everybody went wherever they pleased, sat wherever they pleased in the movie house, ate wherever they pleased, and rode the bus wherever they pleased?"

Even though Gran and Mr. Stokes have lived in the same town and worked side by side all their lives, the only space they *really* share, the only place they can be open friends, is the orchard.

"Who *wouldn't* want to go wherever they pleased without worryin' about getting throwed in jail or beat bloody?"

He didn't say it hateful, but I feel like a small person for even bringing it up. I stay quiet for a bit, thinking of how the Stokes family rope and the Neely family rope have spun out for a hundred years alongside each other. And I'll bet Gran and Mr. Stokes know all the knots that come over the past sixty years in each other's ropes.

I know better than to sound like I'm prying, so I try fishing instead. "It's nice hearing you and Gran talk about old times. There are probably a lot of stories I haven't heard yet."

"I reckon so."

Of all the things Gran has danced sideways about in the past, one mystery sticks out.

"Did you know Granddaddy James's brother, George?"

"How you know about George?"

I've hit on something. "Oh," I say casually. "Gran and I were looking at photo albums a while back and I saw his picture. Gran and I had a nice chat about him."

He gives me that sly look again. "You did, did you?"

"Yes. She said Great-Grandmother James wasn't very tolerant of him."

"Um-hmm."

"Everybody must have been worried when he left with no word."

He stops again and stares down at me hard enough to give me goose bumps. "Your granny tell you that?"

"Well, not exactly. I just figured . . ."

He starts walking again. "Hurry on up. Them berries ain't gonna jump off the cane, you know."

I trot to catch up, knowing time's getting short before Gran shows up. "I bet it made Granddad James especially sad, bein' his only brother and all."

"Your Granddad had a blue streak in general. So I can't say."

The back of my neck tingles. Neither Gran nor Dad has ever said Granddad was sad. But then, I don't go around telling people about my dad's hurricanes, either.

"Is Dad like Granddad James?" I ask.

"Those dark-haired James looks are strong in both your daddy and Griffin."

"I don't mean in how they look. I mean in nature."

"Some."

"Like the blue streak? The hurricanes?"

He frowned and looked at me. "Hurricanes?"

"Griff and I call it that when Dad is all energy and ideas, so full he can't even sleep for it."

Mr. Stokes's mouth gets tight. "These are questions for your granny." He drops two pails onto the ground. "You start pickin' here. I'll start over yonder."

He leaves me standing there, wondering about Granddad's and Dad's natures. And then a horrible thought comes to me. If Granddad and Dad share a blue streak and hurricanes, what about Griff?

I pray that's not why he's been so strange lately. I'd be able to tell, wouldn't I?

11

Even before the church bells ring noon, we're done picking blackberries and I've changed into my prized possession of the moment, a lemon-yellow-with-white-polka-dot spaghetti-strapped dress that Gran made from a Vogue pattern. I feel like a grown woman on the streets of Paris. Too bad my shoes don't send the same high-fashion message. But at least they're new, bright-white Keds.

I'm feeling pretty sassy as I walk to town with my church-bazaar-bought straw purse clutched in my white-gloved hand. I even snuck some of Margo's Picardy Peach lipstick and put a little tease in my hair and sprayed it with Aqua Net before adding a yellow clip-in bow. I'm enjoying myself so much, I almost forget I'm on a serious mission.

The sun is hot, so I keep to the shady side of Eudora Avenue, passing the white picket fence and rose bushes in front of Judge Delmore's house, wondering about Maisie working inside. That starts to drag my mood, so I shift to wondering if Paris also smells of roses right now, too.

I hear the rumble of the car before I hear the wolf whistles and catcalls. I know every well-bred Southern girl is supposed to be offended, but I have to say it gives me a little rush of satisfaction. I finally feel like I'm shaking off my coltish, awkward in-between-ness.

Gran says I shouldn't be in a hurry to grow up. But I've always been grown up on the inside. It's nice that the rest of me is catching up.

The rumbling gets louder, the car coming up behind me is obviously a jalopy. I keep my eyes straight ahead as they pull up alongside me.

"Hey, sugar, how 'bout a ride?"

Out of the corner of my eye, I can see a form hanging out the rear passenger-side window.

"Well, shit, it's that James bitch!"

Grayson Collie.

The whistles die and sounds of disgust pour from the car. It swerves to the curb, rubber squealing against the concrete. I walk faster, holding my breath, not giving them the satisfaction of glancing their way. It's broad daylight. Even Grayson Collie wouldn't be so nervy.

And yet . . . there isn't anyone out in the big front yards on either side of the street, not even a gardener.

Downtown is only four more blocks.

A car door slams, followed by two more.

My heart stuffs itself up into my throat. I let loose my held breath and break into an unladylike trot.

"Hey! Slow up. I still owe your brother something," Grayson calls, vengeance in his voice.

I run, thankful I'm wearing tennis shoes.

Thundering feet pound the sidewalk behind me.

My arms pump, my purse swinging wildly. If I waste the breath on a scream will anyone come?

Suddenly I hear a car horn; one long, blaring note. Tires squeal on the pavement.

Oh, God! More of them!

I smell burnt rubber and find speed I didn't know I had. Just as I open my mouth to scream, I hear a car hop the curb. The guys behind me all swear.

Then a car is alongside me. "Get in! Tallulah!"

Ross!

I glance over my shoulder. Grayson and his toadies are scattered, a couple of them on the ground, Grayson is just getting back to his feet.

"Tallulah!" The red Corvette convertible paces me. He's trying to reach the passenger-door latch.

I don't wait for the door to swing open. I put one hand on the top of it and vault into the passenger seat.

Ross takes off so fast that dirt clods spray up behind us, then downshifts and turns a corner. "You okay?"

I take a moment to arrange my skirt and pat my hair, *regain a little dignity*, as Gran would say. "Of course." The words stick slightly on my dry tongue.

He looks over at me and bursts out laughing.

"If you're going to laugh at me, let me out!" I can't find the door latch.

"It's that little round knob. You just pull it backward. But I wouldn't." He presses on the gas and picks up speed as we head out of town. "And I'm not laughing at you. It's just you're the only girl I know who could be chased down the street by hoods and then sit there as if nothing happened. How do you do it?"

"Practice."

"Why were they chasing you?" There's a hard edge to his voice, like he wants an excuse to punch someone.

"They were just fooling around." I really don't want to explain Griff's and my long-running issues with Grayson Collie.

"The way you were running says you didn't think they were fooling around."

"It's nothing. They just like scaring people."

"Tallulah." He reaches over and takes my hand. I'm glad I have on gloves so he can't feel how sweaty my palms are. "If there's something going on, I want to help."

"Really, they're just idiots. Bored idiots. Why are you in town?" I change the subject.

"I was headed to the hardware store." Ross used to shop in Columbia, which is closer to the Saenger cottage than Lamoyne. But since he and Griff have started palling around, he always comes here. "But now that I've found you, I'm open to other suggestions. Mom went home for a couple of days. I've set ridiculously low expectations for progress on the painting. I was hoping to see you—although not in such a knight-in-shining-armor way."

There's something in his tone that makes me blush. "Sorry. I need to get to the bus station."

"Where are you going?" The question is more than what Dad calls a throwaway remark, asked out of politeness. "You don't have a bag."

Until this very moment, it hadn't struck me how unprepared I am. What did I think I was going to do, ride up to Jackson, find Margo in an hour, and convince her to turn around and drive us both home? But I *have* to go. The blackness I felt in my chest when she told me she was going has done nothing but grow, darker and heavier and more alive with fear. The last time I ignored my gut feeling I almost drown.

"I'm just taking something to Margo up in Jackson." I pat my purse as if it carries something important. "She's there working. I plan on getting the last bus back."

"I'll drive you."

"To the bus station?"

"To Jackson."

A spark of panic hits me. "Oh, no. I can't ask you to do that. Just drop me at the station. I still have plenty of time before my bus."

"Griff would kill me if I let you take a late bus all by yourself."

Before I can protest further, he does a U-turn and heads toward the highway.

The only thing worse than my fear for Margo is the idea of Ross watching me beg her to come home. But, after being chased by Grayson Collie, my worldly confidence is shaken. And those were just stupid kids. What is it going to be like if I have to face the KKKers and police dogs?

No matter the embarrassment, I'd rather have Ross standing beside me than go it alone.

* * *

When we reach the sign for the Jackson city limits, Ross asks me where we're going. I just stare at him for a moment, wondering if he's having amnesia or something. Then I realize he means where *exactly*.

"The bus station." I'm praying it's like the sit-ins where protesters hang around the bus station all day and night, refusing to leave. Otherwise, I have no idea how I'm going to find her.

"Is your mother meeting you there?"

I look out the passenger side and give a vague nod.

When we reach downtown Jackson, I try to keep my mouth closed and a *ho-hum* look on my face. Dad would have a hissy if he knew I was thinking in such unintellectual terms, but jeepers, my vocabulary is buried under the number of cars and people and buildings. I counted ten stories on one of the buildings we passed, and that wasn't including the clock tower and the statues perched on the corners. Busy as they are, the streets are so peaceful I have a hard time imagining police dogs and picket signs, bloodied Negroes and shouting whites. Maybe Margo exaggerated the situation.

The newspaper pictures of the burning bus in Anniston on Mother's Day were real enough, though.

When we stop at a light, three girls wearing fine dresses and carrying expensive-looking handbags cross in front of us. Here I sit in my homemade dress and secondhand straw purse, and they're looking at me with a kind of envy. They think we're on a date! A cute boy and a racy car must trump brand-new dresses and handbags. I feel a little perkier.

One of the girls is wearing sunglasses. As she passes, she slides them partway down her nose and eyes Ross. Her cherry-red lips smile, showing movie-star teeth. I feel like the shabby girl that I am and steal a look at Ross. At least his eyes aren't following those girls across the street the way I've seen Griff's do when we're on campus and a pretty group of coeds walks past.

As the light turns green, my cheeks burn with irritation at myself for dallying in such foolish daydreams. What if Ross happened to look at me and saw what was going on inside my head? *Oh, the humiliation.* If life in Lamoyne has taught me anything, it's that you can never let people see what's on the inside. It just gives them a nice, easy target.

"There's a motorcycle patrolman parked at the next corner," Ross says. "Ask him where the bus station is."

When Ross pulls alongside, the officer looks our way.

"Excuse me, sir," I say.

He takes off his sunglasses with a polite smile. "Yes, miss."

"Can you tell us where the bus station is?"

His smile wilts, and the sun suddenly feels hotter on my head.

"You taking a trip?" he asks, shifting his weight on the motorcycle seat and planting his feet more firmly on the ground.

"No, I'm looking for my mother."

"And you think she's at the bus station?" His brows draw together, leaving a deep crease between his eyes.

I glance behind us, hoping to see backed-up traffic and angry drivers. But there's plenty of room and everyone is politely rolling around us.

Before I can put together a harmless reason my mother is at the bus station, the officer asks, "Where y'all from?" There's now suspicion in his eyes.

Suddenly, I can smell the black rolling smoke from that burning bus. My and Griff's acquaintance with Chief Collie has taught me that just because a man wears a badge doesn't mean he's above letting his personal feelings interfere with his law enforcing.

"Lamoyne," I say. "And he's from New Orleans."

"And why is your mother at the Jackson bus terminal?"

Ross leans around me and says, "Excuse me, sir, but we're holding up traffic, so if you could just tell us where the station is?"

"You look like nice kids, so I'll just say this once—for your benefit. There's no good come of hanging around the bus station. Do your business and move on."

I get that oily feeling in the pit of my stomach.

Ross says, "Of course, sir. The station then?"

The officer points down the street and tells us to take a left in two blocks and go to Lamar Street, then turn right. Then he narrows his eyes and says, "Y'all remember what I said."

Before I can say anything, Ross is pulling slowly away. I hear the motorcycle start. When I look over my shoulder, he's pulling into traffic. Butterflies take flight around my heart.

Ross isn't stupid. He has to know what's going on, the lunch-counter sit-ins, James Meredith, the Freedom Riders, and the Tougaloo Nine. I haven't found the courage to ask him what he thinks about any of it. And I can't tell if he notices the patrol officer following us. He certainly hasn't given any indication that he does. But then, he's not the one keeping a secret about why we're here.

It's easy to spot the bus terminal from down the block because of the tall sign in the center with *G-r-e-y-h-o-u-n-d* written vertically. As we get closer, the blue two-story building reminds me a little of a movie house with windows, with rounded corners and a marquee over two sets of double doors. It's definitely more impressive than the brick storefront in Lamoyne with a bus pull-through in the back alley.

"You can just pull to the curb and let me out," I say, my hand already on the round white knob. "I'll be fine from here."

"The whole point in my driving you was so you don't ride the late bus home."

"I might stay with Margo overnight."

"Okay. But I'm not leaving until I know you're safe with her. You have no business being in this city alone."

"I'm not a child." I'm kind of proud of the steel-edged offense in my voice—very adult. I pull the door lever back, even though the car is still moving.

Ross grabs my left arm. "Hold on! Close the door. That officer is following us. Let's not give him a reason to stop."

Ross goes around the corner, then finds a parking place at the curb. He gets out and comes around to open my already half-open door. My cheeks warm up a bit. Gran has drilled manners into my head for years—*always wait for the gentleman to open your car door.*

If he doesn't, keep waiting. If he doesn't get the hint, he's not worth your time. I never thought I'd actually be in a situation where it counted. Ross takes my hand and helps me from the low car, as casually as if we did this every day.

The motorcycle patrolman putters past, slowing to nod gravely at us as he does.

"Creepy," Ross says behind his smile.

"I'm really fine. No need to stay."

He looks down at me. "I never took you for thick-headed, so I'm assuming it's stubbornness talking." He offers me the crook of his arm. "Shall we?"

I feel upside down, sideways, and inside out when I settle my hand on his arm. The warmth of him sets off new and surprising things inside me. I nearly drag my feet down the sidewalk, unsure if it's because I want to draw out the feeling, or because I'm dreading Margo won't be there.

The inside of the station is cool and full of smooth, curved lines, just like the outside. Also, just like the outside, it's quiet as a tomb. There is a man attending the counter, an old woman sitting and reading a Bible, a couple of ladies with kids busy with *Highlights* magazines, and a janitor pushing a mop so slowly that if Gran were here she'd give him a scowl saying, *Snap to it.* They're all white, certainly not "sitting in."

"What time is your mother expecting you?" Ross asks, his voice low and yet still echoes in the space.

I break away from him and go to the ticket agent.

"Can I help you, miss?" He seems kindly.

I keep my voice almost to a whisper. "I'm looking for my mother, Margo James."

"Coming from where? I can give you an arrival time." He looks down at a schedule book.

"Um, no. She . . . she, well, she's working with . . . for . . . ."

Slowly his eyes come up to meet mine again. "She one of them protesters?"

I lower my eyes. "Yes, sir."

"Buncha them troublemakers showed up in here yesterday. Police asked 'em to leave."

"And they did?" I can't mask my surprise.

"You'd think a mother would be home taking care of her children, not out upsetting law-abiding folk." He shakes his head like he can't believe the state the world is coming to. "You just take yourself right back out that door." His voice gets louder. "And don't be comin' back."

Trembling, I turn around and walk quickly past Ross and out the doors to the sidewalk.

I can barely see the passing cars for my tears. I have no idea where to look. No idea how I'm going to admit my foolishness to Ross. I hear the doors open behind me but don't turn to look at him.

"Tallulah?"

Then I hear the door open again and figure it's the ticket agent coming to make sure we leave.

Then I hear a small, sweet voice say, "Excuse me, young lady."

I turn to the old woman standing beside Ross, holding her care-worn Bible to her chest. "Are you looking for someone? Perhaps I can help."

I swipe my tears before I turn around. "I don't see how, ma'am."

She steps closer and in an even smaller voice says, "I work with the Student Nonviolent Coordinating Committee."

"Student?"

"Yes, well." She smiles with a mischievous twinkle in her hazy blue eyes. "Not *all* the volunteers are students. I'm just keeping a quiet eye on things. Most of the Negroes here to protest are staying with families around the area. The white volunteers are out at the Moonglow Motor Court."

I search Ross's face, looking for disapproval, but he's as blank as a new sheet of paper. He asks her for directions and then thanks her. Then he silently takes me by the arm and directs me back to the car.

We're on the edge of the city before I find the courage to say anything.

"If you don't want to take me to the motel, I understand."

His jaw flexes a couple of times before he says, "I don't mind taking you. But I do mind you lying to me." He looks my way. "I thought we were friends."

"We are! I didn't lie, exactly. More of an omission of detail."

The tips of Ross's ears turn red and his fingers tighten on the steering wheel as he shakes his head, like I've disappointed him. "That's the kind of game you want to play? Really? With *me*?" He says it as if he and I are special, like we owe each other honesty.

"I . . . I just—" His sharp look kills the excuse in my mouth. "I don't know how much Griff has told you about our mother."

"Nothing at all."

"Guess that's no surprise."

"What's to tell?" he asks.

"She's . . . different," I say.

"Yeah, I noticed. So?"

"It's more than the way she dresses." After all, Ross only met her once—and things on Mother's Day certainly didn't give opportunity for normal conversation. "After Dad's craziness at the crawfish boil, I suppose I thought if you knew what she's up to, it . . . it might just be too much. Things might change—friendship-wise." Then I mutter, "It usually does."

I keep my eyes on the road but can feel his gaze boring into my head, feeling around inside there, looking for more than I want him to know.

"I don't know what kind of friends you've had . . ." He pauses. "I'm not against the fight for civil rights, if that's what you're concerned about."

I feel myself standing at a fork in the road. If I say anything less than the full truth, I'm pretty sure Ross will be finished with me.

"Partly." I search around for the words to explain Margo to someone who can't possibly have any frame of reference. Griff says Ross's mother bakes cookies. She wears pearls. I almost laugh out loud—*I* have no frame of reference for *that* kind of mother.

"The truth is"—I lick my dry lips—"if it wasn't civil rights, it'd be some other cause. She always has something else to do, somewhere else to be." When I realize how pathetic and whiny I sound, I rush to add, "She's dedicated to making the world a better place."

"Well, that's nothing to be ashamed of."

I sit up a little straighter, feel a little brighter inside. It's *not* anything to be ashamed of. I used to believe that. Back when she first stopped making popcorn for Saturday-night TV and started missing reading to Griff and me at bedtime. Griff pretends he doesn't remember the time before. It's easier to stay angry that way.

"You're right." Maybe being from a big city *does* give Ross a different perspective. I breathe easier, happy I'm not going to have to make excuses and hide things about Margo for him to stick around.

Now all I have to do is convince her it's too dangerous to be here, that we all need her too much for her to take the chance. I'll promise to help register voters. Yes. That'll be a good positive argument. I'm not asking her to give up the fight, just to do it on safer ground. And she should be happy that I'm joining the cause, too.

I'll get her to come home. I know I can.

12

When Ross pulls under the carport outside the office of the Moonglow Motor Court, I see a bunch of people inside the chain-link fence surrounding the swimming pool in the center of the U-shaped motel. It looks like a bunch of college kids on vacation: loud music, beer bottles, and lots of splashing.

"I'll go ask which room," Ross says.

"No," I say, pulling my eyes away from a show-off doing a jackknife off the diving board. "I'll go."

"Not alone."

"Stay here!" My words are sharper than is polite. And all Ross is doing is *being* polite. "I'm going to be less than ten feet away . . . on the other side of a glass window. I'll be fine."

He raises his hands in surrender.

A little bell on the door jingles when I open it. It takes a few seconds, but a man who looks like he belongs in a boxing ring comes out of a back room. "Help you, missy?" He has a stubby cigar clenched between his teeth and smells like fried onions.

"I was told Margo James is staying here. I'd like her room number, please."

He squints one eye. "And you're lookin' for her because . . . ?" He drags out the last word.

"I'm her daughter."

I'm not sure if the bark that comes from his throat is laughter or just surprise. "So she's got a kid, huh?"

"Four. Four kids." I start to squirm under his gaze; I feel like a puzzle he's trying to take apart and put back together with his eyes.

That's when I notice there's a hole worn in one of the square gray tiles under my feet and the windows are hazed with grime. Wishing I still had my gloves on, I take my hands off the counter and resist wiping them on my yellow dress. "Will you please give me her room number?"

"You don't need her room. She's right out there." He nods toward the pool. "Surprised you didn't see her. A doll like that stands out."

I glance over my shoulder. Not only is she out there in a bathing suit that borders on indecent, she's leaning with her elbows on the top of the fence pushing her chest in Ross's face and laughing like a teenager. I thought I'd already experienced all the ways Margo could embarrass me, but I was wrong.

My ears and cheeks burn as I head toward them.

"I was just coming to get you," Ross says. "I wasn't sure it was your mom at first."

I can see why.

"What are you doing here?" She's no longer laughing.

I'm breathing so fast, I'm light-headed. "Can I talk to you for a minute?"

"Here I stand," she says with a flip of her hand and a laugh. She's obviously been drinking.

"In private."

"Margo! Your poker hand is getting cold," a man in swim trunks and a matching shirt calls from a little table under a faded metal umbrella in the far corner.

Over her shoulder she says, "Be right there."

"I thought you were doing a *protest* at the bus station," I say, my voice shaking. I can't even look at Ross. "You're *supposed* to be working."

"The next Riders aren't due for a few days," she says, as if that explains everything.

The man comes over from the umbrella table and puts his arm around her, and she leans into him a little. "This is Robert. Our fearless leader."

I want to knock his hand off her shoulder. I want to scream and rant and stomp my feet. "A few *days*? And you couldn't come home in the meantime?" I think of poor Walden and Dad and the blackberries, and I want to pull out all her hair.

"Don't use that tone with me, young lady! You don't know a thing about what's going on here."

"Then why don't you tell me! Tell me why you're drinking and playing poker while Walden is crying himself to sleep at night! Tell me why you don't care enough about *your family* to drive home for those few days! Tell me about the *important work* you're doing right now!"

Griff was right. I feel dizzy and sick.

"You don't fight the fight every second of every day," Margo says. "We have to strategize, plan. We have to be ready—"

"Stop! Just stop!" I spin around and run back to Ross's car, hoping he has the decency to follow and get me out of here.

He's in the driver's seat before I get my door closed. Margo isn't a crusader but a . . . a . . . floozy.

Poor Daddy. What am I going to do? If I tell him it'll break his heart. Margo's already driving him really and truly insane. What if this pushes him into a shadow time he can't come out of?

But what if this really is the way protesting works and I'm jumping to the wrong conclusion about Margo and that . . . that Robert. Hard to believe, considering . . . but, still.

Maybe I should tell Griff and see what he says.

You know what he'll say.

As Ross drives silently back toward Lamoyne, I keep my unfocused eyes on the roadside and just want to die. About halfway home, he turns off the highway onto a deserted dirt road and slows to a stop.

"Why are we stopping?" I can't look at him.

He shuts off the engine. "Because I have something to say and I want to do it before we get back to Lamoyne."

I sniff. "Please, just take me home."

"No."

"Ross—"

"Look at me, Lulie."

The name only Griff uses surprises me enough that I turn.

"Maybe you jumped to a hasty conclusion back there."

"You don't really think that, do you?"

He shrugs.

"Griff's right. She's not full of *convictions* and *principles*. She doesn't love us. She doesn't want to be a mother at all." I've been hiding from the truth, burying it under excuses. And now, finally saying it out loud, it slides under my skin like a hunter's knife.

"Maybe not," he says softly.

I'd expected at least a little resistance, reassurance that something so awful as a mother not wanting her own kids couldn't be true.

"But this is on her, Lulie. Not you. Not Griff or the twins. *Her*," he says, taking my hand. "She's the one with the holes inside, not you."

With his words, something twists and rolls in my chest. The tears I've been choking on evaporate. I don't have to want her to love me. I don't *have to* care! Suddenly I understand how free Griff must feel since he gave up on her.

"I'm sorry about what happened back there, but it has nothing to do with you." Ross surprises me by wrapping an arm around my shoulders and pulling me close. "Nothing at all." His lips press against the top of my head and I am free.

My sense of lightness and freedom lasts all of eight hours, when I awaken at midnight to shouting.

"I don't know what Tallulah told you—"

"She didn't tell me anything. But you just did!"

She came home because she was afraid I told?

"*You* don't trust me?" she shouts. "You! With your coeds and—" She breaks off in a growl followed by breaking glass. Margo is a thrower.

Walden scurries into my room with his raggedy stuffed dog. I lift the covers, and he jumps into bed with me. I hold him close, and his face burrows into the curve of my neck. It's a drill that no longer requires words.

I wish he'd closed the door. The hurricane of their voices is so much louder, sharper . . . *clearer* without the wood filter. I don't want to hear. I don't want to understand.

Walden's panicky breath brushes my neck. He's trembling. I feel terrible because my going to Jackson set this in motion, this fight, those hateful words.

I'm glad we live far away from anyone who could hear the storm raging through our screens. All I want to do is go and curl up beside Griff. I doubt he's sleeping—he just doesn't need me to get through these nights.

Lately he only needs Ross.

After today, I'm afraid I do, too. How can I resent one boy so much, and long for him, too?

At dawn, I peel myself away from a sweaty, sleeping Walden and get ready for berry picking. My head throbs from lack of sleep, and my insides feel raw. The house didn't fall quiet until sometime after three. I'm half afraid to come out of my room and face the wreckage. After nights like this I like to have it cleaned up when Dad and Margo wake up, so there's no reminder that they're mad at each other.

At first, when I come into the dim living room, I stop short, fiery shock shooting through my veins. They've finally killed each other.

Then one of the legs in the naked tangle on the floor moves. I realize Dad is snoring softly. Thank the Lord a gray-and-yellow crocheted afghan from the davenport is draped across them, covering from bare shoulders to midthighs.

Other than the disturbing sight of naked parents, there's an overturned bottle of bourbon on the coffee table, two broken glasses on the hardwood, a few books knocked from the shelves, and a ceramic ashtray lying at the baseboard beside the fireplace in three chunks. Toss pillows have landed like grenades all over the room and the lampshade is knocked askew.

I get a towel and mop up the bourbon, the sharp smell stinging my nose. When I start picking up the broken glass, a shard pricks my thumb, drawing a bright bead of blood. As I go get a Band-Aid, I'm wondering how I'm going to keep Gran outside when she gets here. I can get the mess cleaned up, but I can't scoop Dad and Margo off the floor and deposit them behind the closed door of their bedroom where they belong.

But it isn't Gran who shows up before I finish sweeping up the glass. It's Ross. The sound of his car is unmistakable. I rush out the back door into the hazy morning to intercept him before he knocks. Yesterday was humiliating enough; I can't let him see this.

He peers beyond me as I approach. "Griff ready?"

And you thought he came for you, the little mocking voice comes from the back of my mind, knocking my heart down a peg or two. "Oh. Um, no. I'll go get him."

As I turn to go back inside, he snags my arm. "Wait a minute."

I wish I didn't feel so unbalanced when I look into his eyes.

"I see your mom's back." My stomach jumps before I realize he can't see through the French doors but is nodding toward the Chevy parked crookedly on the lawn. "Are you okay?"

"I'm fine." The two words are sharp, cutting the air between us.

"Lulie, I can tell just by looking at you, you're not. Did you even sleep?"

I think of the party at the motel . . . that man, of Walden's fear, of the words my parents hurled at each other in the night, of the mess in the living room, and I want to throw myself into Ross's arms and cry until I no longer have the strength to stand.

But he's already seen too much of the truth of me, of my family. He says he's the kind of friend who won't be scared off by my parents' craziness, but he has no idea how bad it can get. I force the echoes of last night out of my head and put a smile on my face. "I'm fine. I'll get Griff." I turn and hurry into the house before I weaken and say more.

Once I'm back in the kitchen, I look out the window. He's leaning against his car with his arms and ankles crossed, calm and quiet, like the orchard in the early morning. I feel such a tug of longing that my throat swells. Tears? Shame? Love? I can't tell.

I close my eyes and fight the urge to go back out and beg him to take me today and leave Griff here to fight the blackberry thorns and clean up the wreckage.

Then I turn away and go to wake Griff.

I wait until I hear the Corvette start before I head to the sanctuary of the orchard. After a night like last night, Dad and Margo move in a world that is exclusive to the two of them, locking the rest of us out. Which will set Dharma in attention-grabbing mode. The unpredictability of our family is so predictable.

As I move through my morning, I want Maisie. I want her sly way of looking at things to entertain me through the tedious hours of picking. I want to ask her if she thinks Griff will ever come back to the way he was. I want to talk to her about Ross and the strange way he makes me feel.

But I am alone.

When I'm finally done with blackberries, I head to my secret place, toward the river that separates the pecan orchard from the wildness beyond.

If only I could keep walking west, away from family chaos and this town, to a new me with palm trees and sunshine and endless stretches of sand.

13

After tucking the dusty jars of mayhaw jelly back in the closet, I got up off Gran's foyer floor. I couldn't even look Ross in the eye as I headed for the stairs, saying I was going to pack Gran's bag. So far, all I've done is wander from room to room, visiting the memories made in them. Unlike everything else I've encountered since I knocked on Ross's front door, this place truly is frozen in time.

I poke around the old nursery where Griff and I played with the same toys Gran and even Great-Granddaddy played with as children. From there I head to the sewing room, where Gran fitted and hemmed my dresses and sewed recital outfits for Dharma and holiday-themed vests for Walden. The only open bedroom other than Gran's is where Walden must have spent the past nine years. I'm not strong enough to face the detritus of boyhood he left behind, so I turn back around and take a quick peek inside the two closed-off rooms where the furniture is covered with white sheets, just as they have been for as long as I can remember.

The full width of the rear of the second story is a sleeping porch, the old balcony screened sometime around the turn of the century.

During the hottest months when I was a girl, Gran used to set up the same portable cots her family used when she was a child. Those were the best nights: Griff, me, and Gran—and sometimes even Daddy—sleeping on our cots, lined side by side, Gran spinning ghost stories handed down from her own grandmother about the lost souls bound to the river behind the house.

Now there is just a single cot on the porch. It makes my heart ache to think of Gran dragging it from storage herself and spending long dark nights out here alone.

As darkness falls, I breathe the mud scent of the river, listen to the bugs tap against the screens and the rising voices of the crickets and tree frogs—a familiar, beautiful symphony that lulled me to sleep all the summer nights of my childhood.

I swipe the quiet tears from my cheeks and head to Gran's room. Everything is just as it's always been. The rose-covered wallpaper, the handmade quilt covering the bed, the yellowing tatted doilies scattered on all horizontal surfaces. Everything in the exact same place. There's something comforting about it. But it's strange, too. I can't quite put my finger on what makes it feel off. As I walk slowly around the room, it becomes clear. I have never been in Gran's room without her. Things look the same, but the warmth and vitality are missing.

The house is still hot, so I open the windows. There's no stir of breeze, just more heavy, moist air and pressing darkness. Gran's absence echoes in every inch of this place. What if I'd been too late and this was all I had to return to?

To give myself a reprieve, I head to the bathroom to collect her toiletries. Many of them are missing, her toothbrush and toothpaste, her lavender bath talc, her lipsticks, the train case she keeps in the small closet. I wonder if Mr. Stokes was the one to gather her things and take them to the hospital. It seems oddly intimate, and yet I can't imagine her letting anyone else do it.

Thinking of him makes me yearn for Maisie in a way I haven't for years.

I take the things I've gathered to Gran's bedroom and focus my thoughts on the task at hand, filling the spaces where the memories are trying to roost. Turning on her old AM radio, I rotate the yellowed plastic dial. The only nongospel station that comes in with more music than static is playing Alice Cooper. It feels so horribly wrong in this room, I switch it back off.

I lay Gran's blue suit and a soft cream blouse on the bed, along with two other dresses that look like they'll pack well. All the clothes are a size smaller than I remember. I choose a couple of blouses and a pair of slacks. As I pull them out of the closet, I pause, surprised by the hollowness in my chest.

I'd thought I was done with this place for good. Apparently, it isn't done with me.

I move to the dresser to gather undergarments, stockings, and jewelry. Even when working in the orchard, Gran's clothing was tastefully accessorized.

Opening the beautiful inlaid-wood jewelry box Granddad gave her when they were married, I poke through the clip-on earrings, brooches, and bracelets. I don't see her pearls. She'll want them for the courtroom. *Nothing says solidity like a good strand of pearls*, she always said.

There are three shallow drawers in the top row of the long dresser. The one on the right holds her underthings, the one on the left socks and stockings. I don't remember her ever getting into the one in the middle. I pull the knob, but the drawer doesn't budge.

There's a brass-rimmed slot for one of those tiny keys, but no key. I look in the small cut-glass dishes on the dresser, lift the lid of the little Spode box, feel around in the bottom of her lingerie drawers searching for the key. No luck. I check her nightstands and every decorative vase and knickknack that could serve as a hiding place.

Returning to the dresser, I lift out the top tray and check the lower compartment. No key. I lift the mirrored tray holding decorative perfume bottles and check underneath. No key. I look at the jewelry box again. Could there be a third compartment?

I lift out the top tray again, then try the lower. It's snug but finally lifts out. Near the back is a small ribbon loop, the same dark burgundy as the velvet lining the box. I pull and the bottom panel swings open. The space below isn't deep, maybe an inch or so. No pearls. But there is a large gold filigree locket. At the sight, I feel the cold of the dedication day, hear this locket clattering onto the steps of the stage, experience the sting of Gran's unusually sharp reaction as she snatched it away. I never found the courage to question her about it.

I pick up the locket, hoping it might reveal its secret. The etched lines are time-darkened, making the design easy to see. Tiny flowers. Forget-me-nots. Gran's favorite. The back side is inscribed with a date, October 13, 1920. Gran's birthday—her eighteenth.

The latch is so delicate, I use my pinkie nail to open it, expecting to see a picture of Granddad inside. But there is no photograph, just another engraving. Initials in delicate, swirling script. There are so many curlicues that I have to study to make them out. The middle initial is the largest. *LNC and WJG Never Forget.* Lavada Constance Neely. I snap it closed with a smile. "So Granddad had some competition, did he?"

Why on earth did she bring it to the dedication?

Maybe this time I'll find the courage to ask her about it.

The only other thing in this compartment is a small brass key with a fine gold cord through its eye. I replace the locket and pick up the key, then try it on the drawer. It takes some finagling in the old lock, but it finally slides open. The drawer is filled with faded and yellowing black-and-white photographs, some whole, some cut, all of the same young man.

My gaze moves to the bottom shelf of the nightstand. There, right where it's been my entire life, is the old black album with *James* on the front, the one with nearly all of the photos of Uncle George missing. I open it and flip through. The photos from the drawer are the missing puzzle pieces. Gran said Great-Grandmother James destroyed those photos because George was a disappointment. And yet here they are, locked away like Gran's secret locket.

LNC. WJG. Could that have been Uncle George? Was George his middle name? Why, after listening to Gran's family stories for years, do I not know that? Why did she erase Uncle George?

* * *

The telephone is ringing when I come downstairs. I don't hurry, thinking Ross will pick it up in the kitchen. But the ringing goes on.

I run into the kitchen and give him a nasty look.

"Hey," he says, holding his palms toward me. "I'm not here."

Right. I snatch the wall phone off the hook—it could be Amelia with news about Walden.

"Tallulah, dear," Gran says.

The questions raised by the pictures and the locket ricochet in my mind. But I hold them. I want to look her in the eye when I ask them. "Yes?"

"I want to make certain you bring the cream blouse, not the print one. I don't want to look too flashy." She's speaking as if we've been chatting regularly every day for the past nine years. As if she doesn't have a drawer full of secrets in her bedroom.

"I already have the cream one packed." I pause, then can't help a tiny probing comment. "But I couldn't find your pearls."

She's silent for a beat. "Did I *ask* you to bring my pearls?"

"Well, no. I just assumed. You usually wear them with a suit."

"And how would you know what I *usually* do? It's been quite some time since you left." Her tone is conclusive.

I feel Ross's curious gaze on me and realize how long I've been silent. I turn my back to him. "Do you want any of your other jewelry?"

"No. Thank you." Her everything-is-hunky-dory tone is back. "You get some rest, and I'll see you tomorrow. Good night, dear. I love you."

I hang up the phone, those last three words echoing in my head and my response locked deep in my heart.

"Soup's on," Ross says. "You look a little rattled."

"Just adjusting to feeling like a helpless kid again."

He pulls out my chair, reminding me once more that I'm back in the South, where things are left unsaid and men behave like gentlemen.

He holds up the bottle of wine. "Found this in the back of the pantry. Think she'll mind?"

Wine hidden in the pantry? Gran is just full of surprises.

"Go ahead."

As he draws out the cork, he says, "Why helpless?"

"What?"

"You said you feel like a helpless kid again. I had the impression your grandmother was the one stable element in your childhood. Which would make me think she would make you feel stronger, more secure, not helpless."

I pause to think. "You're right. For most of my life, Gran and the orchard were my constants. Which made it all that much harder when she refused to let me stay. Of course, Griff was all set with a new life already."

He pours my glass of wine, and then his. "It must have felt to you like he got the good end of the stick at the time—if there could be a good end with all that happened. But believe me, it wasn't a new life, not like you imagine. It was purgatory. He blamed himself for everything."

"But that's ridiculous! He was as much a victim as any of us—more so."

He looks me in the eye. "I think you said it right there . . . 'any of us.' Don't you think your grandmother should be included in that number? When horrific things happen, it's natural to want to blame someone. Maybe your someone was your grandmother."

"I thought you weren't going to analyze me."

"If I were analyzing you, it'd be a whole lot more intense. And a whole lot more painful. I'm just making an observation—as a friend."

The word *friend* strikes close to my heart. There is something between Ross and me that I've never had with anyone, not even Griff, an understanding that needs no words. I can feel it now, just as I felt it when I was fourteen. When I look back on that time, I wrote it off as a girlish crush, a teenage infatuation. But now? Why do I feel less able—or less compelled—to defend my inner self from Ross than I am everyone else?

"What are you thinking?" he asks, a bemused look on his face.

I take a long sip of wine before I answer. "I was just wondering if there's some mysterious connection between people when one saves the other's life."

He's quiet a moment. "I've wondered that a million times myself. I'd convinced myself it wasn't true—until I saw you on my front porch yesterday."

I force myself to meet his eyes and I feel it, a bond that has stretched over time and distance. "So you think it's true now?"

"Now. Back then. What made me follow you that day? Is fate something we just throw out there to absolve ourselves of responsibility? Or is it a true force? Something that in order to alter you have to beat back and slay like a dragon?"

I think about it for a moment, more focused on the *us* of it than the existential question. "I look at life as a long circuitous line of dominoes," I say. "Take out any one and the course will be altered. And I don't think it takes dragon slaying to change it. It's a simple moment, a split second that affects the rest of your life. I think putting it all in the hands of 'fate' is cheating. So yes, it's absolving yourself of the responsibility of your choices. I am where I am because of my *choices*. Not because of some otherworldly hand moving me around the chess board of life."

"And yet, you blame your grandmother for your leaving Lamoyne. You didn't have a hand in *that* choice?"

"Hey! Margo and Gran were sending me away one way or the other. I had only one choice—*how* I left." I calm myself down. "Which, as you now see, had horrific repercussions for Walden. And I take responsibility for it." Every time I think of him, the regret nearly drowns me. I have to figure out a way to make it right. To save him.

"You're saying *you're* responsible for Walden's actions? Your decisions are yours, but you're to blame for his?"

I wave a hand in the air. "This conversation is way too deep for me right now."

"Okay, but here's one more thing to think about, since you're hanging everyone's troubles on choices. You took off on your own, took a path of your *choosing*. And yet, that path took you away from Lamoyne, away from Griff. Away from me." The passion in his voice startles me. "Did you have to hide for nine damn years?" He stands up. "And why didn't you talk to *me*?" He thumps his palm against his chest. "We were friends. I *cared* about you."

I shoot to my feet, blinded by pain. My losses. "You and your family took Griff from me! He was all I had!"

He comes toward me, not aggressively, yet there's a change in him. "Did I? Or did I just shovel up the pieces after he was broken and no good to you or anyone else?" He casts a quick glance toward the ceiling. "Griff's leaving had nothing to do with you and everything to do with his inability to deal with the shit storm around him. My guess is, he started pulling away long before—"

"He did! After he met you!"

"Come on, Tallulah. You're seriously angry with me because I was his friend?"

Ross rushes on, the pain in his voice so raw, so true. "If you'd only *talked* to me, Lulie. I know my mom would have taken you in. That's the kind of woman she was. But you *chose* to leave, alone, with no thought of how it made the rest of us feel. We spent those first months calling hospitals and police stations all over the country, every damn time fearing we'd find you raped or beaten or dead. My mother hired a private investigator, but you left no trail. If you're looking at choices that had an effect on other people, that's the one!" He pokes the air with his index finger. "Right there. That's the choice that hurt us all."

His outburst leaves my knees weak. Years of well-tended anger becomes a molten pool at my feet, leaving me drained and wanting.

He runs a hand through his hair and puts a step of distance between us. "I'm sorry. I shouldn't have unloaded on you like that. Not with everything else going on."

"You're right," I whisper. The walls I've so carefully tended are useless when it comes to Ross. "About all of it." Hot tears roll down my cheeks, but for once, I don't feel the need to hide them.

Ross steps to me and holds me close, his hand cradling the back of my head.

Against his shoulder, I say, "I was so hurt, so angry. I *didn't* think about anyone else."

"It was a horrible situation. At that moment, all any of us were thinking about was Griff. You were lost in the shuffle because you always looked after yourself and everyone else, too. No one stopped to think about you—and then you were gone."

Hearing his acknowledgment lifts a weight from my shoulders—the burden of fostering my own bitterness, convincing myself that I was beyond it when I simply locked it in a trunk and tied it to my back.

I gather myself enough to pull away. Ross reaches over and plucks a tissue from the box on the kitchen counter and hands it to me.

As I wipe my face, I say, "Margo was leaving no matter what. I thought the twins would be better off with Lamoyne behind them. I really did. They were young enough they'd be able to forget." I look up at him. "I'm ashamed to admit it makes me feel good knowing you were upset by my leaving."

He smooths my hair away from my face. "Yeah, well, don't test me by doing it again."

"Maybe I *wanted* everyone to feel bad."

"Of course you did, you were a teenager. At least you packed a bag and wrote a note, so we knew you left on your own."

I think of the phone calls to hospitals and police. Of Mrs. Saenger hiring a private investigator. I never imagined. "What about Margo? Did she look for me?"

He looks uncomfortable. "Margo was of the mind that you were forging a life for yourself, living an adventure. She almost seemed . . ." He stops.

"Just say it."

"Envious."

"Do you know if she ever came back to see Walden?"

"I don't think so."

"She finally got what she'd been wanting for years, to be rid of us. Complete and absolute freedom."

"I told you a long time ago, she's the one who didn't deserve you, not the other way around."

I think of Griff, finally in a stable home with a loving mother in Mrs. Saenger. And yet he still left. Maybe Margo created such a hole in each of us that it can never be filled.

"I wish I could apologize to your mother, for causing her so much trouble."

"I guess that's the thing. We never know if we're going to get that opportunity."

His tone holds a warning. And I am willing to take heed.

14

As I hurry Ross out Gran's front door, he says, "Heading to a fire?"

"I want to make sure we're back in New Orleans as soon as possible. In case Amelia gets me in to see Walden."

"Don't get your hopes up for today. She said—"

"I know, I know." I keep moving toward the Mercedes. I didn't sleep at all well, my mind a revolving kaleidoscope of the people in my life and the damage I might have prevented, of cut-up photographs and old lockets. "Sorry for being so edgy."

Ross puts Gran's bag in the trunk while I climb into the passenger seat. I put on my seat belt because Ross's fancy car nags with an incessant chime until you do.

Ross gets in the back seat.

"You're kidding," I say.

"Drive to the motel first. I'll drive from there."

"Seriously?"

"Humor me."

With a sigh, I throw open the door. The seat belt—such a nuisance—grabs my hips and refuses to let me out. I give a growl of frustration and unclip it.

As I'm buckling myself in the driver's seat I say, "Perhaps you'd like me to cover you with a blanket? You know, in case someone gets close enough to see you hiding back there. Which, I might add, will cause more tongues to wag than if you'd just sit up here and drive."

"Nah. The side windows back here are tinted."

"I was being facetious."

I ignore his sniggering.

We're halfway to the motel when I hear the blip of a siren. I glance in the rearview and see the cherry on top of a police car rotating. Out-of-state license plates were always targets in Lamoyne.

I hear another chuckle from the back seat. "Bet you wish you'd covered me up now."

"Oh, shut up. And sit up like a normal person."

I finally see his head in the rearview. He's grinning.

The officer taps on the window.

I reach for the crank, then remember the Mercedes has power windows and fumble for the toggle.

"I'm sorry, Officer. I just realized I was speeding. I promise to slow down."

Ducking low, the policeman looks at Ross in the back seat, then back at me. His hand moves to rest on his gun.

"Are you all right, miss? Any trouble here?" He tilts his head toward the back seat.

"I'm fine, thank you. My friend just thinks it funny to ride in the back."

He eyes Ross for a second before he says, "License and registration."

He's wearing sunglasses, so I can't see his eyes. I glance at his nameplate, Officer Murray. He has a dimple in the center of his square chin.

"Tommy? Is that you?"

He slides off the sunglasses and studies me for a moment. "Tallulah?"

"Yes! Gran's in the hospital—"

"I know. I've been visiting." He's speaking in his regular voice now, slow and thick with accent instead of his serious-officer voice.

"I would have contacted you, if I'd known how." There's a hint of condemnation riding in the last words.

"It's kind of you to visit her."

"I keep an eye on her."

"Like in a police kind of way?"

"In a friend kind of way—for Griff."

I get a tingle of excitement. "Have you heard from him? Do you know where he is?"

His eyes shift away, just for a second, the way they always did when he wanted to avoid a subject. It strikes me that I once knew Tommy as well as I knew my own brother. I never counted him among the people I left behind. Maybe I should have.

"I don't know where he is. And I do need to see your license and registration."

He's developed a by-the-rules attitude he certainly didn't have back then. I dig in my purse and produce my driver's license.

"San Francisco?" Tommy is writing on his ticket pad.

"Yes." I wonder how much of Walden's defense fund this ticket is going to take.

"Are you staying at your grandmother's house?"

"As soon as I pick her up we're heading to New Orleans." I'm certain Tommy and everyone else in Lamoyne knows about Walden, but I don't want to get in a conversation about him. I want to get on the road and *see* him.

"Registration?"

"You remember Ross Saenger," I say, hitching a thumb over my shoulder. "This is his car. We drove up from New Orleans yesterday."

"So, you two . . . ?"

"No," Ross says quickly. "Strictly on the up-and-up."

"Ross would prefer the whole town think he spent last night in the motel—for my honor and Gran's sense of propriety."

Tommy grins. "I swear not to blow your cover." He hands back my license and steps back from the car, tapping the top. "Slow down. The next guy who pulls you over might get caught up in a different kind of nostalgia."

The truth in that statement gives me pause.

"Tell Mrs. James I hope she's feeling better."

Not one to look a gift horse in the mouth, I thank him and start the car.

As I drive away, I wonder why he insisted on seeing my license and the registration after he knew who I was and had decided not to give me a ticket.

The rest of the way to the hospital, that just keeps nagging me.

It's early *and* a Sunday morning, so the visitors' parking lot at the hospital is nearly empty, except for an old truck that looks like Mr. Stokes's. The beekeeping equipment sticking up from the bed confirms it's his even before I see him behind the wheel. My spirits lift at the sight.

By the time I pull into a space and get the car turned off, he's there, opening my door for me. He hasn't changed a bit. "Miss Tallulah, glad you come home."

"Hello, Mr. Stokes." I get out and have to restrain myself to keep from hugging him. "It's so good to see you. You remember Ross Saenger? You spoke on the phone yesterday."

Ross steps forward to shake Mr. Stokes's hand.

"I hope you didn't come to take Gran home," I say. "I assumed she called to let you know her plans to go straight to New Orleans with us."

"Oh, she called. I'm here to see you."

Ross touches my arm. "I'll be over by the doors."

Mr. Stokes suddenly swipes his hat off his head, as if he's just remembered his manners. "About your granny. There's things sitting heavy on her soul, and I'm afraid it's caused her sickness."

No kidding. And the list just keeps getting longer. "Such as?" Years ago Mr. Stokes admitted he and Gran shared secrets. Maybe I'll get the answers about my recent finds in her bedroom.

"First off, I want you to know she took your leavin' hard."

"She's the one who wouldn't let me stay."

"You gotta know, she had her reasons. All of them good-intentioned. Mostly, she wanted you freed from this place and the things that are draggin' her down."

"Which are?"

"It'd be wrong for me to say. I made promises. But I can tell she needs free of it. She's a proud woman and was raised a certain way. That pride is breakin' her. She'll try to push you away, but don't you allow it."

"Do any of these things weighing her down have to do with Uncle George?" I realize the man has been a quiet drone in the background my entire life. Every time Gran shifted the subject away from him, when her whole life was about family stories and traditions, the town's attitude and innuendo, the missing pictures—all of these things hummed in the background like white noise. *Things that must never be mentioned.*

His eyes widen just a bit. "These her things to tell. It's a long time comin', but you got a chance to help each other."

"I don't need her help now."

"That may be, but plenty of times when you did, she was right there. Now you can do the same for her."

The rawboned truth of that hurts. "What makes you think she'll tell me anything?"

"You just ask her why she keeps paintin' a storefront that got no goods to sell. No need anymore. The shelves been stripped bare."

"I don't know what you mean." I glance over my shoulder, wishing Ross was closer.

"She know," Mr. Stokes says. "You just do as I say. Use those words. Don't let her close up. It's eatin' her from the inside and not helpin' nobody."

"And what if she does as she always does?"

"Well, you can back down, or you can stand up like the strong, grown woman you are. Reach out a hand, pull her out of the past. You and her got a chance to mend things. And she needs it—even more than you do." He nods and puts on his hat. "That's what I come to say. Don't forget my words. Those are the ones that'll open her up."

"I'll try. But I don't imagine I'll get anywhere."

He puts on his hat and gives me a smile. "Have faith in ole Mr. Stokes. He taught you how to talk to bees, didn't he?"

"So you're saying you know Gran's secret language, too?"

"A shared lifetime teaches you a few things." He winks, and I suddenly feel strong, just as he always made me feel when he took the time to answer my bothersome questions. "Now you tell your granny we all prayin' for Mr. Walden, just like we been prayin' for you all these years." He turns and starts toward his truck.

"Mr. Stokes?"

He stops and turns his head.

"Thank you."

He gives me a slow nod.

"Did Margo ever come back?" I need confirmation.

"Nobody seen your momma since the day she left to take the twins north."

I'm torn between concern and anger. I wonder if I'll ever know where to place my emotions when it comes to my mother.

"Tell Maisie I said hello and I miss her. She and Marlon move away?"

He turns the brim of his hat in his hands. "No, miss."

I'm disappointed. I wanted her life to be free of this place, too. "I'd love to see her, but we have to get back to New Orleans."

"Maisie miss you, too." He puts on his hat. "You do what I say with your granny."

He ambles toward his truck, and I notice he might look the same, but the years have him moving more slowly. He pauses with his hand on the truck's door handle. "Don't make a choice you gonna regret. Everybody need family—including Miss Lavada."

Gran's hair and makeup are done to perfection, her small train case packed and on the bed beside her. The nurse—not Nurse Busybody today—is there with a wheelchair ready to wheel her out as soon as she gets dressed.

"Don't you look like the first day of spring," Ross says gallantly. Gran actually blushes.

"You do look much better today, Gran." I'm relieved. The situation with Walden will be hard enough on her.

When we get her to the car, Ross opens the front passenger door, but she says, "I prefer sitting in the back, thank you."

"All right." Ross opens the back door and holds her hand as she gets in. I'm glad to see she doesn't look as if she needs the steadying.

Once we're in the car, I say, "Since you're going to be gone for a couple of days, I locked your house. The key is in your purse."

"I hardly think that was necessary—" She seems to catch herself. "Thank you for your thoughtfulness."

"You're welcome."

As we pull onto the highway, she says, "Now, Ross, perhaps we should go by the bank before we leave town. I'll need to make arrangements for your cousin's fee."

"I'm covering the legal bills, Gran. I have a good job." I cringe a bit at the inflated pride in my voice—sort of a *so there*.

Ross says, "Amelia isn't worried about getting paid at this point. She'll come by the house after she sees Walden, and we can go from there."

Gran sits up straighter. "Well, I'm sure this will be resolved quickly—"

"I wouldn't count on it, Gran." I twist and look at her in the back seat. "I know the gossip in town is hard for you—"

"I thought I raised you not to listen to gossip," she snaps.

"You raised me to pretend it didn't exist. There's a difference."

Her face settles into that familiar detachment, the one that closes the door. "We can discuss this at a more appropriate time." She looks pointedly at the back of Ross's head. Then her face settles into a pleasant countenance. "So, tell me all about California, Tallulah."

I do a good job of spinning a golden tale about my job, my life, and her eyes light up. I'm aware that I'm doing just as she always did, glossing over unpleasantness. I justify that it's for the sake of her health.

"Doing for others always did suit you, Tallulah."

The pride in her voice affects me so strongly, I have to take a moment before I can answer. "Well, the foundation is a paying job, so I can't call it altruistic."

After a moment, she says, "I don't see a ring, so I assume you're still a single woman."

"And I plan to stay that way."

"Why, Tallulah Mae, what about children? Surely you want children."

"I do not. I made that decision a long time ago."

She and Ross both say, "Really?" at the same time.

"Why is that so surprising? Considering our family history. The madness stops with me."

I feel Ross's gaze on me. "Madness? Why do you say that?"

"I don't mean insanity, per se. I mean I don't have the proper foundation for raising emotionally healthy children. And what if I turned out to be a mother like Margo?"

Gran says, "Your mother was . . . exceptionally selfish. You are not. She and your father were *never* good for each other—gasoline and a match, those two. You'll be smarter. Choose a better partner. You're too young to be making such unbending decisions. Aren't I right, Ross? You want children, don't you?"

Ross doesn't look the least put on the spot. "I haven't really thought about it. I have to find the right woman first, then that's a decision we'll make together."

"See," Gran says. "He agrees. You can't make an iron-clad decision at this point in your life."

I shake my head. "Margo might not have been well suited to motherhood, but I, on the other hand, am not well suited to relationships. If I can't manage that, I certainly cannot raise a child." I steer the conversation elsewhere, closer to Gran's doorstep. "We passed the farm on our way in town. It didn't look like anyone has been there in a long time. Why would someone buy it and just let it fall into ruin?"

"What makes you think it was sold?"

"Well, you're not working it, so I assumed the taxes would have forced the sale if nothing else."

"The land still belongs to you, Griffin, Walden, and Dharma, equally. It's your legacy."

I'm a little surprised at the relief that washes over me. "If that's so, why weren't you and Walden working it? He loved the orchard."

"He loved the orchard because you loved the orchard. His adoration for you has never wavered. Without you here, he didn't have any interest. And, to be perfectly honest, I think he was a little afraid."

"Afraid of what?"

"Failure. He needs his people around him to make him whole. Without them, he has no purpose. Maybe it's because he's a twin, never alone, even in the womb."

"Did you at least try to get Dharma to come back with him?"

"Why would I do that? She was happy. Those people made it so she could reach her dreams. If she'd been here . . ." She purses her lips and shakes her head. "If I had my way, none of you would have come back to this place that never forgets and never lets a whiff of scandal die."

"If that's true, why didn't you just sell the farm?"

She looks surprised. "Because it isn't mine to sell."

"How did you manage the taxes?"

"I suppose I owe you an apology for that. I sold the Neely pearls. They should have belonged to you."

I don't know how to respond, so I turn and face the road ahead.

Ross reaches over and gives my hand a squeeze, but I pull away.

I don't deserve any of it, the farm, the pearls, Walden's adoration, because I left them all behind and never looked back.

15

Every week or so, I "happen by" the judge's house at six o'clock, quitting time, just to get a life-sustaining dose of Maisie, who's been working full-time at Judge Delmore's for about a year. When I'm early, like today, I wait inside the clematis-covered lattice gazebo in the Delmore's big yard. It's easy to slip in through the gate on the alley and not be seen from the house. And, since Maisie comes and goes by the back door and alley, I can't miss her. While I wait, I'm working on my *Wuthering Heights* essay. All I want to say is: Shame on Catherine. Shame on Heathcliff. And why are people so stupid? I know from real life that spitefulness is just a fact of human nature. But that would make for a short essay.

Finally, I hear the back screen snap closed. I fold up my paper, stick it in my book and wait behind the gazebo. I hear Maisie coming like a freight train, huffing and muttering. She's in a mood, which happens frequently when Mrs. Delmore is finished with her.

I wait. Listening. Timing.

As soon as her right arm swings into my sight, I grab it and pull her behind the gazebo with me.

Instead of a surprised, happy giggle breaking her mood, I get an elbow in the eye and "Get off me!" She flails around as I double over and clutch my eye.

Suddenly, she stops. "Dang it, Tallulah! What're you doin'?"

"What're *you* doin'? I think you blacked my eye!"

"Well, serves you right, sneakin' up on me like that! For all I know you were that creep Grayson Collie."

I straighten and blink to clear my blurry vision. "He been bothering you?"

"No more than every other female in town. And you oughta know better than to pull a childish trick like that. Lemme see that eye." There's nothing at all apologetic in her voice for slugging me. But Maisie is like that, never wanting to back down or admit fault when she's with me—even when it's obvious she's in the wrong.

She squints and frowns as she studies my face. "Mmmm-hmmm. That gonna shine. Lucky your momma don't pay attention, or you'd have to come up with a story 'bout how you come by it."

"Guess sometimes it pays to be ignored," I say. Maisie complains her momma watches her like a hawk on a field mouse. She should feel lucky. The list of people ignoring me is growing. Griff has turned into a phantom, and Daddy's gotten so he doesn't see *anybody* but Margo—when she's not around all he does is pace and fret and talk about her.

I don't want to waste our precious minutes together, so I offer an apology of my own. "I shouldn't have surprised you like that when you sounded all bothered coming down the back walk. What's the problem today? Silver not shiny enough? Spines of the books not perfectly straight?"

She starts toward the alley. "I swear that woman has measuring sticks for eyeballs. It's beyond just bein' particular. There's somethin' *wrong* with her—she breaks out in a sweat if the furniture isn't in the *exact* same spot after a floor cleaning. I don't know how she can tell, 'cause it always looks the same to me. I checked the floor just to be sure there aren't any secret marks to tell her. They're *aren't*." She picks up speed down the alley.

Maisie's too smart to spend her days worrying about book spines and not what's inside those books. Back when talk about her quitting school first came up, I begged Gran to intervene. She made it clear I was no friend to Maisie if I made her feel unhappy with her situation. Gran said Maisie was lucky to have this opportunity for job security with the judge and she'd be working with her momma, which is always a comfort to a girl.

Maisie is tearing along like there's fire nipping at her heels. I catch up and loop my arm through hers. We march along that way for a bit, quiet with each other, me thinking on limitations made just by how you happened to be born.

There was a time, back when Margo began her civil rights work, when I thought she would fight for Maisie to go to college, maybe work on getting her a scholarship, too. Of course, that was before I realized Margo only works for the people she *doesn't* know, the ones her "groups" pick out for her. I think it's quite nice of Maisie not to point that out to me on a regular basis. Margo wouldn't even take me and Maisie when she went to the March on Washington to hear Dr. Martin Luther King Jr. talk last month. We had to sneak and watch it on television while Mrs. Delmore was at bridge club.

Gradually, Maisie slows down. After another half block, she nudges her shoulder against mine, as close to an apology for my black eye as I'm going to get.

"I'm going to tell you a secret," I say. "But you have to swear not to tell anyone."

She stops dead and looks at me with a frown. "Since when do you need to say that? I never shared a secret of yours."

"I know." I take her hand. "Guess I'm just skittish because I want it so bad." I take a deep breath. "Griff and I are going to California when I'm finished with school." This is the first time I've said it out loud. I like the way it tastes on my tongue.

"A trip?"

"A new life." I squeeze her hand. "What if you come, too? Things are different out there. Not boxed in by tradition. The three of us can get an apartment—"

"Stop right there! I doubt it's different enough that the three of us can live in the same apartment. Besides, I got my own new life coming on, Tallulah James. And it's right here in Lamoyne—at least for now."

"Marlon?"

"Maaaaybe." She's grinning like a fool, and I know Marlon is *the one*. My heart gives a little zip. Marlon just might be good enough to deserve her. He's a senior and has already applied to several colleges. He's not flashy like her last boyfriend, who Pappy Stokes called a no-account. Marlon is serious, wants to be a doctor. And that will make a good future for Maisie—maybe one away from Mrs. Delmore and her measuring-stick eyeballs.

Maisie's grin tells me he's good for her heart, too, and that's the most important thing.

I do admit, I'm a little jealous. The only boys interested in me are either pimply creeps who still pick their noses or hound dogs (thanks to the rumor Grayson Collie started about me being fast). I can't wait to go to California, where I can be whoever I want and no one will have a say otherwise.

"You two going to the Muscadine Jubilee?" I ask.

"Of course. How 'bout you?" Maisie bumps my shoulder again and gives a sly grin. "You gonna ask that boy from down in New Orleans?"

"Of course not," I say. "Griff's practically a stranger thanks to him. I hope when Ross goes to college next year he never comes back to Mississippi." Then Griff will have time for me. We'll get back to being biscuits and honey. We'll spend our time planning our escape, and as soon as I get my diploma . . . goodbye, Lamoyne.

I steer the conversation in a different direction. "So, did you ask your momma?"

She gives me a confused look. "Ask what?"

"Maisie! You said you would!" Then I see the twinkle in her eye. "You did! Tell me. What did you find out?"

When I was at the library two weeks ago, doing research for a paper on the history of Marion and Pearl River Counties, I was

reading about the white families who first settled here. I was surprised that the James name wasn't listed. Gran said both sides of
Daddy's family settled here when this area was still wild with Choctaw. I did find the Neely name. But not until 1827, when the wildness was on the run and the Choctaw were already being pushed
west of the Mississippi River. After digging around, I found that
the James family showed up in 1854. Apparently, my first James
ancestor in Mississippi was a scoundrel from New Orleans who
won Pearl River Plantation from a man named Julien Doucet in
a poker game. Hardly the "founding fathers" kind of beginning I'd
been led to believe.

I was shocked by this discovery. After all, the past three gen-
erations of James men have been *historians*. Although, now that
I think of it, Dad never talks of his heritage. That was always
Granny James.

I looked to see what else I could find in the library about the
James family. I focused on the things Gran always steps sideways
about. Granddad's accident and Uncle George. There are no microfiche files going back to the twenties, which would have been before
George left. And the librarian wouldn't allow a "nonprofessional" to
put destructive, oily hands on the actual newspapers because they're
too delicate. She was quite cranky about the whole subject, like the
library and all of the books and documents in it were her personal
property she was being forced to share.

The newspapers for the year 1934 *had* been put on microfiche.
So I spent half a day straining my eyes on that machine looking for
something about Granddad James's accident. Since he was hunting,
I assumed it happened in the fall. But week after week there were
no reports of an accident, no obituary for Elliot James. It had to
be 1934 because Daddy was ten. He was a New Year's baby—first
one born in Lamoyne City Hospital in '24, I've heard *that* story a
thousand times.

So I went back and started at January first. I was smarter this
go-around and read the obituaries first. Once I found it, I could
look for an article about the accident.

Old-fashioned obituaries were shocking and creepily addictive, filled with gruesome details and too much private family business. For instance, Sherman Boyd was a fourteen-year-old kid who died "hours after a fire burned off all the skin on his face, chest, and arms . . . Flames burst forth and engulfed the room, including Sherman and his younger brother, Walter." Walter ran from the home, "his clothes ablaze, and was doused by an alert neighbor." He was "not expected to survive." Good golly, they'd written poor Walter off in an obituary before he was even dead.

I finally found Granddad's on June 7, 1934.

James, Elliot Forrest Lamoyne resident, history professor at Wickham College, and landowner, aged 34 years, died in a freak accident sometime on June 5. Missing for nearly a full day, Mr. James was discovered in the woods approximately a mile from his home at Pearl River Plantation by his wife, Lavada (Neely) James. Full particulars as to his death are lacking.

The widowed Mrs. James is the daughter of the prominent and respected Mr. and Mrs. Rudell Neely. The pioneering Neely family founded Hawthorn House in 1827, First Planters Bank in 1850, and have been pillars of charity and public service. Many condolences and much sympathy comes from this paper and the Lamoyne community.

A beloved father and husband, Mr. James will be mourned by his wife and his son, Drayton Neely James, aged 10 years. Mr. James was preceded in death by an infant sister, Elizabeth Jocelyn James, and his parents, Frederick and Cecelia James. Mr. James served his country during the Great War, working in the War Department in Washington, DC.

Mr. James's body was returned home to Pearl River Plantation and laid to rest in the James family cemetery next to his sister, beloved parents, and grandparents.

There wasn't a single article or report of the accident in the newspaper between June fifth and July first. The *Lamoyne Ledger* reported on everything: Rotary Club minutes, Bridge Club scores, Clyde Pickrell's flat tire on Eudora Avenue, even a stray dog stealing long johns off a clothesline. I suppose, considering how private Gran is about family business, it's not surprising that there weren't any gory details regarding Granddad.

So I asked Maisie to ask her momma about it, hoping she'd be more interested in gossiping than Mr. Stokes is. If Granddad died in June, the blackberry harvest would have been in full swing. Mr. Stokes would have been there, and probably Maisie's momma, too.

Maisie says, "Momma remembers that day all right, 'cause Pappy Stokes had to help cart Mr. James home and lay him out."

The image her words bring to mind makes me glad we have McClure's Funeral Home and don't have our dead lying around in the parlor waiting to be buried anymore.

"And?" I prod. The more Maisie knows, the harder she makes you work for it.

"She and Pappy Stokes were there working the harvest that day."

"I surmised that. What was Granddad hunting?"

"How would my momma know?" She sounds almost perturbed.

"What *did* your momma remember?"

"She say your granny came straight to get Pappy Stokes about two hours after the work begun. Pappy dropped his pail, grabbed a couple of strong boys, and told everyone to keep to work. He hurried off with Mrs. James. When they come carryin' your granddad out of the woods, Momma say it look like Pappy Stokes was workin' to hold Mr. James's brains inside his head."

My stomach pitches. Poor Gran, finding her husband like that. Margo said that if anything happens to Daddy she'll kill herself and be done. Griff says she's being dramatic, which is true enough. But I think there might be something deeper than show. It's hard to describe. Despite all the fights and Margo's running off, she and Daddy are as interdependent as lightning and thunder. And if anything—or anyone—gets between them, it's going to get shocked out of the sky.

"And then?" I say.

Maisie lifts a shoulder. "He was boxed up right quick and buried the next day. That's it."

"What about Daddy? Where was he?"

Maisie shrugged. "Dunno. Momma didn't say."

"The obituary said Granddad went out the day before. He was missing."

"I *told you* what she *said*. You want more, maybe you oughta ask your daddy. He was same age as Momma."

I've never asked Dad about his father's death. When I was little I never thought much about it. And then when I was old enough to be curious, I was also old enough to know to avoid bringing up painful subjects for fear of pushing him into shadow time.

We walk in silence for a little while, the only noise the sound of our shoes on the gravel alley and the swish of Maisie's purse against the side of her starched uniform dress. I can't stop thinking about Gran finding her husband bloody and dead in the woods. There's no way I can ask her to tell that story. Besides, Gran only talks about the things people did while they walked this earth, never, never, *never* about how they left it.

"What about Uncle George? Did she know anything about him? The obituary didn't even mention him."

Maisie says, "Told me to hush, like she does when she's tired of questions."

I'm beginning to think I'll never figure out anything about Uncle George.

"I got two dimes burning a hole in my pocket," I say. "How about I buy you a Co'Cola?" The Sinclair station, where Griff works, isn't exactly on Maisie's way home, but close enough. Sometimes we swing by there for a cold drink. I pull them right out of the ice bath in the big red cooler sitting in front of the station office and we drink them while we walk. Then I drop the empties in their squares in the wood crate on my way back. No deposit needed.

The good thing about getting Cokes at the Sinclair is that I can talk to Griff and he can't find a way to run off. Like I said, he's never home, and at school he might as well be made of moonbeams he's so intangible.

"Never turn down a free Co'Cola," Maisie says with a smile.

Turns out Maisie and I aren't the only thirsty girls at the Sinclair. There's a black-haired girl in a tight, pink short-sleeved sweater holding a bottle and leaning against the big red cooler. She reminds me of Elizabeth Taylor in *Cat on a Hot Tin Roof* (a movie that had Granny and Margo at odds for months: Granny angry over the unfair depiction of old Southern families as shallow, greedy, and manipulative; Margo, of course, was a big fan of the "truths" it told).

Elizabeth Taylor is talking to Griff while he cleans the windshield of a robin's-egg-blue convertible parked in front of the green pumps. No driver, so it's likely hers. She's looking at Griff in that hungry way I see lots of girls look at him. And I'm struck with the same strange mix of incredulity and possessiveness that I always am when I witness it.

Maisie hangs back while I go up and lift the hatch on the cooler and pull out a couple of bottles. I slide my two dimes into the coin collector, then finally have to ask the girl to move so I can use the opener on the front. I snap off the caps and they fall into the catcher with a little clink. The girl doesn't stop talking, or bother to look at me, until Griff turns and notices me.

"Lulie. What are you doing here?" He barely looks at me as he tucks the dark-red oil rag into his back pocket. It hangs there like a lopsided tail.

"Hello to you, too."

I hand one of the bottles to Maisie.

Griff nods. "Maisie." Then he looks at Elizabeth Taylor. "You're all set, miss."

She sends a peeved look my way before she walks to her car. She puts a hand on his shoulder as she passes Griff. "Don't forget." Her hand trails off his body in a way that suggests she's a fast girl.

The guys at school stopped looking at Griff like he could move mountains when he quit baseball and football, but girls are all still cow-eyed over him—and apparently not just those in high school.

Elizabeth Taylor gets in the convertible and puts on a pair of white-framed cat-eye sunglasses, taking a moment to pull them down and give me a look over their green lenses, which reminds me of that girl in Jackson looking at Ross—all sophistication and confidence.

Maybe *I* need to get a pair of sunglasses.

"Don't forget what?" I ask.

"Nothing."

"Sooo . . . Someone special?" I say, looking after the car as it drives away.

"Nope. Just another college girl with a fancy car and no common sense about how to take care of it."

I hear his words, but I also notice the way his eyes stay on that car as it pulls away.

16

I walk Maisie farther than I should, well past the little section of colored businesses that stay open late for folks coming home from work. The man who owns the drugstore gives me a respectful nod through the window, but his eyes tell me I have no business in this part of town.

It's dusk when I head back, the streetlights would be coming on if they had any on this side of Lamoyne. I'm almost to the railroad tracks when I hear a car rolling slowly up behind me. My entire body snaps to alert.

I glance over my shoulder, better to sacrifice a little dignity than have the likes of Grayson Collie and his goons sneak up behind you.

It isn't Grayson. But it might as well be.

The black-and-white car paces alongside me. Chief Collie leans across the seat and calls through the open passenger window. "Tallulah James, you know better than to be down here, girl."

Maybe it's the disdainful way he's looking at me. Or maybe it's the memory of the police chief's *own kid* chasing me down on a street in the part of town I *am* supposed to be in. In any case, I keep my steady pace and use a haughty tone when I say, "No law against walking along the street minding my own business."

He slams on his brakes, his tires grinding on the dirt street. I stop, too, my heart suddenly beating hard and fast.

Moving so quickly that he leaves the car door standing open, he comes and stands so close I can feel the heat coming off him. He looks down his nose at me, gritting the same horrible, overlapped teeth he gave to his kid. His breath is fast and angry through his hairy nostrils.

"I didn't hear you correct, girl," he says. "Care to answer me again?"

I swallow hard. "I'm just heading home, sir."

"Ah, there's a little respect. Why are you down here in Coontown? And what happened to your eye?" He glances around, as if looking for a place to lay blame.

"I'm not doing anything wrong." I keep my chin high and make to step around him, but he grabs my upper arm, squeezing until I can feel his nails digging into my skin.

I try to pull away. "You can't just—"

He jerks me around, slamming my back against the door of his cruiser. His body presses against mine, pinning me tight. One hand grips my chin, his fingers and thumb holding so tightly my mouth puckers. "There's where you're wrong, missy. I can. And nobody here will stop me."

Out of the corner of my eye, I see a man skitter off his porch and close the front door behind him. Chief Collie can do whatever he wants. Just like Grayson can.

I hold my breath. But this trouble isn't going to pass.

"You look scared," he says, a lilt of joy in his voice. "If only your Granddaddy Neely was here to see how far his family's fallen. Him always thinkin' he was better than everyone else. You know he foreclosed on my daddy's farm? Threw us all out in the cold. Just. Like. That." He emphasizes each word with a squeeze. I feel my teeth cutting into the inside of my mouth. "Not a care that my momma was ailing, or that it was the middle of the Depression. No matter to a rich man like him. *No*, sir!" He leans his nose close to mine. "But now see who has the power in this town."

He hovers there, a breath away. Waiting for me to say something.

"I . . . I'm sorry." The words are slurred because he's pinching my face.

"Oh, I bet you are."

"Are you arresting me?" At this point, I'm hoping so. Arrest me and take me to the jail where there are other people around.

"Oh, gettin' arrested's least of your worries. Who knows what could happen to a sweet young thing like you down here, stirring up these boys' wild blood." He turns my chin, glaring at my bruised eye. I taste blood in my mouth. "Looks like maybe somebody already had a try."

My rushing blood turns into a cold river. "I walked into a door. It was a stupid accident."

"That's not the way I see it. I found you, beat up and scared, too afraid to point out the colored who attacked you." He shoves my chin upward, snapping my teeth together. His jaw flexes as he stares at me. "There," he says. "There it is. True fear."

Suddenly, he barks out a cruel laugh and shoves me to the side. I hit the ground, rocks digging into my elbow. Looking down at me, he practically growls the words, "This is *my* town!" He shakes a finger at me, his face purple with anger. "Your family's no more than a canker on its ass." As he stomps around to the driver's side of his cruiser I hear him muttering. "Lavada Neely ain't so high and mighty. . . ."

I'm still on the ground when he spins the tires, covering me with dust as he pulls away.

I reach over to my dropped copy of *Wuthering Heights*. I clutch the book against my wildly beating heart. Heathcliff's hate and festering anger have nothing over that roiling inside Chief Collie.

I've finally stopped trembling and can once again feel my feet as they hit the pavement as I near Wickham College. The cuts inside my mouth are swelling, and the skin on my right elbow and forearm screams like a rug burn. I rub my thumb across the reassuring solidness of Griff's arrowhead, thinking how much I'd like to slash Chief Collie's face with it. Now I know how Griff must feel with the chief dogging him at every turn.

I can't believe the man's holding a grudge over something that happened thirty years ago. Granddad Neely died before I was even born. Besides, Gran said her daddy always gave folks every chance before his bank foreclosed, which is why the bank went under in the Depression. I doubt the chief's parents bothered to tell him that part.

A shudder comes over me. After Griff and I are gone, will Collie turn his nastiness toward Walden and Dharma? Poor Walden won't be able to stand it. He felt so guilty when he left the milk out of the refrigerator that he took money from his piggy bank to pay to replace it.

I have to tell Dad what happened.

As I cross the quad, heading toward James Hall, I smell the bonfire and see a flickering yellow glow over the football field. Everyone is headed in that direction for the kickoff for homecoming. Only one office has lights showing behind the textured half-glass door on the second floor of James Hall. Dad's. I try to turn the knob. It won't budge, but I can hear him rustling around in there.

I gently peck on the glass and say in a low voice, "Dad, it's me. I can't get the door to open."

There's a flurry of movement, but no response.

I peck again, and the noise echoes down the hall. "Dad? I really need to talk to you."

Agitated footsteps move toward the door. I wait for the knob to turn. It doesn't.

The footsteps retreat.

I look down at my feet. There's a torn corner of paper. It reads, *Go away.* The handwriting is sharp and frantic.

His hurried footsteps don't stop. Occasionally, I hear a thud and curse.

"Dad. Something's happened."

Feet hurry back to the door. It opens a crack. One wild blue eye looks out. "Margo? Did something happen to Margo?"

I'm standing here bruised and disheveled, and he's asking about Margo? "No. She's fine."

The tension leaves the visible sliver of his face.

He closes the door.

I grab the knob and turn it before he can lock it again. There's resistance when I try to push it open. "Dad! Let me in." I shove. The resistance is gone, and the door swings wide.

I barely recognize his office. I can't see him—only stacks and stacks of books, taller than me, some teetering on the brink of tumbling, some carefully constructed pyramids. I see a book disappear from the top of one pile, then reappear on another.

I close the door quickly behind me. "Dad?"

Near the baseboard behind the door is a stack of cube-shaped boxes marked *Rawlings, Official League*. There must be two hundred baseballs.

"Dad?"

"Can't stop."

"What are you doing?"

His head pops from behind the wall of books. "I finally have them all."

"Them?"

"Books! Can't you see?" He disappears again.

"Dad, I need you to stop for just a minute. Something happened today—"

"Of course it did!" His words are as rushed and frantic as his handwriting. "Something happens every day. Then *people* get involved. Twisting. Manipulating. Interpretations. Lies." He holds up a book and shakes it. "Let the fire eat the lies! Paper. Lies. Fire." He keeps talking, muttering, his words jumbled.

Two years ago he had wild accusations of conspiracies and the manipulation of history. That was the last time I heard anything about the topic, or the book he was supposedly writing.

"Where did all these books come from?" I ask.

"Here and there. Library. Bookstore. Offices. Dorm rooms." He stops restacking one pile into two and cocks his head. "Hear that?"

"What? I don't hear anything."

"They're hiding them." He stops and taps his finger against his lips as he scans the stacks. "I have to start with the most inflammatory. Now. Before they find out."

His skittering gaze settles on one pile. He rummages in a mound of papers, magazines, and a couple of empty bourbon bottles on the floor and picks up a canvas duffel bag stamped with the college logo and marked as property of the athletic department. Then he begins to shove books into it. "I'll burn these first. Yes. That's the right plan. These and then . . ." His eyes sweep the room, but his hands keep putting books in the bag. "Those. Trips. Lots of trips. Fire's big enough."

I fall to my knees next to him and grab his wrists. "Dad! Stop. Please stop for just a second."

His gaze settles on my face, and I see a change in his eyes.

"You're going to lose your job if you do this." Does he think he can just run back and forth between here and the bonfire, tossing on a bag full of books without anyone stopping him? But I don't ask the question. "We can lock them in here. No one will get them tonight."

He sits back on his haunches. "I'm doing this for the school! We'll lead the charge to the new day. They'll build a monument to me." He pulls his wrists free; his fingers flutter at his temples. "So much in my head. Noise. A tornado. I can't keep it straight. Help me. Please help me."

The pain in his eyes scares me more than Chief Collie did. I put my hands on his cheeks. "It's okay, Daddy. Let me take you home. We'll take care of the books tomorrow." I'm not sure how, but at least he won't be burning them tonight.

His gaze sharpens with shock. "You're with them!" He jerks back as if I'd hit him. A tall stack of books falls into another, making an avalanche of noise as they hit the floor.

Dad scrabbles across the floor, grabbing books, furiously restacking.

"Wait!" I scramble for something to stall him. "Let's call Griff." I move toward the phone. "With all these books, you'll never get them all burned tonight. Griff and I will help."

"Good idea. I'll just take this bag down."

"No!"

He stops, but that look of suspicion is back.

"We don't want anyone to know what we're doing until we can get the job done quickly," I say. "We can't risk someone stopping us."

"Right. Okay. I'll go get more bags." He drops the one he's dragging and hurries past me.

I find the phone buried on Dad's desk and call home. Walden answers and tells me that Griff isn't home. Margo's not there, either. I tell him to have Griff call Dad's office as soon as he gets home.

Next, I call Gran. Thank God she answers.

To keep myself from losing my mind while I wait for Gran, I start sorting the books with a library stamp from those without. Inside one book I find a receipt from the college bookstore for $754.63. How will we pay it when the last electric bill had FINAL NO-TICE stamped on it?

I poke around trying to find the bookstore copies, hoping we can return them. Maybe we can just dump the rest in the quad in the middle of the night and everyone will assume it's a fraternity prank. I'm trying to figure out how to tell which ones are new and which have been pinched from dorm rooms and common areas, when there's a tap on the door.

"Tallulah. It's me." Gran's voice is calm, sure. The sound of it settles my racing heart.

I open the door.

"Good gracious! What happened to you?" Her hands go to my shoulders as she looks me over.

"I'll tell you later. Right now we have to find Dad. He should have been back thirty minutes ago."

Gran's eyes take in the room. She seems to be sizing it up with a sense of relief. "Just this nonsense with the books, then?"

Just? I nod. "At least as far as I know. He's been"—I hesitate, feeling disloyal to Dad—"frenetic, for a couple of weeks. Not sleeping, either."

"Your poor father has been working too hard. Carrying too large a burden." She sounds like it's as simple as needing a vacation. But the semester has barely started.

With her head shaking and her hands sorting through the piles of papers on Dad's desk, she says, "The stress of being overlooked for department head . . ." She stills, after opening a folded sheet of paper with a dark stain covering one corner. She looks up.

Now I see some panic.

"Go find your father." Her mouth is tight.

"What did you find?"

"Nothing. You said he went to the athletic department?" There is a note of hope in her voice.

"Yes."

"I'll wait here in case he comes back." She motions for me to go. "Hurry now."

I'm at the door when she calls, "Tallulah."

I turn around.

"If he gives you trouble—about coming back with you—just . . . just get him to stay where he is and come fetch me. Don't push. Don't make a fuss."

The uncharacteristically wary tone in Gran's voice reverberates in my head as I trot down the stairs and out into the smoky-smelling night.

17

The only light in the darkened gymnasium comes from the trophy case. Dad is slumped on the floor with his back against the block wall, his stillness more alarming than his previous agitation.

"Dad?" I drop to my knees beside him. It's not until I register he's breathing that I realize I was afraid he was not. "Daddy?"

He draws his knees up and grasps the sides of his head as if he's in pain.

He's having a stroke. Finally blew out an artery in his brain.

A frantic rush of whispers comes from his lips. Dates. Names. Something that sounds like "losing the thread."

I cast a useless look around for help. The place is deserted.

Lobby pay phones. Call the operator for an ambulance. But Gran said . . .

"Almost had it . . . unraveling."

"What's unraveling?" I ask.

His head jerks up, eyes wide with fury. He yells so loudly I fall back on my heels. "*I'm* unraveling!" He hits his chest with a fist. "Me!"

He fists both hands in his hair, pulling his head from side to side. A groan rumbles around in the depths of his throat. Then he pushes himself to his feet sluggishly.

"Are you in pain?"

"Leave me alone!" The three words are a lion's roar. "You don't know anything." He disappears into the men's locker room.

I follow him, curling my nose against the smell of dirty socks and sweaty boys. The locker room is cast in gray gloom, dimly lit through the big windows to the coach's office, where a desk lamp has been left on. As I pass the office, I try the knob. But the phone stays out of reach behind a locked door.

I hear a metal wastebasket tumble and roll, echoing against the locker banks. A string of expletives, also echoing. I move forward but don't call out, for fear of setting him off.

Dad falls silent. All I can hear is that rocking trash can.

I move toward the sound and find him sitting on a bench with his head cradled in his hands. I sit next to him and put a hand on his back. He shrugs me off.

"Gran's waiting at your office," I whisper softly.

"Stop whispering! I can't stand it!"

"Okay. Sorry." My voice is small, but I manage something stronger than a whisper.

He turns to me, his eyes reflecting the meager light. He looks like a man who's been waging war. His voice is defeated when he says, "Something is wrong with me. Really, really wrong."

Hearing him admit what I've secretly feared causes the world to drop from beneath me. He isn't just moody, but broken. And there truly is no hand on the rudder of our family.

I open my mouth to comfort, to reassure. But instead, a strangled noise of despair comes out. I snap my mouth closed, diminishing but not extinguishing the sound. I have never seen the pendulum swing from too much Daddy to too little Daddy so abruptly. And I have never been so afraid.

"So tired." It's as much moan as declaration. "The vortex—my mind—is killing me." These last words are small and drawn out. And I wish I hadn't heard them.

We're perched on the crest of the roller coaster, poised for a steep fall no matter which way we go. *What if I say the wrong thing?*

"Help me." His voice is so thin I almost think I imagined it. But from the way he's looking at me, I know he spoke.

He's folding in on himself right in front of my eyes. The shadow is descending.

I stand. "Let's go find Gran."

He looks away. "Don't tell her."

I help him to his feet. He stops before we exit the locker room and grabs my elbow. "Promise me."

"I promise." I won't need to tell. Gran will be able to see for herself. She'll know the right thing to do, how to help him.

When we return to his office, Dad is like a sleepwalker, dully going where prodded, eyes as empty as warehouse windows. I want Gran to be alarmed. I want her to show shock at his behavior, the 180-degree turn that has occurred within ninety minutes. But Gran is matter-of-fact when she says, "I'll just take him with me tonight. A good night's sleep. That's what he needs."

Can't she see? She *must* see!

"You lock up his office, Tallulah. Then go on home."

"But, Gran—" I stop myself. I promised. I wave my hands to indicate the chaos in the room. "He was so . . . busy. Now . . ."

"He's burned himself out, poor dear. One can only run so long on fumes."

Dad's standing at his window, as still as daybreak, shoulders slumped, looking out on the dark quad.

"But, Gran—"

"Hush now. Your father needs rest. Lock up. We'll deal with the books later."

That seems to get Dad's attention. He turns slowly, his hands buried in his pockets. "The bonfire." But it's a vacant statement, apparently spurred by the mention of the books, but not necessarily linked to his desire to burn them. He looks perplexed at even having spoken.

"Come, Drayton." Gran takes his arm and he moves alongside her with neither purpose nor resistance. "Do as I say, Tallulah. And not a word of this to anyone, you hear?"

I stare at her, looking for a sign that she understands how bad Dad is.

But she just stares back. *"Do you hear me?"*

"Yes, ma'am."

They leave the office, Gran talking softly to Dad, as if he's a confused little boy. I'm wound so tight I'm ready to scream. As I go to get Dad's keys from his desk, I recall the paper that struck panic in Gran. I poke around, but only find another empty bourbon bottle, the usual class papers, and a doodle pad nearly black with various symbols: a pyramid with an eye in the center and a circle around the apex, a strange fleur-de-lis with a rope wrapped through it like the number 8, a Freemason's symbol, a British flag, a swastika, a Star of David, the stars and stripes, something that looks a lot like an old-fashioned ship's wheel, a crescent and star, an Egyptian ankh, a pentagram, the hammer and sickle, and a Christian cross. Signs of power. Signs of belief.

I pick up Dad's keys and my copy of *Wuthering Heights* and walk toward the door. Eyeing the stack of boxed baseballs, I wonder what on earth he plans to do with so many of them. Griff doesn't play anymore, and Walden is about as athletic as I am. Then I see, there on the floor near the baseboard, half hidden behind the stack of boxes, an edge of black satin. I reach down to pick it up.

Ugh. I drop the panties with a burning face and a disgusted shudder, trying to erase the obvious from my mind. I start for the door, then think of someone, maybe even Gran, finding them. I pick them back up between my thumb and forefinger. Thankful for the deserted building, I take them down the hall and drop them in the trash in the ladies' room.

I'm halfway across the quad before I stop quivering in revulsion and begin thinking again. And I don't want to think.

So I follow the smell of smoke and the dull echo of a crowd toward the football field. I want to lose myself in the sound and movement and simple reality of normal kids—normal kids celebrating something as common and clockwork as homecoming. I bet none of them even appreciate the predictable sanity of their lives.

Gravitating toward the sound of music, I thread my way through the bodies and the smells of smoke and perfume and beer. Near the tall chain-link fence is an old car with its windows down, doors open. "Mashed Potato Time" is blaring from the radio. I wade in, focused on the beat and the movement of dancing. I begin to move with the music, pretending I'm normal. Pretending I'm happy. Pretending I am free.

The radio DJ announces a song for lovers. "Blue Velvet" flows over me. I relish the feeling of anonymity, the primal nature of dancing in a crowd of strangers on a dark and smoky night. The horrors of the day fall behind me as I close my eyes, shift and sway, my arms wrapped tight around my partner, *Wuthering Heights*.

The music changes again, yanking me from my floating mood. "Do You Love Me" blares. The couples around me make the leap from dreamy to jazzed-up as smoothly as shifting from a walk to a run. Some of them are doing normal *Bandstand* dances. But others are shimmying and touching and rubbing against one another in a way that makes me think of those panties in Dad's office.

And then I see one of the shimmying couples is Elizabeth Taylor and Griff! He has a beer bottle in one hand and the other is on her . . . someplace it shouldn't be.

I barely form a thought before I'm grabbing his arm, pulling him away from Elizabeth's gyrations.

"I need to talk to you!" Even I'm surprised at the nastiness in my voice. But I'm spinning with a hurricane of my own, one of anger and disgust and self-pity.

"You shouldn't be here." He takes a swig from the beer bottle, as if challenging me to say something about it.

I glare at Elizabeth Taylor. Everybody gets a piece of Griff but me. "Neither should you."

Elizabeth glares back.

I refrain from socking her in the jaw.

"What do you want?" he asks, but not like he really cares. This Griff just wants me to disappear.

"I need to talk to you in private. Something bad's happened."

I finally see a spark of concern in his eyes. He turns his back on Elizabeth and walks me toward the chain-link fence. When we stop, he leans close. "Is that a black eye?"

My fingers touch the sore area. "What do you care?" I can't keep the childish antagonism out of my voice. He was so busy ogling Elizabeth Taylor he didn't notice it in broad daylight.

His jaw flexes and in his eyes, I see a hint of what I saw when he beat the crap out of Grayson Collie in junior high. I'm ashamed at the flare of satisfaction it gives me.

"Who did that to you?" he asks with a hard edge.

The violence I see in his face scares me enough that I admit, "It has nothing to do with what happened today. Maisie accidentally caught me with her elbow."

"Truth?"

There's my brother. "Truth."

"So, what happened?"

I nearly tell him about Chief Collie, but it's obvious the risk of him doing something stupid is too great.

"It's Dad." I tell him the whole story, including my astonishment that Gran seemed so blind to it. "We have to figure out how to get all those books back where they belong. Dad's gone to shadow time, so he's not going to be any help."

"His office is locked." Griff takes a swig of beer and shrugs. "The books can wait until he snaps out of it. No doubt Gran will call the department head and feed him some excuse about Dad being sick. None of this is our problem."

"How can you say that? What about the huge bill at the bookstore? Dad could lose his job!"

"Not going to happen. He's tenured. Gran'll handle it."

"I don't think you understand. I've never seen him this bad."

"Stop!" He raises his hands. "Just stop. Stop thinking you can fix everything. You can't fix *anything*. They're fucked-up beyond help. All of them. The sooner you figure that out, the better off you'll be. Just let it go, Lulie!"

The whip of his anger cuts me to the bone. He's angry at me! Because I *care*.

I stare at him, my body quivering. "Fine for you—keeping away with your job and your friends. What about me? And what about Dharma and Walden?" I give him a push. "Go on. Get back to your fun. I'm sorry I bothered you."

He tosses the beer bottle over the fence, the liquid casting an arc from the neck. Before I can walk away, he grabs my shoulders. "All right. Okay. I'm sorry for being an ass."

I don't look at him, but I don't break free, either. I feel as if I've been turned inside out by this day, flayed and stinging.

He sighs. "Go home, Lulie. We can figure it all out tomorrow."

I grab onto the *we*. Tomorrow he and I will put our heads together. Together. Us. A team. I nod, still choking on the tears I refuse to let fall.

"Okay." He releases me. "'Night." He starts to walk away.

I get a glimpse of Elizabeth Taylor. She's already dancing with another guy.

"Just come home with me!" I call.

"I'll be home later." I watch his back as the crowd swallows him up.

18

The next morning I'm sitting in sophomore chemistry, the only student interested in Mr. Neiman's lecture—the man *can* drone on, but I love the predictable surety of chemistry. You know exactly what will happen with any set circumstance just by counting the electrons. Out of the corner of my eye, I see two police cars stop out in front of the high school. Chief Collie and three other officers—probably the full day shift—get out and stride up the front steps with grim faces under their uniform caps. I'm not the only one who's noticed their arrival. Even Mr. Neiman has stopped talking about covalent bonds and is staring out the window with his chalk stilled in his hand.

A short time later, Floyd Beeson calls from his seat near the window, "Hey, it's Griff James! The cops have him in handcuffs!"

My stomach whips upside down.

Everyone jumps to their feet and surges toward the window.

By the time I squeeze up to the window, Chief Collie is putting Griff in the back seat of his cruiser. I can't see my brother's face because the three other officers are crowding close, as if they're afraid he's going to make a break for it. My ears are so full of my own heartbeat that I can't untangle the jumble of voices around me, but the drone is full of condemnation and judgment.

Suddenly, I feel the attention shift to me. Without looking at a single face, I push my way through my classmates and run from the room, leaving my books and purse behind.

Chief Collie's cruiser is pulling away when I burst out the school's front door. I fling myself halfway into the window of the second police car. "Why are you taking him?"

Lanky, nineteen-year-old Teddy Gibbs is the officer in the passenger seat. He won't look at me, his profile is all nose and Adam's apple. The driver, a bristly, gray-haired officer I only know by sight, puts the car in gear. I feel it shift slightly under my hands. Inching forward.

"Get away from the car," the driver says. "We need to stick with the chief."

I hear voices behind me, filtering through the open windows. I'm not strong enough to turn and face them. Instead, I take off at a sprint toward Gran's house.

By the time I burst through her front door, I have a sharp pain in my side and I'm so out of breath I can't even call her name. But I don't need to. The racket of the slamming screen door draws her out of the kitchen.

"What on earth?" She rushes toward me. "What's happened?"

Through gasps, I tell her, and her face drains of color.

"Is Dad still here?" I ask.

"Asleep." She gestures upstairs with a lift of her ashen face.

I start for the stairs, but she grabs my arm. "Don't! He's in no shape to deal with this. I'll go down to the police station, figure out what's going on."

I nod. When I follow her to the closet, she turns and says, "You stay here."

"I'm going!"

"Tallulah—"

"I have to go! It's *Griff*." I feel a tear track around the curve of my jaw. "Please!"

She puts on a hat and her gloves. They look ridiculous with her housedress. Then she picks up her pocketbook. "All right, come. It's just a misunderstanding. It *has* to be a misunderstanding."

"Or Chief Collie just being a bastard." The memory of his hateful face so close to mine makes my stomach lurch again.

Gran's eyes snap. "Watch your language!"

"But it's true. You don't know what he's like when no one is watching." Should I tell her about last night's run-in? No. It won't change anything and will just upset her more.

Gran tugs her gloves and lifts her chin. "We will not lower our standards of behavior just because the chief does. We will comport ourselves with dignity. You will listen and not speak once we're there. Can I trust you to do that?"

"Yes, ma'am."

Gran's comportment lasts right up until Chief Collie tells us *why* Griff is sitting in jail.

She shoots to her feet, her voice raised to the roof. "You can't be serious!"

"We have a dead girl. Griff was seen with her last night." There's an inappropriate amount of satisfaction on his face considering he's talking about a dead girl.

"Who?" I ask. "Who's . . . dead?"

He shoves a photo across the desk.

Elizabeth Taylor. Not the real one. Griff's.

My head gets fuzzy, and I sway sideways in my chair. "Griff wasn't the only one with her last night!" I say. "She was dancing with other guys, too."

Gran cuts me a killing look, and I snap my mouth closed.

"So, she was cheating on him?" Chief Collie looks like I just handed him the final piece to his puzzle. "Jealousy is a powerful motive."

"That's not what I said—"

Gran cuts me off, her voice steady and cool. "My grandson wouldn't harm anyone, especially a young woman. What happened to the poor girl? And what evidence do you have that says Griff had *anything* to do with it?"

"We have a case," Chief Collie says. "That's all I'll say at this moment." He leans back in his chair. "Apparently, you don't know your grandson as well as you believe. He has a reputation for violence."

Gran snaps the back of her hand in front of my face to silence me before I can start. "I would like to see him. Get this all straightened out."

"Sorry." The chief lifts his hands as if helpless. "Only parents or legal guardians are allowed."

My God, is he *smiling*?

"Has he been charged?" Gran asks.

"We're working on it."

"Don't you dare do anything—no questions, nothing—until I get back here with his father!" Gran says as she grabs my hand and pulls me out of my chair. "*And* a lawyer. Not one question!"

We're halfway home before I can find my voice. "Chief Collie is lying. Griff didn't hurt that girl. I heard him come in at ten thirty last night. He took a shower and went straight to bed."

"Of course it isn't true. This is insanity. Pure insanity. How could they have possibly done any kind of an investigation if she died just last night?" There is an undercurrent to her tone that speaks of a fear she's not admitting. And it scares me to death.

"There were tons of kids at the bonfire. She was dancing with more guys than just Griff."

Gran snaps her head to look at me. "You are *not* to be hanging around college activities. You're far too young. People will get the wrong impression. You must protect your reputation; no one else will do it for you. Once the damage is done, there's no going back."

"I wasn't hanging around. I had to walk home, remember? And *I'm* not the one who's been getting in trouble." I can't help my anger. Why does Griff get to do whatever he wants without a care, and I have to protect my reputation? *And* worry about Daddy, and Margo, and everydamnthing else?

"You're a young lady. Things are . . . more delicate for you."

I take a deep breath and closet away my arguments. Helping Griff is all that matters right now. He must be so scared. "What lawyer will we get? And where will we get the money?"

"I'll call Charles Gaylord. He's the only one I trust. Your father and he will get this all straightened out, and Griff will be home in a few hours."

I close my eyes and send up a prayer that she's right.

When we get home, Dad's unmade bed is empty. So is the bottle of aged bourbon on the floor of his room. His shoes lay right where they fell last night when Gran pulled them off.

Gran makes some phone calls, his office and our house, while I run around outside looking for him. Neither one of us turn up a clue.

"He's barefoot," Gran says. "He can't have gone far."

"Did you call Margo?" I ask. "If we can't find Dad, she can at least get in to talk to Griff."

"I don't want her anywhere near the police station! She'll just make things worse."

I wonder how much worse they can get. But then, I thought the same in Dad's office last night.

"Did you call Mr. Gaylord?" I ask.

"Yes, but he's on a fishing trip and gone for the rest of the week."

"We can't just leave Griff in jail without a lawyer for a week!"

"I know, I know. I just need time to think. The criminal lawyers in this town aren't used to doing more than defending bar brawlers and shoplifters."

True. Murders—a clammy chill runs across my skin at the word—just don't happen in Lamoyne. Impossible to believe that twenty-four hours ago, Elizabeth Taylor was driving her convertible and last night she was filled with life, dancing wildly. Now she's gone. Forever.

And Griff could be, too.

"What about Ross's family?" I say. "It's filled with lawyers. Maybe one of them can help, or they can at least recommend someone." My heart lifts with the idea of a city lawyer, a good lawyer, one who doesn't play poker with Chief Collie. For the first time since I saw Griff in handcuffs, I feel a spark of hope. Collie thinks he's all-powerful in this town. A good city lawyer will put him in his place. "I think I should call him."

Gran's quiet for a few seconds. "Yes. Do. We must get this taken care of before the damage is irreparable."

The maid answers at the Saenger residence in New Orleans.

"This is Tallulah James, is Ross available, please?" I let out a breath of relief when she asks me to wait.

"Tallulah?" He sounds somewhere between baffled and concerned.

I'm not sure I'm making sense as the words rush from my mouth, but I must be because when I stop talking, he says, "That's insane! Griff would never. Are *you* all right? You're not alone right now, are you?"

"Gran's with me. You were the only one I could think of to call. Can your dad help?"

"I'll call him right now."

"Okay." I can't believe how much better he makes me feel, even with nothing done yet.

"It'll be okay, Lulie. We'll get him out."

Ten minutes turns into fifteen. When the phone rings, I pounce on it like a cat on a cricket. "Ross?"

"This is Samuel Rykerson's office in Jackson," a woman's voice says. "Mr. Rykerson asked me to inform you as soon as he's finished with a client, probably fifteen minutes, he'll be headed to Lamoyne. Should he meet you at the house on Raintree Road, or at the police station?"

I ask Gran and then relay her answer. "We'd like to meet here first. Then go to the station together."

"I'll tell him. Good day."

"We have a lawyer!" I feel like jumping up and down. I have no idea who Samuel Rykerson is, but he must be good. We'll get Griff free, then figure out a way to pay.

Gran doesn't look nearly as relieved as I feel. "Now I need to find your father."

Oh my gosh, I'd forgotten about Dad. "Should I come?"

"No, you stay here in case he comes back."

"What if you don't find him?"

She sighs, and for the first time I see how tired she looks. "Let's not borrow trouble. If I can't find him, at least he's not setting anything on fire."

Book burning isn't the only troublesome thing he might be up to. There are things more—indiscreet. But I keep that to myself, at least for now.

After she leaves, the elation of finding a lawyer ebbs. I hover near the phone, just in case Ross calls. The fifteen-minute intervals of grandfather-clock chimes seem to have stopped, but the pendulum is swinging, the inner works ticking. It's my sense of time that's distorted.

Feeling fragmented and adrift, I wander from room to room in the old house, my feet feeling the concave paths worn in the hardwood by generations of Neelys, my fingers trailing on chipped doorframes, looking at heirlooms that survived hurricanes, floods, tornadoes, Yankees, and a depression. The Neely family has finally worn itself out, just as they've worn out this house. Now there are just Jameses. And us Jameses are destroying ourselves.

A knock on the front screen startles me. Taking a breath, I steady myself to meet Griff's lawyer.

When I open the front door, it's no stranger. It's Ross. The screen bangs against the house as I throw myself into his arms. "Oh my God, I'm so glad to see you!"

I burst into tears. His arms squeeze me tight, and he says something against my ear I can't understand over my sobs. I cry for my brother. Cry for my dad. Cry because Margo is so oblivious that she doesn't even call to find out where Griff and Dad are. Cry because I'm truly terrified of Chief Collie and I can't tell a soul, not now.

I finally gather myself and stand on my own. My face must be a mess, but I don't care. Ross is here.

He frowns. "What happened to your eye?" He gently touches my cheek, then trails his hand down my arm, looking at the scrapes before he takes my hand.

"Nothing that matters. An accident." That's when I realize his mother is standing three feet away.

She smiles her Harriet Nelson smile. "We came straightaway. Of course, we know Griff had nothing to do with this. Our poor boy. He must be terrified."

I'm not quite sure how I feel about her talking about Griff as if he's hers. Especially when we haven't even *told* Margo yet.

"Please, come in." As we go into the parlor Ross continues to hold my hand, and I can't think about anything but the reassuring strength of it.

"Can I get you anything, Mrs. Saenger? Sweet tea? Coffee?"

"No, thank you, Tallulah." She takes a seat in the worn wing chair beside the fireplace. "As soon as Sam gets here, we'll all go to the station and get this matter in hand. Do you know any more than you did earlier?"

I shake my head. "The police aren't telling us anything." Every time I think of Chief Collie, a pool of black dread floods my stomach.

"Well, I want you to know, Sam is a *very* good lawyer—and my cousin. He and I have already discussed his fee. It's taken care of, so your parents don't need to give that a thought. Are they at the station waiting?"

"I—I'm not sure where they are at the moment." I stop short of making up some excuse. Habits die hard. "Gran will be back any minute. We appreciate your generosity." Truth be, I'm torn between being grateful and feeling intruded upon.

Mrs. Saenger smiles warmly. "Oh, my dear. We *love* Griff. I always wanted a brother for Ross, but that wasn't to be. Griff is such a blessing."

That ripple of possessiveness passes through me again. But the harsh reality is, without Ross and his mother, odds are high that Griff will end up in prison for the rest of his life.

Ross pulls me with him and we sit on the davenport. "It's going to be all right, Lulie."

I look into his blue eyes, and for the first time in nearly two days the world stops whirling beneath my feet.

And then Gran returns with no word of Dad.

19

Chief Collie tries to stonewall Mr. Rykerson from talking to Griff, standing with his badge puffed out and his hands on his hips. But Mr. Rykerson isn't someone to be cowed by a small-town police chief. It takes about five sentences, only one of which sounds even remotely like a threat to me, for Mr. Rykerson to disappear into the deeper rooms of the police station. It's all I can do to keep from running after him and trying to slip through before the door closes.

While we were still at Gran's house, Mr. Rykerson explained a few things about a person being arrested. I didn't like any of them. The police don't need solid proof that Griff killed that girl in order to hold him. All they need is what Mr. Rykerson called "probable cause." They can keep him in jail for a couple of days before the district attorney even files charges.

Gran said, "At least the district attorney doesn't have a chip on his shoulder concerning every leaf on the Neely family tree."

I gave her a surprised look. Apparently, the fact that Chief Collie *does* isn't news to her.

While Rykerson is meeting with Griff, I stand at the front window watching normal life on the other side of the glass. I feel so strange, as if that world is completely separate from mine. I'm in an episode of *The Twilight Zone.* I can almost hear Rod Serling narrating: "You're traveling to another dimension . . ."

But this dimension is real.

When I feel a sharp pain in my finger, I realize I've gnawed my nail to the quick. If I had my arrowhead, my nails would be safe. Up until this second, I'd completely forgotten about my abandoned purse. I hope Mr. Neiman gathered my things. Who knows what happened if he put one of my classmates in charge of them.

Gran and Mrs. Saenger wait silently side by side in hard chairs, their backs straight, pocketbooks on their laps, under their folded hands. Their faces are as blank as if they're waiting in line at the bank. I wish I could cover up my fear like that.

Ross is more like me, pacing and fretting. I'm ashamed of how much I've been resenting him. It's not Ross's fault that Griff would rather be with the Saengers than at our house. I mean, who wouldn't? How often did I want to go with him and abandon Walden and Dharma to whatever upheaval was happening at home?

The fact that Mrs. Saenger hasn't asked about either of my parents since just after she and Ross arrived tells me Ross has filled her in to some degree that Dad and Margo aren't normal parents.

I am glad Margo isn't here with her pushy outspokenness. But I can't decide if I'm disappointed or relieved that Dad's not here. Normal Dad would be good. Hurricane Dad, a disaster.

Finally, Mr. Rykerson comes back out. I can't tell anything from his face. Gran and Mrs. Saenger stand, and Ross comes to my side.

Mr. Rykerson says to Chief Collie, "I have told my client not to answer any questions without me being present. And now *you* have been informed. *No* questioning."

He motions for us to head out the door.

I feel sick. Griff isn't coming home today.

Mr. Rykerson insists we wait until we're back at Gran's house to talk. I'm nearly coming out of my skin by then.

"I want to make a call to my assistant first." He and his briefcase walk right past us, up the front steps, and into Gran's house.

"Use the phone in the library," Gran calls. "Off the main hall to the left."

Gran makes coffee. Ross sits on the stairs, bouncing a knee. I pace, making closer and closer passes to the closed library door, until Gran shout-whispers my name and calls me into the parlor.

Finally, Mr. Rykerson emerges. Gran hands him a cup of coffee. Ross and I stand, our nervousness quivering in the air between us.

"First of all, Griffin was arrested without a judge's warrant. That's a good thing. It means the arrest is based solely upon what the *police* feel is probable cause. The prosecutor, or a judge, could see things differently and decide there isn't enough evidence to press charges. Griffin says he was with Miss Colbert in a group, never alone, at the bonfire. He insists they were not dating or involved intimately."

Gran has a sharp intake of breath. "Gracious, I would hope not."

I whisper to Ross, "*Were* they dating?" The words are bitter on my tongue. *I* should be the one who knows.

Ross leans close. "I don't know."

I should be ashamed of my immature sense of satisfaction.

Mr. Rykerson says, "He said he left the bonfire—alone—about 10:00 p.m., went straight home, showered, and went to bed. According to him, she was still at the bonfire with a large group of friends the last time he saw her." He gives Gran an apologetic look. "There was a large amount of alcohol involved."

"She was with other people when he left!" I say, as if my team just scored the victory point.

Mr. Rykerson holds up a broad hand. "We need more corroboration than your and Griff's account of his timeline. That's why I made that telephone call. My assistant Phillip is very good at ferreting out witnesses and information. He'll be down here tomorrow to do face-to-face interviews."

"Chief Collie wouldn't tell us anything about the case," Gran says. "Did they tell you anything?"

"We'll get the police department's take on all of this soon enough. I'm more interested in what *we* can discover at this point. This is a small town and things get around—again, my man is *very* good." He looks at his notepad. "These are our indisputable facts. The young woman's body was discovered at 6:00 a.m. at the base of the stairs in the bell tower. It appeared she fell from a considerable height and had been deceased for a few hours."

I think of those stairs, wrapping around the square walls of the tower. When I was little, Griff and I used to climb up there and look down the open center all the way to the bottom. It always made me so dizzy I would crouch down until the handrail was at my neck.

"I saw her drinking," I say. "She must have fallen."

"Maybe," the lawyer says. "We'll know after the autopsy report. It will establish time and cause of death and if there are any, um"— he casts an uncomfortable glance my way—"*other* physical findings vital to the case. And of course, Phillip will track down her friends, collect their accounts of the evening, particularly regarding what happened after Griff says he left the bonfire."

"Griff didn't just '*say*' he left the bonfire. He *left*. I heard him come home!"

"I'm not arguing against that," Mr. Rykerson says in the bland, even tone that is setting my teeth on edge. I want him angry, indignant. I want him to sound like he's fighting!

Mr. Rykerson is still talking. "I have court in the morning but will be free to come back later in the day if we get a preliminary hearing. But the prosecutor can take another day or two if they deem it necessary." He stands and picks up his briefcase.

"You're leaving?" I shout.

Ross's hand wraps around the fist at my side.

I yank my fist free.

"Tallulah!" Gran scowls at me, then addresses the lawyer. "We're so very appreciative that you have made time for us on such short notice. Is there anything we can do here?"

"Just keep faith, ma'am."

"Do you feel we have a strong chance?" It breaks my heart to hear the naked hope in her voice.

"We'll know more tomorrow." He looks at all of us in turn. "Until then, don't discuss any of this with anyone. You never know how things will be construed."

Mrs. Saenger says, "We'll walk you out, Sam." She takes Gran's hand. "We'll be at the cottage until this is all sorted out. Call if you need anything at all."

"Thank you," Gran says. "We owe you more than words can say."

"Nonsense. We would never abandon Griff. Come, Ross."

For a long moment, Ross stares into my eyes. "I'll see you tomorrow. You know where I am if you need me."

My emotions are so balled up in my chest, I can't open my mouth because I have no idea what will come out—words or a scream.

I watch him follow his mother out the door, then I face Gran. "That's it? We just sit around and wait?"

Gran's eyes flash a warning. "We will do whatever Mr. Rykerson instructs us to do."

"How can you be so calm?"

"I've lived through enough to understand that making decisions in an emotional state does not yield positive results. So you take a few minutes to get yourself under control. You and I still have things to do."

I turn away and close my eyes. I wish we didn't have to tell Margo. She'll be just one more thing to deal with. And Dad. The news has to be all over campus—all over town—by now. Wherever he is, he should know about the dead girl, about Griff's being arrested. So why hasn't he come back or at least called?

Instead of Margo's usual detachment from our family troubles, her let-them-learn-by-their-mistakes mantra and life-lessons-are-good-for-you attitude, I'm heartened by the power of her raw outrage. This is the kind of reaction I wanted from Gran. It reflects what's lashing my own soul. Margo rants at the unfairness of Griff's too-swift arrest and tosses threats around in a way that confirms Gran was right about keeping her away from Chief Collie.

I've never loved my mother as much as I do at this moment.

Feeding on her fury, I'm ready to roll into town and tear that place down.

Gran, on the other hand, is making preemptive arguments. "Calm down. We must put Griffin's welfare first and be cautious in our actions. Of course, Drayton's position at the college must be protected. Mr. Rykerson said—"

"No!" Margo shouts. "Nonononono. This is how they win! When people remain silent. We have to rise up, hit them where it hurts. We will not tolerate this injustice."

"I understand your anger. I'm angry, too," Gran says in an understanding voice I've never heard her use with Margo. "But we can't let our anger overrule our good sense. This is a small town, everything we do will be scrutinized and affect Griffin. Care must be taken!"

"I'll call my people." Margo goes on as if Gran hasn't spoken at all. "Get a movement going."

Is she thinking about Griff at all, or just spouting long-practiced rhetoric?

She's pacing, pounding her fist into her hand with every point. "We'll contact television stations, the newspapers, not just here but *big* papers." Instead of asking for Gran's keys so she can drive to the station to see her son and reassure him, she heads to the telephone. "I have to call Robert. He can mobilize—"

"Oh my God!" I shout. "Will you listen to yourself? Griff is sitting in *jail.* Alone. They say he *killed* someone! And you want to make phone calls to protesters!"

Defensiveness blooms on her face. "We have lawyers—"

"Griff has a lawyer. He needs a mother!"

From behind me I hear Walden's small, choked voice. "Griff killed someone?"

I spin and look at his stricken ten-year-old face, his green eyes wide under his fair hair, his freckled cheeks flushed. Then I look at Margo, foolishly thinking perhaps she'll say something to reassure and comfort him. But she's fumbling with a pack of cigarettes.

I take his shoulders. "Of course Griff didn't kill anyone. There's been an accident. Griff is at the police station trying to help them figure out what happened to his friend."

Walden's eyes widen. "Ross died?"

"Oh! No."

"Tommy?" His lip begins to quiver.

"No, buddy. This was one of Griff's new friends. Someone you don't know. It's all going to get sorted out, but Griff won't be home for a couple of days. Where's Dharma?"

"She went home with Tracy after school." He sounds relieved. Twins are supposed to have a special bond. But Dharma's personality is so big, she doesn't let any light shine on Walden. Sometimes I worry he's shriveling inside.

I hear a match strike behind me. Then Margo says, her lips around the cigarette, "Did anybody tell Dray?"

I realize in that moment, she hasn't asked a single question about the details of what happened; *when* Griff was arrested, who the girl was, the circumstances of her death, if we've been able to talk to Griff ourselves, any question at all about the qualifications of the lawyer.

I put an arm around Walden and lead him outside. "Let's take a walk."

Gran can deal with Margo.

Dad, too, for all I care. My brothers and sister are all that matter now.

I'm up with the chickens and dressed so I'll be ready to go downtown if we get the call from Mr. Rykerson. It's too early for the phone to ring, but I hope my gnawing worry will ease if I'm moving.

A foolish thought. In fact, everything I do—teeth brushing, walking past the checkerboard, putting away Griff's favorite Tomorrowland glass (from Tommy, after his family vacation to Disneyland several years back)—breeds a panic that there will be no more regular-life memories made with my brother.

My solitary suffering ends when Ross arrives on our doorstep, looking as if he didn't sleep any better than I did. I push open the screen. "Come in. I'm the only one up."

He hesitates on the threshold. "Um, have you been out here this morning?"

I get a sick feeling. "No." I step onto the porch and follow his gaze to the front of the house. The word *murderer* is spray-painted in blood red. Three feet tall. The sight freezes my lungs.

Ross grips my arm. "Are you all right?"

I'm drowning again. I feel the pressure of the water in my ears, against my chest.

"Lulie?"

I'm starting to see stars.

"Hey!" He gives me a little shake and that somehow knocks my body back into functioning.

After a couple of ragged breaths, I say, "I'm okay."

He starts toward the steps. "Do you know if there's any house paint around?"

"I doubt it." I can't even remember the last time the house was painted.

"Backwater morons." Then he comes back and stands before me. "Don't worry. Sam will get him out today."

"That won't make any difference," I say through numb lips.

"Of course it will. Once word gets out that the police don't have any evidence against him."

He doesn't understand, *can't* understand. Lack of evidence isn't going to change the minds of the people who did this. Not in this town. Not when it comes to our family.

I head inside. I can't imagine having to go back to school to the sneers and stares. How can we send Walden and Dharma to school to face this kind of stuff alone? Walking into the kitchen, I stand motionless. It feels wrong to put on coffee and pour cereal as if it's a regular day.

Ross takes me by the shoulders and presses me into a chair. He empties the old grounds from the percolator and fills it with water. I watch as if I'm a guest as he measures the coffee into the basket and plugs it in.

Before the coffee is done perking, Gran comes through the back door. I look past her to see if Dad's with her. But it's just Gran and a tray of blackberry muffins.

"Tallulah, I have a coffee cake and a breakfast casserole in the car. Would you bring them in?"

Apparently, Gran spent her sleepless night baking.

Ross helps me bring them in. As we come back inside I ask her, "Did Mr. Rykerson call?"

"Not yet," she says with a hollow smile as she sets the butter on the table. "But it's quite early. He has the number here, too. Is anyone else up?"

She doesn't mention the graffiti on the front of the house, so I don't, either. "Dad's not here." I don't want to get into all of that in front of Ross, but I want her to know he hasn't shown up yet. For now, I've decided to park myself on the side of anger rather than worry. "The twins are still asleep. Margo was on the phone until the wee hours trying to start a movement."

Gran makes a disgusted sound deep in her throat. "Any luck?"

I shake my head and I pick at a blackberry muffin, watching the minute hand move sluggishly around the face of the clock.

A half hour later we're still listlessly poking at cold food. The phone rings. I jolt out of my chair as if it were electrified and snatch the receiver off the wall. "Hello?"

"Killerrrrsss." The word is drawn out so that I feel it rasp across the back of my neck. The voice is gravelly, an old person, or a smoker. "Vengeance is come. Blood always tells. You'll all burn in hellfire and damn—" I slam the phone back in its cradle.

"Wrong number," I say to Gran's expectant face. "I'm going to take a walk." Only the orchard can wash me clean of that call.

"I'll come with you." Ross stands. "Thank you for the breakfast, Mrs. James."

"Ring the dinner bell if Mr. Rykerson calls."

I make for the pecan orchard at a regimental pace. I can't get that voice out of my head. Cold fingers of death brush my shoulders. In my worry over Griff, I haven't even thought about a dead girl who won't have another birthday, another Christmas. And if someone did push her, he's still out there and the police aren't even looking for him.

I thought I'd outgrown my secret place, or just grown so accustomed to upheaval and hatefulness that I don't need it. But right now, I don't want to be anywhere else. I haven't been here since junior high.

Ross keeps a bit of distance, but I hear his footfalls at a steady pace behind me.

Reaching the corner of the pecan orchard, I climb quickly, the movements as instinctive as breathing. I pull myself up to the sanctity of the familiar thick branch.

Ross climbs up on the fence but stops there. When I glance over my shoulder, he's sitting on the top rail, as if he knows this place is precious and private and should not be intruded upon without invitation.

I settle my gaze on the river below and toss my bright-burning anger and dark fears into the current. And then I wait.

Finally, the hypnotic ripple and flow of the river eases conscious thought from my mind. As the tension leaves my shoulders, I realize how raw and beat up I am. The physical toll of emotional turmoil surprises me. A person would think I'd be used to it, like a runner who no longer gets sore muscles.

As I sit in the quiet blessing of birdsong and soft morning air, I gain a new perspective. I cannot change the course of my family. I am bone weary from trying. This town is going to come after us until there is nothing left. Margo doesn't care; in fact I think she *likes* it. Gran thinks if we pretend everything is perfect it will be true. I've always thought no matter which way Dad's moods swing, he'd be there when we really needed him. Well, Griff needs him, and where is he?

There is only me. And I am about as effective as Don Quixote jousting windmills.

I keep my focus on the ever-changing ripples of the river. "You can come up."

Silently, Ross moves to sit beside me. I lean slightly into him, welcoming the crutch of his strength.

For some time, we sit staring at the water. I can tell he wants to say something. The unspoken words crowd the air around us.

"Just say it," I finally say.

His gaze turns my way. "Say what?"

"Whatever it is you've been thinking for the past twenty minutes."

After a pause, he says, "I was just wondering about your dad."

Time to surrender. No sidestepping. No pretending to misunderstand. I look him squarely in the eye. "You mean where he could possibly be that he hasn't heard about Griff's arrest? And if he has, why hasn't he called or come home? I'm wondering the same thing."

"Are you worried that something has happened to him?"

"Oh, something *has* happened to him." I think of his broken plea in that dark locker room. "But nobody wants to see it." I tell Ross about the books and the crazy theories and the drinking. I *don't* tell him there's a very real possibility that he's somewhere screwing a coed. Of course, Ross might already surmise that considering Dad's Mother's Day show two years ago.

Ross's eyes show concern, not judgment. "You said he left your grandmother's without his shoes."

A bark of laughter bursts from my mouth. "After everything I just told you, his leaving barefoot is what you find noteworthy?"

He offers a sad smile. "Well, I don't think we're going to figure out why he did any of those other things. But we might figure out where he may have gone."

"Oh, Ross. You can't apply logic to his thinking. First of all, we don't know if he was in shadow or hurricane when he left."

"If he was what?"

"His behavior. Hummingbird or slug. So full of energy you can't scrape him off the ceiling, or buried in anguish so deep he won't get out of bed. Usually his moods settle in for a while, but the other night he swung like he was on a trapeze. I've never seen him like that."

"So he's always one or the other?"

"No. Sometimes he's just a regular dad for so long I think maybe the roller-coaster moods are gone forever. And then Margo will do something, or she'll go away for a long while, and he gets really sad. I'm not sure what brings on the hurricane. Sometimes it's fun. Once, before the twins were born, he got us all up in the middle of the night and said we were going to the beach. We didn't get dressed or pack a bag, just piled in the car and went. It was vacation season, so there were no motels with a vacancy, so we lived in our pj's and slept in the car for two nights, lived on bologna and Wonder Bread we kept in a Styrofoam cooler. 'An adventure in resourcefulness and ingenuity.'" I smile at his phrase. It all seemed so wonderful when I was four. "So, you see, the fact that he left barefoot isn't much of a clue."

"Griff never said a word."

"Of course not. All he's doing is counting the days until he can leave this insanity behind."

Ross looks at me, steady and deep. "And you? What do you want?"

No one has ever asked me that before, not even Griff. Life has always been navigating through the surprises and challenges of the current day. The future is nothing but that blue glimmer of the Pacific Ocean Griff has promised.

"You mean, like right now?" I finally ask. "Or over the long haul?"

"I'm pretty sure I know what you want right now. But once this is all behind you and the door to your future opens up. What's on the other side of it?"

"If I could do *anything* I want? No limitations?" It's such an impossibility that I've never considered it.

"Well, within the realm of semi-reality. No fair using the Miss America answer of 'achieve world peace' or 'eradicate hunger.' What would you choose for yourself?"

"Well, if you're going to ruin it with semi-reality . . ." I shrug, but I'm really buying time. I don't want to throw just anything out there. Not to Ross.

"I've never really taken the time to think of it clearly, in detail."
I've never had to, I let Griff do that thinking for me. "Truthfully,
the entire concept of a future based solely on my unrestricted choice
scares me to death."

He's quiet for a moment. "I get it. I never chose to be a lawyer—
which is, in essence, our family business—but there's something
safe in having other people already laying that path in front of me,
the choices already made."

"So you *don't* want to be a lawyer?" I can't imagine tossing away
a life of Ivy League schools and unquestionable respect.

And then I look at it through Ross's eyes. A boy with his wealth,
his intelligence, his opportunities, can easily be anything he wants,
Jonas Salk inventing the polio vaccine, John Glenn circling Earth.
What would that feel like, having *everything* as a viable possibility?

He shrugs. "It's not that I *don't* want to be—exactly. It's more
the weight of the expectation, the idea that it's a foregone conclusion that bothers me."

I never considered a family *caring* could be a burden. I lean my
head on his shoulder. His arm comes around me and, despite everything, I feel at peace.

Then the dinner bell echoes across the orchard.

20

Ross and I are sitting on the front steps waiting. My mouth is cottony and I'm picking my cuticles.

"He's here!" Ross says in a near whisper and grabs my elbow.

We stand. Feet thunder through the front hall and onto the porch. Gran, Margo, and Mrs. Saenger burst out the door right behind the twins.

Mr. Rykerson's Cadillac comes up the drive. The windshield has a huge spiderweb crack on the passenger side. Griff is only a dark shape behind it. As the car pulls closer, I see a foot-size dent in the passenger door and understand why Mr. Rykerson insisted he go alone to pick Griff up from jail. I'm shocked by the violence that marks the car, and yet deep down not truly surprised.

"My Lord." Mrs. Saenger's breathless voice comes from behind me.

The twins run past. I follow them to the car, my insides a whirl of contradictory emotions: relief, worry, happiness, anger, anticipation, dread. Overshadowing them all is a protective rush of love for my brother.

Walden and Dharma don't know exactly what's going on, but have clearly caught the elation of Griff's homecoming. Bouncing with excitement, Dharma reaches the passenger door and yanks it open. But Griff doesn't jump out. He just sits there, his face ashen, his mouth grim.

Dharma grabs his hand from his lap and pulls. "Come on! We're having a party."

As always, Walden is more intuitive. He steps close to me and whispers, "What's wrong with him?"

I lean to his ear. "He's just really tired." But he is changed. I can tell from the set of his shoulders, by the way he won't look at me.

He finally gets out of the car and gives Dharma a strained smile that borders on a grimace. Pulling his hand from hers, he walks past me as if I'm a part of the landscape. He passes Ross, then Gran, Margo, and Mrs. Saenger without a word, not once looking at any of them.

Gran has the sense to be quiet and let him go, but Margo makes the mistake of reaching for his arm. "We're going to make them—"

The look he gives her is chilling enough that she lets go and takes a step back.

"Why isn't Griff coming to the party?" Dharma takes it as a personal affront.

He goes into the house and a few beats later I hear his bedroom door slam.

Mr. Rykerson says, "Let's go inside and I'll fill you in."

Gran says, "Dharma and Walden, the burlap sacks for the pecans arrived yesterday. You two go on out to the barn and unpack them. You know where to put them. Then I want you to break down the boxes and take them to the burn pile."

"I thought we were going to have fun today!" Dharma stamps her foot. Silently, Walden tugs her hand. As he leads her to the barn, she must be giving him an earful because her pigtails are bouncing and about every fifth step she stamps her foot again.

In the parlor, we gather around Mr. Rykerson as if he holds the Ten Commandments sent down from God.

"As I explained on the phone, the district attorney has decided not to press charges against Griffin. Of course, that could all change if there is new and compelling evidence—"

"They can't just let this hang over his head forever!" Margo says.

"Unfortunately, they can. And yet, it's highly unlikely that they will rearrest him, all things considered."

"What do you mean by 'all things considered'?" Margo asks.

I wish she'd disappear like she usually does.

Mr. Rykerson continues. "First, they would need enough clear-cut evidence to contradict the medical examiner's cause of death, which is traumatic injuries to the head and spine from an accidental fall and establishing a window for death between midnight and 3:00 a.m. We have eyewitness corroboration of Griffin's departure from the bonfire around ten—thanks to Phillip's good work—and Tallulah's confirmation of his arrival home at ten thirty.

"And honestly, with public sentiment"—his gaze casts through the front window toward his car—"and the upcoming election for the district attorney, if they had *anything*, they would have pressed charges and hoped for a biased jury.

"Now, there was another finding at the autopsy." He clears his throat. "Miss Colbert was approximately three months pregnant. This, combined with lack of witnesses and the time of death bolsters the argument for suicide—if it comes to needing to argue the case."

"Wouldn't it also bolster the argument for murder?" Margo asks. "What if the father killed her?"

"Margo!" Gran holds a palm up.

"I'm just stating facts." Margo snatches a pack of cigarettes off the coffee table. "What if she was about to name the father? What if he'd do anything to keep it from becoming public? We need to be realistic about the possibility they could come after Griff again."

My head is reeling. "You think Griff is the father?" A girl as fast as Elizabeth Taylor appeared could have a long list of possible fathers. "He would never—"

"Be quiet, Tallulah!" Margo snaps. "You have no idea how boys—"

I raise my voice. "I was *going* to say he would never hurt someone he cared that much about! He would take responsibility—"

"Enough!" Gran is visibly trembling. "Hold your tongues and listen to what Mr. Rykerson has to say."

Mr. Rykerson appears unbothered. "Griffin has assured me it is not possible for him to be the father. If she'd been home in Tupelo at the time of conception and not here attending summer school, that would erase that possibility altogether. But right now, they have nothing but Chief Collie's 'gut feeling,' and the fact that she was dancing with Griffin at the bonfire. Frankly, I'm surprised they picked him up at all. I still thought you should know—about the pregnancy. These things tend to come out. I didn't want you to be blindsided."

Gran says, "So that's it? They cast this pall over Griffin's reputation based on Chief Collie's gut?"

Margo pipes in, "They need to be held accountable for false arrest! We need to bring suit."

"It's fully within the law for them to hold possible suspects in a suspicious death. Anyway, it's all part of the process," Mr. Rykerson says. "Of course, anyone can file a civil suit, but your chances of getting anywhere are marginal at best."

Gran says, "Yes, yes. And it will just keep gossip alive. It will do Griffin no good at all."

"He's *my* son . . ."

I can see the rabbit hole this conversation is headed down and back silently out of the room. For a long moment, I look down the hall, toward Griff's closed bedroom door. Then Ross comes up behind me.

"You can bet he's in the clear," he says. "Sam's cautious. If he wasn't positive, he wouldn't have said it's unlikely they'll come after Griff again."

Right now, I just want my brother back. "Did you *see* him? Do you think this broke him?"

Ross sighs. "I think it's been a hell of a couple of days. Anybody would be a wreck. Are you going to try to talk to him?"

"Not yet." I'm afraid. If I knock on his door and he sends me away, I couldn't bear it.

We turn around and head out to the front porch and stare at that horrible accusation scrawled across our house. What must that have done to Griff, seeing that hateful word there?

* * *

The Saengers and Mr. Rykerson are gone. Griff won't come out of his room, won't eat. Gran and Margo are in a round robin of accusation and blame. I listen to Dharma complain about being cheated out of a party about as much as I can stand. I get her and Walden parked in front of *The Flintstones* with Swanson TV dinners, then creep outside into the cool twilight, forgetting my sweater.

It's the first time I've been alone all day, so I don't risk going back inside to get it.

As I push myself back and forth on the porch swing, I watch the bats dart against the purpling sky. Halloween is in two weeks, and I haven't made Dharma's and Walden's costumes yet. Walden's easy. He's happy with a sheet thrown over his head and being a ghost. But Dharma, every year she wants something more elaborate, more dramatic. I'm wondering if any of Margo's old prom dresses can be cut up and reworked for her request for Cinderella. I, however, have drawn the line at her request for a glass slipper.

Headlights creep slowly up the drive. After the events of the past twenty-four hours, I ready myself to flee inside and bolt the doors. But as the car gets closer, I see it's Tommy's family's station wagon.

I'd almost forgotten there's a friendly face left in this town. Getting up, I meet him at the front steps. In his arms are a stack of textbooks and folders, on top of which sits my purse. Thinking of the arrowhead inside, it's all I can do to keep from snatching it out of his hands.

Holding them out to me, he says, "I volunteered to bring them. I figure you won't be back at school for a few days."

I take my things, hiding my irrational eagerness to get that piece of flint back in my possession. "Thanks. Griff's home. He didn't have anything to do with hurting that girl."

Tommy shifts his gaze away from me and rubs the back of his head—a sure sign he's uncomfortable.

"What's going on?"

"Nothing. I'd better go." He starts to back toward the car.

No matter how things sit between Griff and Tommy, and re-gardless of his general shyness around girls, he has never been this standoffish with me.

"Did you ever see him with her?" I call out.

"Who?"

"Come on, Tommy, don't play dunce."

He takes another swipe at the back of his head. "Not with him exactly, but around. Sometimes she parks at the Wig-Wam and talks to the guys cruising there." The Wig-Wam Drive-In is the high school hangout; the college kids all hang out at Eddie's—their carhops wear short skirts and skates.

"Why would she be there?"

He shrugs. "Guess she likes high school guys." He takes another step away. "I really gotta go."

"Don't you want to see him?"

"I have to get back home. My folks . . ."

"Why are you in such a hurry?"

"Look, Tallulah, I just wanted to give you your stuff and see how you're doing."

"Me?"

He looks directly at me for the first time. "People just seem to . . . overlook you. With all of this going on, I know it's been rough." He comes back up the three steps and grabs me in an abrupt hug. "Take care of yourself." He turns and trots down the steps and to his car.

The finality of his goodbye hits me hard. My knees buckle and I sit on the steps to watch our childhood drive away. Just one more casualty amid the wreckage.

After Gran leaves, I knock on Griff's door. Margo downed a full bottle of wine and locked herself in her bedroom.

"Griff," I loud-whisper. "It's me. Let me in. Please."

I hear him moving. He stops on the other side of the door and then it sounds like his forehead thumps against the wood. "Not tonight, Lulie."

I can hear him breathing, but he doesn't move away.

"Please."

His slow, heavy footsteps move away from the door.

Not tonight. I read a lot into those two words . . . maybe tomorrow.

As I cross the hall, a flash of headlights arcs across the wall. My pulse kicks up. My mind is filled with broken car windows and spray-painted accusations.

I press myself against the wall and inch toward the front of the dark house.

A police car sits in the spill of the porch light I left on in case Dad shows up. The only reason for the police to be here is to arrest Griff again. I wish with all my heart it was just vandals with more paint.

Before I can decide whether to get Margo, a knock sounds on the front door and she bursts from her bedroom pulling on a robe.

"Who in the hell is knocking at this hour?"

I'm right behind her when she opens the door. Chief Collie, that sanctimonious, two-faced monster, is standing next to a county sheriff's deputy.

I step beside Margo. "You can't take him! He didn't do anything!" All of Mr. Rykerson's arguments jumble in my head: eyewitnesses, time of death, suicide.

"Mrs. James," the sheriff's deputy looks at Margo and takes off his hat. "May we please come in?"

"No, you may not." She steps in front of me again. "Not without a warrant."

"A warrant, ma'am?"

"Search or arrest. Otherwise, you can just climb back into your car and go back the way you came."

Chief Collie says, "I'm afraid you misunderstand—" There's an unfamiliar tone in his voice that grabs my stomach—not with an aggressive fear like when he came after me, or a frustrated anger like at the police station. This is a rancid, curdled dread.

"Oh, I understand all right!" Margo's voice rises. "You just won't stop until you ruin his life, you small-town, narrow-minded—"

"Margo." I don't care what she calls the chief, but I realize those are not the faces of police officers here to haul someone off to jail.

The deputy says, "If we could just step inside, ma'am."

I push open the screen door. "Come in." I'm not sure if the clammy chill crawling across my skin is from the chief's proximity, or fear of what they're going to say.

"They don't have a warrant—" Margo blocks them with her body.

"Mrs. James, please, we're not here about Griffin." The chief sounds almost nice. And that scares me more than anything.

"What then?"

The deputy says, "I'm afraid we're here to inform you that your husband's body was discovered early this evening in the Pearl River about three miles downstream."

Margo's scream is so horrible, it brings Griff running from his room.

21

The pecans lay moldering on the orchard floor as the days pass in a fog of pain. All I can think of is how alone Dad must have felt, how much he suffered. Was he in the river from the very first hours he was missing? Could I have found him before it was too late if I'd looked harder, searched farther?

I'll never again hear his laugh. Never have the chance to rail against his demand for logical, unemotional debates. Never have another vocabulary word.

When the carousel of casseroles (from every hypocrite in town), hymn selections, and flower-arrangement arguments (Gran and Margo fought tooth and nail over whether the casket spray ribbon should say father or husband) finally stop, my guilt overshadows my grief like an alp over an anthill. If only I'd pushed Gran about Dad. Maybe she *didn't* see.

After Griff was arrested, I didn't even worry about Dad. And now my heart yearns for him, the wound so wide and so deep it will never heal.

Margo is on her own roller coaster; either sobbing and carrying on like a madwoman, or blanketed under a thick layer of Valium—a new drug the doctor calls a miracle for overwrought women. I thought when the shock wore off and the funeral was behind us, she would improve. If anything, she's gotten worse.

Her hysterics frighten the twins so much, I personally deliver a Valium to her every six hours. At least when she's huddled alone in her bed, unwashed and unmoving, Walden isn't wild-eyed with panic.

This is the first time I've been thankful she was never a day-to-day mother. We learned to live without her a long time ago.

Today, I sent Dharma and Walden to school for the first time in nearly two weeks. I hope their teacher has enough compassion to protect them from the cruel things third graders will no doubt say, little parrots of what they hear at home.

I only venture out to go to the grocery store. I might never go back to school. Maisie called one day when Mrs. Delmore was out. She said her momma's been down with sickness so she's had to head straight home after work, but promised to come and see me as soon as she can. I know Maisie has burdens of her own, so I assured her I'm doing fine. In truth, hearing her voice just emphasized how little time she and I share these days.

The spray-painted accusation remains scrawled on the front of our house, a stamp of hate, a stain of disgrace. We all pretend it isn't there. Not even the death of our father has slowed the flow of anonymous letters, creepy phone calls, and unpleasant surprises left on our property. Dad's drowning was no accident, despite Gran's vehement claims, and everyone knows it. The discoveries the police made in his office—the stolen books, his paranoid scribbles, love letters from an anonymous student, bits and pieces of evidence spun as moral corruption and sexual misbehavior—have fueled an entirely new level of ridicule.

At nine thirty I knock on Griff's door. Although he has been among us, helping with the twins, comforting Gran, carrying Margo to bed after she passes out on the davenport, he hasn't done much talking.

"Come on in, Lulie."

When I open the door, Griff is standing on the braided rug between the twin beds. It takes me a second to process what I'm seeing. "Why are you packing?"

"Sit down." He moves the battered tan suitcase across the navy-blue plaid spread toward the head of the bed, making a place for me to sit.

"No! Tell me what's going on!" I don't recognize my own voice, shrill and desperate.

His hands tighten around the vertically striped cardigan he's folding. "Mrs. Saenger invited me to stay with them in New Orleans. She's picking me up at noon."

"You're leaving?" I can't believe my ears.

"Lulie—"

"You can't!" My fist slams the solid muscles of his chest. He stumbles backward a half step. "You can't just leave me here!"

"It's just for a while. Until things settle down."

"Uh-uh. No." My index finger waggles under his nose. "Margo and Gran won't let you, anyway."

"They already know. Gran was harder to convince than Margo."

"I can't believe Gran agreed—"

"If I'm gone, the calls and letters will stop. People will stop harassing the rest of you."

"Don't you *dare* try to make it sound like you're doing this for me. You sound just like Margo."

His face hardens. "Don't say that. Don't ever."

"Why shouldn't I? It's true. You're leaving because you want to get away from everything here, to live in Ross's perfect world, not because you're trying to protect me. Just admit it!"

He sits heavily on the bed and cradles his head in his hands and says something so low and muffled I can't understand.

"What?"

"What if I am like Dad?"

"I don't understand."

"You've heard it. People say Granddad's brother was like Dad. Crazy moods. Chasing after girls."

I cringe at the mention of Dad's promiscuity. How could he and Margo be so obsessive about each other and still cheat? I don't understand love at all.

For a moment I study a jagged crack in the plaster over the closet door. "Do you think Dad was with that girl, you know, in *that* way?"

He frowns. "You mean Lena?"

I'm so unfamiliar with Elizabeth Taylor's real first name it takes me a second to make the connection. "Do you think that's who the love notes were from? Was he . . . responsible for her baby? I mean, maybe her suicide and his are because of the same thing." As soon as I say it my conscience pipes up: *Maybe you're just looking for a reason you couldn't have saved him.*

"She wasn't the kind of moon-eyed girl who fell in love with her professor—or love at all, for that matter." He pauses and then looks up at me. "And I don't believe for a minute she committed suicide."

I instinctively glance over my shoulder to make certain no one heard him. "Why not?"

"Because if there's anyone on this earth who didn't give a crap about her reputation, it was Lena. In fact, she seemed to revel in going against convention and making sure everyone noticed—especially her parents."

"So you *do* think she was murdered?"

"I don't know! Suicide just doesn't seem possible. Maybe she was just drunk and fell. Not that it matters. Everyone thinks I threw her over that railing."

"Why don't you tell the police what you just told me?"

He looks at me, his eyes suddenly cold as winter frost. "I did. Her parents painted an entirely different picture of their beloved daughter to the police, pure as the driven snow and just as delicate." He puts the folded cardigan in his suitcase. "You missed my point entirely."

"Which is?"

"What if it's true? What if I'm crazy like Dad and George? What if it's just a matter of time before I lose all control? The best thing I can do is get away from you and the twins."

My heart takes flight. "I asked Gran once if Dad was always full of shadows and hurricanes. She said brilliant people are often moody."

"So?"

"She didn't say he got that way, that he *changed*. He just was always that way. You're completely normal. You're in the clear."

He doesn't seem convinced as he reaches into the scarred old chest of drawers and pulls out a worn envelope. "There's a hundred and thirty-three dollars in here." He hands it to me, and I stare at it dumbly. "I wish it was more, but at least you won't go hungry." He snaps the latches on the suitcase, leaning his full weight on it to get it to close.

Then he straightens and gives me a look that finishes off my already battered heart. "I can't stay here, Lulie. Not even for you."

If I had drowned that day, I wouldn't be any worse off. Dead might be preferable to being alone with my guilt, resenting Gran, hating Ross for taking Griff, hating Griff for leaving me, hating Margo, hating this town. I would leave today if there was someone else to take care of the twins. Dharma is resilient enough to get along on the crumbs Margo offers. But Walden, he needs more.

I sit in my pecan tree, trying to cast the guilt and the hate into the river. After an hour, I feel as raw and angry as I did when I climbed up here. Maybe there's just too much even for a river to carry away. I give up, but I won't go back to the house until I'm sure Griff is gone.

Spinning around, I swing my legs to the other side of the limb and face the orchard. Squirrels are busy gathering a winter cache of nuts. Gran always leaves a few of the late ones on the orchard floor, an offering to the wildlife. But this year the animals aren't even having to search. The floor is a carpet of stripped husks and untouched fruit.

I could probably still save the harvest, at least some of it. I should.

Looking out on the old trees, my heart aches even more. I love this orchard. But not enough to stay. Not anymore.

When Dharma and Walden are old enough to care for themselves, I am gone.

* * *

For nearly three weeks, I keep thinking Griff will call. He does not. I am a link to the darkest parts of his life. He is the brightest part of mine.

I tell the twins to hold their heads high, to ignore anyone who teases them, to live their lives honorably and bravely. And then I spend my school days with my head down, scurrying along the walls like a mouse, hiding behind the church across the street with my sack lunch. My hypocrisy makes me sick.

And then, on the twenty-first of November, while I'm obsessing over how horrible Thanksgiving will be, Margo drops a bombshell.

She calls the three of us into the living room because she has an announcement—an unprecedented occurrence that sets off alarm bells. But even my panicked imaginings can't compare to what she says. "I've made arrangements for you kids to go to live with my family in Michigan."

Walden sucks in a breath.

Dharma asks, "The rich ones?"

"You can't! We . . . we need . . . we don't even know— You said they're—" I can't believe she was functional enough through her Valium haze to arrange such a thing.

"Stop! I can't do this." She rubs her forehead as if suddenly struck with a migraine from our protests.

"Do what?" I shout as I jump to my feet. "You don't do *any-thing* for us! What difference can it make to you if we're here or there?"

"You have no idea what it's like—losing your father is *killing* me. He was the love of my life!" Her arms go dramatically wide and her eyes cast heavenward. Suddenly I see Dharma in twenty-five years.

"Well, you sure had a funny way of showing it."

She moves so quickly I don't see the slap coming before the sting on my face. "How dare you!"

I won't give her the satisfaction of clutching my cheek. "You always said how awful your family is. How can you send us there?"

"Well, *here* is pretty awful right now, too, isn't it? I have to get away from this place, the pain. Everyone will be better off—"

"*You're* leaving? Leaving, but not going to your family. You just want *us* to have to deal with their selfishness and greed—"

"They aren't that bad. And they can provide for you. Dharma can have all the lessons she needs to be an actress. You and Walden will have the best educations—"

"You don't believe in education!" If Maisie can survive in the world quitting school at sixteen, so can I.

"Well I might not, but the rest of the world does. And—and it would please your father, make him proud." She says it as if she stumbled on the best argument ever. "Besides, how am I going to feed you now that Dray is gone?" She chokes on his name, as if just saying it is too painful. "I need time to heal."

"So where *are* you going? And how are you going to afford to feed *yourself*?"

"I'm going to stay with friends. I can't heal in Michigan."

"But we can?"

"What about Granny James?" Walden asks in a small and broken voice.

"Yes, what about Gran?" I say. "Who will take care of her? Who will take care of the orchard?"

"Your grandmother doesn't need to be cared for. She's not an invalid. And the orchard is going under, there's no stopping it. This is an *opportunity* for you kids. It'll just be for a while—this school year, maybe next. Then we'll all settle somewhere together." She doesn't even try to make it sound convincing.

I want to scream the truth: that she doesn't care about us and never has. But for me that awareness came in stages, and I don't want to hasten Walden's and Dharma's painful understanding. So I storm out of the house and down the road.

Walking so fast that I'm huffing and puffing, I pass Judge Delmore's. I don't see Maisie anywhere. Moving through downtown, I'm barely aware of people and cars around me. By the time I walk into Gran's kitchen, I'm sweating and red-faced.

She sets down her teacup, alarm on her face. "Tallulah! What's wrong? What's happened now?"

I tell her the whole horrible tale, pacing the kitchen and gulping the glass of water she pressed into my hand. When I stop, she's sipping her tea as if nothing is amiss.

"I spoke to Margo's brother, Roger, and his wife, Carol, on the phone," she says. "They seem like nice people."

"If they're so nice, why didn't they come to Daddy's funeral?"

"Their relationship with your mother is complicated . . . as you might imagine."

"Wait. When did you talk to them?"

"Last week. When all of this got started."

"You knew last week and didn't say anything to me?"

"There was no reason to tell you until things were certain."

"Well, they're not certain. I'm not going. If Margo has to go off and 'heal,' let her. We can stay with you."

Gran stands and comes before me, settling her hands on my shoulders. "Tallulah, my sweet child, I can't possibly take on ten-year-old twins. I'm too old. You'll all have every advantage with Margo's family. Your aunt Carol is quite excited to have you all. She and your uncle are childless. You'll go to a good college. Your father would want that for you."

"No fair using Dad's imaginary wishes against me. Send the twins. Let me stay with you. This year and next and I'll be graduated and out of your hair." I can't believe I'm arguing to stay at Lamoyne High. "You and I can run the orchard. We can't let it go to ruin."

"We need some time to let things die down here—for people to stop talking. Maybe someday—"

"So all your talk about the James family legacy is just that, empty words? You don't really care."

"The legacy only matters if there's someone here to live it. Griffin won't ever come back. Honestly, the way things are now, I can't wish that burden on you or the twins. Lamoyne is no place for any of you, not any longer." Her shoulders slump and her voice is filled with defeat. For the first time, she looks old. "It's time to go."

"What about you? Why don't you and I go somewhere together

and start over? Or you can move to Michigan, too. You're all we have left." Tears sting my eyes.

She shakes her head. "This has been my home for my entire life. I won't leave. Besides, I can't afford to start over. And truthfully, I have no interest in doing so. But you have your whole life ahead of you. Take this opportunity and make the most of it. You'll have security, a boundless future."

"You're giving up on us."

"Never. I am doing quite the opposite. I'm sacrificing the joy of having you near me because I believe in you—your future." She pulls me close and kisses me on the cheek. "We'll write. You can come visit on school holidays. This isn't the end, Tallulah. It's your beginning."

The next day, as the world goes mad after President Kennedy's assassination, I do begin my new life. But not in Michigan.

22

Shortly after Ross, Gran, and I arrived at his house, Amelia called. All she would say was that she'd gotten us approved for a visit today and to come right away. The tall, blue-eyed blonde greets us in the lobby of the Orleans Parrish jail. The family resemblance between her and Ross is significant. She's wearing a black skirt suit and pearls. She looks way too Southern-girl sweet to be the barracuda Ross claims.

After Ross introduces us, she gets right to the point. "We have a serious problem. Walden has refused counsel—mine or anyone else's. I'm afraid he'll put up no defense at all."

"What does that mean?" Gran asks.

"Unless he changes his mind, I can't do anything to help him. Hopefully, you two will be able to get him to see reason."

"Why doesn't he want to put up a defense?" I ask as we all head toward the door that'll lead us to my little brother.

"He's very detached. He's refusing to participate in a court that has no authority over him or his brothers."

"Isn't sitting in jail enough proof that the courts do have authority over them?" I ask.

"I'm not sure logic has anything to do with it," Amelia's eyes are troubled. "You'll see."

We leave Ross in the lobby and follow Amelia and a deputy down a gray hallway with harsh fluorescent lighting to an equally gray room with the same awful lighting, a battered metal table, and four chairs. We sit and wait.

Gran looks completely out of place in this visitation room at the jail, an orchid in a field of dandelions. If she's uncomfortable, she's not showing any sign.

We both jump to our feet when the solid metal door opens. There's a rushing in my ears as Walden is led in wearing a striped jumpsuit and handcuffs. His hair is long and tangled. He's grown tall but is whippet thin, his face hard angles and jutting bones.

Gran sucks in a shocked breath, confirming his appearance isn't what it was the last time she saw him, either. Instinctively, I take her cold, fragile hand.

They don't take off his handcuffs, and we've been instructed not to touch him. My body is literally aching with the need to wrap him in my arms.

His eyes are skittish, passing quickly over Gran, then me, but not lingering on either one of us. I'm not even sure he recognizes me.

The deputy makes Walden sit in a chair across the table from us. "You have ten minutes." He nods to where Amelia is sitting in a row of chairs behind us.

Ten minutes won't give us time to crack the shell, let alone find the boy we know underneath. "It's me, Walden. Tallulah."

His gaze lifts to my face briefly before sliding away. "Neither of you should have come." His voice is deep and yet so soft-spoken I have to strain to hear. It's full of disdain.

"We had to come," Gran says.

She starts to reach across the table.

The deputy says, "No touching."

Her hand returns to her lap as quickly as if it had been slapped by a ruler.

I eye the harsh tension in his mouth and lead with contrition. "Walden, I owe you an apology." My throat swells and I have to force the words. "I never should have left you and Dharma. If I'd gone with you to Michigan, things would have been different."

He keeps his chin tucked and looks at me from beneath his fair brows. "What makes you think I want different?" His voice is so cold that it strikes like a fist.

I lick my lips and swallow my pain. "I know Mr. Smythe is—"

Walden's fists pound the table, the handcuffs clanking like knives against the surface. "Do not say his name!"

The deputy takes a step closer.

That Smythe's name sparks anger gives me hope.

Then Walden says, "You haven't earned the right."

My heart sinks. "I'm sorry." I allow a repentant pause. "But I'm sure he wouldn't want you to refuse legal counsel. He wants what's best for you."

Walden's eyes are two frosty panes. "You don't know what he wants. Or what I want. Just go back where you came from." He stands and starts for the door.

Gran looks at me in a panic.

"Wait!" I say. "I don't know anything, you're right. But you're my brother, and I want to understand."

He looks over his shoulder. "I am a brother, but not yours. I belong to the Scholars and no one else."

"What about Dharma? This will break her heart."

His half smile is accompanied by a disbelieving huff. "She's like Margo. She doesn't have one."

I stand, frantic. "Walden, please! Don't make a rash decision. Accept the counsel . . . at least for this first hearing. You'll have time before the trial to fully decide."

"A trial is inconsequential to my spirit." He walks to the door and waits for the deputy to open it, then leaves without looking back.

Gran's pale. There's a fine sheen of perspiration on her upper lip.

I squat down so I can look her in the eyes. "Gran? Are you all right?"

She shakes her head. A tear slips from the corner of one eye and her hand covers her mouth. "He wasn't like this before. I've failed him. I've failed you all."

Wrapping my arms around her, I feel how bony she's become. "No, Gran. You did your best. It was Margo who failed us all."

And for the first time in nine years, I see clearly. I have blamed and cursed and accused Gran, when we were not her children to raise. Even so, she threw herself into the job, doing the best she could, making hard decisions with no good choices available.

But Margo simply abandoned a sinking ship with all four of her children still aboard.

We return to the lobby, where Ross is waiting with an expectant look on his face. I keep Gran moving toward the car and give him a disappointed shake of my head.

Amelia took a taxi to the jail, so she rides home with us. I sit in the back next to Gran, alert for the first sign of physical distress.

Gran says, "Perhaps I should contact Mr. Smythe. Walden respects him. Maybe he'll have luck changing Walden's mind."

My heart breaks for her naïveté. "Oh, Gran, I'm pretty sure this is exactly what Mr. Smythe wants. The evidence against him destroyed and those three kids taking the full punishment."

"I'm afraid you're right," Amelia says. "He's already made a public statement expressing his shock that three of his followers could stray so far from the path." She pauses, as if to calculate whether to continue. We must look solid enough to take the blow. "I found out something from one of the deputies while I was waiting. Smythe locked them out of the compound and called the police himself. That, along with the eyewitness who puts Walden and the other two at the scene of the fire that killed Mr. Moore . . ."

"Oh my God! And Walden still acts if this guy is the Dalai Lama!" Angry, bitter tears fill my eyes. But they can't fall. I have to be strong for Gran.

"I just don't understand." Gran sounds like a lost child. "He was so good for Walden, cared so much about him."

Ross's voice is patient and gentle when he says, "Men like Smythe seek out kids with difficult childhoods."

I nearly choke on the gentle term for the carnage of our early years but appreciate his sensitivity to Gran.

He goes on, "Lost souls. Runaways. Kids looking for a place where they feel like they matter. These guys tailor their bait, figuring out what the person needs the most. Then they give it to them in a way that makes them feel grateful, indebted. Once that confidence is gained, the real brainwashing begins. It's not Walden's fault—and it's not yours. Men like that are clever, charismatic predators."

"He did seem brainwashed," I say. When I glance at Gran, I can't stand the agony on her face. "Ross is right. Walden's loving nature made him vulnerable, not anything you did or didn't do."

She wraps her hand over mine and gives a wavering smile that tears at my soul.

We reach Amelia's house, not far from Tulane. "We can request a psych evaluation, but it's going to be difficult in these circumstances—he's an adult and he's refused counsel," she says. "And it won't postpone the arraignment."

"Thank you." Gran's voice is tired. "For your help."

"We'll talk tomorrow," Amelia says to me. "I'll give Walden another try first thing in the morning. But I wouldn't hold hope that he'll change his mind."

After I get Gran settled in a bedroom in Ross's house, I return to him making coffee in the kitchen.

"I hope that's not decaf. I don't think I can drag myself back up those stairs without some sort of a boost," I say.

"Why would anybody drink decaf?"

I chuckle. "You're the doctor."

I lean against the counter while he gets out cream and a couple of nice big coffee mugs—I do appreciate a person who doesn't mess around when it comes to coffee. And then I tell him every detail of our meeting with Walden, as if by saying it aloud I'll be able to make sense of it.

"Guys like Smythe have endless ways to break a person down and then rebuild him the way that suits them: loyal, obedient, and at least a little scared."

"Walden was under this man's control when he set that fire—he still is." Every time I blink I see Walden's cold, gaunt face. Then I get a glimmer of hope. "Maybe he didn't set it at all! Smythe turned those kids in. Maybe they're just scapegoats and Walden's brainwashed enough to accept it."

"Possibly. I'm sure that will all be part of the case, if we can get that far."

"What do you mean, 'if'?"

He freezes. "Walden didn't tell you?"

"What?"

"He's going to plead guilty. The other two are as well. Amelia told me on the phone, but he asked her not to tell you so he could do it himself."

"He doesn't know what he's doing!" I push off from the counter. "I need to go back there, try again. Call Amelia."

"They don't let prisoners have visitors whenever they feel like it. And after what you told me, I doubt Walden would see you anyway."

"I have to do something!"

"You did. You went in there and tried. At this point we'll work on getting him to accept a lawyer before the sentencing. Then Amelia can get a psych evaluation. We can argue the circumstances and press for leniency."

"But he'll go to prison."

"Yes."

My voice rises with desperation. "You're a psychiatrist. Can't you declare him incompetent?"

"The court makes that declaration. The doctor just offers an opinion based on his evaluation. And it can't be me anyway, they'll attack my bias."

"If you could have seen him, you'd know there's no hope he'll change his mind by tomorrow." I pace from the stove to the basement door and back. "If only I could go back in time . . ."

Ross steps in front of me, takes my hands, and looks into my eyes. "Walden lived his life, just as you lived yours, by making choices in the circumstances that presented themselves. You're his sister, not his parent. The responsibility is not now, nor should it ever have been, on your shoulders. You were in the same situation he was. None of this was your doing."

"You don't understand. He always counted on me." My chest is so tight I have to force in a breath. "He came to me when he was scared. Not Griff. Not our parents. Me. And I left him when everything was at its worst."

"You're punishing yourself for things that you couldn't control and you can't change now." He takes me by the arm and guides me to the table. "Sit down, I want to tell you something."

"This had better not be more bad news. I'm not sure I can take anymore today."

"It's not." He sits down in the chair closest to me. "Remember the first time I went to your grandmother's? The Mother's Day after we met."

"Of course. My mortification is branded into my memory."

"It stuck in my memory, too, but not for the reasons you imagine." He looks bemused. "Actually, it makes me think of your toppling-domino theory. About a year before that, I'd gone with my dad to a conference—he was always trying to jump-start my faint interest in law. I sat in on a seminar addressing criminal psychology and how it can influence a trial. It was fascinating. Not the trial part, the psychology. And then seeing your dad like that, and when you told me about his hurricane and shadow time—"

"Oh my gosh, you remember what I called it."

He looks directly in my eyes. "I don't think you have any idea how much I care about you and Griff. Maybe it's because I'm an only child. Maybe it's because I admire you so much." He leans closer. "From that very first day. I mean, you nearly drowned and all you could think about was saving those damned mayhaws—because they would make someone else happy. What teenager is that selfless? And then I saw you with the twins, filling in the empty place left by Margo. You're an incredible person, Tallulah."

As I stare into those blue eyes, time collapses in on itself. I'm fourteen and so infatuated I can barely function. My mouth goes dry. Finally, I mutter, "You're kind to remember it that way."

"I should have told you back then, back when you really needed to hear it."

Maybe I need to hear it now. For the blink of an eye, I have the urge to kiss him.

"When disaster hit your family, you were still a child," he says. "Sixteen, yes, but not a fully formed adult by any means, no matter how mature you were.

"Your parents were passionate, volatile people. Who knows what made Margo so detached from motherhood. Maybe something in her own childhood. There's no way to know. But your dad . . . I think he was probably suffering from an actual illness, what we call manic-depressive disorder. Extreme highs and lows, brimming with unending energy, wild spending, periods of grandiose ideas, paranoia; the mania. Other times utter, bleak despair."

"That describes him perfectly. He would obsess, not sleep for days." I tell Ross about Dad's crazy theory that all history had been manipulated by a consortium. I sit for a moment, sorting through the snippets and scraps of my memory. "I always blamed his dark moods on Margo."

"Their relationship could have been a trigger. But the way he spiraled so low that he was incapacitated was likely the disease."

"This feels like a rescue come years too late."

"Too late for him. Not too late for you. I want you to try to put your childhood in perspective. You tried to take care of everyone, and you did a great job, but there's only so much a child can do, especially up against odds like that."

There was a *reason*. It was an illness. "Margo was too self-centered to care. And Gran either made noble-sounding excuses or ignored it altogether. And now you're telling me Dad could have been *fixed*?" We let him live in torment until he finally couldn't stand it anymore.

"First of all, your grandmother came from a different generation—one where mental illness wasn't well understood by most people, they covered it up or locked it away. Asylums. Disappointment rooms. Hell, sometimes I think we've only taken baby steps from that now. As for fixing him, it couldn't be done back then. Up until about three years ago, there wasn't even a good treatment. Electroshock therapy was about it. That could wipe out the symptoms for a time, but often takes a whole lot else with it."

I think about Gran covering up Dad's issues. Then I think of her comments about Uncle George and how his mother didn't have tolerance for imperfections.

"Does it run in families?" I ask.

"There can be a familial component."

"Do you think it could have anything to do with Walden's behavior?"

"I don't have enough information to even make a guess, let alone a diagnosis. But people with manic depression aren't usually good candidates for cult recruiting. Too undisciplined. Too unpredictable."

"Do you think Griff . . . ?"

"I didn't see any signs of it before he left."

"There were always so many whispers about Granddad's brother and how the James blood carries certain . . . traits. What if he left because he was worried it could be him, he didn't want to burden anyone?"

"You're taking quite a leap. And right now, we need to focus on Walden. Don't overload yourself."

I bury my face in my hands. "Everything is so tangled together."

"It always is, Lulie. That's why you can't blame yourself for things other people do. And remember, whatever happens"—he pulls my hands from my face and holds them tight—"I'm right here with you. *I* won't leave you."

For the first time in my life, I let myself believe that could actually be true.

* * *

As evening turns to night, Ross and I sit beside a burbling fountain in his back garden. The smell of jasmine is thick and sweet. The moon casts a silver sheen on everything. We turned off the first-floor lights before we came out, to deter bugs. With the heat of the day gone, the humidity is more tolerable to my adopted San Franciscan nature. We gave up coffee some time ago and are now sharing a bottle of pinot noir. My exhausted mind is overcome with the past three days, so the conversation has been spotty, and yet the silence between us is comfortable.

Sitting here in these pleasant surroundings, I think of Ross saying Griff's time in this house was purgatory, and of how angry I was as I scrounged my way to California alone, thinking he was living in the lap of luxury with people who loved him. People who meant more to him than I did.

"Was Griff unhappy the entire time he was here?" I might have been angry, but that doesn't mean I wanted him miserable.

Ross is quiet for a long while, then he says, "I think he *tried* to be happy. As I look back on it, he probably made the effort more for Mom than himself. He played football and baseball because it made her think he was involved and well-adjusted." He shakes his head. "Man, was he a good athlete. Even if he didn't want to accept my parents' help for college, he could easily have gotten a scholarship. He made all the right noises about wanting to go to school—Mom was terrified he'd get drafted and sent to Vietnam if he didn't have a student deferment—but whenever a college scout came to town, he always had a bad game. A *seriously* bad game."

"Self-sabotage?"

"Took a while for me to see it, but yeah. And it seemed the more popular he got, the more disconnected he tried to be."

"Why would he squander such a great opportunity? For years all he wanted—all either of us wanted—was a normal life."

Ross looks over at me, his face an odd color in the moonlight, his eyes shining that vivid blue. "Because he let you down."

"Is that supposed to make me feel bad?"

"You *asked*. And you already know my thoughts on being responsible for someone else's situation. But a little communication could have made things different for both of you. If he'd known you were running away, he'd have gone with you—or better yet, you both could have come here." He pauses. "But then, you were teenagers." Ross smiles. "Your brains weren't ready to make rational decisions."

"Thanks for the out."

"All part of my complementary housing package."

We're quiet for a while again. Then he says, "It wasn't all terrible. That first summer, before I left for Harvard and his senior year, my Corvette blew a head gasket. He and I spent a couple of weeks out here in the garage working on it. He taught me a hell of a lot. As you might guess, I didn't have much experience with mechanical things. But Griff, he could almost become one with the engine; the tools, so clumsy in my hands, were like an extension of his. And man, that kid could drive like a demon."

"He and Tommy were always building stuff. I think they were about eleven when they rebuilt a lawn tractor they found at the junkyard and made a wagon out of an old truck bed to pull behind it. To make up for not letting me go scavenging with them—they insisted girls got lockjaw easier than boys, but I'm pretty sure it was because they were stealing half the stuff from Prescott's Salvage— I was in charge of aesthetics. They weren't happy when I painted flowers on it, but they stuck to the deal. Hot summer nights, Griff and I would drive it out to the pecan orchard and sleep in the truck bed."

"I know your childhood was difficult, but in a way, I'm envious."

"What are you talking about?"

"The way your crazy childhood bonded the two of you together."

"I can't imagine what it would have been like without him." After a moment, I say, "Where do you think he is?"

"He didn't leave any better trail than you did. Someplace racing and working on cars, I hope." Then he adds, "If Tommy doesn't know, then nobody does."

"Oh, he and Tommy had drifted apart that last year." *But did it stay that way?* I think of how sketchy Tommy looked when I asked if he knew where Griff was, and of his scribbling when he looked at my license.

Ross says, "Those bonds formed in childhood and adolescence tend to stick, even if you don't see each other. That's why people have high school reunions."

I nearly spit out the sip of wine I just took. "You can't be serious. High school reunions are so the ones who were sitting at the top can show that they're still at the top."

"Now how would you know?"

"Because life has taught me how to assess ulterior motives and judge a person's true nature—which never changes, by the way." I don't look at him, but I feel his gaze on me.

"It sounds like you didn't leave all that behind when you left Lamoyne."

"Oh, Lamoyne was just kindergarten. I earned a graduate degree." I get up, unwilling to end the night talking about things that will give me nightmares. "Thanks for the wine. I'm going to bed while I can still navigate the stairs."

He stands and grabs my hand before I can walk away. His eyes are so intense on mine that I take a small step toward him.

"*Our* bond has stuck, hasn't it, Lulie? Years apart and still . . ."

"And still." I leave the understatement hanging. Smiling softly, I touch his cheek.

Then I walk away, my head slightly dizzy, knowing, thanks to Ross, tonight there will be no nightmares.

23

December 16, 1963

My first glimpse of the Pacific Ocean nearly makes me cry. Not because of its sapphire beauty or its violent, crashing majesty, but because I always imagined this moment with Griff by my side. But Griff chose the easier path as soon as it opened up for him, leaving me with only the unfulfilled dream he planted and left to wither in the drought.

Standing on a rocky prominence, facing a cold wind, I am alone and bone weary. I drop my Wickham College duffel, now showing the scars and stains of a long journey. From my pocket, I dig out my arrowhead. Wrapping my heavy sweater tightly around me, I clutch that piece of flint over my heart and breathe in the salt air.

Everything I know of California beaches comes from the movie *Gidget*, Coppertone ads, and the images the Beach Boys created with their lyrics: palm trees and beach volleyball, blond-haired surfers and blazing sunsets. But gray clouds hang over my head. The crescent spit of beach below is empty, surrounded by dark, craggy rocks, the water dotted with the same. The palm trees, at least, are as advertised.

As I shiver, it comes to me that the myth of perpetual summer is as true about California as it is the South. Is there anywhere in the world that can live up to that golden expectation?

I wonder about the twins. Are they experiencing their first snow, snug inside their safe, clean new home in Michigan? Are they finally getting tucked in at night by a grown-up? A deep-down part of me—beneath feeling betrayed and discarded—is jealous.

For the first few days of my journey, my feet pounded the earth with anger. Then reality elbowed past the fury, and sadness weighed my steps. There would be no more Griff. No more Daddy. No more Maisie. No more orchard. Before those thoughts could take me down, I refocused. No more Grayson Collie. No more looks of pity. No more whispers.

Still, I miss Dad so much it hurts, feeling particularly forlorn when I use the more obscure vocabulary words he assigned. And I miss Walden's boy-puppy smell after he comes in from playing, his sweet thoughtfulness, and the way he looked at me as if I had special powers to protect him. I might even miss Dharma's constant demand for an audience.

None of those things are in Lamoyne anymore.

These past weeks, the flags at half-staff for our president reminded me that I'm not the only one who is sorrow-filled. That shared mourning probably opened many a car door as I hitchhiked west.

To conserve my money, I limited my bus ride to the miles through the desert. And motels were out of the question. After camping with Griff, I know how to pick a good spot and am okay sleeping in the open.

After living in Lamoyne, I know how to read people; my two-thousand-mile trip has been uneventful because of it. Well, I did have a bit of a close moment at a gas station in Louisiana with a couple of alligator poachers. Once I noticed the way they were looking at me, I locked myself in the bathroom until they left.

Gas station sponge baths broken by the occasional camp ground shower has left me in a state that would send Gran into apoplexy. But then, I don't care what Gran would say anymore. My new life is going to be about living free.

I'm still about seventy miles north of Huntington Beach, a place

Griff picked out for us after listening to the forty-five of *Surfin'*
Safari last summer. I tuck the arrowhead back in my pocket, pick
up my duffel, and walk toward the southbound lane of the Pacific
Coast Highway, where I raise a thumb to finish my trek.

An odd-looking little orange convertible with its top sensibly
up stops. A blonde wearing sunglasses, even though there's no sun
in sight, dips her head to look across the car as I open the passenger
door. Although I've been lucky, I adhere to caution, taking a step
back to assess before I accept the ride.

"Where are you headed?" she asks with a smile accentuated by
a friendly dimple.

"Huntington Beach." I try to sound as if the name is not unfamiliar on my tongue.

"I'll get you a good part of the way there. Just put your bag in
the trunk."

The name on the trunk says Karmann Ghia. Foreign. Exotic.
Like my new life.

She calls out, "Not back there. It's in the front."

Stopping, I begin to reassess my impression that she's a nice,
friendly girl.

"Really," she says. "It's a Volkswagen thing."

It does sound like the clattery-hum of the engine is coming
from the rear, so I turn around. Sure enough, when I open the hood,
there's a spare tire and empty space. I put my duffel inside and climb
into the passenger seat.

"I'm Barbara," she says. "Barbara Hurst. But everybody calls me
Bobbi—*i*, no *e*."

"Tallulah."

"Hello, Tallulah." She lets out the clutch and off we go. "I'm
headed back to Hollywood—spent a disappointing weekend in
Santa Barbara fending off a disingenuous producer." She makes it
sound trivial and commonplace. "I'd take you on down to Huntington Beach, but I have a drama class this afternoon."

"You're an actress?"

"I am." Then she shrugs. "Although unknown and mostly unemployed. Where are you from—wait, let me guess. Georgia . . . no, Mississippi."

"Good guess."

"I'm an East Texas girl, myself."

"You don't sound like it."

"Years of practice and countless diction lessons."

"I didn't know a person could get rid of an accent." I'm quite intrigued by the idea—stripping away everything that makes you easy to decipher, anything that might give a hint of your vulnerable underbelly.

"You'd be surprised what you can leave behind." After a pause, she says, "Please tell me you're not here to become an actress. Don't get me wrong—you're pretty enough. There's something too . . . sweet and soft about you. This town will eat you alive."

"You don't know anything about me." I don't want to be sweet. And I certainly am not soft.

"Do you have family in Huntington Beach?"

"I don't have any family anywhere." I use the tone that usually puts an end to questions.

"Staying with friends?"

"Does it matter?"

She turns on both her headlights and windshield wipers, and her head tilts to the side as the gray sky begins to shed its tears. "Listen, I know what it's like to land in this town with no place to stay. The weather is ridiculous. I don't want to dump you in Santa Monica and have you catch pneumonia."

"I'm sure I can get a lift for the last few miles easy enough."

"It's forty miles. And the beach traffic is nonexistent today. Why don't you come home with me? I have a double at the Hollywood Studio Club, and my roommate is away for the week. Have some hot food and a shower. The weather is supposed to clear tomorrow. You shouldn't have trouble getting a ride the rest of the way."

I open my mouth to refuse, then think of a real shower with shampoo and soap. I'll have a better chance of finding a job if I don't smell like a gymnasium. "I don't want to be an imposition."

"If you were an imposition, I wouldn't have invited you."

There's something nice about how direct this girl is. "Okay, then. Thanks."

"Good!" She turns left, away from the ocean. "There's a washing machine, too—if you need it."

I wonder just how bad I smell. At least she hasn't rolled down the window yet.

I don't know what I was expecting, but the Hollywood Studio Club, a stuccoed, tile-roofed YWCA with tall wooden doors, is like a college sorority house, girls and drying stockings draped everywhere. Bobbi explains it was created for aspiring actresses in the twenties. There's a reception lobby, a dining hall, and huge living room with a massive fireplace and a stage, even the air holds the promise of stardom. Dharma would love it here.

As we leave the living room, I overhear someone make a comment about Bobbi finding another stray, but they sound admiring, not judgmental.

Bobbi's room has two twin beds with mismatched bedspreads and a sink. One side is bare and tidy, the only decoration a stuffed autograph hound on the bed. The other is piled with clothes, curlers, and a bonnet hair dryer like I wanted last Christmas.

"Don't worry, the messy side is mine." Bobbi chuckles. "Karen is a saint for putting up with me. She's at a modeling job at a trade show in Vegas." She hooks a thumb over her shoulder. "Showers are down the hall, on the left. Feel free to take my shower caddy—oh, where is that thing?" She reaches under her bed. "There!" She pulls out a wire basket with a sticky bottle of Breck shampoo, matching cream rinse, and a squishy-looking bar of Dove soap. "All of the face stuff is strictly off-limits due to budget constraints." She plucks out a couple of bottles. "There's a robe hanging on the closet door you can use. The yellow one." Bobbi smiles and heads toward the door. "I should be back around six. Make yourself at home."

I'd been considering taking a shower and then leaving while

Bobbi is at class. But after seeing the security of this woman-filled place, I decide to sleep in that clean, crisp-looking bed.

After my blissfully hot shower, my clothes are all too nasty to put back on, so I stay in Bobbi's robe. I pick up the autograph hound and read the signatures: Doris Day, Jerry Lewis, Cary Grant, Sandra Dee. Wow. Just silvery images in Mississippi, all real flesh and blood here in California. I set the dog gently back in place.

I pull out my sketch pad and sit on the roommate's bed, leaning against the wall. The first drawings are people and places I don't want to forget from home: Maisie and all the tiny details that make her face special; the orchard barn; my pecan tree. Then my drawings move west: the twin ironwork bridges in Natchez that took me across the Mississippi River; the motel in Oklahoma with an office shaped like a wigwam; miles of waving prairie grass; different kinds of cactus; the gaping maw of the Grand Canyon (out of my way, but one of my rides was headed there, and I thought, *What the heck*); a roadrunner; the scrubby pines on the mountains between the desert and the coast.

I pull out my pastels and begin what will be the last two sketches: the place I first saw the Pacific Ocean and the Studio Club. The end of my journey and the beginning of my new life.

As soon as I get a job, I'll buy a new, California pad.

The next thing I know, Bobbi is shaking me by the shoulder.

"Time for dinner," she says. From the pile on her bed, she tosses me a sweatshirt and a pair of wrinkled navy slacks. From a drawer, she pulls a pair of panties. "You can wear these until we get your clothes washed. Don't think my bra will fit you, but it's just girls. Half of them go braless anyway, so don't sweat it."

Braless? Where people can see you?

And then, I realize, anything that would make Gran shudder qualifies as a step toward my plan for unconventional freedom.

Bobbi and I sit down at a table for six with two swanlike girls—Wendy and Ginger, "because of the hair, not my real name." As soon as I take my first bite (prolonged and frequent hunger has a way of making every bite ecstasy), I forget all about being self-conscious. Wendy and Ginger are friendly enough, but I catch a whiff of jealous competition hiding just under the surface as they eat tiny bites of broccoli and poached chicken.

As the room fills, the noise rises and the talk and laughter at the table make me forget I'm a plain-Jane outsider. This inclusiveness is foreign, as foreign to me as the Grand Canyon. I keep my forays into the conversation brief and banal, trying to figure out the rhythm and rules. As much as I hate to admit it to myself, I'm afraid of making a misstep, becoming an outcast here, too.

I remind myself, I am reborn. I will move through the world according to my judgment alone. I will not form myself to fit someone else's mold. I sit up a little straighter and project my pride at being homeless and braless.

It feels right. It feels good.

I feared I'd feel regretful once my journey west was over. But my heart is not full of longing or loneliness. I have closed the door on the past, my family.

And all I feel is relief.

24

It began with Bobbi saying, "You don't want to spend your first Christmas in California alone. Karen is heading back east for the holidays as soon as she's finished with the trade show, so the bed is free—at least until she comes back and you need your own. Then it's fifty dollars a month." She ended with a wink.

Back when California was just a dream spun by Griff, I let him do all the planning and problem-solving for me. Now I had to set my own future. Bobbi's friendship made me see that a life of self-imposed isolation holds no more appeal than one lived as an involuntary outcast.

So I stayed.

We decorated Bobbi's bedroom with silver tinsel from the drugstore, and made hot chocolate and Jiffy Pop on a hot plate. There were no presents, but there were also no arguments or bitter undercurrents. It was the kind of holiday I'd always dreamed of.

Even so, at the end of Christmas Day, when the sound of Bing Crosby's "Silver Bells" had faded, I found myself slipping into a grayness, missing Dad, thinking of his tortured last days and what I might have done to help him. I spent a little time doing tiny sketches of the things that I wanted to remember most about him; James Hall, his briefcase, him standing on that carousel horse with his arms wide, the pecan sheller he invented, the thick old dictionary from which he assigned our vocabulary words. As always, drawing made me feel better, but I still wondered how my three scattered siblings had fared in their first Christmas away from Lamoyne.

Bobbi and I rang in 1964 at a party in a Hollywood Hills apartment on Franklin Avenue. Hot and crammed with people, the air blue with cigarette smoke, the booze flowed like water, but food was skimpy—definitely not run by a Southern hostess. People clustered in little knots, laughing and talking loudly to be heard over the hi-fi. Couples filled the corners and, I discovered shockingly, the unlocked bathroom, making out like they were in guarded privacy. Once I discovered the peculiar smell was marijuana, I was so worried about getting arrested that I spent most of the chilly evening skulking near the bushes outside in case I needed a quick hiding spot. I did slip back in for the stroke of midnight and was grabbed by a guy and suffocated with a beer-tasting kiss. My first. Memorable, but not in the way I'd always imagined.

Now that the New Year is under way—and Karen's on a bus back to Hollywood—it's time to find a job and my own place. Bobbi is the first to give voice to my inner fear: I am too young and inexperienced to get much of a job at all.

She taps her chin. "Let's capitalize on the fact that you're *not* an actress using this job as a temporary fix against hunger—a job to be jettisoned as soon as a part comes along. That should give you an edge." She moves to the door of her closet, then reaches in and pulls out a dress that looks like something Jacqueline Kennedy or Audrey Hepburn would wear. Turquoise with black embroidered vines rising from the hemline, it has elbow-length sleeves, a black patent leather belt, and a wide, rolled neckline. "With proper makeup and a sophisticated hairdo, I'm sure you can get something at one of the high-end department stores. Oh, and when you fudge your age, don't say eighteen. Nineteen sounds less like a lie. And play up that Southern genteel accent of yours. Let's say you're from a prominent, but overly traditional, family. You came west to become a modern, independent woman. Dazzle them with that vocabulary of yours."

She sounds like she's creating a part. I suppose she is: a new, re-invented me.

"I don't know anything about being a sales clerk."

"Smile and tell ladies they look fabulous. Couldn't be easier." She begins to tease my hair.

When Bobbi's finished, I don't even recognize myself. I lean close to the mirror and examine the expert stroke of eyeliner, the startling fullness of my mouth under a bright coral lipstick. My hair is upswept. I *do* look nineteen.

"Stop batting your eyes, for goodness' sake."

"I can't help it. These false eyelashes are heavy, and they itch."

"Well, don't scratch!" She grins like a proud sister. "Now dress and shoes."

I give the black heels a wary glance. I've never worn heels.

"They're perfect," she offers. "Low enough you won't break your neck, yet high enough you don't look like a grandma. You're sophis-ticated, yet not showy. Perfect for Saks."

"Saks? Tell me you're kidding." I've been in the Studio Club long enough to learn the department store pecking order, even if I haven't set foot inside one.

"Of course, that won't be your first application. We'll work up to it. Practice applications first. Then you'll have a job to fall back on if you don't get on at Saks."

"You sound like this is no big deal."

"It isn't." She points to the shoes. "Now step into those and I'll drive you."

The job interview process isn't nearly as awful as I expected. And it quickly reaffirms what I've learned about the value of hazily shaded truth. It's all about reading people to gauge what they want to hear. And even as angry as I am with Gran, I must admit she prepared me well when it comes to etiquette and manners. Now I understand what she meant by, "A moment of empty silence *always* works in your favor. Don't be in a rush to speak." Most times people move on out of either respect or their own discomfort.

It is amazing how simple things are when no one knows you. Four days later, I'm filling out paperwork for my first day of work at I. Magnin—half a block from Saks and nearly as prestigious. I'm starting in hosiery, the breaking-in ground for new clerks. The department is basically Loretta, a divorcée in her thirties, and me. She teaches me how to write up a sales slip, use the levered embosser to run a charge plate, and the proper way to match a stocking to a woman's skin tone.

"And over here," she motions to a small display in the corner. "Are panty hose—stocking and panty all in one. But hardly anybody will ask for them. We're carrying them temporarily to see if they find a market."

Looking between the garter belts and that new panty-stocking combination I say, "I bet everybody would want them if they knew about them."

"Well, don't count on it. Our ladies require *proper* foundation garments."

Maybe once I'm comfortable here, I'll move the display to where people can see. As short as the skirts in California are, soon there won't be any room for *proper* foundation garments.

I soon discover very few wealthy women spend time in our department. Instead, they send someone from the dress department or their personal secretary to pick up their stockings, which allows me to cut my teeth slowly, without much danger of being bitten back.

Before long, I no longer feel like I'm pretending. I am a working girl with no past and an infinite future.

My other stroke of fortune—and I feel more than a little guilty thinking of it as that—is Bobbi's roommate, Karen, came back after the holidays with the news that her parents gave her a six-month trip to France for Christmas. Bobbi and the other girls suspect "France" is a home for unwed mothers in some godforsaken place like Minnesota. I'm sorry for her, but I was happy to officially become a resident at the club just the same.

After only three months, I understand why Southern California is the subject of songs and the location for movies. The air sits feathery on your skin, the sun casts a flattering light, the streets are clean, and there are so many different kinds of people around that if you ever feel out of place, you won't for long.

Today I'm finally going to make it to Huntington Beach. It's a perfect Sunday afternoon—although Bobbi assures me it's warmer than usual for late March—so the top is down on Bobbi's car. She loaned me a triangle scarf that she insisted should be tied in the back under my hair instead of beneath my chin. Being a California girl now, I have my own sunglasses. The radio in the dash is tuned to KRLA. We sing "Surf City" at the top of our lungs. I throw my arms in the air and feel as light as a kite.

As we roll into Huntington Beach, I'm a little disappointed. There are ugly oil derricks along the beach, although Bobbi says not as many as there used to be. The buildings along the highway aren't much different from the outskirts of most towns I passed on my way west. Other than the blue Pacific to my right, there is nothing magical about this place, not like I'd imagined.

Near the pier, things get livelier. Motels. Seafood. Colorful surf shops. As we pass a twenties-type stucco-and-tile building, Bobbi points to it. "That's the Golden Bear. As much a part of Huntington Beach as the pier. Music and drinking—the most beloved things next to surfing."

We park in a lot next to a vehicle that looks like a cross between a station wagon and a delivery van with a surfboard tied on top. I get a little thrill-tingle—I'm about to see real live surfing! Bobbi grabs a blanket and her transistor radio. I pull out the small, red metal Coca-Cola cooler, and we make our way toward the beach. A few surfboards are propped against the elevated lifeguard stand, but I don't see anyone riding the waves.

As we walk across the sand, Bobbi says, "I wish you'd bought a swim suit."

Looking at the girls in their bikinis, I'm glad I didn't. I'd looked at Woolworth's, but even the most modest two pieces made me feel naked. "I told you, I don't like getting in the water."

She waves a hand. "Do you see any of those girls in the water? It's too cold to swim this time of year. It's all about getting tan and looking cool."

I glance down at my Bermuda shorts and sleeveless shell. "Guess it's too late to look cool, so I'd better hope for a tan."

Once we get settled on our blanket and have the radio on, I lie back on my elbows and enjoy the warmth of the sun. "Thanks for driving down here. I really wanted to see it." I haven't told her about Griff, or why I came to California. Thankfully, she hasn't asked.

"That guy over there is looking at you." She lifts her chin in the direction of the pier.

"Don't be ridiculous. He's probably just shocked at my inability to look cool. Or more likely, he's looking at you."

"You really don't know how pretty you are, do you?"

"Funny."

"Oh my God, you're not just feigning modesty." She sounds genuinely surprised. "From the second I first saw you, I knew you didn't belong in this town. I just wonder how long it'll be before you figure that out."

I lift my sunglasses and look at her. "I'm not sure if I should be flattered or insulted."

"Definitely flattered. Once you're here a while, you'll see."

This city is a million things, not just a single, small-minded organism like Lamoyne. Before I can argue, I'm thumped on the back of the head with something that bounces off and lands on the blanket between us.

"Sorry!" the voice comes from behind me. "Are you okay?"

I turn and words evaporate from my tongue. The guy is tall and tan with sun-bleached longish hair. He belongs on a surfing poster.

Bobbi pipes up. "This lovely lady you just beaned is Tallulah. And you are . . . ?"

"Cody. I really am sorry, Tallulah."

I manage an inelegant shrug.

"Tallulah might feel better if she had a Sno Cone," Bobbi says. "They sell them up at the Pav-a-lon."

"I'm fine." I force myself to make eye contact. His are green. And incredible. I pluck the Frisbee off the blanket and hand it up to him, hoping he can't see the artery in my neck telegraphing my rapid heartbeat. "And I don't need a Sno Cone."

"Well . . . thanks, Tallulah." He takes it and trots off.

"He was the one looking at you," Bobbi whispers. Then she calls loudly, "A gentleman would bring back a Sno Cone."

"Shhhh."

"Hey, Cody!" she yells louder.

He stops and turns.

"Do you surf?"

"Nah. Guitar's my thing. Come on over to the bonfire later and see." He points to a pit dug in the sand. "Sunset."

"We won't be here that late." I'm rewarded with an elbow from Bobbi.

"Ignore her, she's new in town. We'll be there." She waves him on. Then she says to me, "Lesson one: you don't come to the beach and not stay for sunset. Lesson two: you *certainly* don't turn down a cute guy's invitation to a bonfire."

When we join the group at the fire pit, I steer clear of Mr. Green Eyes. Bobbi engages in a conversation with a dark-eyed boy, and I talk with the other girls. I tread warily, keeping an eye out for the sly look, waiting for a joke at my expense. But the girls act as if I'm just like them. Even as I begin to relax, I can't shake the feeling that sooner or later, they're going to turn on me. Maybe Lamoyne will never leave my blood.

A couple of boys join our side of the circle. I grow quiet and stare into the fire, unprepared for the way it draws me in. Yellow flames grow, climbing higher, broadening to a massive size. A tinny version of "Blue Velvet" suddenly plays in the recesses of my mind. A chill begins at the nape of my neck and creeps across my skin. Even a life filled with chaos and uncertainty did not prepare me for the way my family imploded the night of the Wickham bonfire. I thought I would never recover, never leave it behind. And yet, as I sit on this beach, I feel the distance more than the suffering. Maybe I am truly reborn.

Cody sits down next to me and drapes an arm over my shoulders. "How's your head, Tallulah?"

I'm so flustered by his boldness, it takes me a few seconds to craft my oh-so-clever response. "Fine."

He pulls his arm away. "Sorry. I didn't mean to upset you."

"You didn't . . . I mean . . ."

"You're from the South." He lifts a shoulder. "More rules, I guess."

I manage a half smile and feel a little less brittle. "You could say that."

"How long have you been in LA?"

"Just over three months."

"So are you an actress, singer, or student?"

I smile. "Sales clerk at I. Magnin. No ulterior ambitions."

His laugh sounds like California itself, full of life and free. "I'm happy you're not an actress awaiting discovery. That feels too close to a damsel in distress awaiting rescue."

"Hey, those girls work hard! They take classes and hold more than one job and sit for hours at open calls. They *are not* waiting to be rescued."

He raises his hands. "Okay, okay. I stand corrected."

"What about you?" I ask. "Do anything other than play guitar?"

"Nope. Well . . . I sing and write songs. I play the piano, too—but I can't fit one in my bus."

I turn to him. "You have a bus?"

"Not like a bus bus. A V-dub." I must not be hiding my confusion as well as I think because he raises his eyebrows and adds, "Volkswagen."

"I know. You make it sound like you live in it, that's all."

"I kinda do. My folks live up in Monterey, so when I'm down here or traveling to perform, it's home sweet home."

"You play a guitar *for a living*?" He sounds like a gypsy.

He shrugs. "I don't need much."

"Guess not."

He looks west. "There it goes."

I look up just as the last sliver of orange disappears and brilliant pink flares on the undersides of the few, spotty clouds. "Wow."

"Every time." He says it in a way that is sweet and a little heart-breaking.

After the sun disappears, it gets chilly quickly. I stand and brush the sand off my shorts.

"Where are you going?" he asks, looking up at me, firelight dancing in his eyes.

I don't like the way he pulls me off-balance just by looking at me, as if his eyes have gravitational properties to which only I seem to be susceptible. I suddenly get a terrifying glimpse of what bound Margo and Daddy. My stomach turns.

I remind myself, plenty of people have relationships without that horrible tangle of love and hate, relationships not ruled by extremes. But I *do* feel extreme when he looks at me. Maybe I've inherited the defective James genes everyone is always alluding to. Drawn to the destructive. Helpless against the winds of emotion.

"I'm cold. And tomorrow's a work day." I look around for Bobbi but don't see her.

"Here." Cody hands me a sweatshirt. "Take a walk with me."

"I thought you were going to play guitar."

"I can play anytime. I'd rather walk with you. C'mon."

"I should wait here." I make a show of glancing around for Bobbi again.

"She took a walk with Greg." He points, and I see them about a quarter mile down the beach. "We'll be back before they are. I promise."

I want to walk with him so badly my whole body is vibrating. I slip the sweatshirt over my head. "All right." I'm surprised my voice sounds calm and reasonable, when inside I'm full of grass-hoppers.

As we walk, he angles us toward the water. He asks me questions, not regular get-to-know-you things, but about what I think about life and the wider world, if I believe in fate or if we're totally creatures of free will. He's interesting. He acts as if what I have to say is important.

He talks about Woody Guthrie (whose name I know but whose music I do not) and Bob Dylan (who I've never heard of) and the poetry of Leonard Cohen (which he recites, and I feel it reach deep into both our souls). I imagine Cody writes deeply serious songs, not about catching waves and fast cars. He says music is a form of poetry and songs like "I Want to Hold Your Hand" and "She Loves You" and the Beach Boys in general are lyric larceny; crimes against the power of words.

My only experience with music is radio hits and *American Bandstand*, so I focus on the thing I *do* understand. "My dad taught us to believe words are arsenals and require skill in wielding them wisely—just like any other weapon."

"Exactly!" Cody says, excitement in his voice. "Is he a writer?"

"History professor . . . at least he was. He passed away last year." *Passed away.* Two words far too innocuous to describe what happened to Dad.

"Oh, I'm sorry. Is that when you came to California?"

"I hitchhiked out here a short time later."

He stops and looks at me. "Seriously? You hitched alone all this way?"

"I did."

"Wow. You're one brave girl."

I shrug. I wasn't brave. I was desperate.

We approach a woman who looks down on her luck, even in this light. She has a worn paper sack with the top rolled down next to her and is huddled in a holey sweater. Cody must notice me looking at her because he whispers in my ear. "That's Mary. Pretty much lives on the beach. Has for years."

A coffee can sits in front of her. As we pass, I see it contains coins and a few dollar bills. After we've gone on about two more steps, I stop and go back. I dig out three ones, all I brought with me, from my pocket. "Stay safe," I say softly, as I drop them into her can.

She smiles her thanks, and I hurry back to Cody.

He stands for a moment, looking at me . . . no, not at me, *into* me. "That was nice."

I wave away the comment and start walking.

Full darkness descends, which somehow intensifies the sound of the waves. The water feels bigger, more powerful, ominous. I try to veer away from that dark, grasping mass. Cody playfully nudges me with his shoulder, and I take two stumbling steps. The cold grabs my ankles. I give a deathly squeal and shove past him for the security of dry land.

His arms wrap around me. "Hey, are you okay? You're shaking."

"I . . . I had an unpleasant experience with water once. Not so fond of it anymore." My racing heart freed up more than I intended to offer.

He holds me tighter. "Oh man, I'm sorry. I was just joking around. I would never—"

"I know." I push slightly away. "I didn't know how bad it was myself until a few seconds ago. Don't worry about it."

He takes my hand and walks us up into the dry sand before turning around and heading back toward the bonfire.

The solidness of his hand around mine affects me in a way I've never felt before. My heart is filled with song; my skin is on fire; my soul reaches out to his poetic heart. I feel naked and vulnerable, standing on the edge of a high, rocky cliff.

And I cannot let myself fall.

25

I'm getting ready to go to a party with Bobbi—who's out on a liquor run because it's a BYOB apartment gathering and not a Beachwood Canyon shindig—when there's a knock on my door. Pamela from down the hall sticks her auburn head in. "You have a visitor downstairs."

I turn from the mirror with an eyeliner brush in my hand. "Must be a mistake."

"You're the only Tallulah within thirty miles, so I'm pretty sure it's not."

I throw on my new white shift dress but don't bother with sandals. When I make the last turn in the stairs, I stop dead.

"Cody?" I'd forgotten how good-looking he is. Maybe because I wanted to.

He grins. "Surprised to see me?"

He's called three times in the three weeks since we met. I feel less vulnerable talking on the phone than when I'm looking into his eyes, but I'm frightened by the way my heart races and my body tingles at the sound of his voice. What frightens me more is how he fills my mind when I'm falling asleep and when I'm handling delicate lingerie at the store.

I've never felt so out of control.

Dad probably didn't either before he met Margo.

Forcing restraint, I walk slowly down the last few steps.

He says, "I was hoping you'd come to the strip with me, hear some music."

Most of the clubs require you to be twenty-one. I don't want to scare him away with even my pretend age of nineteen. "I have plans."

He closes some of the space between us. "I wanted to spend time with you before I leave."

"You're leaving?"

"I have shows at some colleges up north—a few clubs, too. I'll be gone for at least a couple of months. Three if I can get more dates locked down."

"But you're coming back to LA?"

He looks at me so intensely, I can't breathe. "Depends."

"On what?" The two words are choked and quiet.

"Will you still be here?" His smile is so sweet it lifts my heart.

I try to strip the naked eagerness out of my voice. "Don't have any plans to the contrary."

He steps close and gives me a quick kiss on the lips. "Good."

That's when I remember my hair is still in the shape of rollers, stiff with Dippity-do, and only one eye has liner. "Ugh! I—"

"Rival a sunset." He runs a finger along my cheek. "Eclipse the moon."

I want to call him a liar. But the gravity of his green eyes steals my voice.

"I'll call you whenever I can," he says as he takes a backward step.

We stand sharing the same air, looking at each other. I feel greedy, hungry. Nothing else matters but moving closer to him, into him.

Then I do and he's kissing me, sweetly, unhurried.

The desperation that washes over me is staggering. I want to claw and cling. My fingers dig into the back of his neck. As I feel the soft flesh give and hear his sharp intake of breath, I freeze and jerk away, horrified.

Granny's words echo in my head. *Your momma and daddy are dangerously obsessive. Sometimes with love, sometimes loathing, but always full to the brim with each other. It's unhealthy. No, it's sick.*

That's what I feel. Sick. My trembling hand goes to my mouth. I've never been so afraid of myself.

Cody looks perplexed, his head slightly to the side.

I turn away and run up three flights of stairs, then slam the door safely between me and him.

Now I have to figure out a way to banish him from my mind.

For the next week, I feel as if I'm mourning, a papery shell of the person I should be. The pain of losing Cody has reopened the door to all things lost to me. Maybe it's because I'm finally still enough for the sadness to catch up with me. The hole Dad left in my life seems even greater than it did after he first died. My yearning for Griff more intense.

When Bobbi asked me about it, I was less than nice. I feel too raw to talk. Griff and I *never* talked to each other about the insanity in our house and what it did to our insides. I suppose once you survive something horrible, you're not inclined to talk it to death afterward. Maisie is the only person who's seen my deepest wounds. So I add her to my litany of sorrow.

One evening when I'm feeling particularly low, I call information to get the number for Judge Delmore's house. Maisie's family doesn't have a phone, plus, the judge doesn't have a party line, so no one can listen in and spread our words all over town.

The next day I call.

"Judge Delmore's residence."

The comfort that surges through me at the sound of Maisie's voice astonishes me.

"Maisie, it's me. Can you talk?"

"Tallulah Mae! Sweet Jesus, where are you? You all right? I thought you might be dead, too." She's talking so fast her words trip over one another.

"Dead, too!" My flesh crawls with alarm. "Who else is dead?"

"Nobody new. But your Daddy's dyin' and all that went around it is still on the lips of every gossip in town. It's shameful. Let the man rest in peace. You should be glad you're gone. But shame on you for not tellin' me you were leaving."

"I'm sorry," I say, surprising myself with the truth of it. "I'm in California. LA. I have a job and a nice place to live. I'm starting over."

"Seventeen is mighty young to need a clean slate, but in your case, I say it's the right thing. Forget Lamoyne."

My recent birthday didn't even cross my mind. Maybe I did leave everything about the old me behind. "I miss you."

"I miss you, too. But that don't change anything. Your brother took his way out. It's good you found yours. You sure you're okay?"

"Yes. Well, no. Um, I don't know. Mostly I am. It's just there's a boy—"

Her whoop nearly breaks my eardrum and confirms that she's alone in the Delmore house. "Hallelujah, Jesus! I'm so happy you have someone like I have my Marlon. Just so you know, when he's done with college, we're gettin' married."

"Oh, Maisie, congratulations! I'm happy for you. But it's not like that for me. I sent Cody away."

"He a no-good?"

"No, he's . . . he's wonderful. He's kind and gentle and writes music."

"Drunkard?"

"No.

"Womanizer?"

"I don't think so."

"So why'd you send him away?"

"Because I . . . I . . . he makes me feel wild inside."

"He supposed to!"

"No. I mean, in a bad way. Like obsessive and reckless. Like—"

"You nothin' like them! You're just feelin' what new love feels like."

"No. No. It's more. It's bad."

"You can't have known this boy long. Give it some time and see. You can always change your mind."

"That's just it! If I only know him a little and think about him all the time, what's it going to be like after . . . after I love him?"

"Tallulah, you've never been like your momma, and you never will be. Enjoy that boy—" Her words cut off, then she whispers, "Missus Queen Bee's home. I gotta go. I'm glad you're safe."

"Maisie!"

"What?"

"Don't tell anyone where I am."

"You forget we're blood sisters?" She hangs up.

I wander out to the courtyard and sit in the shade. I start to feel sad for a different reason. What if Maisie's right? What if I made a horrible mistake? It isn't as if I can just write Cody a letter or call him on the phone. He. Is. Gone.

I bury my face in my hands and sob for the loss of something that my fear and my foolishness killed before it had a chance to bloom.

Three weeks later, a postcard arrives. The Golden Gate Bridge.

Tallulah,
    The road is long. The music strong.
    The mysteries of the universe great.
                     Cody

What the hell? Could he be more ambiguous?

I wish he hadn't sent it at all.

I arrive home from work early with a throbbing headache, which I'm pretty sure was caused by what I've come to think of as my co-worker Loretta's *neurosis du jour*.

Bobbi looks startled when I walk in. "You're home!"

I drop my purse on the floor and flop down on my bed, kicking off my heels as soon as I land. "Killer headache. You look like you're heading out."

"Um, yeah." She busies herself putting on earrings. "I'll leave so you can rest."

"Where're you going?"

She hesitates. "I have a date."

"Anyone I know?"

She sighs and sits down on her bed. "I didn't want to tell you, but I'm dating Greg."

"Huntington Beach Greg?"

"Yeah. He works up this way, a sound guy for Warner Brothers."

"How long have you been dating?"

"Over a month." Her cheeks pinken, from the shame of secrecy or the thought of Greg, I can't tell.

"A *month*? How did I not know?"

"You've been mooning over Cody—"

"I have *not* been mooning!" A lie.

"Okay, okay." She raises her hands. "You've been a little down since he left. I didn't want to rub your nose in the fact that I'm dating Greg."

"Why should I care?" I think I sound detached, convincing. Truth be, the very thought of Greg makes me miss Cody more. Proof that I'm unnaturally vulnerable when it comes to him.

"Tallulah. I've never seen you like this over anyone you've gone out with."

As if there have been scores. She's right, though. I've never had someone turn me inside out like this, not even when I was fourteen and crushing on Ross. "You don't need to hide your dates from me, for God's sake." I'm ashamed of how snippy I sound.

"Why don't you come with us tonight? We're going to a cocktail party for some studio people. It'll be fun. Maybe you'll even meet some movie stars."

I throw my arm over my eyes. "This headache is making me see my own stars."

"Okay, then, don't try to make yourself feel better. Lie there on your fainting couch and pine over a guy you saw twice."

I pick up a book from the nightstand and throw it. It sails past her and crashes into the things on top of the chest, knocking her lighted makeup mirror onto the floor. I roll over, turning my back before I see if it's broken.

Inside I'm a mass of quivering revulsion. Maisie was wrong. Cody *has* turned me into Margo.

26

August 1964

Ever since the cat climbed out of the bag that Bobbi's dating Greg, I hardly see her. Some nights she doesn't even come home. I've seen Greg just enough to get a sense that he doesn't like sharing her with anybody. So it's a happy surprise when I get home from work and find her in our room leafing through a magazine.

"Hey there," I say. "How about a movie tonight? *Marnie* is playing."

"I promised Greg I'd see it with him."

"Okay, how about *A Shot in the Dark*? After today, I could stand a good Inspector Clouseau laugh."

"He wants to see that one, too."

I try again, "Maybe we can forgo the dining room and go out for Chinese?" Until I came to LA, my only experience with foreign food was Chef Boyardee spaghetti from a box.

"I'm low on cash."

That's a first. "Okay. We stay in. We can get a couple of girls and play cards?"

"Sure. Unless Greg calls."

She stays quiet as I change out of my conservative gray dress and into a turquoise-and-yellow giant-flowered tunic top and pants. New to my wardrobe and very mod.

"Any new audition prospects?" I finally ask.

She shrugs. "A couple of commercials. But Greg's keeping an ear to the ground over at Warner."

"That's nice of him."

She lowers her magazine and looks at me for the first time since I walked in. "What's that supposed to mean?"

"It means he's being nice by keeping an eye out for roles for you. What else?"

"You sounded annoyed that he's helping me."

"I'm not annoyed he's helping you. But every statement you've made since I got home is centered around what Greg wants."

"Oh boy. Greg said this would happen."

"What?"

"You're jealous."

"Jealous? Of your *boyfriend*?"

"It's just that you have so few friends and you've counted on me so much. With Cody taking off and leaving you . . . it's natural for you to feel abandoned."

"Cody's been gone for four months. And he did not 'leave' me. We never even dated, for God's sake. And, for your information, *I* walked away from *him*." Technically true, and a moot point to boot. "I'm not jealous of Greg. I'm worried about *you*! You've changed."

She throws her magazine on the bed. "What are you talking about?"

"You can't seem to do anything without Greg's permission, or blessing, or whatever it is you get from him. And"—I decide to jump in with both feet and address the most concerning issue— "the drugs. You always stayed away from them. But now you're obviously . . . not." She came home so high on acid one night she was picking pink fairies out of the air.

"What's wrong with expanding your mind a little? It's no big deal."

"Maybe it's not a big deal, but it's a big change from your 'drugs just make you stupid' and 'I can't risk my career.'"

"All said from a place of naïveté." She waves a dismissive hand. "Before I discovered *everybody* around movies is using drugs. It fuels creativity. It has nothing to do with Greg."

"Okay. Okay. I don't want to fight. I'm just concerned because I care about you and it seems you're letting him control you."

She shakes her head. "Greg said you'd say that, too."

I grab my purse and leave the room before I say things I'll regret. In walking off my anger, I find myself in front of the El Capitan. While I'm waiting for *A Shot in the Dark* to start, I calm down enough to ask myself, *am* I jealous? Do I count on Bobbi too much?

All of my introspection ruins the movie and I'm sorry I wasted my dollar.

I leave the theater and head back to the Studio Club to apologize to Bobbi. It isn't my place to tell her what she should or shouldn't do, any more than it's Greg's. She seems happy. That's all that should matter.

But when I get back to our room, Bobbi isn't there. Most of her stuff isn't, either. There's a folded note taped on the mirror with my name on it.

> *Greg asked me to move in with him last week and I've decided now is as good a time as any. I'll be by to pack up the rest of my things this weekend. I've given notice to the Studio Club.*
>
> *Bobbi*

I crawl into bed feeling almost as alone as I did when I first set foot in California. I was deluded for a time, but now I see, no matter how nice they seem, people are the same everywhere.

My neck is in knots when I step out into the mid-September night. Loretta has turned into a most tedious coworker, full of complaints and gossip. It's becoming a full-time effort to avoid being drawn into the petty conflicts between different cliques of clerks inside these walls. That, along with the strict rules of etiquette and behavior required at I. Magnin are beginning to mirror life in Lamoyne.

At least they don't roll up the sidewalks here at 6:00 p.m. When I get off at seven, the street is busy with diners and moviegoers, even though it's a weeknight. The sight of people laughing together makes me feel starkly alone as I move toward the bus, where I will sit silent among strangers. Daytime-gathered heat is still radiating from the sidewalk. Although the mercury has nudged over ninety most days the past few weeks, it isn't anything like the sticky, cloying heat of home that drains energy and bogs the mind.

I usually keep everything Mississippi and all its chaos locked in a dark, windowless cellar. But as I stare out the bus window, I wonder if there *was* blackberry picking this year or if the birds finally got the whole crop. Is Gran lonely without any of us around? Quickly, I kick that cellar door closed before too much crawls out.

When I arrive at the Studio Club, I'm dreaming of getting out of my stockings and into a pair of shorts. Shorts and a nice bottle of Coke. I've missed dinner in the dining room, but I'm too tired to eat anyway.

Entering the lobby, I hear the piano in the big common room. Not a classical piece or show tune, as is the norm, but something sweet and haunting and unfamiliar. I veer away from the stairs. The lights are low in the room. When I see who's seated at the baby grand, my heart falls to my feet.

The notes die in the air as Cody's eyes meet mine. He stands in a relaxed, unhurried way that makes me touch my lips at the memory of the way he kissed me. My ears grow warm thinking of how I fled. How I rejected him without the courtesy of words.

"I told you I'd come back." He steps away from the piano and walks toward me.

"It's been five months. I thought maybe you were dead." Which I decide sounds much less petulant than grousing about no phone calls and just a single, cryptic postcard.

"You didn't get engaged or anything, did you?"

He's right in front of me now, causing my heart to thunder and my breath to halt. I'm torn between throwing myself in his arms and running off like a frightened deer. I will myself into stillness. "The proposals have been legion, but I haven't accepted any yet."

With a crooked smile, he cups my face and leans close. "I want to kiss you, but I'm worried you'll bolt again."

"I suppose you'll have to take that chance sooner or later." *As will I.*

When his lips touch mine, I swear I can hear music, his music, those beautiful chords he just played. Need wells up in me, dangerous, frightening.

You've never been like your momma and you never will be. Oh, Maisie, I hope you're right.

Just to prove it to myself, I give myself over to the kiss and keep my hands on his waist, softly touching.

I will never grasp for love again.

Cody and I sit holding hands in the wee-hour quiet of the Studio Club courtyard. The night air is warm and comforting. We've talked the evening away, him sharing stories of his tour and me talking of work and how Bobbi and I fell out.

"I'm sorry I couldn't be here for you," he says.

"You make it sound like something *kept* you away."

"It did. While I was at Berkeley at the end of May, I got involved with CORE."

"Oh my God, you went?" That acronym needed no explanation after the national news of the missing civil rights workers last summer. A wave of cold fear washes over me, even though the danger to Cody has long passed.

When the three voter registration workers disappeared in Mississippi, I had no doubt those boys were dead in a swamp. Or at the bottom of an old well. Or burned to ash. But I kept my mouth shut and avoided talking about it. Which made for some uncomfortable moments. It was a lot like being back home—conversations fell quiet when I walked into a room, people cast sideways looks and whispered after I passed. As if everyone with a Southern accent was a murdering bigot.

"I did. And I'd do it again," he says. "They prepared us for harassment—trained us how to handle it. But until I got there—" He shakes his head. "I had no idea things could be like that in this country."

I pull my hand from his, trying not to feel tainted by association, but his words make me defensive.

He looks directly into my eyes. "All the time I was there, knowing that was your home, I wondered—"

"If I'm a racist, too?"

"Don't be ridiculous. I've seen how kind you are, how sensitive to anyone in need."

I'm quiet for a moment, recalling the argument Gran and Dad had years ago. "I'm not defending what's going on there, but like everywhere else, some people are small-minded and terrified of change. They've been taught, cradle to grave for generations, that life is a certain way. For someone to come and tell them that they and all their ancestors are wrong-minded is hard to swallow. The ones who make us all look bad"—people like Grayson Collie— "don't want to lose their easy targets."

"Is that why you left after your father died?"

"There are a lot of reasons I left. Civil rights and the Klan never entered into it."

"I see." He sounds disappointed.

"No, you don't. When my best friend and I got old enough, our friendship just couldn't continue because she's Negro and I'm white. So the only racial motivation I had was my own personal deprivation, not anyone else's." I lift a shoulder. "It sounds selfish."

"It sounds complicated." He takes my hand again. "We've spent so little time together, I know so little about your life, but I feel so, so—connected to you."

"You've probably filled in the blanks with things that make you think I'm a better person than I actually am." *Just like I've probably done with you.* "Maybe we should just leave it at that." The idea of stopping this before it goes further is both painful and a relief. Crazy and disparate emotions. A combination that leads to nothing but volatility and pain.

"How can you say that? I want to know everything about you."

If that's true, why did you disappear for five months and not write more than thirteen words to me?

"It's 4:00 a.m. I'm too tired to tell you everything," I say in a teasing tone that I hope will lighten things up.

He leans in and kisses me gently. "I'm a patient guy."

My new mantra: *I am not Margo. I am not my father. I will not be that weak.* Although the hours fly when Cody and I are together, I haven't handed him the key that unlocks my ability to draw breath.

On a Saturday in mid-October, Cody picks me up directly from work. I change clothes in the back of the bus as he drives to beat the sun to the water.

Now we're sitting shoulder to shoulder on the beach north of the Santa Monica Pier. We've walked to where the wide sand narrows and it's more private.

Each beach I've been to has its own personality. Malibu is an outlier, staid and quiet. Huntington Beach is surf and music centered, low-key and plain-Jane with its oil derricks and quaint City of Huntington Beach Pav-a-lon. Just over two miles south of where we now sit in near seclusion is the noisy, lively Pacific Ocean Park, where for $1.91 (their claim to fame) Cody and I spent a whole Saturday enjoying the rides. No one seems to mind that the park is an unlikely mix of nautical and space-aged themes; its Diving Bells, Sea Serpent roller coaster scrambled in with Space Wheels and Trip to Mars. But I found the incongruity of it unsettling.

Before we left the amusement park, he put a dime in that creepy robotic gypsy fortune-teller and had me pull the lever: *Your past will collide with your future; a new nightmare begets a new dawn.* He laughed. "Lame. Whose past doesn't collide with their future every damn day?" But something in those words sent a shiver down my spine. Maybe because I'm working so hard to keep my past back where it belongs.

I wiggle my bare feet deep into the sand just off the edge of our blanket, enjoying the solid feel of his side pressed against mine as we drink half-warm beers. Maybe that's one of the things I like about Cody, no incongruities. He says what he thinks, voices his passions, and there is no tangled rope of opposing emotions. His feelings are well defined and stay in their proper lanes.

"So now are you going to tell me what's in the bag?" he asks.

I pick up the brown grocery sack and unroll the top. "Drumroll, please."

He obliges by drumming his hands on his thighs.

Reaching in the bag, I pull out an I. Magnin box filled with peanut butter fudge with chopped peanuts on the bottom and chocolate chips on the top.

His face lights up when I pull off the lid and lift the wax paper. He reaches right in. "Where did you find it?" He pops a piece in his mouth. "I thought my mom was the only one who made it like this."

"I hope it's close. I found a peanut butter fudge recipe, but had to guess at the rest."

"You made it?"

"I did." I can't help smiling my pride. "The kitchen at the Studio Club doesn't have a candy thermometer, so I had to use the drop of syrup in cold water method. Is it the right consistency?"

"Perfect!" He gives me a peanut butter flavored kiss. "Thank you."

"I wanted to do something special. It's been a month." As I say it, I feel silly and girlish. Adults probably don't celebrate something as commonplace as dating for a month. But every day since he returned, I wake with happiness in my heart.

"It has. But I count longer, from the day we met." He kisses me again, then leans his forehead against mine. "The Frisbee was no accident, you know. Somehow I knew you were special, different. And your heart is even bigger, you're even stronger than I could have imagined." I lay my head on his shoulder and his arm comes around me. "Still, I hope you don't expect me to share this fudge."

I chuckle as the flaming orange sun inches closer to the water. The upper parts of the few fluffy clouds go a deep, vibrant blue as their rippled undersides show various shades of electrified purple and pink. I haven't felt this calm and at peace . . . well, ever. I'm in the perfect place, not longing for time to push forward or lingering over things past. I'm not even dithering over whether Cody is making me feel this way, or if it's the infinity of the ocean and the reliability of the arc of the sun.

Cody calls sunset nirvana for surfers, a mystical time when the link between soul, sea, and sky is strongest. If what I feel now is anything like that, it's no wonder they paddle out there regardless of frigid water or failing light.

I open my mouth to tell Cody that I understand. Then snap it closed. If I tell him what this moment is making me feel, the release of the tightly wound barbed wire that has been within me my whole life, I'll have to explain why it's there in the first place. He thinks I'm fearless. Strong. Perfect.

I'm so lost in my own thoughts, his voice startles me slightly when he says, "As long as I live, sunset will remind me of you."

A beautiful sentiment, but a flutter of panic disrupts my perfect peace. I stay silent and keep my eyes trained on the colorful western sky, but I can feel his gaze still on me.

Touching my chin, he turns my face toward him. His eyes look even greener, his dark lashes in sharper contrast, in the declining golden light. That sensation of falling hits me hard. I can't retreat. My only defense is to close my eyes.

His hand slips behind my neck, and his thumb caresses my cheek. "Look at me, Tallulah."

Instead, I lean forward and kiss him. Then I try to settle back, put some space between us, but he holds my face close to his. I fight the urge to close my eyes against the intensity of his gaze once again.

"Sunset is supposed to be the dying of the day," he says in a near whisper. "Since I met you, it's where the day begins." His kiss is restrained, a question of its own. "I need you. More than I've ever needed anyone." He's waiting. Waiting for me to speak. Finally, he says, "Tell me what you're thinking."

Your intensity makes me want to break away and run. And yet, I want to climb inside your skin and become one person. I'm terrified of myself.

I cannot fall into the vortex of my own emotions. "We're missing the sunset." I manage to wriggle down and resettle my head on his shoulder.

He places an arm around me, and I hear his sigh of disappointment. But I can't speak the words he wants to hear. Not now that I know that with a few simple words he can wreak havoc on my hard-won inner peace.

The bottom of the sun hits the water and I hold my breath, waiting for this fear to pass, my nirvana to return.

One by one, the surfers disappear until Cody and I are totally alone under a dark moonless sky, listening to the hypnotic roll of the surf.

Finally he says, "Tell me something you've never told anyone else."

So many things flash in my mind: My parents loved so wildly, they destroyed each other. My father was a tormented man. My brother betrayed my trust. My mother is a self-centered hypocrite. My grandmother has secrets so dark she'd rather lose me than reveal them. I'm afraid if I love you, you'll destroy me. Instead, I stay safe and say, "I used to think that if I held my breath, bad things wouldn't be able to touch me."

"Did it work?"

"Probably about the same percentage of the time that doing nothing did."

"Huh. Imagine that. So, what were these bad things?" He ducks his head close to my ear. "Monsters under the bed? Boogeymen in the closet?"

"Nothing quite so imaginary." My voice is flat and cold, far from the flippant air I aimed for.

"I don't like the sound of that." He twists so he can look at me. "Tell me."

"Spiders. Tornadoes. Math tests."

"Tallulah." He pushes my hair away from my face, and I can see his frustration-laced disappointment. "That list could belong to anyone. Talk to me. *Share* with me."

It won't change anything except how you look at me.

"I want to know the little girl who grew into this woman. Don't hide her from me."

He told me part of what he dislikes about performing is the way girls grasp at the idea of what he is, having no interest in *who* he is. He says he liked the way I didn't fall for an idea, that I held myself back waiting to *know* him.

He gives of himself so freely—his trust, his soul, his love. I know the name of the teddy bear that lost an arm when Cody was five; of his best friend in grade school; of the first girl he kissed (in fourth grade, little Casanova). He told me about his terrible fights with his father and the handful of words he regrets saying but will never apologize for. I know his baby sister nearly drowned and his mother has never forgiven herself—mostly because his father won't let her. I know he thinks his parents should have gotten divorced, but stubbornly remain mired in their misery because they think it's better than giving up. I know he values beauty over money, principle over success, truth over everything.

And I have stingily meted out only the things I want him to see. He wants more—deserves more. Yet fear keeps my words locked inside.

I lace my fingers behind his neck. "My time with you is special. I don't want to waste it talking about my boring childhood."

"I want to know every tiny, boring detail of your life. I'm in love with you, Tallulah."

Tell him. Tell him now how you feel.

But I can't. Instead, I show him with a kiss full of love and need.

We lie back on the blanket, his hands gentle yet echoing the hunger in my kiss as they slide under my top and pull it over my head. As his kisses trail down my neck, across my collarbone, I realize this is the moment I've been waiting for since I fled from his first kiss, the moment that will bind us together forever in my memory. There is a fire in this need, burning so hot and bright it cannot last. But we have this moment. Now.

All I can think about is getting closer to him. I unbutton his shirt and run my hands over his skin. He's trembling. I'm breathless. I slide my hand between us, caressing him through his shorts.

"My God," he breathes, his forehead against mine. "You'd better stop that."

He's said it before and I have. But this is the place. This is the time. "No."

That one small word leads to soaring joy.

We stay on the beach, cocooned in our blanket, chilled but warm in each other's arms, until the sky begins to lose its inky darkness.

27

Colors are brighter. Smells stronger. The lyrics to love songs at last reveal their hidden meanings. Every brush against my skin sets off erotic thoughts of Cody under that endless velvety sky. Not even the dullness of the hosiery department or Loretta's cattiness can bring me down.

Tonight Cody's playing at Pandora's Box, an outlandishly painted building right in the mix of the strip where music people come to scout out talent (*and* it's not an over-twenty-one venue). I've never seen him onstage, and the prospect makes me a little nervous—for him or for me, I'm not sure. As I wait in the long line out front, everyone is talking about the headline band, but occasionally I catch Cody's name floating around. It's all I can do not to claim him as mine.

The decor inside is bare bones. I find a beat-up bentwood bistro chair near the front.

By the time Cody steps up to the microphone, the house is packed, which fills me with personal pride, as if I have anything to do with his talent. Girls exclusively fill the first few rows. They're not Beatles kind of crazy, but they're vocal enough that I know they're swooning over Cody before he even opens his mouth. I think about what he said, how none of these girls mean anything to him.

As he begins to sing, instead of the crowd ramping up to the level of insanity that keeps anyone from hearing the Beatles when they perform, the room falls quiet. What I see on the stage is a doppelgänger, he looks exactly like Cody, but there's something ethereal about him as he loses himself in his music. The emotions he paints are so real, so compelling. And his voice—rich and rangy, plaintive, deliciously restrained, then powerful. I lean forward, straining to grasp every nuance. And I'm not alone.

When he begins the last number in his set, he locks eyes with me and sings the song I heard bits of on the piano the night he returned. A song so hauntingly beautiful and heartbreaking, not only am I crying, so is every girl in the building . . . even a few guys are wiping their eyes.

As he bows his head with the last note, the silence hangs in the air for so long I begin to panic. Did I misread the crowd?

And then, the whole place erupts. Cheers. Applause. Whistles.

I cannot believe he's in love with me. I feel unworthy.

Girls rush the stage. The manager can't get things back under control so the headlining band can get set up. Finally, he resorts to squawking the mic long enough to get the attention of even the deaf. Cody finally extricates himself and pushes through the crowd, straight to me. He's holding his guitar by the neck with one hand, his other arm wraps me tight. His voice is hot in my ear. "Did you like it?"

I pull back and look at him. "I. Am. In. Awe."

His smile carries as much potency as his performance. Good thing he's holding me, because my knees go a little weak.

"Is it always like this . . . the crowd reaction, I mean?" I ask.

He shrugs. "Sometimes. Other times I'm playing to a room with four people in it, two of them asleep, the other two playing a game of chess."

"I can't imagine how anyone can pay attention to anything but you when you're on that stage."

"Believe me, it happens. But I'm happy you liked it. I was worried."

"Oh my God! You have to be kidding."

His eyes grow serious. "You're the only thing that matters more to me than this music." Before I can deflect his intensity with a glib comment, his lips are on mine, and I forget we're in a room full of people.

But Cody soon remembers and hurries us outside.

We barely get the VW door closed behind us before we're naked in his bed in the bus. Our first lovemaking is all fire and desperation. The second is something so tender I feel uneasily defenseless afterward and turn away. He pulls my back to his chest. "God, I love you."

I wriggle free and start gathering my scattered clothes. "We'd better get dressed before the police come knocking on the steamed-up windows."

He grabs my hand. "Come to Berkeley with me."

"Berkeley?" I slip my dress over my head, shielding my vulnerability. "For a show?"

"There are plenty of music opportunities up there, sure. But there are also a lot of important things happening. Last week they arrested a guy for handing out fliers for CORE. The college administration has no right to control what their students *say*. Anyway, the students blocked the police car he was loaded into for two days. The car became a podium for free speech and civil rights. The police finally let the guy go. People are making a *difference* there."

The very idea of a crowd pressed around a police car in protest makes my entire body revolt. Too much anger. Too many bodies. Too much uncertainty.

I think of Griff's sullen form behind Mr. Rykerson's shattered windshield.

"Was there violence?" Back in July, there were riots in Harlem. Six days of yelling and rocks and bottles and nightsticks and fires. So much hatred. Just seeing it on the news ignited the same dark, oily sickness in my belly that living in our house on Pearl River Plantation sometimes did.

"No," he says. "That's what's so great about it. If enough people band together and show their will, speak their piece, violence isn't necessary."

I've seen plenty of violence wrought with just two people who refused to budge. I think Cody is being naive, but I don't say so.

On the other hand, if simply standing for free speech and civil rights can do some good, shouldn't I get involved? I think of Maisie and how she could have a different life, one with more choices.

"When will we come back?" I ask.

"Does it matter? Maybe never."

Can I just run off with Cody because I feel like it?

"I don't have much money saved up," I say. "I need to work."

"Don't they say two can live as cheaply as one? I'll be able to keep us fed and gas in the bus. What more do we need?"

Just pick up and go? This is so far from anything I've ever considered. But isn't this what I came out here for? To be free? To live how I choose?

"Come on, Tallulah." He cups my cheek. "We're good together."

"Maybe we're good together because we're still new." Daddy and Margo could go a long time with things being good—until they weren't. "And what happens if I give up my job and my room and a week down the road you change your mind and want to be rid of me?"

He takes my face in his hands and kisses me. "I'll never want to be rid of you. Come with me."

Then it hits me. He's going. With or without me, he's going. The idea of another long separation makes me light-headed.

He says, "You didn't have a job or a place to stay when you came to LA, did you? It's the same—except you won't be alone. You'll have me."

"What if I say no?"

The hurt in his eyes is clear and immediate. "Don't ask me not to do this, Tallulah. I want to be involved. Don't you?"

"I'm not asking you not to. I'm asking what happens to us if I don't go with you?" As I say it, I realize the only thing holding me here is a meaningless job.

I *need* to be with him, near him, beside him as he makes his music and fights for what's right. I want it so much, I can't trust myself.

He scrubs his hand over his face. "I don't know. I want you with me. If you stay here, I don't know how long I'll be gone."

"You make it sound like it could be months." Months of here, alone, working my mind-numbing job, going to parties I don't care about with people I don't really want to know. *Or I could be doing something that matters.*

"That's why I live in my bus. I want to be able to go anywhere. And I don't want to be with anyone but you. What's tying you here?"

A thunderbolt hits me: I am not bound here just because Griff picked it years ago. As always, I'm complicating the simple by worrying about what other people want, instead of what I want.

And I *want* to go with Cody. I *want* to do things that matter. That will help Maisie. If Cody and I don't work out, I'll figure out the next step on my own, just like I did when I came to LA. I am young. I am free. Unlike Margo, I'm not abandoning anyone to fight for this cause.

Before my self-talk can change direction, I throw my arms around his neck and say, "I'm tied to nothing but you. So yes, I'll go."

It turns out two might live as cheaply as one, but two adults living in a VW bus is too cramped, even for Cody. By the end of November, we're renting a room with a kitchenette and a bath in a house near Berkeley's campus on a week-to-week basis. I'm volunteering for CORE and filling in part-time at a coffeehouse where Cody sometimes plays. The best nights are the ones when he's performing, when I feel as if he's singing only to me.

If someone had told me when I left Mississippi a year ago I'd be this deliriously happy, I would have laughed in their face. But I am. Our life is simple. Uncomplicated. Spontaneous. Finally, I have the freedom my California dreams promised.

As we leave the coffeehouse late one damp chilly night, the air between us is electric. I can't wait until we walk the few blocks to our room. I grab his hand and pull him into a small neighborhood park surrounded by a brick wall.

"Why, Tallulah James, are you trying to take advantage of me?" He sets down his guitar case on a picnic table and wraps his arms around me.

"Indeed I am."

"Remind me to sing to you more often." His words are slurred and breathless as his hands roam over my secret familiar places.

Making love out in the open reminds me of our first time. It must for him, too, because it drives him deeper and just a little wilder. Afterward, our disheveled clothes are soaked with sweat. The chilly air is welcome against bits of exposed skin. His forehead is pressed against mine, our foggy puffs of breath mingling between us. He gently rearranges my clothes before his own.

His arm is tight around me as we walk out of the park. "I can feel you drifting away already," he says softly, not unkindly.

"What do you mean?" I tighten my grip around his waist, confirming I'm right here.

"It's always like this. Just when we should feel the closest, when you should be able to share everything in your soul, you back away."

I can't become my parents. It seems no matter how I try to maintain the wall between then and now, something dark and ruinous always seeps through.

"You're imagining things," I say. "I'm just . . . content."

"All right, so, tell me one special thing about your life in Mississippi."

"Welllll." I draw the word out, as if I'm sorting the vast number of special things my home held. But all I'm doing is looking for one that won't change the way he looks at me.

I decide to tell him about Maisie. I tell him about our summers in the orchard, about her Pappy Stokes and his bees, about the long connection between our families, about her quitting school and going into domestic service even though she was way too smart to be polishing silver and being bossed around by Mrs. Delmore. As I speak, a cold emptiness sits just below my heart. I realize how very much I miss her. I miss having someone who already knows the dirty secrets in my family, someone who understands my life without me having to drag it out for show and tell.

As we walk into our room, he says, "She sounds like a good friend. But you've spent the past twenty minutes telling me about *her*, not about you."

I kiss him on the cheek. "I'm exhausted and need a shower to get rid of this cigarette smoke." I drop my coat on the bed, hurry into the bathroom, and close the door. I lean with my back against it and close my eyes.

The door pushes against my back. I step away and let it swing open.

"What happened to you that's so horrible that you can't trust me with it?" he asks with pain in his eyes.

I stand there for a long moment, reaching deep but once again falling short of being able to drag the past out and lay it before him. "Nothing horrible happened. I'm just tired."

"What am I to you?" His tone borders on cold.

"What do you mean?"

"I love you with all of my heart. But I have no idea what I mean to you."

I am terrified what I feel for you will overcome me, wipe out my will to live if you leave. If I admit it or if I let you see the ugliness hiding in my blood, it will give you a weapon to destroy me.

"I feel the same." As soon as I say it, his face hardens.

"Well, it doesn't feel that way. For you, this relationship is all sex and no substance."

I reach for him, as I always do, to show him what I can't seem to find the strength to say.

He pushes me away.

I'm so hurt, I lash out. "I thought that's what guys call the ideal relationship. Why can't that be enough for you?"

"You are unbelievable." He turns around and slams the bathroom door behind him.

I allow myself a good cry in the shower and convince myself it's unfair of Cody to demand more than I can give. When I come out of the bathroom, he's in our bed asleep, or pretending to be asleep.

We spend the next few days in a mix of exaggerated politeness and silence.

Finally, time and our chemistry wear us down and, without acknowledgment or apology, we go back to the way we were. Me pretending I'm giving as much as I'm getting, and him letting me believe it will be enough.

28

The day is overcast, the air San Francisco chilly. I'm filled with snakes and shards as we approach the antiwar protest. I spent my childhood living with this walking-through-a-minefield tension and hoped never to experience it again.

As always, Cody reads my mood. "Relax. This is a march for *peace*. Civil disobedience, remember?"

Every month I hold my breath, fearing Cody will be called up for the draft. LBJ's escalation in Vietnam has increased the number alarmingly. Unprotected by student deferment or the Canadian border, how long will Cody's luck last? But the draft isn't the only shadow creeping at our backs. A distance is growing between us. And in the dark of night when I can no longer distract myself, I fear we are simply a habit, one Cody doesn't have the will to break, and I don't have the strength to heal.

"I'm fine." A lie. I'm back in my bedroom closet on Pearl River Plantation waiting for the hurricane of my parents' violence to pass.

He puts an arm around my shoulder. "I can tell you're nervous. Talk to me."

What good will it do to shine a spotlight on my fears? Without the illusion of strength and fearlessness, will there be anything left in me for Cody to love?

"I'm really okay."

He stops dead and the stream of people heading onto campus flows around us. "Dammit, Tallulah. I'm sick to death of being shut out."

Does he think I want to lay my soul bare in the middle of thousands of people?

"How much farther in do you think you can get?" I say suggestively, and start to walk on.

He grabs my arm and stops me. "Why do you always do that?"

"Do what?"

"Dodge. Deflect. Hide. I swear to God, sometimes I feel like you're a stranger."

"How can you say that? We've lived together for months."

"And that's what makes it so fucking sad." He walks away, leaving me dry-mouthed and angry.

I consider turning around and going back to our apartment. But the idea of Cody being shipped off to die in a jungle halfway around the world fills me with so much fear that I move forward to add my voice to the chorus against the draft. I keep Cody's blond head in sight in the crowd. As I move in tandem with him, fearing being separated by more than a few feet, it strikes me how dependent I've allowed myself to become. How long will it be before I slip into Daddy's kind of immobilizing gloom when Cody's physically or emotionally unavailable?

The mass of people becomes dense. Cody's talking to a girl I recognize from the coffeehouse—Stephanie, or Samantha, or something feminine and S-ish. She's touching his arm; no doubt baring her innermost emotions and insecurities, speaking directly to his heart. I'm used to girls flocking around him. Today for the first time, it sparks panic.

Can I give him what he wants? After all this time, am I going to admit my lies of omission—that I'm only eighteen, when he thinks I'm twenty-two? How will I explain that I don't want the children he talks about because of the twisted sickness that runs in my blood? Is truth—Cody's most precious commodity—delayed so thoughtfully and in such a calculated way better than no truth at all?

The crush of people is suddenly on the move, marching our parade of antiwar chants and placards. I shuffle along, my mind on Cody and not the war or the draft or any higher cause. Suddenly there's a flurry of movement off to my right. Two men push into our ranks, flailing fists, shouting that we're all communists and cowards.

More people surge in from the sidelines, shoving, shouting.

A kid is on the ground, curled and covering his head from the kicks of a burly man in a seaman's jacket. I throw myself at the man, trying to knock him away, give the kid a chance to get back to his feet. The man catches me with a forearm and flicks me off like a flea.

A knot of struggling bodies knocks me to the ground. My cheek hits the pavement. A heavy foot lands between my shoulder blades, knocking the breath out of me.

Get up. Get up. You're going to be crushed.

A scuffling foot kicks my thigh.

Tennis shoes, loafers, and boots engage in brutal dance before my eyes.

My breath gone, I'm drowning just like I drowned in that river. But no one is here to save me.

The movement around me ebbs. I don't know how long I've been on the ground. Sixty seconds? Six minutes?

Then gentle hands come to my rescue. Cody?

But it's a stranger. Cody's moved on with the crowd.

I sit on the curb and wait for the shaking to stop, waiting for Cody to come looking for me. But he doesn't. He cares more about the march than about me. And that crushes me more than the boot in my back.

After a while, I pick myself up and walk back to our apartment, where I clean the scrape on my cheek and lift the back of my shirt to see a foot-size bruise.

Cody knew I was afraid in that crowd. And still he left me.

I sit on our bed in the dark, waging an inner war of my own. The entire day points to one thing: Cody and I are in serious trouble. Do I want to fight or surrender? To fight means to give up even more of myself. And I already feel far too dependent.

The door to our room opens. "Tallulah?"

"I'm here."

He flips on the overhead light. "Oh my God! Are you all right?"

Sitting next to me on the bed, he pushes my hair away from my scraped cheek.

"I got knocked down." I pull away from his touch. "And you left me."

"I figured you came home, since you didn't want to be there anyway."

I'm so furious I can't breathe. "When that fight broke out, you didn't even look for me!"

"I should have made sure you left. But dammit, you are wearing me down."

"You're trying to make this," I motion to my cheek, "my fault? You knew I was nervous, and you just walked off with that girl."

"Treat me like a stranger long enough, and I suppose I begin acting like one. I can't love enough for both of us, and God knows I've tried."

"You're saying it was okay for you to abandon me out there because I don't love you enough?"

"I'm saying it's time to stop dragging the carcass of our relationship around and bury it in the ground. I've seen what not giving up on a lost cause did to my parents. I won't do that to us."

"You're leaving me?" I remind myself I was just ready to leave *him*. Easy to think when it's not really happening.

"I never really had you, did I?"

"I love you!"

"You love me?" He jumps to his feet, shoving his hands roughly through his hair. "*Now* you love me?" He shakes his head, and I'm stunned by the anger I see in his eyes. "Do you know how you've made me feel, declaring my love for you, never hearing it in return?"

"Haven't I shown you that I care? I moved here. I was at that march, a place that terrifies me, because of you."

"And yet, still I don't know the *reason* it terrifies you. Or any other fucking thing about what's going on under your skin. I don't know what you think love is, but to me it means sharing everything."

"I do love you, Cody. I just . . ."

"I've respected your boundaries, thinking one day you would trust me enough to let me see the wounds you're hiding, let me help you heal them. But it's clear you don't want me to. Now I'm bonedry. There is no more love in me."

My whole body is shaking. *If I had shown you the truth, you would have been gone long before now.*

He grabs a canvas duffel and starts throwing his lyric notebooks and clothes into it. I watch in silence as he picks it and his guitar up. He stops with his hand on the doorknob, perhaps offering one last chance for me to open a vein for him.

"Take care of yourself, Tallulah."

And then he's gone. Out of my life in an instant, wrenching my heart from my chest and throwing it in the dirt.

29

August 1972
New Orleans, Louisiana

Unable to sleep after leaving Ross in the garden last night, I surrender the effort at 5:00 a.m. I drag myself to the kitchen in search of coffee. Gran is already sitting at the table, fully dressed, the cup of coffee in front of her cold enough the cream scums the top. She's so lost in thought that she startles when I speak to her.

"You unable to sleep, either?"

She pushes herself up from the table. "Let me get you some breakfast. Ross has a nicely stocked refrigerator for a bachelor."

"Sit, Gran. I just need to start with a good dose of coffee."

"You know how I feel about breakfast."

"I do. And I believe you. But this morning, I'm not sure my stomach will accept any donations." I pour my coffee and sit across from her. As I do, I recall Ross's promise not to desert me. I hold on to it. I *could* do this alone, I know I could. I've survived worse alone. But I'm surprised to find I don't want to. In fact, I'm tempted to wait until he comes down to tell Gran about Walden's guilty plea.

As if conjured by my thoughts, Ross comes through the back door wearing shorts and running shoes, hair and gray T-shirt drenched with sweat. He pulls up short. "Excuse my appearance, ladies. I thought I'd be back and cleaned up before anyone was up."

"You always run this early?" I ask.

"In the summer. Can't stand the heat once the sun comes up." He fills a glass from a water pitcher in the refrigerator. "Do you run?"

"Only if I'm being chased by a bear."

He leaves the room chuckling.

"I know yesterday got away from us," Gran says, turning her coffee cup in slow circles on the table. "But I think we should call Dharma as soon as the hour is decent."

"Want me to heat that up for you?" I start for the Mr. Coffee, hoping to dodge the subject of Dharma.

"No, thank you." She waves a hand over her still-full cup. "I don't really drink coffee anymore. It just gave me something to do. It's an hour later in New York. So do you think if we wait until seven?"

"Gran, I'm not so sure calling Dharma is that urgent right now."

"I know she can't get here in time for this morning's hearing, but she'll want to talk to him. And she'll need to plan, so she can be here for the trial."

I kneel in front of her. "Gran," I take her hands in mine. "There won't be a trial. Walden is pleading guilty. He asked Amelia not to tell us because he wanted to do it himself. But that was obviously just a way to keep us from knowing ahead of time and arguing with him."

She sits blinking, and I'm not sure she understood me. Then her face clears. "Then we must call Dharma right away! If she can speak to him before the hearing, he'll change his mind. Call your uncle and get her number."

"Has she kept in touch with you or Walden at all?"

"You didn't keep in touch, and you still came when you knew Walden needed you." She pauses. "I understand why you did what you did, Tallulah. I made my choice, and you made yours. But that's behind us. I'm sure Dharma—"

"I already called Uncle Roger. He as much as threatened me if I called Dharma about Walden's arrest."

"Don't you think we need to give her the *chance* to decide on her own?"

If only Margo had let us weigh in before tearing our family apart, maybe we all would have been better off. "Yes," I say. "Yes, I do. I just hope she's listed."

"If not, maybe Ross's private investigator can help." The hopeful note in Gran's voice tells me she's in for a huge disappointment. Even if I do find Dharma.

"I'll use the phone in the library." I pause at the doorway. "Maybe you should be the one to talk to her."

Gran offers a watered-down smile. "Oh, I don't think it matters. She never heeded me any more than anyone else."

She never heeded *anyone*. "I'll do my best to convince her. But, Gran," I pause on my way out of the room. "Don't get your hopes too high that we'll get Walden to change his mind."

Her eyes cloud. "I saw what he's become. But we have to try."

I nod and go to look for one of my needles. At least I know this one is in the New York City haystack.

I first have Information look for Dharma James. Then I nearly smack myself in the head for my stupidity. She was adopted. I have a stroke of luck when the operator finds just one listing for Dharma Vandervere in Manhattan. I'm not surprised she's not using just her first initial as many single women do—Dharma always was about being noticed. And *of course* she's in Manhattan and not the boroughs. Roger Vandervere would never have let his *darling* live anywhere but the best.

The phone rings so many times, I almost give up. Then a groggy, "This had better be fucking important." Unlike me, she has completely shed her Southern accent. She sounds so much like Margo it takes me a second to orient myself.

"Dharma, this is Tallulah."

There's silence for several seconds. "I figured you were dead."

As with Walden, I extend the hand of atonement. "I'm sorry. I just discovered Uncle Roger never gave you my letters. I've thought of you both so often, but felt calling would be bringing Lamoyne too close to your doorstep."

"So why are you bothering me now?"

"Something's happened and I, we, think you should know."

"And by *we* you mean?"

"Gran and I. Walden is in some serious trouble and he needs—"

"I watch the news."

The detachment in her voice is chilling.

"He's going to plead guilty," I say. "He's protecting that cult leader. We were hoping you could try to talk to him, convince him to change his plea. Then we can work on getting him to accept legal help."

"It looks to me like he *is* guilty."

I still can't get myself to admit my sweet brother could have done something so barbaric. "He won't have a chance at all if he pleads guilty. He's been brainwashed."

"He's obviously as batshit crazy as Dad was, so it's probably safer for everyone if he's off the streets. Who knows what he'll do next."

"Jesus, Dharma, he's your brother."

"I am an only child now. And it suits me just fine. If this carries on, there are people in Michigan who might make the connection to the Vandervere family. So the quicker this is out of the news, the better. Besides, there's nothing I can say that's going to change his mind—not if his *favorite* sister can't."

Jealous as ever. "Won't you try? Please. For Gran."

"No. Not for Gran. Not for you. Not for Griff. Not for Walden. Not for Margo."

I grasp at my only remaining straw. "Do you know where Margo is?" If Dharma won't get involved, maybe Margo will.

"Some commune out west, last anyone heard—but that was five years ago, when she contacted Daddy needing money."

Daddy. Dharma finally has the undivided adoration of a parent. "Where out west?"

"I have no idea. Neither does Daddy, so don't call him. He cut her off. I have to get back to sleep. I have a performance tonight."

The phone goes dead in my hand, and my heart goes cold in my chest.

About five minutes later, Ross sticks his head into the library. "Lavada said you're trying to find Dharma."

"Oh, I found her."

He comes and sits on the edge of the desk as I recap for him.

"I'm sorry," he says, then looks at his watch. "We need to head to the courthouse."

The phone on the desk rings. Before I remember this is Ross's house, I snatch it up. "Dharma, I knew—"

"Tallulah, this is Amelia. I'm afraid I don't have good news."

I reach out and grab Ross's hand. "He won't change his plea."

"All we can do now is look toward sentencing."

I hang up the phone, feeling weak and gut-punched, even though I knew this was the likely outcome.

Ross pulls me out of the chair and holds me close.

"I don't know how I'm going to tell Gran about Dharma."

"Just like you wish she'd always dealt with you. With unflinching honesty."

I stand back, taking his hand again. "You'll help me?"

"Lulie, I'd do anything you ask."

And just like that, calm, steady Ross Saenger opened another door inside me.

My mouth goes dry looking up at the massive limestone Orleans Parish courthouse where Walden's fate will be decided. The stairs to the colonnaded entrance rise in a daunting mountain. My reservations about Gran's ability to climb them are short-lived as she grabs a handrail and starts up before either Ross or me. Inside, the arched hallways echo footsteps in a nerve-racking way.

We take seats right behind the defendant's table. The row is empty but for us and a man with a sketch pad sitting at the far end. I suddenly wish I had the comfort of my own sketch pad.

Walden is led into the courtroom looking exactly as he did yesterday, handcuffed, unkempt, and detached. Gran grabs one of my hands, Ross the other. Walden doesn't look at us. He sits alone at the defense table, still as stone.

The judge is a grouchy-looking man with a head like a bowling ball. I spent last night thanking God for the moratorium on the death penalty imposed by the Supreme Court a couple of years ago, still fearing a charge of first-degree murder. I feel a little weak with relief when the charges are aggravated criminal damage and manslaughter. According to Amelia, that was the best we could hope for.

The judge then asks Walden to confirm that he has refused counsel. It takes three times to get him to respond verbally. The judge urges him to reconsider. To this, Walden stands mute.

The judge asks for his plea.

Just buy us more time. Please. Please. Please.

Walden holds his silence.

"If you do not enter a plea," the judge says, "the court will record not guilty."

"Guilty." Walden's voice is loud and strong.

My stomach takes a slow roll.

Beside me, I hear a stifled whimper from Gran, but I don't have the courage to look at her.

The judge remands him to the county jail to await sentencing, bangs his gavel, and it's over. Walden has surrendered his future and his freedom for a man who used him and then betrayed him.

The deputy steps over to escort Walden from the court.

I stand, hoping the motion will draw his attention. But he never turns. A tingling numbness takes over my body as I watch him saunter from the courtroom, once a beloved, sweet innocent, now an unfeeling, murdering stranger.

I glance down at Gran. She looks like someone just pushed her off a cliff. She took my report of my conversation with Dharma (a fully honest recounting) so well that it was obvious she had little hope of a different outcome. But she clearly hadn't given up on Walden's plea.

Ross and I each take an elbow to help her stand. She wobbles slightly but holds her head high as we walk out. As soon as we step outside the courthouse doors, we hit a wall of cameras and reporters thrusting microphones in our faces. They are pressed so close, we can't move forward.

"You're the family of Walden James?"

Before I think, I nod.

Camera flashes flare. Shoulder-held TV cameras nudge closer.

The questions are rapid and overlapping:

"Can you tell us anything about the cult he belonged to?"

"Does his guilty plea surprise you?"

"Do you have reservations about him refusing counsel?"

"How long has he been a disciple of Westley Smythe and the Scholars of Humanity?"

Ross leads with a shoulder and pushes us through. "Excuse us."

The questions keep coming, the voices louder, more condemning. The television cameras pace us all the way to the bottom of the long flight of steps and halfway to the parking lot.

By the time we get Gran settled in the car, she's trembling and pale. "What is wrong with those people? How can they be so heartless?"

Even as I attempt to calm her, it astounds me that after spending most of her adult life as grist for the Lamoyne rumor mill, she can even ask this question.

30

There was no shock in the outcome of today's hearing, and yet Ross, Gran, and I are acting just that, shocked. Consequently, the afternoon has been extraordinarily quiet.

Amelia told us it could be a month or more before he's sentenced, depending on the court calendar. There are no phone calls to inmates in the Orleans Parish jail, and no one can force Walden to accept visitors. I'll keep trying to convince him to accept help through letters, but it appears Walden has made his bed and wants to lie in it.

Gran is in her bedroom, presumably napping, but I hear her moving around up there occasionally. Ross disappeared into the library to catch up on paperwork. I've been drifting through the high-ceilinged rooms, studying the art, looking at magazines—I found *Psychology Today* particularly fascinating. I walked the garden, reacquainting myself with funnel-shaped, vibrant hibiscus blooms and glossy-leaved white-flowered camellias, restless and unfocused—yet glad to be alone.

My life in San Francisco is a series of planned movements with little variance to my well-worn path, a disciplined work schedule and a quiet apartment. I'm well suited to it, much more than to the footloose life I had with Cody. But until now, I never realized how much I need solitude.

It's nearly four o'clock when I knock lightly on the library door.

"Come on in," Ross says.

"Sorry to interrupt, but I need to get a rental car. Gran seems done in, so I'd like to wait until morning to drive her home. That is if you don't mind having houseguests another night?"

He stands and walks toward me. "I'd have you both stay forever." The look in his eyes is serious enough that it sets off those teenage flutters.

"What car rental is the most convenient?"

"I'll drive you two up in the morning."

"Thank you, but no. You've already disrupted your life too much for us. Besides, it's nearly a six-hour round trip, and I have to get back to New Orleans to fly home anyway. Renting a car is the only sensible option."

"Leave it to you to be sensible when it comes to protecting someone else's needs." He surprises me by giving me a quick kiss on the forehead. "I'll arrange for the car."

"Thank you." I turn away and peruse the bookshelves. "I've always wanted a home with a library—such a sense of stability, a place too refined for bad things to happen."

He comes up behind me, close enough that I can feel the heat of him on my back. "I wish I could take away your painful memories."

I think of my domino trails. Painful events set me on every one of them. I turn and face him again. "Just lately I've realized those memories made me who I am. Who would I have become without them?"

His hand cups my cheek, and his eyes hold mine. "You might be a little freer, more open, and less guarded. But still you."

I have a strange sense of falling as I stare into his eyes.

The phone on the desk rings and we both jump.

"That's a call I scheduled," he says. "I need a file from my car." He moves toward the door. "Will you pick it up and tell him I'll be right there?"

"Sure." I pick up the receiver, still a little off-balance from the kiss that almost happened. "Saenger residence."

"Mrs. Saenger?"

"No, I'm a houseguest. Dr. Saenger will be right with you. He just went to get a file."

"Doctor?"

"Oh, I'm sorry. Aren't you the call he scheduled?"

"No." There's a pause, long enough I begin to think he cut the connection. "Lulie, is that you?" That voice, familiar, yet different.

"Griff?" I sit down hard on the desk chair.

"Oh my God!" There's a break in his voice. "When Tommy called and said he saw you with Ross, I couldn't believe it." He takes a shuddering breath. "I was calling Ross's mom to get his number . . . and . . . and here you are."

I imagined this moment so many times. Here it is, and all the words I planned to say evaporate from my mind. What's left is an accusation. "Tommy *called* you. Because *he* knows where you are."

"He has a number. I've been—" He cuts off abruptly. "Who are you to complain about not letting anyone know where you are?"

"I suppose that's a draw. Although I never would have left if you hadn't deserted me."

"You know I couldn't stay." His voice is soft, apologetic.

I can't bear this conversation right now. "You know about Walden?"

"Yes."

"The first hearing was this morning. That's why Gran and I are staying with Ross. She wanted you here, too." Even though I know it's unfair, I can't keep the censure from my voice.

Ross walks back into the library, and his brow creases with curiosity. I cover the receiver and give a wide-eyed whisper. "It's Griff!"

Ross tosses his files on the desk. "He's okay?"

I raise my palm in a *Who knows?* gesture.

Griff asks, "How did Walden, of all people, end up in a cult?"

As I fill him in on Walden, the shock of hearing his voice begins to subside, and I begin to gather more solid footing.

"You don't think there's much hope of getting him to accept a lawyer?" he asks.

"Not at this point. But I'm not going to give up trying. Maybe now that he's away from that man's influence, we'll have a chance. Once you get here, maybe he'll respond to you."

"What about Dharma? Maybe she can get through to him."

"She's in New York, on Broadway. Not coming. Imagine Margo multiplied by ten."

"Shit."

"Exactly. So it's just you and me."

"Lulie," Griff says. "I—I can't come."

"What do you mean you can't come? If it's the money, I'll buy you an airline ticket. Gran needs you here."

"It's not the money. I just can't come. Maybe in a couple of months."

My temper spikes. "A couple of months will be too late for Walden! What am I going to tell Gran?"

"Don't tell her anything."

"That's just cruel—do you want her to go on forever not knowing if you're dead or alive?" *Did I just say that? Would she know I'm alive if not for Walden's mess?* "She's grown so much older. Can you please at least talk to her?"

He's quiet for a moment. "I just can't right now. It wouldn't be fair to talk to her and not be able to answer her questions. But I will. I promise."

"Why are you being so cryptic? Are you in jail?"

He laughs. I hear the old Griff in it, and it makes me realize how un-Griff-like he's sounded.

"If you're not coming, at least give me your phone number so I can contact you with updates on Walden . . . and hunt you down if you break your promise."

"You can get a message to me through Tommy. Once you're back in San Francisco, I'll call you there."

Now Tommy's scribbling when he checked my driver's license makes sense. "Why is Tommy the one with the secret number?"

"I needed someone in Lamoyne to be able to contact me, in case you came back, or something happened to Gran."

"Well, both happened. So now what?"

"I'll come as soon as I can."

"Are you a spy or something?"

"Something." I hear rustling and a muffled groan. "Listen, I have to go. I'm so relieved you're safe."

It strikes me then that his voice has grown weaker as we've talked. I feel a riffle of panic. "Dammit, Griff. Tell me where you are."

"I can't see anyone right now. I have to go."

I hear someone talking in the background.

"Griff? Please."

There's a hitch in his voice when he says, "I—I want— Lulie, I'm sorry I didn't take you to California."

The line goes dead.

I whisper, "Oh, Griff, California wasn't the land of perpetual summer, either."

I thought this wound had healed. But it's as raw and bloody as it was nine years ago. I might not be that broken girl, but I do still long for my brother to take my hand and lead me away from the pain. And I want to do the same for him.

Ross is waiting with expectation on his face. "So?"

"He says he can't come." All my anger has been supplanted with worry. "He won't tell me where he is or what he's doing."

"What *did* he say?" Ross asks.

"Nothing about himself. Just not to tell Gran because it'll be better for *her* and that if I need to tell him anything to go through Tommy."

"I'm sure he has a reason."

None of my suppositions make me feel any better. Jail keeps coming to the top of the list. Or . . . "Oh God, maybe he's in an institution somewhere. What if he is dealing with manic depression? He wouldn't want Gran to know; it'd be too upsetting. But why didn't he trust me?"

He takes my left hand, turning it so the cut on my palm is facing him. Running a finger over the thin, red line left by the arrowhead, he says, "Sometimes the thing you need the most can hurt you the worst."

I look up into his eyes.

"For a long time," I say, "I thought the only way to protect myself was not to allow myself to need."

"And did it?" he asks. "Protect you?"

"It just hurt me in different ways."

He brings my hand to his lips and places a gentle kiss on the palm. "We all hurt, Lulie. Every damn one of us. It's better if we don't do it alone."

The truth of that slices to the bone.

The telephone rings. "That's my call," he says, disappointment coloring his voice. "I'm sorry, I have to take it."

I wave off his apology and leave the library, wondering if what Ross and I share is truly different, or if I'm just so worn down I want someone else to carry the load.

Ross is in the kitchen making a fruit-and-cheese plate when I come downstairs after a long hot shower in which I schemed on how I'm going to get Tommy to give up Griff's number.

"I thought we needed appetizers." A bottle of wine is open and the small television on the kitchen counter is tuned to *Nightly News*. I imagine he spends many evenings like this, making a solo meal with the national news for company, just as I do—with the exception that I have my television tuned to the nonupsetting *Beat the Clock*.

"When I get back to Lamoyne," I say, "I'm going to get that number from Tommy, then I'm going to track down my brother."

"Are you sure you want to do that? Griff said he'd be in touch, right? If he can't come now, maybe he's right about waiting to tell Lavada."

"You're taking his side?"

"I didn't know there were sides."

"Sorry. I'm just so frustrated."

"It is frustrating when a person you care about won't be open with you—won't let you know where they are."

I eye him. "Point taken."

I pick up a grape and roll it between my fingers, thinking of my brothers, both alone by choice, as I have been. It suddenly seems foolish and wasteful. A sense of control can foster the soul only so long. I feel it now, the vacuum of my inner self, where nothing stirs, so nothing changes.

Gran says family traditions are what give meaning to life. But that's not it. The family itself, if we accept it for what it is and not condemn it for what it is not, can be the fiber that weaves a rope that pulls us out of ourselves, and into a world where we're willing to take an emotional risk.

As I'm musing, a cacophony of noise and movement draw my gaze to the television. It's a mob. I hear Walden's name. Ross, Gran, and I fill the screen, trying to get out of the Orleans Parish courthouse. Gran holding her head high. Me looking like a terrified child.

Once the horrendous footage is over, the anchor John Chancellor comes back on and says. "According to our sources, this is his grandmother, Lavada, and his sister, Tallulah, along with prominent New Orleans psychiatrist, Dr. Ross Saenger. They had no comment on his guilty plea. The other two suspects will be arraigned tomorrow. Speculation is that they, too, will plead guilty. But what of the mysterious Westley Smythe? No one has been able to reach him for comment. The question remains, are the Scholars of Humanity a benevolent organization, a fraternity, or a cult?"

The grape explodes between my finger and thumb. "Oh my God. How did they get our names?"

Ross grabs a towel and wipes up the pulverized grape. "I should have shut it off. But this could be good, the media is calling out Smythe."

"There is *nothing* good about this." My body is hot, my hands shaking. My boss, Mr. Capstone, never misses *Nightly News*.

"I need to make a phone call." I head for the library, trying to decide what I can say that will make a difference. Mr. Capstone's most stringent rule is to keep everything that touches the foundation above reproach.

I call him. Any hope of his not having seen the broadcast is destroyed by the chilly tone of his voice.

"Mr. Capstone, I want to apologize for not explaining the situation before I left. I wasn't sure there was validity to the charge at that time."

"And you didn't think to call me between then and now? Bruce has already called in an outrage."

Bruce Buckman, of *the* Buckman family. "I'm sorry, sir. I've been estranged from my family for years. I had no idea—"

"You know my hands are tied. Keith has already called and offered to take over your responsibilities, so nothing will be disrupted."

That was fast. Sharks always are.

Mr. Capstone goes on, "The announcement to the press is going out tonight. You can collect your personal belongings at the security desk whenever you return."

I hang up the phone, sick at heart. I *love* that job. It's all I have. *And whose fault is that?*

31

Ross gave me the space I needed last evening after my conversation with Mr. Capstone. Even this morning he asked no questions, only extracted a promise that I would call him to let him know when Gran and I arrive safely in Lamoyne. I suppose to most people someone expressing concern over their safe arrival wouldn't be extraordinary. But to me, it's as foreign as living underwater.

I missed his reassuring strength the second I drove away. Seeing him again, feeling that sense of connection, has made me reassess the way I've chosen to live. Keeping people at a distance has a cost, one I'm not sure I want to continue to pay.

Coming here has awakened the girl I buried when I left Mississippi. And I miss her, even her vulnerability.

As I drive north, I glance over at Gran. All her efforts to hide the truth, bury the imperfections, preserve the facade, have done nothing but leave her standing with only her pride for company.

I dig deep for the resolve to do as Mr. Stokes urged, unburden Gran of the secrets she's carrying. She'll no doubt resist, but I have to try.

What if, back in my childhood, we'd talked about the ugly parts of our lives, lashed ourselves together with the rope of family, instead of floundering around in our individual storms, allowing those ropes to twist into nooses and shackles? The what-ifs behind me are a mountain I can't unbuild. All I can do is examine myself openly, move forward. I suppose that's been my problem, I've been running away from and not toward for nine years.

When we get to Lamoyne, we stop at the grocery store. The stares and whispers are back with the force of my childhood. I pity Gran as she moves with her cart, back straight, pretending she doesn't notice. I wonder if there was any time during the past nine years when talk of our family died down enough that she was relieved of the burden.

Once at Hawthorn House, Gran unpacks while I throw together a couple of salads. Then we sit at her kitchen table, talking about our times at the orchard, Mr. Stokes and Maisie, happy topics. She needs some breathing room before I bring up the things in her locked bureau drawer.

After we've eaten, she looks tired.

"Gran, why don't you take a nap while I clean up?"

"I wouldn't mind a few minutes to rest my eyes. I think I'll rest in the chaise on the front porch."

"Good idea. I'll join you with some sweet tea in a while."

Once the kitchen is set in order, I creep like a thief up to her bedroom. Perhaps the gentlest way to open this door is with the James family album.

After I take it from the night stand, I eye the drawer of secrets. I retrieve the key and open it to look through the photographs of Uncle George again. I pull the locket from her jewelry box and open it, thinking of the young girl Gran had been when it was given to her. Had she been in love? Had George declared himself, then left her?

As I swipe the depth of the drawer to draw out all the photographs, my finger catches a folded paper in the back. It's slightly yellowed, but not old and brittle like the photographs. Unfolding it, I see the Wickham College letterhead with Dad's name under the embossed college logo. There's a large dark stain on the lower right corner.

It's that stain that gives me chills. I saw it the night of the bonfire and recall the panic on Gran's face when she read it. I always assumed it was a note that tied Dad to Elizabeth Taylor (I'm ashamed I never remember that poor girl's real name). But I was wrong. It was from Dad *to* Gran.

The writing is in pencil, heavy, dark and smeared. The letters, uneven, angular and sharp-edged, frantic.

> **I know why he did it. I heard you. George. Dad.**
> **You could have stopped him.**
> **I can't stand the whirlwind in my head. The chaos in my soul**
> **Make it stop Stop Stop Stop St——————**
> **I know why he did it I know why he did it I know why I know I know**

How he must have been suffering when he wrote this. I stumble-sit on the bed. We didn't help him. We just shuffled him out of sight.

Gran had to know how desperate he was after reading this. My fingers tighten on the paper. All of the forgiveness I've been trying to foster evaporates on a single breath. She knew. And did nothing to ensure he wasn't going to hurt himself.

I sit staring into space for a few minutes, angry at both of us for failing him. Then I look at the note again. References to both George and Granddad. George was long gone by the time Dad was born. Could he have come back? Was there trouble between the brothers?

I won't let her continue to ignore this like she's ignored every other unpleasant thing in our lives.

I force myself to calm down, organize my thoughts. I have to remember all she has lost. I cannot go out there and slap her in the face with my discoveries.

Finally, I walk out on the front porch, without bothering to bring the album, the locket, or the discoveries from the drawer. Gran is sitting in the swing, staring into the distance.

I sit next to her, and we rock silently for a few minutes. Then I say, "I've been thinking a lot about the James family."

"That makes sense in our current circumstances, I suppose."

"Is it true that Dad and Uncle George were alike?"

"What do you mean?"

"Ross said he thinks Dad had a mental illness. Manic-depressive disorder."

"Your father was a brilliant, creative man. He was *not* mentally ill."

"Gran, when you hear the symptoms, you might see it differently. There's no shame in it. It's not a character flaw; it's a disease."

"Drayton could have his moods, but married to that woman, who could blame him?"

I see myself sitting in her skin not that long ago, blaming everything about Dad on Margo. It's hard not to, she earned her position as scapegoat. But she was not the sole cause of his destruction. I force myself to speak without judgment, hoping I can lead Gran to acceptance by example.

Gran keeps her gaze fixed on the gnarled oak in the yard as I explain the symptoms as I saw them in Dad. But her hands, restless in her lap, show her agitation.

"Don't you think it's a possibility?" I ask. "Remember his office at the end, his paranoia, the notes, his promiscuity. What if he was sleeping with that student who died?"

"Really, Tallulah! How can you even speak of such things?"

"Because they're true. Not facing them is poisoning all of us."

Her lips tighten. "Margo was the poison. Drayton would have been fine if he hadn't—"

"Gran! I know you want to believe that. For years, I did, too. But can you honestly say he showed none of his *moodiness* before they were together?"

I glance at her hands. The beds of her fingernails bloom crimson as she clenches them. I reach over and put my hand over hers. "It's all right, Gran. There's no one here but you and me. We loved Dad, nothing will ever change that."

She refuses to look at me. Although she blinks, her tears stay dammed in her eyes.

I give her a minute before I press on. "I ask about Uncle George because Ross said there can be a familial aspect to the disease. You said George wasn't well suited to running the orchard or being a professor. I believe you said he was too scattered. Did any of the symptoms Ross described fit him, too?"

"What good does talking about George do now?"

"If we can face the truth, we can accept it. If we accept it, we can let it go. Ignoring it has only made things worse."

"Talking about these things only inflames! I don't want to discuss George, or your father. Please stop."

Even in her profile, I can read her pain. I have to ask myself if I'm really doing this for her, or because I want answers to my own questions?

Mr. Stokes knows Gran better than anyone on this earth. His friendship has been a mainstay her entire life. I know he wants the best for her. He's carried her secrets with love and honor for years. And he thinks it's vital for her to let them go.

Oh, Mr. Stokes, I hope you're right. Because this feels cruel.

"I know things were different when you grew up. You said Great-Grandmother James wasn't tolerant of imperfections and that's why George left. But ignoring and hiding things doesn't fix them. It makes them worse."

She starts crying, real crying.

I feel horrible. "When I was looking for your pearls the other day, I unlocked the center dresser drawer in your bedroom."

Her body goes rigid. "You had no right."

"I don't suppose I did. But I'm not sorry. I found the locket. George was his middle name, wasn't it?"

She nods, her eyes taking on a faraway look and a noticeable tremble takes over her chin.

"*You* cut George out of the album, not Great-Grandmother James."

"This is none of your business." There's more pain than reprimand in her voice.

"It might not be, if it wasn't affecting everyone I love. Including you. You were in love with George."

Her eyes close, forcing fresh tears from their corners. "I was."

"Did you ever look for him, after he left?"

She's quiet for so long, I don't think she's going to answer. Then she whispers. "He never left."

My skin flushes with hot prickles. "What happened to him?"

"You'll never understand."

"Not if I'm not allowed to try."

She's quiet for a time. I simply wait.

"George wasn't like Drayton," she says in a small voice. "I never saw George dark and withdrawn. He was sparkling light and energy, the life of the party. Everybody loved him—until those last months when he went too far."

She takes a deep, shuddering breath and continues to stare into the yard.

"You can tell me," I say softly.

She shakes her head. "It doesn't matter now. Leave it lie."

"I honestly would, if I didn't see the pain keeping it inside is causing you. It's time for you to stop standing alone. So we can help Walden. So we can help Griff. So we can help each other."

Again, her eyes close. When she opens them, she turns away.

Finally, I use Mr. Stokes's words. "Why do you keep painting a storefront that has no goods to sell? There's no need anymore. The shelves have been stripped bare."

Her head whips around. Her eyes are huge, her mouth open. After a second she says, "Why are you asking me, if he's already told you?" The words come from between gritted teeth. "He promised."

"He didn't tell me anything except to ask you that question."

Her hand covers her trembling mouth. "Why are you doing this to me?"

I slide closer and put an arm around her. We sit like that for a minute before I say, "Mr. Stokes is right. There's no one left to protect in Lamoyne. It's time to cut that secret out like the cancer it is."

After a choked sob, she says, "Elliot was just trying to calm him down. If he'd left George alone like I wanted, everything would have been all right."

Her shoulders quake.

I suddenly wish I hadn't started this conversation out here. We should be inside where the security of family heirlooms surrounds her. And then I think, maybe this *is* the right place. Out in the open, where the grasp of the past isn't quite so strong.

"It's okay, Gran. There's no one left for it to hurt."

"I need some time. Please."

I'm reluctant to leave her alone. Yet I know from experience there are some things you have to face alone before you can face recounting them to others.

"I'll go in and get us some sweet tea and be back in a few minutes."

Her whispered thank-you leaves a mark on my heart.

She dabs her eyes with the tissue I bring before she accepts the glass of tea. She holds it in her hand until the sweat from it dampens her skirt.

Finally, she's ready to talk. "Your Great-Uncle George proposed to me on my eighteenth birthday—completely out of the blue. With the locket, not a ring. I told him I needed to think it over because I knew my daddy would have a fit. George couldn't hold a job outside the orchard—and even that he did infrequently and haphazardly. But worse, he hadn't asked Daddy for my hand. And we'd only been courting for a couple of months." She tilts her head slightly, as if just struck by a thought. "I wonder if he would have asked me at all, had he not been so . . . outside himself."

"He would have, Gran. I know he would. Those words on the locket. He loved you."

She gives me a shadow of a smile and pats my hand. "Perhaps." After a pause, she says, "When I looked back on it, his behavior had been escalating for weeks. Maybe even the entire time we were seeing each other." Her expression darkens. "Rumors began surfacing in late May. Just a few at first, and people were careful to keep them away from me. But then the dam burst. He was careening out of control and so was the gossip. He bought on credit all over town—things he didn't need and certainly couldn't afford, trading on his family name, which, at the time, was highly respected.

"He bought *sixteen* straw boaters. All the dry goods store had. When I asked him why, he laughed and said you never knew when one might blow off your head. It seemed funny and cavalier at the time, so refreshing after living with my straitlaced parents." She pauses. "I learned the hard way there are reasons for rules, for structure. Without them, a person can ricochet out of control."

I begin to see her rigid emphasis on social protocol in a different light.

"The whole town was talking by my birthday," she says softly. Then she straightens her back. "His mother was trying to keep him on the farm, away from trouble and the eyes of the gossips. She'd arranged a Saturday family picnic as a birthday celebration for me. We were halfway through the meal when George got it in his head that the butcher was cheating them. He was going to town to put an end to it. He wanted my car keys, but I wouldn't give them to him. His mother had already hidden the keys to their car and the farm truck.

"We thought he'd just gone to the orchard barn, that's where he hid his bootleg. But when I went after him, he wasn't there. Your great-grandmother sent Elliot after his brother. Because I might have more luck in getting him to come back, I drove. We caught up with George on the bridge between the orchard and town." She dabs her eyes and releases a long breath. "He resisted when Elliot tried to get him in the car. I jumped out and said to let him go. The town was already full of rumors about him, what was one more?

"But Elliot had been sent by his mother, and you didn't return to that woman with a job unfinished." She swallows hard. "It was h-horrible."

I've never heard Gran stammer.

"Elliot was a year younger than George," she says, her eyes distant and unfocused, "but still a little bigger. As they scuffled,

George's strength seemed almost inhuman. When they broke apart, he lunged at Elliot. Elliot dodged to the side. He didn't plan it. It was reflex. And George . . . George just kept going, right over the railing." She covers her eyes and bows her head. "I can see it as clear as if it were yesterday. For a moment, he almost seemed to fly."

"Oh, Gran." I scoot closer on the swing, put my arm around her and hug her close.

For a few seconds, she cries into her hands. Then she raises her face and uses the tissue to dab her nose.

Her voice is as distant as the past when she says, "He didn't hit the water because we were near the end of the bridge. We knew immediately his neck was broken. Even then, we didn't give up. We rushed down. His eyes were wide-open." Her shudder tells me she's seeing it all play out in her head. "Elliot was wild with grief, clawing the mud and begging George to come back. He blamed himself. And I was so shocked and stricken; I couldn't say anything to comfort him. I just sat there holding George's hand and wailed."

"You were in shock, too, Gran. You couldn't help Granddad."

She turns slowly and looks at me. "If I'd just spared a kind word for him at that moment. It might have made a difference; it might have eased his soul."

"I doubt he would have absorbed anything you said." As those words leave my lips, I think of Dad in the locker room. Knowing what I know now, nothing I could have said would have altered his course. The truth is heartbreaking and freeing at the same time.

"You asked me about regrets—that's one of my biggest," she says. "If only I could go back and reach out to Elliot, ease his pain, let him know I didn't blame him and he wasn't alone."

I think of the locket. Of George asking Gran to marry him. "Granddad was in love with you then, wasn't he? He loved you, even when he thought you were going to marry his brother."

"I don't want you to think I didn't love him back. I did, in time. But when George was around, I couldn't see anyone but him.

"Elliot never believed me when I assured him that George and I would never have married. I was besotted, but he was tomcatting all around the county. I just hadn't worked up the nerve to break it off with him. Elliot always believed he only got me because he killed his brother."

"How horrible for him. But you were happy, weren't you, you and Granddad?"

"We were as happy as two people can be with a ghost standing between them. If George had lived, I believe Elliot and I would have been truly happy."

"So sad for both of you."

"Don't feel sad for us. We had more happiness than many married people. And we had Drayton. But there was so much that weighed us down."

"It was obviously an accident."

Gran took her tissue and blew her nose in that delicate, ladylike way I'd never been able to master. "Of course it was." She pauses. "It's what came after that ruined your grandfather."

God, how could it get worse? And then I realize. George left town. Only he didn't. "You covered it up."

Her nod is slow and tired. "Your Great-Grandmother James . . . I know you think I'm too concerned with propriety, but that woman . . ." Gran's fingers begin to shred the damp tissue. "I waited with George on the riverbank while Elliot went back to the farm for help. I was so relieved when Ezra—Mr. Stokes—came with Elliot and his father. Ezra was like a brother to me, such a comfort.

"By the time we got back to the farm, Elliot's mother had already created a story and a plan. We all went along—shock, I suppose. None of us were thinking clearly. And once it was done, there was no undoing it."

"The story that George ran off," I say.

"He'd been acting so erratic, so wild, it was believable."

"And his body?" *Please say they at least buried him in the family plot.* But I knew in my heart that wasn't what happened. Someone might have seen the disturbed dirt, link it with George's disappearance.

"Great-Grandmother James decided Elliot and Mr. Stokes would bury George deep in the woods. They weren't to tell any of us where." She pauses. "There was no funeral. No place to mourn. No place to pay respects. I still can't understand how a mother could be so callous about one child or so cruel to the other."

The death of a child. The same loss Gran suffered when Daddy died. "That had to be so horrible for you and for Granddad."

"Worse for him. I was only burdened with the secret. Elliot and Mr. Stokes had to bear the sin. But, ever the faithful son, Elliot kept his promise to his mother. He never told anyone, even me, where George was buried."

I swipe tears from my cheeks with my palm.

"But I know," she says bitterly. "George was buried right where Elliot had his accident."

"An accident that wasn't an accident at all," I say. Poor Gran, so much tragedy. So much loss. So many secrets to carry.

"Just another lie attached to a James death. A lie of convenience that was meant to spare pain, not cause it." She takes a deep breath and blows it out. "I suspected what Elliot was up to that day. We argued about him going. I said some things, things I later found out your father overheard. I wish I had cut my tongue out before I said any of it."

"The note you found on Dad's desk the night of the bonfire—he *knew* Granddad killed himself—over guilt about George."

"*And* he knew I didn't stop him."

"But you tried. You said you argued."

"But my last words to him were hateful. I told him to go ahead and put us all out of our misery." A sob breaks loose in her throat. I hold her close and let her cry.

Finally, she regains herself. "I was never sure exactly how much Drayton heard. More than a ten-year-old should. When I tried to talk to him, he pulled farther away. So I stopped and we went on with our lives, repeating the same lies to ourselves and everyone else."

I tighten my hug. "All to protect a family name that was ruined anyway."

"I thought in time people would forget. It's unfair you children paid the price for us who came before. And now, Ezra is right. There is no one left to protect."

It seems strange to hear her call Mr. Stokes by his first name. All my life she called him Mr. Stokes and insisted we all did, too, even though most white people didn't give a black man that kind of courtesy. The secrets and burdens they shared drew them so much closer—the same secrets that drove her and Granddad apart.

I feel the tension in her shoulder muscles ease under my hand.

After a moment, she blows her nose again, then looks at me and grabs my hand. "I am so proud of the woman you've become, Tallulah. You did it on your own. You were brave enough to walk away from all this poison. Not the way I wanted, of course." She squeezes my hand. "I truly did think you'd be better off in Michigan. You and the twins would be shed of all this, have amazing opportunities I couldn't provide. I thought it selfish of me to keep you here. Maybe I was wrong. But you. You were strong. You did what you've always done: you took care of yourself. And for that I am so proud."

"Oh, Gran, I wasn't so strong or brave. I was hurt and angry."

"Tallulah, don't you see? Hurt and anger make a strong person brave and a weak person broken."

I lay my head on her shoulder. The sun cuts lacework on the ground below the limbs of the old oak, just as it has for generations of Neelys. As I breathe in the heavy Mississippi air, I realize something else. The locked drawer in Gran's dresser is her pecan tree by the river, the place she puts all the things that molded her but are too painful to bear.

As we sit quietly on the porch swing, a soft calm blooms in my heart. Gran's road was so much more difficult than I ever imagined. I feel so lucky that we are no longer isolated from each other, no longer struggling through our worlds alone.

32

I help Gran upstairs for a rest. I can't tell if the release of her secret has helped or just beaten her down. I pray Mr. Stokes is right, and this will be the beginning of a long-delayed healing.

I've never really thought of Gran as a person separate from myself, one with an entire life of experiences that had nothing to do with me. I now understand the magnitude of her losses and the extraordinary strength it's taken for her to carry that burden. She survived the only way she could. I can't condemn her for it, because I haven't done any differently. Isolating myself is just another form of denial, the one I've chosen to protect my inner self.

As I'm leaving the room, she says, "I don't want to trouble you, but I have a prescription that needs refilling." I open my mouth, but she cuts me off. "Don't look so alarmed, it's just a special salve the doctor prescribed for my eczema. Would you mind running to the drugstore? I've been out for a few days, and the itch is acting up."

"I'm happy to, Gran. Do you need anything else while I'm out?" I'm too agitated to sit still and glad for the errand.

"Pick up a pie at Donna Lynn's. You need some meat on those bones."

I smile as I leave the room. "You're one to talk."

"Make it lemon." Then she calls after me, "Or anything but pecan. Donna Lynn never did learn how to do a proper pecan."

"Got it," I call.

As I pull into a parking space in front of Donna Lynn's Bakery, I realize I haven't had a piece of pie since I left Lamoyne nine years ago. After witnessing Gran's misery today, I thought I might never be hungry again, but my mouth waters at the prospect of a flaky, lard-laden crust.

A little bell on the door rings as I enter. Donna Lynn comes out from the back, wiping her hands on a towel. The pink uniform dress she's wearing strains across her chest now, but her beaming smile hasn't changed at all. Gran always said that the day Donna Lynn didn't smile was the day the devil would take us all.

"What can I get you, hon?"

"Hello, Donna Lynn. Tallulah . . . from the orchard."

Her squeal is high enough to break glass as she hurries around the counter with her arms wide. She wraps me in a surprising hug. How could I have forgotten how nice she's always been to us? She was one of the orchard's most loyal customers.

"God bless you for comin' to help your granny." She rocks us side to side. Then she puts me away from her and wrinkles her brow. "How's she doin'? I been thinkin' of her ever' day."

"She's doing well, all things considered."

"You tell her she's in my prayers."

"I will. Thank you." I'm not sure if this exuberance is simply Donna Lynn being Donna Lynn, or her penchant for taking in strays nobody else wants, mangy dogs and one-eyed cats—and Jameses. At a Rotary Club–sponsored dog show when I was eight, she pranced a half-bald, ear-bitten mutt around the 4-H arena as if it was a pedigree poodle. Everybody booed, but Griff and I clapped and whistled our hearts out.

I can't help but grab her in a quick hug again. She giggles.

"I need a lemon pie."

"Comin' right up. If it's just you and your granny, I have tarts, instead."

The case is *full* of whole pies. "We'd like a whole, please. Aaaandd . . ." I look over the merchandise. "Is that a chess pie back in the corner there?"

"Yes, ma'am."

"Let us have that one, too."

She hands the tied boxes over the counter to me. "Tell your granny Donna Lynn says hello."

As I walk back out to my rental, it strikes me that there was more good in Lamoyne than just the orchard and Maisie. I've let the shadows overcome the light.

Thinking of Maisie, I drive down Eudora Avenue for old time's sake. I crane my neck as I approach the Delmores'—foolishly, I know. Married to Dr. Marlon Springer, I doubt she's still here suffering Mrs. Delmore's crossness.

The Delmores are on their front porch. The judge in a rocker; missus on the swing. The place looks as meticulous as ever, but they're both white-haired and shrunken. The front screen swings open. I can scarcely believe my eyes when Maisie comes out carrying a tray with two tall glasses, the mandatory sprigs of fresh mint bright green on their rims.

I swerve to the curb. I manage to keep from running up the front walk, but barely. I'm to the front steps before Maisie looks my way.

Her eyes widen, and the smile she gives me warms me even more than Donna Lynn's hug.

"Tallulah James! Is that you?" Then she glances at Mrs. Delmore. "May I have a minute, ma'am?"

I nod politely. "Mrs. Delmore. Judge."

Mrs. Delmore doesn't look happy, but she flips a bony hand in dismissal.

Maisie rushes down the steps, and I grab her in a hug.

"Come 'round back where we can talk," she says, grinning.

As we walk to the backyard, she links her arm with mine, just like the old days. "I reckon it's your family troubles that brought you back," she says.

"Seeing you takes some of the sting out of it."

"Pappy Stokes been real worried about Miss Lavada, says it was the blood pressure that took her to the hospital. She doin' better?"

I think of how exhausted she was when she laid down. "Everything is weighing on her."

"I never thought I'd see Walden be the one in trouble," she says. "Haven't seen him much this past year. I hear he moved down near New Orleans."

"Into a *cult*. How in the hell did that happen?"

"That boy was always lookin' for a place to belong—joined every scout, club, sport, and school group in town."

How can she see it so clearly? How could I *not*? "I should never have left him."

"Might not have made any difference," she says with a shrug. "You did right, goin' off to California on your own, making a life away from this place. I'm proud of you bein' so strong."

"Strong would have been staying and dealing with reality."

"As I see it, reality was *you* needed to be away from here and all that happened. Aren't you happy in California?"

"I am, or at least I was. I lost my job—which is my whole life."

"A job isn't a life!"

The truth of those words rattles me so much I turn our talk away. "What about you?" I rub the gold band on her left hand. "Marlon making you happy?"

"He is." Her smile tells me that's an understatement.

"Well, he'd better be! I admit I was surprised to find you still working for missus Queen Bee."

She shrugs. "She's so crotchety, who'd take care of her if I don't? And Marlon's doctoring day and night. We haven't had any luck getting babies, so I figure I might as well stick here for now."

I hear the incessant dinging of a small bell.

"That'd be missus Queen Bee now, ready to go inside. She can't take two steps without fallin'." Her hug reaches deep inside me, touching the void I've been ignoring for too many years. She releases me and gives a caring smile. "I pray for Walden." She starts around the house. "Marlon and I have a phone. Call me!"

I watch her disappear, hot tears of love and longing in my eyes.

A job isn't a life. Leave it to Maisie to shine a light on the lie I've been telling myself.

I wait in the backyard until I hear the front screen snap shut. Then I wipe my face and walk back to my car, wondering if I'm strong enough to do something about it.

33

I'd prepared a list of tactics to convince Tommy to give up Griff's number, tears (always effective on him back in the day) being the last resort. As it turned out, Tommy rolled quite easily. When I called after Gran went to bed, he seemed relieved to tell me where Griff was, even though that was all he knew, a location—and only because of the switchboard answering the call before they redirected it to Griff.

As soon as I hung up, I called American Airlines and booked a flight from New Orleans to San Antonio. This morning I told Gran I have to return to California for a couple of days for work and promised to be back for her appointment with Dr. Scott on Friday.

Now, I'm clammy and trembling as I stand outside the last door between me and my older brother. A white-clad army nurse stops and asks me if I need assistance. I do, but not the kind she's offering. I need the courage to open this door, to discover *why* Griff is in an army hospital in Texas.

I thank her, take a breath, and push the door open.

The window curtains are drawn, so the room is dim. He turns his head my way. His left arm, neck, and jawline are heavily bandaged, the sheet falls flat just below the knee of his left leg. I lean against the wall beside the door, light-headed, and whisper his name.

He's silent for a moment, then he says, "When I get out of here, I'm going to kill Tommy."

"Why didn't you tell me?" I push myself from the wall and pray my knees will hold.

"Because I didn't want this to happen, for the first time you see me to be like this. Besides, you have enough going on with Gran and Walden."

I walk around the bed to Griff's right side, the unbandaged side, and take his hand.

He smiles at me, lopsided due to the wounds on the left side of his face. "I worried I'd never see you again."

I lean over and kiss his forehead. "Me, too." I pull up the chair close to the bed and sit down. "What happened?"

"I had another surgery for the burns. Skin graft."

"I mean to make you need a skin graft in the first place."

"My medevac got shot down in Vietnam. Life's been a string of surgeries since then."

"Oh. I'm so sorry." Of all the things I imagined Griff doing these past years, drafted and slogging through rice paddies in Vietnam wasn't one of them. Just more denial, I suppose. "And aren't they supposed to avoid shooting down medevacs?"

His half chuckle is laced with anger. "They treated that red cross like a target. Can't recall one evacuation from a hot zone without bullets hitting the Huey." Then he squeezes my hand. "I'll be okay. It's just going to take some time."

"Are you alone? I mean, do you have a wife or anything? Is she here with you?"

"No wife. You married?" He rubs his right hand across his forehead. "It seems really weird, asking that."

"Nope. I'm as alone as a person can possibly be. I mean, up until all my recent family reunions in hospital rooms."

"Is Gran really doing okay?" Then his eyes narrow. "You didn't tell her I was here, did you?"

"She's doing great." I almost tell him about her admission but decide this isn't the time or place. "I told her I had to go back to work for a couple of days."

He asks about my life in San Francisco and I sketch it out, which only highlights what Maisie said, a job is not a life.

"Where's home for you?" I ask.

"I don't have one. Not at the moment, anyhow. I've been in one hospital or another pretty steadily since I got back to the States."

"I protested the war . . . the draft. I wish it could have saved you."

"Lulie, haven't you learned that it's not your responsibility to save anyone but yourself? And I wasn't drafted. I volunteered. I was a medevac pilot from early '66 until eight months ago."

"Dear God, why would you volunteer?"

"Why wouldn't I? Guys with real lives—wives and kids—were being yanked into the army left and right. Truthfully, at that point I didn't see a future I wanted to live. I—I was still afraid I'd turn into Dad or George."

At least he said he *was* afraid of being like them, so at least that particular horror must not have visited him.

"I didn't know you knew about George."

"*Everybody* in Lamoyne knew about George—and Dad. And of course, Margo. The holy trinity of Lamoyne social scorn."

"I never thought it bothered you like it did me. You always had friends. You were always out with people."

"Yeah, well, for me the best defense was just what Gran prescribed. Don't try to fix it. Don't address it. Ignore it. I mean, what can a kid do about any of it? And if I'd let you know it bothered me, it would only have made you feel worse. I was trying to *show* you how to plow through until we could get the hell out of Lamoyne."

With that, I'm crying, after I promised myself that no matter what I found behind this door I wouldn't. "Why didn't we talk about this back then?"

"Honestly, I don't want to talk about it now. After Dad, Lena, Margo, Vietnam, I'm only looking forward."

"But I want to know everything that's happened to you."

"I have an ammo box full of letters I wrote to you. I'll send them to you in California when I get out."

"I may not be in California. I'm looking for a new job."

"Just make sure you let me know where you are."

"Always, from now on. Where will you be?"

"I haven't decided. I have rehab and then I have to get discharged. Could be some time."

What kind of work will he be able to do? How will he manage?

"I've been thinking," I say. "Gran said the four of us still own the farm. It's pretty much gone to ruin, but we can sell it. I mean, none of us wants to go back there, and the money can help you get set up somewhere, give you some breathing room."

He's quiet for a moment. "I'm not sure I'm ready to do that yet." Then his voice brightens. "Besides, weren't you the one who was all about honoring the James family legacy?"

"As it turns out, I don't want to look backward, either. Do you really think there's a chance you'll go back there?"

"Probably not. But once it's gone, it's gone. I think we should spend some time considering—and I think we should discuss it with Gran. It was a big part of her life. It seems wrong to make the decision without her."

I wonder how she'll feel about it. Will it be a release from a constant reminder? Or will she mourn its passing?

"And speaking of Gran, I don't want to see her until I'm out of here," he says. "So you can't tell her, or she'll want to come."

"I know. Although if I did tell her, I could stay."

"Please don't. I don't feel much like conversation most of the time. We have the rest of our lives."

"Truth?" I'm swept up on soaring wings at the prospect.

"Truth."

A nurse comes in and says, "I'm sorry, but I have to take Lieutenant James down for some tests now."

"Go home, Lulie. I promise I'll call."

"But—"

"If you go, I promise not to strangle Tommy."

I reach into my purse. "Swear it on your arrowhead." I hold it out in the flat of my palm.

I can tell the smile hurts his face. He puts a hand over the arrowhead. "I swear I'll call—and I won't kill Tommy."

I laugh through my tears. "I'll go. But I'm not staying away. I'll be back."

"Deal. But I say when."

The nurse is unlocking the wheels on his bed and attaching his IV bottle to it.

"Still think you're the boss of me?"

"Always."

I wrap his fingers around the arrowhead and leave it in his palm. Then I give him a kiss on the cheek. "I'll be here when you need me," I whisper. "I promise."

Once back at Hawthorn House with Gran, it's almost impossible not to tell her about Griff. But I promised, and I don't make promises I don't keep. Besides, she seems to finally have some solid footing. We've not spoken of George again, but there's a new lightness in her bearing that makes me hope she's finally healing.

I can't bring myself to book a flight to San Francisco. I'm not doing Walden any good here, but somehow it feels like desertion if I leave. I've written him a pleading letter every day. I fear there aren't enough days between now and the sentencing to do any good. I wonder if a lifetime of days would be enough.

I saw on the news that Wesley Smythe and his followers abandoned their Louisiana compound. The film of the deserted clotheslines and crude huts that made most hunting shacks look like architectural wonders was chilling. The whole thing was made more so by the alligator dragging its tail around the place. It sickens me to think my brother lived there by choice. The news also featured a fine house that Smythe owns not far from the compound; apparently the living conditions of his followers were beneath him. His whereabouts are currently unknown. I made sure I added all that to my letter to Walden with the faint hope he'd see the man for the selfish manipulator he is.

Yesterday morning, I called Amelia, hoping she'd been summoned to see Walden in jail. It was foolish, of course. I know she would have called. But I need to feel like I'm doing *something*.

She said, "I want you to be prepared. The DA is looking for maximum sentencing. He's doing his homework, so I need to do mine. First of all, I'd like all the good character references you can accumulate—testimony from teachers, ministers, if he performed community service, if he was a Boy Scout, that kind of thing. Let's show the court who he was before he met Mr. Smythe. Also, your family history. We want the court aware of all extenuating circumstances that made him vulnerable to a man like Smythe. Now, I know there was some trouble surrounding your other brother years ago, before he came to live with Ross's family. He was arrested, then released and never charged, is that correct?"

"How can *that* be relevant to Walden's sentencing?"

"Walden gave a guilty plea without any bargaining. He's an easy mark for the DA to prove how tough he is on crime. And frankly, people are terrified of crazed cult members since the Manson murders a few years ago."

I thought of Sharon Tate and my blood went cold. It finally hit me. To the world, Walden isn't a vulnerable, damaged boy led astray. He's Tex Watson, reviled killer.

"The prosecution will argue Walden is unpredictable and unstable. He'll claim violent familial tendencies—thus the concern over your other brother's circumstance. The DA wants this to hit big in the papers. It's an election cycle, you know."

My instinctive reaction is to circle the wagons of our family—just like Gran. It was a shock of cold water, finally understanding that she and I aren't so dissimilar.

I take a moment to steel myself and then tell her the ugly truth. All of it, Dad, the night of the bonfire, and how Griff was arrested for murder. But my wagon-circling nature couldn't be completely eradicated. I had to add that Chief Collie's overreach, his jealous hatred of Gran's family, his fervor to blame Griff without adequate proof, led to Griff's arrest before the coroner even ruled on cause of death.

"Collie showed up a few hours after her body was discovered and took Griff from school in handcuffs. Locked him in jail and wouldn't let any of us see him."

"He was a minor! What about your parents? Were they called in?"

"No. Dad was . . . well, he was missing at that point. But Gran and I went to the station. They wouldn't let us talk to him."

"And your mother?"

"She . . . we didn't tell her until after the lawyer got there. Gran was too afraid she'd make things worse—and she would have."

"Hmm. I think I'll look into that case. I don't want to be blind-sided."

I just hope she has the chance to get blindsided. "I appreciate you doing all of this preparation. I hope it doesn't go to waste."

"Me too. I'll be in touch."

So now, more waiting. I should be champing at the bit to find another job, it's not as if I can live forever on my two-week severance.

When I first arrived home, I had a long list of things I wanted to confront Gran about—things I saw as shortcomings that contributed to our family's disintegration. I wanted to make her face the truth of Dad's suicide. But now I am at peace allowing her to believe whatever she needs to about his death to get through the day. Losing a child has to be enough to break the strongest soul.

It's late afternoon when I park the rental car in front of the post office to mail my daily letter to Walden—and one to Griff that I wrote in secret. I'm fishing in my purse for my wallet as I climb the granite steps when someone says, "I heard you were back in town but didn't believe it."

Grayson Collie is standing right in front of me, same cruel smirk, same greaser hair. He's one step up, looking ten feet tall. All the miles between me and my childhood vanish.

It pisses me off that I'm still afraid of him.

I step around him and stop on the step above his so we're eye to eye. "I heard you're still an asshole. And I did believe it."

He looks as stunned as if I'd gut-punched him. Then he rears his head back and guffaws, showing his crooked teeth all the way back to his tonsils. "Ain't you gone to the gutter."

I tilt my head to the side and raise a brow. "Must have if I'm face-to-face with you." He's wearing a green utility uniform with his name embroidered on the chest just beneath the Sinclair dinosaur. "I see you're finally man enough to take my brother's high school job."

"If we weren't here where God and everybody can see, I'd show you how much of a man I am."

"I knew the only way you could get a woman is by forcing her against her will."

He leans closer and his eyes burn with so much hatred, I recoil. He says through tobacco-stained teeth, "I didn't touch that slut— wasn't anywhere near the campus that night."

Even though the sun is beating down on my head and it's ninety degrees, I go as cold as river stone. I try to sound glib when I say, "What made you think of her?"

For the briefest second, I see fear in his eyes. Then he regains his sneer and says, "Griff James oughta be in prison right now."

Not wanting him to see my suspicion, I head on up the steps. "Certainly was great seeing you again. I hope I never repeat the pleasure."

"We thought we'd rid this town of Jameses. Go back to wherever you came from."

"If I didn't hate this place so much, I'd stay just to piss you off." Then I put on the Southern debutant smile Gran taught me. "You have a good day now."

Disgust fills me, and grayness presses the edges of my vision. I barely make it inside the post office before I collapse on the wooden bench in the lobby and put my head on my knees.

* * *

Tommy lives in a little green house on the edge of town, not a full mile from the house where he grew up. I came straight from the post office and have been sitting on the front steps long enough that my backside is numb when he gets home.

"Hey," he says with a smile. "This is a surprise. I was hoping I'd see you again before you leave."

"Well, it's not like you don't know where to find me."

He sits down beside me. "Guess I wasn't sure . . . I dunno . . . I figured you don't want anything to do with this town anymore."

"Maybe not this town, but there are a few people in it I'm still pretty fond of."

"Want a beer?" he asks.

"I could really use one, or six."

"Let's move to the backyard or else the whole town will have you pregnant with my baby by tomorrow—what with the beer and all."

"You do know how this place works."

"That I do. But it's home."

We sit in metal Griffith chairs so heavily oxidized from the sun you can barely tell they used to be aqua. Neither of us seem ready to talk. I wipe down the sweat on the can of Pabst Blue Ribbon in my hand, then slip off my sandals and bury my toes in the grass. The crickets and the tree frogs have already started their evening competition. Living in the city, I'd forgotten how deafening the tiniest creatures can be.

Sitting out here brings back the best parts of my childhood: summer days spent trailing Tommy and Griff. Days when the streetlights determined when it was time for Tommy to go home. Of course, Griff and I had no such limitations.

"Your momma and daddy doing well?" I ask. Mrs. Murray was one of the few in town who never looked at Griff and me with pity or condemnation. When she gave me Tommy's sister's hand-me-downs, it was in the spirit of family, not charity.

"They are. Dad's thinking about retiring . . . as if that will ever happen. Tina has a baby now, Charlotte, after Momma. So you can imagine. She says being a grandma is reward for putting up with all the trouble we caused as kids."

I smile. "She's a special woman, your momma."

"You and Griff were always special to her, too. She worried herself to death when you ran off—we all did."

There's that growingly familiar tingle of regret. "I'm sorry. I was so upset, I didn't think anyone would care—I didn't think of anyone at all."

"Well, it was an unpleasant time."

Now there's a genteel Southern understatement for life being ripped apart by a cataclysmic shit storm.

We drink in silence for a minute, letting the past settle.

I finally get to my business. "I ran into Grayson Collie today."

"I'm sorry."

"Me too. He's just as horrible as ever." As hard as I try to push it away, the image of him leaning close to me, hatred burning in his eyes fills my mind. I swear I can smell his breath again. "He said something that got me thinking. I wanted to talk to you about it, see what you think."

"Can't imagine him saying anything even remotely thought-provoking, but go ahead."

I force myself not to rush into my theory, but lead Tommy on the path and see if he comes to the same idea.

"He was so infuriating!" I say. "He made a disgustingly macho comment, and I responded with a flip retort about him needing to force a woman to get anyone to be with him. And he immediately took a flying nine-year leap to the dead girl on campus. You should have seen him. He was so . . . explosive."

"And?"

"Why go there? And that death was ruled an *accident*. Why react so strongly?"

"He's a hateful man."

I can tell Tommy's thinking.

"Back then," I say, "Griff told me Lena liked high school guys."

"Only the big, athletic ones. Didn't go for those not yet through puberty." He strokes his upper lip. Poor Tommy went through the motions of shaving before he needed to, just to save face.

"You knew?"

"*Everybody* knew—guys anyway."

"Is it possible Grayson was one of them?"

"Could have been."

"What if he was with her that night? The fact that his mind immediately went to her after all these years—"

"*Nobody* had to force Lena."

"No. But somebody might have had to *feel like* he was forcing her in order to . . . you know."

"That doesn't narrow the field to Grayson Collie."

"No. But when you put all those things together it *could*. And his dad *is* the police chief; we both know he covered up plenty of other stuff Grayson's done over the years." I pause, realizing I'm trading on a friendship I abandoned. "You're in the police station, where all the evidence is kept. I was wondering if you would take a look and see if they actually questioned anyone else, if they followed any leads, that kind of thing. Why did they arrest Griff even *before* the cause of death was determined? Why rush to arrest anyone at all when it could easily have been an accident or suicide?"

"I don't want to sound like a coward, but why dredge this up now? Griff was let off."

"He wasn't *exonerated*. It might matter in Walden's sentencing hearing. And, there's a difference in the eyes of this town. We still own Pearl River Plantation. What if Griff wants to come back here?"

He's quiet for a moment. I watch the light come into his eyes.

I don't want to mislead him. "I mean, I don't *know* that he will. But he said he's not ready to sell it."

"You know I'd do anything for Griff."

"I know."

"I'm kind of dating the sister of the evidence clerk. I can probably do it without drawing attention."

"Kind of dating?"

"Okay. Dating."

"Damn good thing we got off your front porch before we broke out the beer, then. Don't want to piss off her brother."

We clink our cans and watch the first stars appear in the deep-blue sky.

34

I'm lying on Gran's front porch swing like a lazy cat, watching the sky-blue ceiling boards shift back and forth hypnotically, trying to point myself in a direction. I spent the last hour looking at my sketchbooks, the diary of my life after Lamoyne. I'm not sure I want to go back to California.

I hear the phone ring. A moment later, Gran sticks her head out the front door and tells me I have a call. Can't be Ross, because he always chats with Gran for several minutes first.

"I'm at the station, so I have to make this quick," Tommy says when I answer, his voice low and quiet. "I got a hold of the evidence box for Lena's death."

"And?" My heart speeds up.

"I found a photo buried in the coroner's report. A picture of fresh bite marks on Lena's neck. Lateral incisors that overlap crooked centrals."

"Oh my God. You linked him with hard evidence!"

"It can prove he bit her not long before her death, not more than that."

"Well, this should help. Amelia called early this morning. She interviewed a retired, very guilt-ridden officer from campus police about that night. He's in Arizona now and—after she used her lawyer skills on him—decided to clear his conscience. He saw Grayson around the bell tower that night. The chief threatened him into silence."

"He'll testify?" Tommy's whisper is excited.

"I don't know for sure. But it'll help you, right?"

"Maybe. I have to be careful how I handle this, so keep it to yourself for now. I don't want this evidence disappearing before we can use it. And I'll need to see if I can find more."

"Be careful."

"I will. Any change with Walden?"

"No—"

"Gotta go. Talk soon." He hangs up, and it's all I can do not to let out a whoop of joy. Even if it doesn't help Walden, it might just get Grayson Collie what he so richly deserves—and clean up Griff's reputation at the same time.

From that moment, it's the falling of dominoes, fast and decisive. Amelia started it at one end and Tommy the other. In the center, caught in the crossfire, was Grayson Collie and his conniving father.

The chief is immediately fired by a very embarrassed mayor. And the prosecutor's office is reopening Lena's case and starting an investigation into obstruction of justice and a couple of other charges against the chief that I've never heard of.

I make a beeline to tell Maisie, thinking of how happy she'll be. Grayson harassed us both throughout our growing-up years.

When I arrive at the Delmores' house, the Delmores are in their respective stations on the front porch and Maisie is in the backyard taking down laundry.

She smiles when she sees me coming around the corner. "If I didn't know better, I'd think you decided to move back here."

"No way. But I can't seem to get myself motivated to go back to face unemployment in California, either." I take the pillowcase out of her hand and fold it and put it in the basket. "You know Grayson's sitting behind bars in his Daddy's old domain right now, don't you?"

"I heard. My hopes ain't high he'll stay there."

"Well, this might raise them. Tommy just called and told me two women came forward claiming Grayson raped them. Maybe now that Chief Collie is out of a job things will change."

She snorts, and I can't really argue with her.

"Have you and Marlon considered moving away? Maybe up north—or west? There are more opportunities," I say.

Her eyes widen. "I love you, Tallulah, but why would I leave? This is our home. Our people are here. Besides, Marlon's practice is here, our community needs a good doctor."

Her words sink deep. Coming home, finding *my* people threatened by things I never imagined, has made me see things differently, maybe clearly for the first time in many years. No matter how much you disappoint one another, or infuriate one another, no one makes you feel as connected to life as family.

"Just a few weeks ago I would have argued with you. But now I see what a person gives up when they leave their people behind."

"So?" She nudges me with an elbow. "Maybe *you* should move back here."

"No matter how far I am from here, I won't go years without coming to see you and Gran again. I promise."

"I know what a promise means to you, so I'm happy with that."

I give her a quick hug. "Life without your friendship is a lonely place."

"Amen to that."

Saturday morning, two weeks after bringing Gran back to Lamoyne, I wake restless. Walden hasn't budged. Dr. Scott said Gran is in the clear. It's time to deal with my own life—reinvent myself yet again. As a grown woman with work experience, I can pretty much plant myself wherever I choose—not a place Griff selected, or where I was abandoned. A choice. Turns out, endless options are nearly as frightening as none.

I put on a scooter skirt (my semiconcession to Gran, who doesn't believe women should wear shorts, even in the home) and my Adidas and find Gran in the backyard pruning her roses.

"I'm going to take a walk," I say. "Get my head back to normal life—whatever that is."

"Why, Tallulah, normal is whatever you make it. You surely know that by now." She looks in my eyes for a long moment, then she smiles. "I think a long walk will do you good." Then her gaze travels to my bare thighs. Her cheeks turn pink, but she doesn't lecture. "You should take the straw hat from the back porch, 'else your nose will burn."

Saturday is a busy shopping day and I don't want to talk to anyone, so I take side streets to skirt downtown. I stick to the shade as much as possible, but I'm glad I wore the hat. The sun is brutal already. Which means the afternoon will bring either scorching temperatures, or a fierce thunderstorm. I remember sitting on Gran's front porch in the summers of my childhood, watching the roiling clouds and jagged lightning. We would stay there as long as we could, watching puddles gather and raindrops plop like sprouting corn shoots. When the wind pushed the lashing rain so hard it reached across the depth of the porch, we'd run inside and Gran would give us chocolate milk and cookies.

I'm hoping for a storm.

It's funny, now that I'm no longer feeding justification for leaving, I recall the good times more and more.

My pace slows and my feet swell in my shoes as I push through the heat and humidity. Sweat trickles down the center of my back and between my breasts.

Soon I'm standing at the lane to Pearl River Plantation without consciously planning to come here. I run my hand over the splintery sign, tracing the ghost of the letters labeling my old life. Then I wade through the stinging nettles in the overgrown lane, wishing I'd worn pants. I try to flatten them ahead of me by pushing them with the side of my shoe, only to be rewarded with a sting on the back of my calf as the occasional plant pops back up in retaliation.

When the house comes into view, it's smaller than I remember. Vines have climbed the brick pilings that support the porch and are taking over the railing. They wrap the posts and snake into the eaves. The windows have been boarded over with weathering plywood, which must have been Gran's effort to protect the interior from the ravages of storm-broken glass and vandals. The only sounds are the whirr of insects and conversation of birds.

I stare at the house for a few minutes, even now surprised I'm standing here, a place I thought I'd never see again. It causes a strange sense of vertigo, this collision of long-ago and now, of childhood pain and adult understanding, of the unchangeable past and the possibilities of the future.

I pick my way carefully up the six warped steps to the porch. Placing my palms on the solid front door, I close my eyes. The rumbles of every emotional storm that raged inside these walls still reverberate within me—and probably always will. Even so, I'm sad that nature is trying to erase this place, erase the legacy of generations of Jameses, of Granddad and Great-Uncle George, of Daddy. Mistakes were made. Lives were ruined. And yet Gran fought tooth and nail to preserve this family legacy for us.

I can only see the peak of the orchard barn roof from the front porch. When I reach it, the vines have been even more aggressive here, covering a good part of the walls and roof. I go behind the barn, looking for Dad's pecan sheller. There's a mass of vegetation with a couple of fingers of rusted metal poking out. Even though I've promised myself to stop the *what-ifs*, I wonder how different life might have been if he'd had the focus to complete it.

The blackberry orchard is impassable, a tangle of thorny cane and wild weeds. But when I reach the pecan orchard, the rows of giant trees are evident even with underbrush and sprouted saplings littering the aisles. I make my way toward the southwest corner, scolded by chattering squirrels, and frightening rabbits and snakes along the way.

The fence is still standing, overtaken by weeds, but standing. I climb up and onto my branch. The river is the first thing I've seen on the farm that is unchanged. The water low and slow, depleted by the long months of summer, making it clearer than usual. Brown, mossy rocks are visible on the bottom in the shallows, along with the occasional fish nosing around. I rest my cheek against the trunk of the tree, close my eyes, and breathe in the smell of the mud. I hear a woodpecker hammering away somewhere nearby and the call of a mockingbird. And suddenly, I feel it.

Home.

In spite of all the misery and turmoil that happened here, I feel a peaceful connection to this place—to Gran, my siblings. Keeping my eyes closed, I enjoy the revelation, the internal stillness that seems so contrary to my childhood.

My eyes snap open when I hear something large moving through the underbrush. A wild hog can't get me up here, but a bear . . .

I look right and left. Then behind me. It's neither hog nor bear. It's Ross. I knew he was coming to the cottage this weekend, but am surprised he's arrived so early.

"You scared the daylights out of me. How did you know I was here?"

"Lavada said you went for a long walk, with the emphasis on long. I took a guess. You left an easy trail to follow from the road." He looks up at me for a moment. "I'll leave if you want to be alone."

"I don't." Ross is the only person who's not an intrusion as I return to this sacred place.

He climbs up and sits on the top rail of the fence, just as he did years ago.

"Come on up," I say. "I didn't expect you until this afternoon."

"I couldn't sleep." He sits next to me. "Too excited."

"Excited?"

"To see you."

I smile at him.

His hands cup my face. "How can I miss you so much in a week, when I lived without you for so long?" Then he kisses me, and it's even more earth-shattering than my fourteen-year-old self imagined.

When our lips part, I look into those impossibly blue eyes and say, "I've been missing you for nine years. I just didn't know it."

He puts an arm around me, and I rest my head on his shoulder. We sit there, the world outside no longer mattering. For the first time in my life, I feel totally at peace, no qualifications, no reservations.

Walden's troubles are ongoing, but he's safer in jail than with that lunatic, Smythe. Whatever happens, I will be here for him. And Griff. Once he is healed, I will support him in getting his life restarted, wherever he wants it to be.

The storm of the past is gone. The future unsure, but I no longer fear the uncertainty, the uncharted path. As long I have my people to care for, each of us bent but hopefully not broken, hurt but not unforgiving, I will find my way forward.

Now I just have to decide where. For certain, not California, a place I now associate with isolation and hiding.

I draw strength from Ross's closeness. I am not afraid to let him see me as I am, for he's always known the worst and still he is here. He is not wild declarations of passion, or demands for concessions I'm not ready to give. Just Ross, caring and constant, his arm around me. Always.

Sitting in his embrace, staring at the flow of the river, I realize that I no longer have any fears to toss into the current.

EPILOGUE

May 12, 1974

There's a new sign for Pearl River Plantation. Ross makes the turn onto the neatly cleared drive, smiling at me as he does. As a child, starting down this lane caused a knot in my belly, not ever knowing what awaited at the end. Back then I didn't notice it, commonplace as it was. Now my happy anticipation makes me starkly aware of the absence of dread. In my lap, I clutch a jar of mayhaw jelly. I didn't risk life and limb to collect the fruit, or make it with my own hands, but I hope Gran will appreciate the sentiment just the same.

Griff and Ross managed to talk her out of hosting the newly revived Mother's Day crawfish boil, arguing that as the honoree she shouldn't be lifting a finger. Her health is good, but her poor eyesight is making everyday life more of a challenge—not that she'll admit it. I can tell giving up the crawfish boil doesn't sit easy with her. She's been responsible for every holiday this family has ever had. I imagine today will be filled with worried glances and gentle suggestions.

Ross says, "This is an anniversary of sorts for us."

I reach across and take his hand. "I thought our anniversary was last Friday. Thirteen years since we met. Thirteen years I wouldn't have had if you hadn't saved me from drowning."

"Guess we're going to have to start a list."

I suppose all couples have multiple anniversaries, but I like to think Ross and I are special. Special in the way we met. Special that from the beginning he saw the worst, not the best of me. Special that we share not only our lives, but our work. Throughout the first year after we reunited, we worked to establish the Drayton Foundation for Mental Wellness. I left off Dad's last name to keep Gran from being too uncomfortable. She and I have learned to accommodate each other that way.

I spend too much time on the road away from Ross, but these first years require a great deal of speaking. Still today, mental illness is too often viewed as a character flaw, something a person can will themselves to get over. My mission is to make people see it's a biological malfunction, just like diabetes. This year we expanded the Drayton Foundation's family support outreach. My favorite project so far.

The house comes into view. It looks better than I recall it ever looking—fresh paint and clean windows, as if someone finally cares enough to do more than slam in and out of its doors and sleep under its roof.

Griff pushes through the front screen. Gran is right behind him. I'm out of the car before it stops rolling. I race up the steps and throw one arm around each of them in a giant hug.

Griff stumbles back slightly, his balance not quite solid on his new, improved prosthetic leg.

"Oh, sorry!" I say as I let him go.

"I have to learn to balance the onslaught of your hugs sooner or later." He grabs me and hugs me again.

When he releases me, I surreptitiously assess the scars on the side of his neck and left arm. The redness is finally easing, but it's still painful for me to look at. I imagine it always will be. Overall, though, he looks good. He's put on some weight and the tension in his face has eased. It seems the orchard he gave new life is returning the favor.

Considering all he's been through with the war, his wounds and rehabilitation, the horrible way people are treating Vietnam vets, I worried he might fall into drugs or darkness like so many. But it seems he's a sword forged in fire, any microscopic weaknesses have been hammered out of him. It breaks my heart to think of the years he secretly feared the day mental illness would sweep him away as it did our father.

Ross finally catches up and gives Griff a hug, not that awkward standoffish hand shaking so many guys do. It warms me all over every time I see them with their arms around each other.

"Is Tommy still coming?" I ask. After all, this is his mom's first Mother's Day as grandmother of twins—and his wife's first Mother's Day ever.

Griff smiles. "When I asked, he said the same thing he said back in the day, 'Why wouldn't I? I come every year.' But he said it might be close to five before they get here. Maisie, Marlon, and Mr. Stokes?"

Maisie is still waiting for a baby. She's starting to give up hope. But I'm proof there is always hope for complete happiness, no matter how bleak things are.

"Yes. She said Mr. Stokes has been counting the days." I extend the jar of jelly to Gran. "Happy Mother's Day."

She smiles as she takes it. "This is the only thing your mother and I ever agreed on." The knowing look in her eyes tells me she understands everything it stands for. She gives me a kiss on the cheek. "I love you, Tallulah Mae."

Gran links her arm through mine and leads me into the house. "Come help me scrub the potatoes."

Once we're inside, standing at the sink, she says, "It'll be so nice when Walden and Dharma can be here for Mother's Day, too."

My heart breaks a little. Walden has eight years before he'll be eligible for parole. He's still refused to see any of us except Ross—and that took months of skillful psychiatric maneuvering. Last month Ross returned from the prison with a letter for me. I opened it with a heart full of hope.

Tallulah,

The only reason I talk to Ross is because he convinced me it will help you and Gran get past everything. I am who I am; but I am not a cold-blooded murderer. I thought the house was empty. We were protecting ourselves from an unfair and unwarranted attack. Moore was manufacturing evidence against an honorable leader of men. I believe in Westley Smythe. I believe in our brotherhood. But I would not kill for any reason.

Walden

Ross assures me this is a breakthrough, a beginning. He thinks in time, he can undo the conditioning of the cult. I hope he's right.

As for Dharma, she'll never return to Mississippi. But I don't ruin Gran's dream by saying it. Sometimes our dreams are all that get us up in the morning.

Hours later, our bellies are full, and the crawfish shells are scattered on newspaper along with the corncobs. After Tommy, Maisie, and their families have gone, I ask Griff to show me the pecan orchard. The uneven ground sometimes gives him trouble, so instead of walking, we ride in an old military surplus jeep. As he points out the changes and improvements I'm still a little stunned that he, of all of us, is the one to come home.

Once we reach the southwest corner by the river, he stops under the boughs of my tree.

"I have a feeling there's something you want to tell me," he says as he shuts off the engine.

"There is." I take a deep breath, still unsure in my own heart. "I found Margo." I watch his face carefully.

"Why in the hell would you do that?" he asks with more bewilderment than anger.

"I'm not sure," I say honestly. "It just felt so unfinished."

"Where is she?"

"An apartment in Tucson."

"Alone?"

"I don't know. All I have is an address."

"I hope she's alone." His face is hard.

"I thought we should decide together if we want to do anything about it."

"Oh, Lulie, I have nothing to say to her. She erased us. Let her live the life she's chosen—whatever it is. I don't care." He takes my hand. "But you do whatever you need to."

I secretly hoped he would make a definitive decision for both of us. A coward's approach, I suppose.

I feel Griff watching me, his hand tightens around mine as I search my soul. The awareness that this is my choice, the power is in *my* hands, seems to come out of the blue, although it's been true ever since I walked off this farm eleven years ago.

Suddenly, I realize this is the first time thinking of Margo doesn't hurt. In this moment, with Griff at my side and Gran and Ross waiting for me, I decide to let my mother go.

It takes me a few precious moments to release a hope I didn't realize I'd been holding. Then I cast the empty place that should have been filled with a mother into the current of the river below and allow it to be carried away.

My road has been long with many losses, some at my own hand, some dictated by others. I've learned to accept my own weaknesses and forgive those I love theirs. I hope that, in time, Dharma and Walden will find their peace, too. Even if the road doesn't lead them back to Pearl River Plantation.

ACKNOWLEDGMENTS

With each book I discover how much I *don't* know. I'm grateful to those who share their knowledge, experiences, and aid my research. They allow me to tell my story with as much truth and accuracy as possible. That said, any artistic license (this is fiction, after all) or errors are on me.

I am indebted to many. I thank Dr. Walter Beaver for insights and fact-confirming. Thanks to Marilyn Thompson for generous assistance in research. My surfing nephew Jeff Zinn was my Huntington Beach and SoCal surfing guide; he taught me so much more than I could incorporate into this book, and always in such an entertaining fashion.

To the brave people who chronicled living with bipolar disorder and to those who shared their stories of living with someone with the disorder. For further reading and insight, I highly recommend *An Unquiet Mind*, by Kay Redfield Jamison, brilliantly written and painfully honest.

To my intrepid and ever-patient agent, Susan Ginsburg, thanks for your hard work, your keen insight, as well as putting up with my snail-like writing pace and false starts.

The entire team at Gallery Books/Simon & Schuster was, as always, invaluable. Editor Karen Kosztolnyik's sharp eye and gentle support were instrumental in the development of this book. Editor

Kate Dresser escorted this project over the finish line and had the difficult job of helping trim this once-bloated beast into shape. Thanks to Molly Gregory for jumping in with cheer and enthusiasm, tending to those pesky details that continuously pop up. My appreciation goes to Jen Bergstrom for her support of this book, as well as the two that preceded it. Thanks to Wendy Sheanin for her amazing marketing efforts. Grateful admiration goes to Laywan Kwan, who designed this amazing cover. Thanks to Michele Podberezniak for guiding and organizing publicity. Hats off to those unsung heroes in sales who fight in the trenches every day to put my books into readers' hands. Of course, homage must be paid to the booksellers who make sure readers and the books they are bound to love find one another.

Fellow authors Karen White and Wendy Wax deserve a round of applause for the brainstorming, eagle eyes, hand-holding, and friendship. I don't ever want to go through this process without you.

Last but certainly not least, my husband and family, who put up with the mental absences, as well as the physical, when the book overtakes all.

the *Myth* of
PERPETUAL
SUMMER

SUSAN CRANDALL

Introduction

When Tallulah James returns to her Mississippi hometown in 1972 after a seven-year absence, determined to help her brother escape a murder conviction, she hopes to avoid the small-town gossip mill and return to California as quickly as possible. But as Tallulah reconnects with her dysfunctional family, she becomes entangled in a web of long-held secrets about their history of mental illness, her tumultuous upbringing, and a terrible tragedy that nearly tore the family apart. Ultimately, the truth forces Tallulah to reckon with her past—and find a way forward.

TOPICS AND QUESTIONS
FOR DISCUSSION

1. Why do you think Susan Crandall opens the novel with Walden's arrest before revealing Tallulah's backstory? How did your impression of Tallulah and her family evolve as the flashbacks unfolded?

2. In what ways are the Jameses a product of time and place? How would the novel be different in another setting?

3. Crandall depicts Margo's activism in stark contrast to her selfishness as a mother. Why do you think Margo is outraged by social injustice but blind to the needs of her children? What fuels her outrage?

4. Does *The Myth of Perpetual Summer* reinforce or challenge any preconceptions you had about the 1960s South?

5. Discuss how the different characters perceive racial discrimination and the Civil Rights Movement. What do their various experiences and responses to racism say about them?

6. While Tallulah envies the stability of Ross's family, she understands that their expectations for him are stifling in their own way. Which would you prefer? Ultimately, is Tallulah's family her millstone or salvation?

7. How are the James children defined by their parents' actions? Discuss how each of the siblings emulate and/or resist Margo's and Drayton's behavior.

8. Discuss how Tallulah's childhood point of view shaped your impression of Drayton's behavior in the flashback chapters. How did your understanding of his mental illness shift over the course of the novel?

9. Drayton tells Tallulah that history is like "dominoes set in motion on one era toppling those in the next" (pg. 72). How does this theory bear out for the James family? What does it take for Tallulah to break from the past and gain agency over her own life?

10. "Gran says family traditions are what give meaning to life," Crandall writes (pg. 304). "But that's not it. The family itself, if we accept it for what it is and not condemn it for what it is not, can be the fiber that weaves a rope that pulls us out of ourselves, and into a world where we're willing to take an emotional risk." Discuss the distinction here between tradition and family. How does the latter empower Tallulah to come out of her shell?

11. Why do you think the "ugly parts" of the James family's history bring some of the siblings together and drive others apart?

12. Toward the end of the novel, Gran characterizes the cover-up of George's death as "a lie of convenience that was meant to spare pain, not cause it" (pg. 316). What do you make of Gran's obsession with keeping up appearances? Do you see her commitment to upholding the family legacy as shortsighted and harmful or practical?

13. Gran tells Tallulah that "hurt and anger make a strong person brave and a weak person broken" (pg. 317). Do you agree with this statement? Why or why not?

14. Discuss the ending of the novel. Were you surprised that Tallulah returns to the South? How is she able to accept the family plantation as a happy home despite her painful memories?

15. What do you make of the title? Did your perception of the "myth of perpetual summer" change over the course of the novel?

ENHANCE YOUR BOOK CLUB

1. Host a Southern-style brunch for your book club discussion. Don't forget the mint juleps and the pecan pie!

2. Read up on the Civil Rights Movement and discuss how your learnings inform the historical backdrop in *The Myth of Perpetual Summer*.

3. Cast your film version of *The Myth of Perpetual Summer*. Which actors would you want to play the main characters, and why?

4. Read one of Susan Crandall's other historical novels (http://susancrandall.net/susan-crandalls-booklist). Discuss which is your favorite, and why.

5. Learn more about Susan Crandall by checking out http://susancrandall.net/ or following her on Twitter @susancrandall.